Praise for _New York Times_ bestselling author Suzanne Brockmann

"Zingy dialogue, a great sense of drama, and a pair of lovers who generate enough steam heat to power a whole city."

—_RT Book Reviews_ on _Hero Under Cover_

"Brockmann deftly delivers another testosterone-drenched, adrenaline-fueled tale of danger and desire that brilliantly combines superbly crafted, realistically complex characters with white-knuckle plotting."

—_Booklist_ on _Force of Nature_

"Sizzling with military intrigue and sexual tension, with characters so vivid they leap right off the page, _Gone Too Far_ is a bold, brassy read with a momentum that just doesn't quit."

—_New York Times_ bestselling author Tess Gerritsen

Praise for _USA TODAY_ bestselling author Barb Han

"Han crafts a wonderful mystery with suspense and action. _Texas Prey_ is an entertaining read that will hook readers at the outset."

—_RT Book Reviews_

"Another thrilling yet emotional story... A page turner with plenty of action."

—_RT Book Reviews_ on _What She Saw_

NIGHT
WATCH

NEW YORK TIMES **BESTSELLING AUTHOR**

SUZANNE BROCKMANN

ISBN-13: 978-1-335-40661-3

Night Watch
First published in 2003. This edition published in 2022.
Copyright © 2003 by Suzanne Brockmann

Hard Target
First published in 2015. This edition published in 2022.
Copyright © 2015 by Barb Han

For questions and comments about the quality of this book, please contact us at CustomerService@Harlequin.com.

Harlequin Enterprises ULC
22 Adelaide St. West, 41st Floor
Toronto, Ontario M5H 4E3, Canada
www.Harlequin.com

Printed in U.S.A.

CONTENTS

Suzanne Brockmann is an award-winning author of more than fifty books and is widely recognized as one of the leading voices in romantic suspense. Her work has earned her repeated appearances on the *New York Times* bestseller list, as well as numerous awards, including Romance Writers of America's #1 Favorite Book of the Year and two RITA® Awards. Suzanne divides her time between Siesta Key and Boston. Visit her at suzannebrockmann.com.

Books by Suzanne Brockmann

Not Without Risk
Night Watch
Taylor's Temptation
Get Lucky
Identity: Unknown
The Admiral's Bride
Hawken's Heart
Harvard's Education

Visit the Author Profile page at
Harlequin.com for more titles.

NIGHT
WATCH

Suzanne Brockmann

For Ed and Eric,
who understand what friendship means.
I love you guys. My heartfelt thanks to the real
teams of SEALs, and to all of the courageous men
and women in the US military who sacrifice so
much to keep America the land of the free and the
home of the brave. And an even bigger thanks
(if possible) to the wives, husbands, mothers,
fathers and children who are waiting for our
military heroes and heroines to do their jobs
and then come safely home. God bless—my
thoughts and prayers are with you!

Chapter 1

Brittany Evans hated to be late. But parking had been a pain in the butt, and she'd spent way too much time trying to decide what to wear—as if it really mattered.

She surveyed the scattering of people standing around the college baseball stadium's hot dog stand as she came out the door that led from the locker rooms.

And there he was.

Standing under the overhang, out of the gently falling rain, watching the players on the ball field. Leaning against the wall with his back to her.

At least she thought it was him. They'd never really met—at least not for more than two and a half seconds. Brittany, this is whatever-his-naval-rank-was Wes Skelly. Wes, this is Melody Jones's sister, Britt.

Hey, how are you, nice to meet you, gotta go.

The man who might or might not be Wes Skelly

glanced at his watch, glanced toward the main entrance of the stadium. His hair was longer and lighter than she remembered—of course, it was hard to remember much from only two and a half seconds of face time.

She could see his face better as he turned slightly. It was...a face. Not stunningly handsome like Mel's husband, Harlan "Cowboy" Jones. But not exactly Frankenstein's monster, either.

Wes wasn't smiling. In fact, he looked a little tense, a little angry. Hopefully not at her for being late. No, probably just for being. She'd heard a lot about Wes Skelly over the past few years. That is, assuming this was really Wes Skelly.

But he had to be. No one else in the place looked even remotely like a Navy SEAL.

This guy wasn't big, though—not like her brother-in-law or his good friend Senior Chief Harvard-the-Incredible-Hulk Becker—but there was something about him that seemed capable of anything and maybe a little dangerous.

He was dressed in civilian clothes—khaki pants with a dark jacket over a button-down shirt and tie. Poor man. From what Mel had told her about Wes, he would rather swim in shark-infested waters than get dressed up.

Of course, look at her. Wearing these stupid sandals with heels instead of her usual comfortable flats. She'd put on more than her usual amount of makeup, too.

But the plan was to meet at the ball game, and then go out to dinner someplace nicer than the local pizza joint.

Neither of them had counted on rain screwing up the first part of the plan.

Wes looked at his watch again and sighed.

And Brittany realized that his leaning against the wall was only feigned casualness. He was standing still, yet somehow he remained in motion—tapping his fingers or his foot, slightly shifting his weight, searching his pockets for something, checking his watch. He wasn't letting himself pace, but he wanted to.

Gee whiz, she wasn't *that* late.

Of course maybe her five-minute delay wasn't the problem. Maybe this man just never stood still. And wasn't that just what she needed—a date with a guy with Attention Deficit Disorder.

Silently cursing her sister, Brittany approached him, arranging her face into a smile. "You have that same 'Heavenly Father, save me from doing favors for friends and relatives' look in your eyes that I've got," she said. "Therefore you must be Wes Skelly."

He laughed, and it completely transformed his face, softening all the hard lines and making his blue eyes seem to twinkle.

Irish. Darnit, he was definitely at least part Irish.

"That makes you Brittany Evans," he said, holding out his hand. It was warm, his handshake firm. "Nice to finally meet you."

Nice hands. Nice smile. Nice steady, direct gaze. Nice guy—good liar, too. She liked him instantly, despite the potential ADD.

"Sorry I'm a few minutes late," she said. "I had to drive almost all the way to Arizona to find a parking space."

"Yeah, I've noticed that traffic really sucks here," he said as he studied her face, probably trying to figure out how she could possibly be related to gorgeous, delicately angelic-looking Melody Jones.

"We don't look very much alike," she told him. "My sister and I."

She'd surprised him with her directness, but he recovered quickly. "What, are you nuts? Your eyes are a little different—a different shade of blue. But other than that, you're a…a variation on the same lovely theme."

Oh, for crying out loud. What had her sister's husband told this guy? That she was a sure thing? Just liberally sling the woo, Skelly, and she'll be putty in your hands because she's lonely and pathetic and hasn't had a man in her bed—let alone a date—in close to a decade?

It was her own stupid fault for giving in to Melody's pressure. A blind date. What was she thinking?

Okay, she knew what she was thinking. Mel had asked her to go out with Wes Skelly as a favor. It was, she'd said in that baby sister manipulative manner of hers—the one that came with the big blue eyes, the one that had enabled her to twist Britt around her little finger for the past several decades—the only thing she wanted for her upcoming birthday. Pretty please with sugar on top…?

Britt should have cried foul and gotten her a Dave Matthews CD instead.

"Let's set some ground rules," Brittany told Wes now. "Rule number one—no crap, okay? No hyperbole, no B.S. Only pure honesty. My sister and your so-called friend Harlan Jones manipulated us to this particular level of hell, but now that we're here we're going to play by our own rules. Agreed?"

"Yeah," he said. "Sure, but—"

"I have no intention of sleeping with you," she informed him briskly. "I'm neither lonely nor pathetic. I know exactly what I look like, exactly who I am and I happen to be quite happy with myself, thank you very much. I'm here because I love my little sister, although right now I'm trying to imagine the most painfully horrific way to torture her for doing this to me—and to you."

He opened his mouth, but she wasn't done and she didn't let him speak.

"Now. I know my sister, and I know she was hoping we'd gaze into each other's eyes, fall hopelessly in love and get married before the year's end." She paused for a fraction of a second to look searchingly into his eyes. They were very pretty blue eyes, but her friend Julia had an Alaskan husky with pretty blue eyes, too. "Nope," she said. "Didn't happen for me. How about you?"

He laughed. "Sorry," he said. "But—"

"No need for excuses," she cut him off again. "People think alone means lonely. Have you noticed that?"

He didn't answer right away. Not until it was good and clear that she was finally finished and it was his turn to talk.

"Yeah," he said then. "And people who are together—people who are a couple—they're always trying to pair up all of their single friends. It's definitely obnoxious."

"Well meant," Britt agreed, "but completely annoying. I am sorry that you got roped into this."

"It's not that big a deal," he said. "I mean, I was coming to Los Angeles anyway. And how many times has Lieutenant Jones asked me to do him a favor? Maybe twice. How many times has he bailed out my butt? Too many to count. He's an excellent officer and a good friend, and if he wants me to have dinner with you, hey, I'm having dinner with you. He was right, by the way."

Britt wasn't sure she liked either the gleam in his eye or that grin. She narrowed her own eyes. "About what?"

"I *was* having a little trouble there for a while, getting in a word edgewise."

She opened her mouth, and then closed it. Then opened it. "Well, heck, it's not exactly as if you're known throughout the SEAL teams as Mr. Taciturn."

Wes's grin widened. "That's what makes it all the more amazing. So what's rule number three?"

She blinked. "Rule three?" She didn't have three rules. There was just the one.

"One is no bull— Um. No bull," he said. "Two is no sex. That's fine 'cause that's not why I'm here. I'm not in a place where I'm ready to get involved with anyone on that permanent of a level, and besides, although you're very pretty—and that's not crap. I'm being honest here as per rule one—you're not my type."

"Your type." Oh, this was going to be good. "What or who exactly is your type?"

He opened his mouth, but she thumped him on the chest as the action on the field caught her eye. It was a very solid chest despite the fact that in her heels she was nearly as tall as he was.

"Hold that thought," she ordered. "Andy's at bat."

Wes fell obediently silent. She knew that he didn't have children, but he apparently understood the unspoken parental agreement about paying complete and total attention when one's kid was in the batter's box.

Of course, her kid was nineteen years old and a college freshman on a full baseball scholarship. Her kid was six feet three inches tall and two hundred and twenty pounds. Her kid had a batting average of .430, and a propensity for knocking the ball clear over the fence, and quite possibly into the next county.

But it had just started to rain harder.

Andy let the first ball go past him—a strike.

"How can he see in this?" Britt muttered. "He can't possibly see in this. Besides it's not supposed to rain in Southern California." That had been one of the perks of moving out here from Massachusetts.

The pitcher wound up, let go of the ball, and...*tock*. The sound of Andy's bat connecting with the ball was sharp and sweet and so much more vibrant than the little anemic click heard when watching baseball on TV. Brittany had never known anything like it until after she'd adopted Andy, until he'd started playing baseball with the same ferocity that he approached everything else in life.

"Yes!" The ball sailed over the fence and Andy jogged around the bases. Brittany alternately clapped and whistled piercingly, fingers between her teeth.

"Jones said your kid was pretty good."

"Pretty good my eye," Britt countered. "Andy's college baseball's Barry Bonds. That's his thirty-first homerun this year, I'll have you know."

"He being scouted?" Wes asked.

"Actually, he is," she told him. "Mostly because there's another kid on the team—Dustin Melero—who's been getting lots of attention. He's a pitcher—a real hotshot, you know? Scouts come to see him, but he's still pretty inconsistent. Kind of lacking in the maturity department, too. The scouts end up sticking around to take a look at Andy."

"You gonna let him play pro ball before he finishes college?"

"He's nineteen," Brittany replied. "I don't let him do anything. It's his life and his choice. He knows I'll support him whatever he decides to do."

"I wish you were my mom."

"I think you're a little too old even for me to adopt," she told him. Although Wes was definitely younger than she was, by at least five years. And maybe even more. What was her sister thinking?

"Andy was what? Twelve when you adopted him?" he asked.

"Thirteen." Irish. Melody was thinking that Wes was Irish, and that Brittany had a definite thing for a man with a twinkle in his eyes and a smile that could light his entire being. Mel was thinking about her own intense happiness with Harlan Jones, and about the fact that one night, years ago, Britt had had a little too much to drink and admitted to her sister that her biggest regret about her failed marriage to That-Jerk-Quentin was that she would have liked to have had a child—a biological child—of her own.

That would teach her to be too heavy-handed when making strawberry daiquiris.

"That definitely qualifies you for sainthood," Wes said. "Adopting a thirteen-year-old juvie? Man."

"All he really needed was a stable home environment—"

"You're either crazy or Mother Teresa's sister."

"Oh, I'm not a saint. Believe me. I just… I fell in love with the kid. He's great." She tried to explain. "He grew up with no one. I mean, completely abandoned—physically by his father and emotionally by his mother. And then there he was, about to be shipped away again, to another foster home, and there I was, and… I wanted him to stay with me. We've had our tough moments, sure, but…"

The look in Wes's blue eyes—a kind of a thoughtful intensity, as best she could read it—was making her nervous. This man wasn't the happy-go-lucky second cousin to a leprechaun with ADD that she'd first thought him to be. He wasn't jittery, as she'd first thought, although standing still was clearly a challenge for him. No, he was more like a lightning bolt—crackling with barely harnessed excess energy. And while it was true he had a good sense of humor and a killer smile, there was a definite darkness to him. An edge. It made her like him even more.

Oh, danger! Danger, Will Robinson!

"You were going to tell me about your type," she reminded him. "And please don't tell me you go for the sweet young thing, or I'll have to hit you. Although, according to some of my patients, I'm both sweet and young. Of course they're pushing 95."

That got his smile back. "My type tends to go to a party and ends up dancing on tables. Preferably nearly naked."

Brittany snorted with laughter. "You win, I'm not your type. And I should have known that. Melody has mentioned in the past that you were into the, uh, higher arts."

"I think she must've meant martial arts," he countered. The rain continued to pour from the sky, spraying them lightly with a fine mist whenever the wind blew. He didn't seem to notice or care. "Lt. Jones told me that you came to Los Angeles to go to school. To become a nurse."

"I *am* a nurse," she told him. "I'm taking classes to become a nurse practitioner."

"That's great," he said.

She smiled back at him. "Yes, it is, thank you."

"You know, maybe they set us up," he suggested, "because they know how often I *need* a nurse. Save me the emergency room fees when I need stitches."

"A fighter, huh?" Brittany shook her head. "I should have guessed. It's always the little guys who…" She stopped herself. Oh, dear. Men generally didn't like to hear themselves referred to as the little guy. "I'm sorry. I didn't mean—"

"It's okay," he said easily, no evidence of the famous Skelly temper apparent. "Although I prefer short. Little implies…certain other things."

She had to laugh. "A, I wasn't thinking—not even for a fraction of a second—about your…certain other things, and B, even if I were, why should it matter when we've already established that our friendship isn't going to have anything to do with sex?"

"I was going with Rule One," he countered. "No crap, just pure honesty."

"Yeah, right. Men are idiots. Have you noticed?"

"Absolutely," he said, obviously as at ease with her as she was with him. It was remarkable, really, the way she felt as if she'd known him for years, as if she were completely in tune with his sense of humor. "And as long as it's established that we're well-hung idiots, we're okay with that." He peered toward the field. "I think they're calling the game."

They were. The rain wasn't letting up and the players were leaving the field.

"Is it temporary? Because I don't mind waiting," Wes added. "If Andy were my kid, I'd try to be at every home game. I mean, even if he wasn't Babe Ruth reborn, I'd want to, you know? You must be beyond proud of him."

How incredibly sweet. "I am."

"You want to wait inside?" he asked.

"I think there's some other event scheduled for the field for later this afternoon," Britt told him. "They don't have time for a rain delay—they'll have to reschedule the game, or call it or whatever they do in baseball. So, no. It's over. We don't have to wait."

"You hungry?" Wes asked. "We could have an early dinner."

"I'd like that," Britt said, and amazingly it was true. On her way over, she'd made a list of about twenty-five different plausible-sounding reasons why they should skip dinner, but now she mentally deleted them. "Do you mind if we go down to the locker room first? I want to give my car keys to Andy."

"Aha," Wes said. "I pass the you'll-get-into-my-car-with-me test. Good for me."

She led the way toward the building. "Even better, you passed the okay-I-will-go-out-to-dinner-with-you test."

He actually held the door for her. "Was that in jeopardy?"

"Blind dates and I are mortal enemies from way back," Britt told him. "You should consider the fact that I even agreed to meet you to be a huge testament to sisterly love."

"You passed my test, too," Wes said. "I only go to dinner with women who absolutely do not want to have sex with me. Oh, wait. Damn. Maybe that's been my problem all these years…"

She laughed, letting herself enjoy the twinkle in his eyes as he opened yet another door—the one to the stairwell—for her. "Sweetie, I knew I passed your test when you asked me to adopt you."

"And yet you turned me down," he countered. "What does that tell me?"

"That I'm too young to be your mother." Brittany led the way down the stairs, enjoying herself immensely. Who knew she'd like Wes Skelly this much? After Melody had called, setting up this date, she and Andy had jokingly referred to him as *the load*. He was her burden to bear for her sister's birthday. "You can be the kid brother I always wanted, though."

"Yeah, I don't know about that."

The hallway outside the locker rooms wasn't filled to capacity as it usually was after a game, with girlfriends and dorm-mates of the players crowded together. Today, only a very few bedraggled diehards were there. Brittany looked, but Andy's girlfriend, Danielle, wasn't among them. Which was just as well, since Andy had told her Dani hadn't been feeling well today. If she were coming down with some thing, standing in the rain would only make her worse.

"My track record with sisters isn't that good," Wes continued. "I tend to piss them off, after which they run off and marry my best friend."

"I heard about that." Britt stopped outside the home team's locker room door. It was slightly ajar. "Mel told me that Bobby Taylor just married your sister... Colleen, wasn't it?"

Wes leaned against the wall. "She tell you about the shouting that went down first?"

She glanced at him.

He swore softly. "Of course she did. I'm surprised the Associated Press didn't pick up the story."

"I'm sure it wasn't as bad as she—"

"No," he said. "It was. I was a jerk. I can't believe you agreed to meet me."

"Whatever you did, it wasn't a capital offense. My sister apparently forgives you."

Wes snorted. "Yeah, Melody, right. She's really harsh and unforgiving. She forgave me before Colleen did."

"It must be nice to know you have such good friends."

He nodded. "Yeah, you know, it really is."

He met her gaze, and there it was again. That darkness or sadness or whatever it was, lurking back there in his eyes. And Brittany knew. The outwardly upbeat Irishman would be fun to hang around with and was even adorable in his own loudly funny way. But it was this hidden part of him, this edge, that would, if she let it, make him irresistible.

He was, without a doubt, her type. But she wasn't his, thank you, God.

Eddie Sunamura, the third baseman, popped his head out of the locker room. His wife—June—was one of the soaking wet diehards. She lit up when she saw him, and he grinned back at her. They were only two years older than Andy, a thought that never failed to give Britt a jolt.

"Give me ten more minutes, Mrs. S.," he called to June, and Brittany couldn't keep from groaning.

"Eddie, you're unbelievably hokey," she said.

"Hey, Britt."

"Have you seen Andy?" she asked him.

He pointed down the hall before he vanished back into the locker room.

And there was Andy. At the end of the hallway. In the middle of what looked to be a very intense discussion with the team's star pitcher, Dustin Melero.

Andy was tall, but Dustin had an inch on him.

"Man, he grew," Wes said as he looked at Andy. "I met him about four years ago, and he was only..." He held his hand up to about his shoulder.

It was then, as they were gazing down the hallway at the two young men, that Andy dropped his mitt and shoved Dustin with a resounding crash against the wall of lockers.

Brittany had already taken three steps toward them, when Wes caught her arm. "Don't," he said. "Let me. If you can, just turn around and don't look."

Yeah, like hell...

Still, she managed not to follow as Wes hustled down the hall to where Andy and Dustin were nose to nose, ready to break both the school rules and each others' faces.

As she watched, Wes put himself directly between them. They were too far away for her to hear his words, but she could imagine them. "What's up, guys?" The two younger men towered over him, but Wes somehow seemed bigger.

Andy was glowering—the expression on his face a direct flashback to the street-smart thirteen-year-old he'd once been.

He just kept shaking his head as Wes talked. Finally,

Dustin—who was laughing—spoke. Wes turned and gave the taller boy his full attention.

And then, all of a sudden, Wes had Dustin up against the lockers, and was talking to him with a great deal of intensity.

The new expression on Andy's face would have been humorous if Brittany hadn't been quite so worried at the amount of damage a full-grown Navy SEAL could inflict on a twenty-year-old idiot.

Dustin's sly smile had vanished, replaced with a drained-of-blood look of near panic.

Finally, unable to stand it another second, Brittany started toward them.

"…so much as look at her funny, I will come and find you, do you understand?" Wes was saying as she approached.

Dustin looked at her. Andy looked at her. But Wes didn't look away from Dustin. All that intensity aimed in one direction was alarming.

She wasn't sure what to do, what to say. "Everything okay?" she said brightly.

"Do you understand?" Wes said again, to Dustin.

"Yes," he managed to squeak out.

"Good," Wes said and stepped back.

And Dustin was out of there.

"So," Brittany said to Andy. "This is Wes Skelly."

"Yeah," Andy said. "I think we're kind of past the introduction stage."

Chapter 2

Remarkably, Brittany Evans didn't jump down his throat.

Remarkably, she didn't immediately demand to know what on earth would possess him to physically threaten a kid more than a dozen years his junior. Forget about the fact that he did it in front of her impressionable teenaged son.

In fact, she didn't say anything about it at all.

Wes took that as a strong hint that he'd surely hear about it later.

But she'd merely talked about her sister's current pregnancy and friends they had in common as they drove to a Santa Monica café, not too far from the house Brittany shared with her kid.

The questions didn't come until they'd sat down to dinner, until they'd ordered and had started to eat.

"You surprised me back at the fieldhouse," Brittany introduced the topic. The table was lit by candlelight, and it made her seem warmly, lushly exotic in a way that her little sister would never look. Not in a million years.

Wes used to think that Melody was the prettier of the Evans sisters, and maybe according to conventional standards she was. Britt's face was slightly angular, her chin too pointed, her nose a little sharp. But catch her at the right moment, from the right angle, and she was breathtakingly beautiful.

Sex was not an option, he reminded himself. Yes, this woman was very attractive, but he wasn't interested. Remember? He definitely had to deal with all the emotional crap rattling around inside of his own head before he went and got naked with someone who would want a real relationship rather than a happy night or two of the horizontal cha-cha.

The odds of her wanting a night of casual sex with him were pretty low to start with. She so didn't seem to be the type. But even if he was wrong, those odds would slip down to slim-to-none after he told her the truth—that he couldn't give her more than a night or two because he was in love with someone else. No, not just someone else. Lana Quinn. The wife of one of his best friends—U.S. Navy SEAL and Chief Petty Officer Matthew Quinn, aka Wizard, aka the Mighty Quinn, aka that lying, cheating, unfaithful sack of dog crap.

Brittany Evans was sitting across the table from Wes, gazing at him with the kind of eyes he loved best on women. Warm eyes. Intelligent eyes. Eyes that told him she liked and respected him—and expected the same respect in return.

Lana had looked at him—at all of the SEALs—like that.

"Yeah," Wes said, since Brittany seemed to be waiting for some kind of response. "I kind of surprised myself back at the fieldhouse." He laughed, but she didn't join in.

She just watched him as she took a sip directly from her bottle of beer and he tried not to look at or even think about her mouth. The bottom line was that he liked her too much as a person to mess around with her as a woman, as hot as he found her. But if she were some random babe that he caught a glimpse of in a bar, he'd make a point to get closer, to see if maybe she might want some mutually superficial sex.

So, okay. He was man enough to admit it. If all things were equal, he'd throw Brittany Evans a bang. No doubt about it. Forget about Lana—because, face it, he had to. She was married, off-limits, verboten, taboo. He couldn't have her, so he took pleasure and comfort wherever he could find it. And he kept his heart well out of it.

But things here were definitely not equal. Not even close. Brittany was Lt. Jones's sister-in-law, which was probably even worse than if she were his sister. A sister wouldn't tell a brother about a night of hot sex with a near stranger. Well, probably not. But a sister just might tell a sister. Provided the two sisters were close. Which Brittany and Melody certainly were.

And word would definitely get back to Jones, which wouldn't be good.

No, this was not going to happen, not tonight, not

ever. Which, on that very superficial and completely physical level, was a crying shame. He would have liked, very much, to see Brittany Evans naked.

"What did he say to you?" she asked, looking at him in that way she had—as if she was trying to see inside of his skull and read his mind. Good thing she couldn't. "Melero, I mean."

"That kid is a total…" Wes chose a more polite word. "Idiot."

Brittany smiled at him. "That's not what you were going to say."

"I'm working hard to keep it clean."

"I appreciate that."

God her smile was a killer. Wes forced himself to stop cataloging everything he wasn't going to do to her tonight. Enough self-torture already. He brought the conversation back on track. "Melero was just being a jerk. That's another good word for him—jerk."

"I've met him plenty of times before," she countered, narrowing her eyes slightly. "I'm well aware that he's capable of extreme jerkdom. But Andy knows that, too. What exactly did this guy say to Andy to piss him off like that?"

"It was about a girl," Wes said, unsure just how much to tell her.

"Dani?"

"Yeah, that's the one."

"She's Andy's girlfriend."

"I gathered that," he said.

"What did he say?" she persisted.

Wes paraphrased and summarized. He'd heard quite a bit this afternoon that he didn't want to repeat. It really was none of his business. "Melero told Andy that he'd, uh, you know, slept with her. Only, he put it a lot less delicately."

"I'm sure." Britt let out an exasperated laugh. "And Andy didn't just walk away? What a lunkhead. That girl is devoted to him—she thinks he makes the sun rise. She's a nice kid. A little low in the self-esteem department in my opinion, but, okay, she's still young. Maybe it'll come. I just hope…" She shook her head. "I'm not sure she's right for Andy and I'd really hate for her to get pregnant. I preach safe sex pretty much nonstop. He just rolls his eyes."

"Yeah, well, you can cross that off your list of things to worry about, at least for right now." Wes finished his beer before remembering he'd planned to make it last all through dinner. Crap. "Apparently Dani is all about taking it really slow." Ah, hell, why not just tell Brittany all of it? It wasn't his business, but clearly this wasn't something Andy would bring up in a conversation with his mother. "She's a public virgin."

Brittany put down her fork. "Excuse me?"

"She's a virgin, and apparently she's not afraid to tell people—you know, make it public knowledge that she has no intention of messing around before she's good and ready."

"Well, you go girl! Good for her. I had no idea she had that much backbone."

"But now Melero's telling everyone he popped her cherry and—" Holy God, what was he saying? And to Lt. Jones's sister-in-law, no less. "Look, he was beyond crude, okay? When I heard what he'd said, I wanted to throw him up against the wall myself."

"You did."

She was looking at him so pointedly, so like the way

Mrs. Bartlett, his third grade teacher had looked at him, he had to laugh. Man, he hadn't thought about Mrs. B. in years, God bless her. "Yeah," he said, "no. I didn't do that until he said the other thing."

"Which was…?"

She wasn't going to like this. "I went into caveman mode," he apologized first. "I'm sorry I did that in front of your kid. That was the wrong message to send, but when that little cow turd started laughing and saying you were hot, and that you were next on his list…"

Brittany looked surprised for about half a second. Then she laughed. Her eyes actually sparkled. "Sweetie, that was just a schoolyard taunt. And your mother, too… You know? This boy is a total jerk and a bully, but he's not any kind of a real threat. And even if he was, I could take care of myself. Believe me."

"Yeah, I picked that up from you right away," Wes said. "And I told him that."

"After which you told him you were a Navy SEAL and if he so much as breathed in my direction, you were going to…what?"

Wes scratched his chin. "I may have mentioned something about my diving knife and his never having offspring."

She laughed again. Thank God. "That must've been when he looked like he was going to faint."

"How is everything?" The waiter was back, but the place was crowded and he didn't wait for an answer. He deftly removed the empty beer bottles from the table. "Another?"

"Yes, please." Brittany smiled up at the guy, and Wes said another short prayer of thanks that his knee-jerk treatment of Melero hadn't made her decide not to like him.

"Sir?"

"Yeah. Wait! Make it a cola."

"Very good, sir." The waiter vanished.

"I'm trying to cut back," Wes felt the need to explain as the warmth of her gaze was focused back on him. "One beer a night. Two becomes six a little too easily these days, you know?"

"I appreciate it," Brittany said. "Especially since you're driving."

"Yeah, well, I'm a sloppy drunk. It's not pretty. It's definitely not a good way to make new friends." Why the hell was he telling her this? He didn't even talk with Bobby about his fears of becoming an alcoholic, and Bobby Taylor was his friend and swim buddy from way back. "This is a very interesting first date. We talk about your son's sex life and my potential drinking problem. Shouldn't we be talking about the weather? Or movies we just saw?"

"It finally stopped raining, thank goodness," Brittany said. "I just rented *Ocean's Eleven* and loved it. When did you quit smoking?"

Damn. "Two days ago. What'd I do? Pat my pocket, searching for my nonexistent pack?"

"Yup."

Crap. He resisted another urge to reach into his pocket. Not that he could've had a cigarette until later. This restaurant was smoke free.

"It must be driving you crazy," Brittany observed. "To stop smoking and cut back on your drinking all at the same time."

"Yeah, well, I've tried to quit before, I don't have a

whole hell of a lot of faith in myself. I mean, the longest I've gone without a cigarette is six weeks."

"Have you tried the patch?"

"No," he admitted. "I know I probably should. I don't know, maybe the idea would appeal to me more if I could get Julia Roberts to glue it to my ass."

Brittany laughed. "Maybe not smoking would appeal to you more if you had a girlfriend who told you that kissing you after you smoked was similar to licking an ashtray."

He forced a smile. "Yeah, well…" The woman he wanted to be his girlfriend was married. He didn't want to think about the one time he did kiss her. As easy as it was to talk to Brittany, he couldn't talk about Lana. This was a date, after all, not therapy.

Not that he'd managed to talk to the team shrink about Lana, either, though. The only talking he'd done was when he was completely skunked.

The waiter brought their drinks to the table and vanished again. Wes took a sip of his soda and tried to like it, tried not to wish it was another bottle of beer.

"My ex used to smoke," Brittany told him. "I tried everything to get him to quit, and finally drew a line. I told him that if he was going to smoke, he couldn't kiss me. And he said okay, if that's what I wanted."

Wes knew what was coming from the rueful edge to her smile.

"So he stopped kissing me," she told him.

The adjectives he used to describe the bastard were blistering—far worse than anything that had come out of Dustin Melero's mouth that afternoon, but she just laughed as he winced and apologized.

"It's all right," she said. "But cut him some slack. He

wasn't entirely to blame. You know, he smoked when I married him, so it was pretty unfair of me to make those kinds of demands. Bottom line, sweetie, is that you've got to quit smoking because you want to quit smoking."

"Or at the very least, I've got to want Julia Roberts to glue the patch onto my—"

"Yes," she said, laughing. "That might do it."

"He was a fool," Wes told her, reaching across the table to take her hand. "Your ex."

The smile she gave him was stunning as she squeezed his fingers. "Thank you. I've always thought so, too."

Brittany took a sip of her coffee. "Melody told me you had leave for a week—"

"Two," Wes interjected.

"And that you were spending that time here in L.A. as a favor to a friend?"

"Yeah." Wes Skelly had a nervous tell. Even sitting at the table, he was constantly in motion, kind of like a living pinball. He was always fiddling with something on the table. His spoon. The saltshaker. The tablecloth. His soda straw. But when he got nervous—at least Britt thought it was nerves he was feeling—he stopped. Stopped moving. Stopped fiddling. He got very, very still.

He was doing it right now, but as he started to talk, he started stirring the ice in his soda. "I'm actually here as a favor to the wife of a good friend. Wizard." He glanced up at her, and she knew it was an act. He was working overtime to pretend to be casual.

"I don't know if your sister ever talked about him," he continued. "She may not know him. I don't know. He's with SEAL Team Six, and he's always out of the country, so… Very hard to find. So he's gone again, and his wife, Lana, she's, you know, very nice, very… We've been friends for years, too, and… Well, she was worried about her sister. Half sister, actually. Her father's second marriage, and… Anyway, Lana's half sister is Amber Tierney and—"

"Whoa." Britt held up her hand. "Wait a sec. Information overload. Your friend Wizard's wife Lana's—" Lana, who was *very nice* "—half sister is Amber Tierney from *High Tide?*"

"Yeah."

"Holy moly." With her heavy schedule at school and exhausting rotations in the hospital, Brittany didn't have time to keep up with the various TV and movie stars who made headlines in L.A. But Amber Tierney had been impossible to miss. She'd been TV's current It Girl ever since her sitcom, *High Tide,* had first aired last September. "Her sister's worried…that she's making too much money…? That Tom Cruise wants to date her…? That—"

"She's being stalked," Wes finished for her.

Britt cringed. "Sorry. That is a problem. I shouldn't have tried to make it into a joke."

"I'm not sure how real the threat is," Wes told her. "Lana says Amber's shrugging it off, says the guy's harmless, he wouldn't really hurt her. But see, Lana's a shrink, and some of this guy's patterns of behavior are freaking her out. It's a little too obsessive for her comfort level. So she called me, and… Well, here I am."

Lana, who was, *you know, very nice* calls and Wes jumps all the way to L.A.? Oh, Wes, please don't be having an affair with the wife of a friend. That was just too snarky and sleazy and downright unforgivable. You're a far better man than that.

Brittany chose her words carefully. "I know Navy SEALs are very good at what they do, but…isn't this a job for the L.A.P.D.?"

Wes finished his cheesecake, and he wiped his mouth on his napkin before answering. "Amber doesn't want to involve the police. It would be instantly all over the news—especially the tabloids. Like I said, she thinks this guy's harmless. So Lana asked me to come to L.A. and quietly check out Amber's security system, make sure it's good enough, make sure she's really safe."

"And the reason that what's-his-name—Wizard— can't do this is…?"

"He's out of the country. He's been gone for—I don't know—ten of the past twelve months."

"So Lana called you."

"Yeah." He wouldn't meet her eyes.

"You must be really good friends," Britt said. "I know you don't get a lot of vacation time, and to spend some of it here, doing this kind of favor…"

"Yeah, well…" Again, no eye contact.

"Although, of course, Amber Tierney… Sheesh. She's gorgeous. And currently single, according to the *National Star.* If you play your cards right…"

Wes laughed. "Yeah, right. No, thank you. That's the dead last thing I need. And Amber—I'm sure she doesn't need another idiot drooling over her."

"You don't think your friend Lana sent you here to set you up with her little sister?"

He looked up at her then, seriously taken aback. "God, what a thought."

"Sisters do those kinds of things," Britt said. "They

know a single guy who's really nice, they really like him a lot, they have a sister who's single, too..."

He was shaking his head. "I don't know..."

Are you sleeping with her? Brittany didn't ask. That was definitely a question that required a friendship that was more than a few hours old. And even if she had known Wes for years, it was none of her business. She kept her mouth tightly shut.

Although, what better way to spend a few weeks with a lover? Husband is conveniently out of town ten out of twelve months a year, but the neighbors might notice if one of his best friends starts coming over for slumber parties. Little sister needs a brave Navy SEAL to check out her security system, so Wes toddles off to L.A. Whoops, there's some kind of a problem, Lana comes to town to "help..." And gee, there they are. Wes and Lana in L.A., away from everyone who knows that she's married to someone else, for two blissful weeks.

Ick. Britt hoped she was wrong.

The waiter brought the check, saving her from asking nosy questions.

As Wes looked it over, he took out his wallet.

Brittany opened her purse, too. "Let's just split it right down the middle."

"Nope," he said, taking out a credit card, sliding it into the leather folder that held the bill and holding it up so the waiter could grab it on his way past. "This one's mine."

"Uh-uh," she disagreed. "This wasn't a date."

"Yes, it was," he countered. "And actually, I think it was the nicest date I've ever been on."

What a sweet thing to say. "Wow, you don't get out much, huh?"

He laughed.

"Seriously, Wes," she said. "It's not fair that you should have to pay for my dinner just because my brother-in-law—"

"How about I let you pick up the tab next time?"

The waiter was back. "I'm sorry, sir. Your credit card's expired. Would you like to use a different card?"

Wes swore as he looked at the credit card. "I only have this one." Brittany opened her mouth, but he cut her off. "No, you're not going to pay. I have cash." He looked at the waiter. "You do take cash?"

"Yes, sir."

He opened his wallet and just about emptied it. "Keep the change."

"Thank you, sir." The waiter vanished.

"Well, that was embarrassing." He looked at the credit card again. "I thought they were supposed to send me a new card before the expiration date runs out."

"What do you do with junk mail?" Britt asked.

He looked at her as if she'd lost her mind. "I throw it away. What do you do with it?"

"Do you throw it away without opening it? Mailings from mortgage companies and insurance companies and…" She paused dramatically. "…credit card companies?"

"Ha. You think they sent me a new card but I threw it away without even opening it," he concluded correctly. "Well, hell, aren't I just too efficient for my own damn good?" He forced a smile as he put the expired card back into his wallet. "Oh well."

Brittany suspected his expired card created a bigger snafu than he was letting on. "Where are you staying tonight?"

"I don't know. I guess I'll drive back to San Diego. I was going to stay at a motel, but..." He shook his head and laughed in exasperation. "I'm supposed to meet Amber pretty early in the morning over at the studio, so if I go home, I won't have time for much more than a short nap before I have to turn around and come back to L.A."

"If you want, you could sleep on my couch," Britt offered.

He looked at her, and his blue eyes were somber. "You may want to learn to be a little less generous with men you just met."

She laughed. "Oh, come on. I've been hearing about you for years. I seriously doubt you're a serial killer. I mean, the word probably would've trickled down to me by now. Besides, what are your other options? Are you going to, like, sleep in your car?"

That's exactly what he'd been planning to do. She could see it in his eyes, in his smile. "Seriously, Brittany. You really don't know me."

"I know enough," she said quietly.

Wes sat there looking at her for many long seconds. She couldn't read the expression on his face, in his eyes. If she were young and foolish and prone to thinking that life was like a romance novel, she would dare to dream that this was the moment when Wes Skelly fell in love with her.

Except they'd agreed that there wasn't going to be anything romantic between them, she wasn't his type, he was definitely connected in some way to the wife of his good friend Wizard, and Brittany didn't really want anyone to be in love with her. She had too much going on with school and Andy's college and getting used to living on the west coast and…

Maybe the man just had gas.

"Okay," he finally said. "Your couch sounds great. Thank you. I appreciate it very much."

Brittany stood up, briskly collecting her purse and her sweater. "You can't smoke inside the house," she told him as he followed her to the door.

"I told you, I quit."

She gave him a pointed look, and he laughed. "Really," he said. "This time is going to be different."

Chapter 3

"Hey, Andy," Brittany called as she opened the door to her apartment.

"Hey, Britt," her adopted son called back. "How'd it go with the load?"

Brittany looked at Wes, laughter in her eyes. "Um, sweetie?" she called to Andy. "The, uh, load came home with me."

Wes had to laugh, especially when she added, "And he ain't heavy, he's my brother."

Her place was extremely small, but it was decorated with comfortable-looking furniture and bright colors. A living room, an eat-in kitchen, a hallway off the kitchen that led to the back where there were two bedrooms.

Britt had told him on his way over that even though the place was significantly tinier than their house in Appleton, Massachusetts, it had the essential ingredient to shared housing—the bedrooms were large, and she and Andy each had their own bathroom.

Andy emerged from the hallway, dressed down in shorts and a T-shirt, his feet bare, and his dark hair a mess. He was trying to play it cool, but the kid practically throbbed with curiosity.

"Hey," he said to Wes. He looked at Wes's overnight bag, and then at Brittany. "Isn't this outrageously unusual."

"He's sleeping on the couch," Brittany told him in her refreshingly point-blank manner. "Don't get any ideas, devil child."

"Did I say anything?" Andy countered. "I didn't say anything." He reached out to shake Wes's hand. "Nice to see you again, sir. Sorry about the load comment."

"It's not sir, it's chief," Wes corrected him. "But why don't you just call me Wes?"

Andy nodded, looking from Wes to Brittany with unconcealed mischief in his eyes.

"Don't say it," Brittany warned him, as she went to a living room trunk and removed sheets and a blanket for the couch.

"What?" Andy played an angel, giving her big, innocent eyes. But beneath the playacting was an honestly sweet kid, who genuinely cared for his mother.

Jeez, that was who Andy reminded him of. Ethan. Wes's little brother. Ah, Christ.

"There was a credit card mishap," Brittany told Andy, putting the linens on the coffee table. "And Wes needed a place to sleep. Since we have a couch, it all seemed to line up quite nicely. I have an extra pillow on my bed that you can use," she told Wes, before turning back to Andy. "Wes is not a candidate."

Wes couldn't keep from asking. "A candidate for what?"

Andy was watching Britt, too, waiting to see what she was going to say.

She laughed as she led the way into the kitchen, turning on the light and taking a kettle from the stove and filling it at the sink.

"This proves it," she said to Andy. "I'm going to tell him the truth, which I wouldn't do if he were any kind of real candidate—not that there are any real candidates." She turned to Wes. "Ever since I adopted Andy, he's been bugging me to 'get him a father.' It's really just a silly joke. I mean, gosh, who's on the candidate list right now?" she asked the kid as she put the kettle on the stove and turned on the gas.

"Well, Bill the mailman just came out of the closet, so we're down to the guy who works the nightshift at the convenience store…"

"Alfonse." Brittany crossed her arms as she leaned against the kitchen counter. "He's about twenty-two years old and doesn't speak more than ten words of English."

"But you said he was cute," Andy interjected.

"Yeah. The way Mrs. Feinstein's new kitten is cute!"

"Well, there's also Dr. Jurrik from the hospital."

"Oh, he's perfect," Britt countered. "Except for the fact that I would rather stick needles into my eyes than get involved with another doctor."

"That leaves Mr. Spoons."

"The neighborhood bagman," Brittany told Wes. "Be still my heart."

Wes laughed as he leaned again the counter at the other end of the kitchen.

"The reason the list is so lame," Andy told Wes, "is because she won't go out and meet anyone for real. I mean, once every few years someone sets her up with the friend of a friend and she grits her teeth and goes, but other than that…" He shook his head in mock disgust.

"The truth is, most men my age *are* loads," Brittany said.

"The truth is," Andy told Wes, "she was married to a real load. I never met the guy myself, but apparently he was a piece of work. And now she's gun-shy. So to speak."

"I'm sure Melody and Jones completely filled in Wes as far as my tragic romantic past goes," Britt said to Andy as she rolled her eyes at Wes. "Don't you have studying to do?"

"Actually Dani just called," Andy said. "She's coming over."

"Oh, is she feeling better?"

"I don't know," he said. "She sounded… I don't know. Weird. Oh, by the way, the landlord called and said he was replacing the broken glass in your bathroom window with Plexiglas." He grinned at Wes. "There's a group of kids down the street really into stickball and they've managed to break that same window three times since we've moved in—which is pretty impressive." He looked back at Britt. "The Plexiglas isn't going to look too good, but the ball should bounce off."

Brittany snorted. "Ten to one says that my bedroom window breaks next."

The doorbell rang.

"Excuse me," Andy said as he went into the living room.

"He's a good kid," Wes said quietly. "You should be very proud."

"I am." She opened one of the kitchen cabinets and took out a pair of mugs. "Want tea?"

He laughed. "SEALs aren't allowed to drink tea. It's written in the BUD/S manual."

"BUD/S," she repeated. "That's the training you go through to become a SEAL, right?"

"Yeah."

"Jones had a few pretty wild stories about something called Hell Week."

Hell Week was the diabolically difficult segment of Phase One training, where the SEAL candidates were pushed to extremes, physically, emotionally and psychologically.

"Yeah, you know, I don't remember much of Hell Week," he told her. "I think I've blocked most of it out. It was hard."

"Now, there's an understatement." Brittany smiled at him, and Wes wished—not for the last time this evening, he was sure—that he wasn't sleeping on that couch tonight. Her smile was like pure sunshine—God, it was trite, but true.

"Yeah, I guess," he said. "Like I said, I don't remember much of it. Although, Hell Week was where Bobby Taylor and I finally stopped hating each other. The guy's been my closest friend for years, but when we were first assigned as swim buddies—you know, we had to stick together no matter what during BUD/S— we hated each other's guts."

Brittany laughed. "I had no idea. Your friendship with Bobby is legendary. I mean, Bobby and Wes. Wes and Bobby. I keep expecting him to show up."

"He's on his honeymoon," Wes told her.

"With your sister." Her eyes softened. "That must feel really strange. It must be hard for you—your best friend and your sister. Suddenly it's not Bobby and Wes, it's Bobby and Colleen."

It was amazing. Everyone who'd heard about Bobby's marriage to Colleen had made noise like, how great was that? Your best friend gets to join your family. Wasn't that terrific?

And yes, it was terrific. But at the same time it was weirder than hell. And Brittany had hit it right on the head. Wes's entire friendship with Bobby had been based on the fact that they were two unattached guys. They shared an apartment, they shared a similar lifestyle, they shared a hell of a lot.

And now, while Wes didn't quite want to call what he was feeling jealousy, everything had changed. Bobby now spent every minute he wasn't on duty with Colleen instead of hanging out with Wes watching old, badly dubbed Jackie Chan movies.

Bobby and Wes had definitely turned into Bobby and Colleen—with Wes trailing pathetically along, a third wheel.

"Yeah," he said to Brittany. "It's a little weird."

From out in the living room, Andy's voice got loud enough for them to hear. "You can't be serious!"

The kid didn't sound happy, and Wes took a quick glance in his direction.

Andy was standing at the open door. His girlfriend hadn't even made it into the living room. She was a pretty girl, with short dark hair, but right now her face was pinched and pale, and she had dark circles beneath her eyes.

"Will you please come in so we can talk about this?" Andy asked, but she shook her head. Her reply was spoken too softly for Wes to hear.

"What, so you're just *leaving?*" Andy, on the other hand, was getting louder.

Wes stepped farther into the kitchen, attempting to

give them privacy. Clearly this was not a happy conversation. It sounded, from his experience, as if Andy was getting the old dumparooney.

He looked at Britt who winced when Andy said, loudly enough for them to hear, "You're just going home to San Diego—you're not even going to finish up the term?"

Again, the girl's reply was too soft for Wes to hear.

"The biggest problem with having a small apartment," Brittany said, as she poured hot water over the tea bag in her mug, "is that there's no such thing as a private conversation."

"We could go for a walk," Wes suggested. "You up for a walk?"

She put the kettle back on the stove, giving him another of those killer smiles, this one loaded with appreciation. "Absolutely. What I really wanted was iced tea, anyway. Let me get a warmer jacket."

But as she went down the hall to her bedroom, the conversation from the living room got even louder.

"Why are you doing this?" Andy asked. He was really upset. "What happened? What'd I do? Dani, you've got to talk to me, because, God, I don't want you to leave! I love you!"

Dani burst into noisy tears. "I'm sorry," she said, finally loud enough for them all to hear. "I don't love you!"

The door slammed behind her.

Oh, cripes, that had to have hurt. Wes met Britt's worried eyes as she came back out into the kitchen. She'd obviously heard that news bulletin, too.

Andy was silent in the living room. He'd have to come past them to get to the sanctuary and privacy of his room.

And even if they were going to go for a walk, they'd have to go out right past him. If Wes were in Andy's shoes, having to face his mother and her friend was the last thing he'd want after getting an *I don't love you* response to his declaration of love.

"How about a tour of your bedroom instead?" Wes asked Brittany. If they went into her room and shut the door, that would give Andy an escape route.

"Yes," she said. "Come on."

She grabbed his hand and pulled him down the hall.

Her room was as brightly colored and cheerful as the rest of the place, with a big mirror over an antique dresser and a bed that actually had a canopy. As she closed the door behind them, Wes had to smile.

"Gee, I wish it was always this easy to gain entry to a beautiful woman's bedroom," he said.

"How could she break up with him like that?" Brittany asked. "No explanation, just *I don't love you!* What a horrible girl! I never really liked her."

They heard a click as Andy quietly went into his room and locked the door. The kid turned music on, no doubt to hide the noise he was going to make when he started to cry.

Brittany looked as if she was going to cry, too.

"Maybe I should go," Wes said.

"Don't be ridiculous." She opened her door and marched back into the kitchen and out into the living room where she started putting the sheets on the couch.

"I can do that," Wes said.

She sat down on the sofa, clearly upset. "From now on, I'm going to screen his girlfriends."

Wes sat down next to her. "Now who's being ridiculous?"

Brittany laughed, but it was rueful and sad. "He was so damaged when I first met him, when he was twelve. He'd been so badly hurt, so many times—shuffled from one foster family to the next. No one wanted him. And now this... Rejection really sucks, you know?"

"Yeah," he said. "Actually, I do. I mean, not on the scale that Andy's faced it, but... So now you want to protect him from everything—including girls who might break his heart." He shook his head. "You can't do it, Britt. Life doesn't work that way."

She nodded. "I know."

"He's a terrific kid. For all the bad crap that happened to him in his life, he's got his relationship with you to balance it all out. He's going to deal with this. It's going to hurt for a while, but eventually he's going to be okay. He's not going to come unglued."

She sighed. "I know that, too. I just... I can't help but want everything to be perfect for him."

"There's no such thing as perfect," Wes said.

Except there was. Brittany's eyes were a perfect shade of blue. Her smile was pretty damn perfect, too.

If she were any other woman on the planet, he would have given her a friendly, comforting hug. But he didn't trust himself to get that close.

She exhaled loudly—a supersigh. "Well. I have to get up early in the morning."

"I do, too," he told her. "Amber Tierney awaits."

Her smile was more genuine now. "Poor baby." She stood up. "Towels are in the closet in the bathroom. Help yourself. I'll get you that pillow."

"Thanks again for letting me crash here," he told her.

"You're welcome to stay as long as you like."

Chapter 4

Wes's car was in the driveway in the late afternoon, when Brittany got home from her last class.

When she'd gotten up in the very early morning to go in to the hospital, she'd left a key on the kitchen table, along with a note telling Wes to help himself to breakfast and to feel free to come back when his meeting with Amber was over.

As she juggled her keys with the grocery bags she was carrying in from her car, he opened the door and took one of the bags from her.

He had his cell phone tucked under his chin, but he greeted her with a smile and a twinkle of his eyes as he carried the bag into the kitchen.

"Is there more?" he mouthed. He was wearing jeans, and he had a barbed wire tattoo encircling his left biceps, peeking out from the sleeve of his snugly-fitting T-shirt.

Dressed up in a sports jacket and nice pants, he looked like an average guy—with a thick head of pretty-colored hair and those dancing blue eyes working to cancel out his lack of height. But with some of his natural scruffiness showing, in jeans that hugged a world-class set of glutes and a T-shirt that clung to his shoulders and pecs, with his hair not so carefully combed, and that tattoo… He was eye-catching, to say the least.

"I can get it," she said, but he shook his head and went out the door and down the wooden steps to the driveway. Wasn't that nice?

She started unloading the groceries, and he returned with the last two bags.

He was still on the phone. "I know," he said to whomever he was talking to. "I understand." He paused. "No, I don't think you're crazy, although, you're the shrink—you should know." Another pause. "Look, I'm on the case. I'm going out to her place tonight—there's some kind of party and…"

Even though he was talking to someone—and Brittany would've bet big money that it was his very nice "friend," Lana—he helped by putting the milk and yogurt in the refrigerator, the frozen vegetables in the freezer.

"No, I only spoke to her for about fifteen minutes—while she was getting her hair done in her trailer," Wes reported. "She said this guy's just a fan who's gone a little bit overboard. He's no big deal." Pause. "No, those were her words, not mine. I haven't met the guy." Pause. "Yeah, she mentioned that she came home last week and he was in her garage. She seems to think the only way he could have got in there was if he wandered in while she was leaving in the morning and hung out there all day, which is—yes, you're absolutely right— it's pretty freaky. I'm with you totally on that, and yeah, she seemed to talk about him as if he was some kind of stray animal—*he wandered in*. It's more likely he snuck in. But she also said that he left immediately, as soon as she asked. And she didn't get out of her car until he was out of there and the garage door was closed, so at least we know that your sister's not a total brainless idiot."

With all the groceries put in the various cabinets, he sat down at the kitchen table.

"Definitely," he said. "I'm going out there tonight. I'll look over her security system, and I'll talk to her again. And I'll call you soon, okay?" Another pause, then he added, "Yeah, you know, Lana, about Wizard…" Wes rubbed the bridge of his nose, right between his eyes. "Yeah. No, I haven't heard from him. I was, you know, wondering if you had?" He laughed. "Yeah, right. Yeah, okay babe, talk to you soon."

He closed his cell phone with a snap and very salty curse. "Sorry," he said as he realized Brittany was still standing there. "God, I would sell my left…shoe for a cigarette."

This time, Brittany couldn't keep her mouth shut. "Are you sleeping with her?"

Wes met her gaze and there was something in his eyes that looked an awful lot like guilt. "Who, Amber? Of course not," he said, but she knew he knew exactly what she was talking about.

Was he sleeping with Lana—who was *very nice*.

Britt just waited, watching him, and he finally swore and laughed, although there wasn't any humor in it.

"No," he said. "No, I'm not. It's not… It's never gone that far. It's not going to, you know? I wouldn't do that to Wizard."

But he wanted to. He was in love with the woman. It had dripped from every word he spoke while on the phone with her.

Brittany's heart broke for him. "Has it occurred to you that she might be taking advantage of you? I mean, asking you to come out to L.A. to do something she should be paying a private investigator to do…?"

"I had to take leave," Wes told her. "The senior chief insisted. And believe me, coming down here was better than staying in San Diego with all that time on my hands. It's not easy to be there—especially when Wizard's away." He laughed again, rubbing his forehead as if he had a terrible headache. "Yeah, like it's easy to be there when he's home. It sucks, okay? Wherever I am, 24/7, it really sucks. But it sucks even more when she's a five-minute ride from my house."

Brittany sat down across from him at the table. "I'm so sorry."

"Yeah, well…" He forced a smile.

"You said… She's a psychiatrist?"

"Psychologist," he corrected her.

"Does she know you're in love with her?" How could Lana not know? How could a trained psychologist not take one look at Wes and know without a shadow of a doubt that he was head over heels in love with her?

But, "No," Wes said. "I mean, yeah, she knows I run hot for her, sure. I've done a few stupid things to give that away, but… She also knows that I'm not going to act on it. You know, my attraction to her. It's not going to happen. She knows that."

Brittany kept her mouth closed over the harsh words she wanted to say. Like, how could Lana use Wes as her errand boy like this, knowing that he'd do darn near anything for her? What kind of woman would take advantage of this kind of devotion from a man who wasn't her husband?

Lana didn't sound very nice to her. In fact, she sounded an awful lot like a snake.

"You know what the real bitch of it all is?" Wes asked. "I found out something today—from Amber—that's really making my head spin. It's…" He shook his head. "I'm sorry. You probably don't want to hear this."

Brittany sighed. "Do I look like I'm in a hurry to go someplace?"

He sat there, just looking at her, somber and weary of life's burdens. This was a Wes Skelly that most people never got a chance to see. Britt realized that he hid this part of himself behind both laughter and anger.

"I've been caught in the middle for years," Wes said quietly. "Between Lana and Wizard, I mean. Wizard—the Mighty Quinn—he doesn't exactly include fidelity as part of his working vocabulary, you know what I mean?"

Britt did know.

"He's been stepping out on Lana for years," he continued, "and when I've called him on it, he's got this 'What she doesn't know won't hurt her' kind of ha-ha-ha attitude about it. So there I am. Do I tell her? Do I not tell her? I was Wizard's friend first, so I've kept my mouth shut, but it's been driving me freaking crazy.

Because if I tell her, it's going to seem as if I'm doing it for selfish reasons, right? But today…"

He started fidgeting, straightening the napkin holder and the salt and pepper shakers.

"I was talking to Amber, you know, about this guy who's been following her," Wes told her, "and how Lana's worried about him, and Amber, she says that Lana worries about everything." He stopped fidgeting and looked up at her. "She said, that's what happens when you have a lying, cheating dog for a husband. You worry about everything."

He laughed. "I was, like, floored. I was, like, 'How do you know about Wizard?' And she looked at me like I was from Mars and said, 'Lana told me.'" There was still shock and disbelief in his eyes. "All this time, I'm protecting Lana from the truth, protecting Wizard, too, and it turns out she knew."

"My ex-husband was like Wizard," Brittany told him. "He couldn't keep his pants zipped. You learn to recognize the signs."

"Just now, when I was talking to her on the phone, I wanted to ask her about it. I mean, why is she still with him? But what was I supposed to say? 'Hey, Lana, so when'd you find out you've been sharing the Wiz with dozens of other women and why the hell do you put up with that?'"

"Maybe she hopes he'll change," Britt suggested. "Of course, if she does hope that, then she's a fool. Men like that don't change."

Britt understood Wes's confusion. Lana had to know that Wes could be hers with a snap of her fingers and a short trip to a surgical specialist—a divorce attorney who could remove her malingering growth of a husband from her otherwise healthy life.

It was so obvious that Wes would be like a pit bull when it came to a relationship. He would never be unfaithful. Boy, he couldn't even be unfaithful to Wizard, in terms of their friendship.

Brittany had no doubt that Wes was going to love Lana until the end of time.

She was envious. If Lana got her head on straight and ditched Wizard for Wes, she was going to have that same, rare happily ever after that Melody and Jones had found.

"So now you know way more about me than you wanted to, huh?" Wes said with a rueful laugh. He stood up. "Well, at least I didn't smoke for three days."

"Oh, no you don't." Britt stood up, too, and blocked his way into the living room. "You are not going out to buy cigarettes. You are quitting. Even if I have to go buy a nicotine patch and stick it on you myself."

That got a smile and a trace of sparkle back into his eyes. "That might be fun."

"It goes on your arm," she told him as he kept moving toward her. She kept backing up, too, all the way through the living room, until she bumped into the door. As she hit it, she spread her arms, as if sealing it closed. As if that would keep him from leaving. "I'm a nurse, remember? I know these things."

"I'm dying for a cigarette," he admitted.

"So what?" Brittany said. "There're lots of other things in this world that you can't have, either." Including Lana. "Suck it up, Skelly."

The door opened behind her with no small amount of force, whacking her hard on the derriere and pushing her forward. It was like being hit by a linebacker. She tripped on the throw rug and would have landed on her face if Wes hadn't moved to catch her.

Brittany was nearly Wes's height and she would've bet big money that his jeans had a smaller waist size than hers. But despite that, despite his being slight of stature and seemingly slender, the man was solid muscle. She didn't even come close to knocking him over. But as a result of his catching her, she couldn't have stood any closer to him if she'd tried.

At least not with their clothes on.

While Wes had caught her, she'd caught herself by grabbing him, too, and as Andy stood looking at them now from the front door, she had to unwrap her arms from around Wes's neck.

"Oops. Sorry." Andy started to leave, closing the door behind him.

"Wait!" Brittany untangled herself from Wes and pulled the door open. "I was just keeping Wes from buying cigarettes."

Andy laughed. "Well, that's one effective way to do it."

Wes laughed, too. "I wish. But she was actually standing right in front of the door. You almost knocked her over, kid."

"Sorry." Andy didn't sound sorry at all. In fact, he sounded entirely too cheerful. But it was definitely forced.

Brittany searched his face, wondering if he and Dani had patched things up.

"You're staying here again tonight, right?" he asked Wes. "I mean, I hope you'll stay again tonight. I was hoping we could maybe, I don't know. Shoot some baskets or something."

In guy-speak, or at least in Andy-speak, *shoot some baskets* meant *talk*.

And talking—man to man—was something Brittany couldn't give to Andy. She turned to Wes. "Please stay."

"Actually," Wes said, "I spoke to my credit card company. They're overnighting a new card to me care of a Mailboxes Plus office here in L.A. But I won't get it until tomorrow. So I was hoping—"

"Terrific," Brittany told him. "And actually, you can stay for as long as you like. Save the money you'd spend on a hotel, as long as you don't mind sleeping on the couch. Just chip in a little for groceries." She looked at Andy, unable to keep herself from asking. "Is everything all right? Did you see Dani?"

"Nah, she's gone." He was almost too flip, too unconcerned. Which meant he was terribly hurt. "She packed up all her stuff and cleared out of her dorm room." He laughed, but it sounded a little too harsh. "Apparently, after spending the past six months talking me into taking things slowly, she really did sleep with Dustin Melero."

And what could Brittany possibly say to that?

Wes swore softly.

Andy went into the kitchen, apparently determined to move on. "What's for dinner?"

He didn't want to talk about Dani. Not now. Maybe not ever—not with Britt. But maybe it was part of the guy stuff he wanted to discuss with Wes.

She hoped so. "You tell me. It's your turn to cook." She followed Andy, pushing Wes ahead of her. "No cigarettes," she told Wes sternly. "You can get through one more day."

Andy put his backpack down on the kitchen table and opened the refrigerator. "Tonight we dine on…pasta."

"Wow! What a surprise. You know, I just got some chicken. We could light the grill and—"

"You guys want to go out for dinner?" Wes interrupted. "Like in about an hour? Because I've been invited to this party where there's going to be a buffet. The downside is we'll have to get dressed up. But I've got to go check out Amber's security system and I kind of promised I'd do it tonight."

"Amber?" Andy asked. If he were a dog, his ears would have pricked up.

"Amber Tierney," Wes told him. "Want to come to a party at her house tonight?"

Andy laughed, his enthusiasm a little more genuine. "Yeah. She's only the hottest woman in America. You actually know her?"

"Amber's sister—half sister, really—is a pretty good friend of mine."

"Don't you have homework?" Brittany asked Andy.

He looked at her. "Don't you?"

"Of course." She smiled. "Race ya to see how much of it we can get done in the next forty-five minutes."

Andy grabbed his bag and bolted for his bedroom. "I don't have a lot—the baseball team's going to Phoenix tomorrow, remember?"

Brittany wasn't too far behind him. "Race ya anyway."

"I guess that's a yes," she heard Wes say as she closed her door.

Chapter 5

There was no doubt about it. Wes was certain that a picture of Amber Tierney's house was going into the next edition of *Webster's* dictionary—right next to the definition for pretentious.

How much house—it was a castle, really—did one little twenty-two-year-old need?

"Are you sure she's not going to mind you bringing two mere mortals to her fancy party?" Brittany asked him as they approached the front gate—also pretentious. The gate itself was iron, but it connected to a high stone wall that had ornate iron pikes sticking out the top, like some kind of fortified medieval keep. The only thing missing were the severed heads of the enemy.

Except the stones in the wall could give even a seven-year-old the toeholds necessary to scale the damn thing. And those pikes, although dramatic looking, wouldn't even keep Wes's grandmother out.

"I'm positive," he told Brittany as they waited for the goon at the gate to find his name on a guest list. "I told her I'd stayed with you last night—I thought maybe she might know Lt. Jones and Melody, but she didn't. When she gave me the invite, she said, bring your friends. And that's a direct quote."

And indeed, they were all waved past the gate and into the yard.

As far as mere mortals went, Brittany really couldn't be counted among them—not dressed the way she was. She had definitely transcended earthly limitations. She was wearing a black evening gown that accentuated her curves in a way that was entirely too distracting. The dress wasn't low-cut or see-through the way some women's were, but every time he glanced at her, it was like, *hello*.

With her hair piled atop her head, and only slightly more makeup than she usually wore, she looked glamorous and elegant—as if she'd stepped out of a movie. Her smile was so damn genuine and relaxed. Everyone else looked tense, as if they had an agenda.

And indeed, everyone was looking at them, no doubt wondering who the heck she was.

"Everyone's looking at you," she whispered to Wes. "Nothing like a handsome man in uniform to create a stir."

He laughed. She needed to visit San Diego and re-acquaint herself with the rest of Team Ten so she could get a clearer picture of what handsome was. "I hate to break it to you, but they're looking at you, babycakes."

"Actually," Andy joked, "they're looking at me."

Brittany laughed and even more people looked in their direction.

And Wes, idiot that he was, couldn't stop thinking about how perfectly she'd fit in his arms. True, she'd only been there for a few short seconds, but she'd hit him with a full-body slam—chest to thighs. It was almost enough to make him regret telling her about Lana.

God, he couldn't believe he'd finally told someone the truth. He'd never told anyone about his feelings for Lana before—at least not when he was sober.

But somehow, telling Brittany felt right. It felt good in a very strange way—knowing that someone else finally knew.

Except here he was now, lusting after that same someone else.

Of course, he'd trained himself to do that. To act on his attraction to women besides Lana. If he hadn't, he'd be in a five-year dry spell instead of one that had lasted only ten months.

Ten months without sex. Something was seriously wrong with him. But he honestly hadn't wanted it.

Correction. He *had* wanted it, but never when it was blatantly available. Although it had been close to forever since he'd wanted it this much.

And right now, God help him, he was finding it hard to think about anything else.

"Did I tell you that that dress makes you look like a goddess?" he murmured to Brittany now.

She laughed, but her cheeks got a little pink. Wasn't that interesting?

He put his hand at her waist, pretending it was to steer her around a series of lounge chairs as they approached a huge swimming pool, but really just because he wanted to put his hand at her waist. She was warm and her dress was soft beneath his fingers, but not as soft as her skin would be, and...

And he had to stop trying to figure out the best way

to get her naked. He liked this woman too much to do anything that could hurt her.

And telling Brittany all about how much he loved Lana and then trying to take her to bed would definitely hurt her.

Or royally piss her off.

Unless maybe he was honest about it...

Yeah, that would be nice. *Hey, Britt, of course you know I'm in love with Lana, but she's not here and you are, and you're really hot...*

Christ, he needed a cigarette. He needed to take his hands off of Brittany and find a beer for one and a cigarette for the other.

But she turned toward him, moving even closer, lowering her voice to say, "Oh, my God! The entire cast of *High Tide* is here. And isn't that Mark Wahlberg? And what's his name, from *Band of Brothers?* And that girl who used to be on *Buffy*..."

"Oh, yeah," Andy said. "That's her."

Britt's body brushed against Wes's and he forced himself to take a step back, made himself let go of her.

She didn't seem to notice, one way or the other. "Whoa, there's that actress who plays that nurse on *E.R.* She is *so* good. Her mother must be a nurse, or maybe she just spent a lot of time doing research. Let's go schmooze in her direction, can we?"

"Why don't you guys schmooze without me for a bit," Wes said. "I should go inside, see if I can't find Amber, maybe take a quick look at the security system. I'll catch up with you later, okay?"

Andy was already drifting off in the direction of the actress from *Buffy*.

"Do you want me to come with you?" Britt asked.

Yes, he most definitely did, in a completely *Beavis and Butthead* kind of way. Heh-heh.

"Nah," he said. "Go talk to your nurse. I'll be back before you know it."

"This is fun," she told him, her eyes sparkling and her smile warm. "Thank you so much for inviting us."

"My pleasure," he said. He let himself watch her walk away, then headed for Amber's castle.

Wes's big mistake was wearing the uniform.

Without it on, in street clothes, he would be easy to overlook in a crowd, especially a crowd like this one, filled with the brightest stars in the firmament. But with all those colorful ribbons adorning his chest, in that white jacket that had been tailored to fit his trim body, his eyes seemed an even darker shade of blue, and his jaw seemed more square.

Or maybe it had always been that square and Brittany just hadn't noticed.

Everyone wanted to talk to him—and not just the twenty-something young women, either. He was surrounded pretty constantly by men, too. And not necessarily gay men.

Brittany had overheard two of Amber's friends talking. "He's a Navy SEAL," one reported to the other.

"A real one?" the other asked. "You mean, that's not just a costume?"

They hurried over to join the crowd around Wes.

Amber wasn't among them, however.

She was holding court herself, on the other side of the swimming pool, and the few times she'd glanced in Wes's direction, she'd seemed a little peeved. Or maybe

Brittany was just imagining that, expecting her to act like the spoiled starlet that she was.

Britt leaned back against the cabana and sipped a glass of wine. She couldn't hear what Wes was saying, or what any of crowd were saying to him, but he was starting to eye a strikingly pretty young woman in a midriff-baring dress who was standing close to him.

No, strike that. He was eyeing her cigarette.

Just at that moment, Wes looked up and caught Britt's eye.

She put two fingers to her lips as if she were smoking, and shook her head, making a stern face at him. Don't do it.

He made a face back at her. And then he said something to his groupies—a fairly long story filled with gestures and big facial expressions. When he was done, he pointed directly at Brittany. And they all turned to look at her, almost as one.

And wasn't *that* disconcerting. Weakly, she raised her wineglass in a salute.

Wes was grinning at her. What had he told them about her?

He gestured to her and although she couldn't hear him, she could read his lips. *Come here, baby.*

Baby?

Those Irish eyes were positively dancing with mischief. *Come on, honey. Don't be shy.*

Honey, huh?

What was it Han Solo always said to Chewbacca? *I have a bad feeling about this.*

But *shy* wasn't a word she'd ever used to describe herself. Curious, however, was.

Britt pushed herself up off the wall. As she approached, the crowd parted for her, as if she were some kind of queen.

"Hey, babe," Wes said when she got closer. "I was just telling everyone—everyone this is Brittany, Britt this is everyone."

"Hello, everyone," she said, trying not to be overwhelmed by the famous faces she spotted among them. Was that George Clooney standing at the edge of the crowd? If it wasn't, it was his even better-looking clone. He nodded to her, his dark eyes nearly as warm as his smile.

"I was telling the old story of how you nursed me back to health after I was injured, you know, when my squad was ambushed by *al Qaeda* forces." Wes managed to capture her complete attention.

"Oh, you were, were you? And when was this?"

"Not the first time," he said. He looked at the crowd and closed his eyes briefly, shaking his head in mock exasperation. "There were actually two times and she always gets them confused—"

"Where will you be honeymooning?" the woman with the belly button and the cigarette interrupted to ask.

What an…interesting question. Brittany looked at Wes, eyebrows raised. Apparently there were parts of that "old" story that she needed to be filled in on with just a little more detail.

"I told them about the second time we were ambushed," he told her. "You know, when the doctors were so sure I was going to die, only I opened my eyes and I saw you, and since the choice was between going to you or going to the light, I of course picked you."

"Of course," she echoed. She had to bite the insides of her cheeks to keep from laughing aloud. And Wes knew it, the devil. "Where will we be honeymooning, Lambikins? Last time we discussed it, it was a toss-up between Algeria and Bosnia." As Wes choked back a laugh, she turned to the crowd. "I'm afraid poor Wesley needs that little extra rush of adrenaline that comes from vacationing in countries with a high incidence of terrorism—to keep him revved up. You know how some men are. And so unwilling to ask the doctor for a simple Viagra prescription. I'd be happy with Hawaii, but, no."

Wes put his arm around her, pulling her so that she was pressed up against him. He kissed her, right next to her ear. "Thanks *so* much," he murmured.

She gave him a big smile. "Any time. Sweetie honey pumpkin pie."

"How do you handle it when he goes off to fight?" a woman with dark glasses asked. Brittany wasn't positive, but she thought she'd seen her a time or two on daytime TV, while on break at the hospital.

"Faith," Britt said. She'd asked the same question of her sister, and Melody had given that exact answer.

"Aren't you afraid he's going to, like, attack you in the night?"

What? "Since I'm not a terrorist," Brittany said, "no."

Wes apparently liked her answer. He gave her a squeeze.

He still had his arm around her, and her entire left side was pressed against him. She could feel the muscles in his thigh, the solidness of his chest. That-Jerk-Quentin, her ex-husband, had been both taller and wider, but nowhere near as well endowed. Muscularly, that was, of course.

"Is it true that in order to marry a SEAL—which stands for Sea, Air and Land, right?—you have to get it on in all of those places?"

Good God. Brittany doubted it, but she honestly didn't know. Was there some secret club she didn't know about? Her sister had managed to get pregnant at thirty thousand feet, but at the time Melody had had no intention of getting married. As for sea and land, well, land was easy enough, and most SEALs had access to a boat. Unless…

"By sea do you mean underwater or on top of the water?" she asked. It was such a ridiculous question, she started to laugh. She turned to Wes. "Because, honey, we've done underwater a few times, haven't we? Once when we were scuba diving off the coast of Thailand, and once in the Bering Strait?"

Wes was making that odd, choking sound again.

"I'm so sorry," Britt said. "But my dearest darling needs some air. War wounds, you know, acting up. Excuse us."

The crowd parted like magic, and she was able to lead Wes into Amber's house, through a kitchen that was twice the size of Brittany's entire apartment, and down a long marble-tiled hallway.

Most of the guests were outside, and once they were alone, Wes leaned back against the wall and laughed until his eyes watered. "The Bering Strait?" he gasped. "Do you know the average water temperature in the Bering Strait?"

Well, considering it was up by Alaska… "Cold?"

"Very cold, my dearest darling. No one's doing anything raunchier than Eskimo kisses underwater up there. Believe me. You go into that water, and you're in a dry suit. Which is even more cumbersome than a wet suit. And then, even within the dry suit, there's the small matter of the effect of freezing temperatures on male anatomy. Pun intended."

Brittany grinned at him. "Men are such fragile, delicate creatures."

"Tell me about it." He grinned back at her. "Look, I'm sorry I didn't ask you to marry me before introducing you as my fiancée, but some of those women were starting to circle like sharks. It was just a matter of time before they attacked."

"And you really don't want that?" Brittany had to ask him, suddenly serious. "I would never say this in front of Andy, and if you repeat it to him, I'll deny having said it, but it's not as if these women are looking for a lifetime commitment right from the start. And you… You can't exactly have Lana, right? I certainly won't think less of you if you—"

"Thanks, but no thanks," he said. "Unless you decide to join the circling sharks." He was only teasing. He wiggled his eyebrows at her as he leaned closer. "I'll be your bait any day, babydoll. Have I mentioned how much I love that dress?"

"Repeatedly," she told him. "Wes, come on. Seriously. Who knows? Maybe one of these girls actually has a soul. Maybe you'll meet her and forget all about Lana. You'll never know if it's even possible if you don't let yourself get close to anyone else."

He sighed. "Britt, these women don't want to discuss philosophy with me. They want to jump me in their car."

"Gee, what's that enormous blob blocking out the sun? Oh, my God, is it your ego?"

Wes laughed. "Yeah, no, I said it wrong. They don't want to jump *me,* they want to jump a SEAL. Any SEAL. It has nothing to do with me. They just want to be able to tell their friends that they got it on with a SEAL. You know, add that to their sexual resume."

Ew. "Really?"

"Yeah. SEALs get laid simply by being SEALs. Anywhere, any time. It doesn't matter what we look like, doesn't matter who we are. And yeah, I've taken advantage of that more than I like to admit and... I don't know. Right now I'm tired of it. I'm going through this phase, I guess, where I want the woman I'm in bed with to like me for me—at least a little bit."

"Well, all they have to do is talk to you for a few minutes," Brittany told him. "I mean, I liked you right away. You're very likable. That can't be too hard to—"

"How many times have you had sex with a stranger, just for the sake of having sex?" he asked.

She didn't have to think about it. "Never."

"And how many times have you had casual sex?"

"Once," she admitted. "It was awful, and I cried for four days afterwards, and I never did it again."

"There," he said, as if it proved his point. "You've obviously got a different agenda when it comes to meeting men. You think in terms of friends or potential lifemates, rather than tonight's quick screw. Walk with me, okay? I want to go check out Amber's garage. I think it's over this way."

They retraced their steps back toward the kitchen and down a different corridor.

"Just for the record," he added. "I like you a lot, too."

The garage was protected by the same high-quality security system that was wired throughout the rest of Amber's castle. There were no windows, so Amber's overly enthusiastic fan either had to have wandered in from the street, or come in through the house.

Wes pushed the button for one of the automatic door openers to verify that, yes, the garage doors were built right into the stone wall that surrounded the place. Although there was a gate and a driveway in the front of the house, he suspected that was mostly used for limousines.

He pushed the button again, and the door slid back down.

Like everything else in the house, the garage was spacious, with three bays. Each was filled, and filled very nicely, with a Maseradi, a Porsche and a vintage 1966 Triumph Spitfire—be still his heart.

Two regular doors led into the house—one was the door Wes and Britt had come through, from the kitchen, and the other... He opened it.

"Jeez, this place is freaking huge."

Britt looked over his shoulder. "Ah," she said. "It's the laundry-slash-ballroom. Of course."

The laundry room had stairs leading down into the basement—an enormous, cool concrete area, complete with a wine cellar.

It took a while, but Wes checked the windows, making sure the security system was hooked into them all, as Brittany trailed after him.

Everything was kosher. All the windows were secure.

"Do you really think a grown man could fit through those tiny windows?" Brittany asked.

"I could fit," he told her.

"Yeah, but you're...in really good shape. Anyone with a tummy is going to get stuck."

He looked at her. "You were going to say *little,* weren't you? Don't worry, it doesn't bother me."

"I don't think you're little," she told him. "I think you're just…more compact than most men."

Wes laughed at that. "My father's a real giant," he told her. "He's six foot four. My little sister Colleen is big, too. She's actually taller than me. So's my brother Frank. As luck would have it, I took after my mother's side of the family. The elfin side. We're short, but we're fast and we're tough."

"It bothers you, doesn't it?"

Yes. "Of course not. I mean, sure, it took me a few years to recover from the shock when I stopped growing but Colleen didn't. And I've gotten into more than my share of fights through the years, you know, proving what a tough guy I am despite my lack of height and…"

Brittany was just looking at him. He'd told her the truth about Lana, for crying out loud.

"Yeah," he admitted. "It sometimes bothers me—it was just a genetic crapshoot, that I should be short and Colleen should be tall, you know?"

"Yeah, I do. I used to hate the fact that Melody was so much prettier than me," Brittany told him. "I love her dearly, of course, but even now I sometimes get envious. It's all part of being human—the envy. I don't pay it too much attention, because I'm at the point in my life where I really do happen to like myself just the way I am. But it's like a holdover from when I was a teenager, when I hadn't accepted yet that there were things out of my control. I mean, yeah, I could get a nose job, but why? I'm really glad now that I didn't."

"You have a great nose," he told her.

"Thank you." She smiled at him. "It's pointy, but thank you."

"I happen to like pointy," he said.

Her smile got wider. "And I happen to like compact."

Bare bulbs lit the basement, but they didn't light it very well. Shadows loomed in the dimness. Shadows and intriguing possibilities.

But the last time this woman had had casual sex, she'd told him that she'd cried afterwards—for days.

"God, I want a cigarette," Wes blurted. No, what he really wanted was to close the distance between himself and Britt, take her into his arms and kiss the hell out of her.

"Well, you can't have one." She started for the stairs. "What's the next step in this investigation, Mr. Holmes?"

"I have to talk to Amber, find out if her alarm system was completely on, on the day that guy got into her garage. It's possible she shunted the system—you know, had it only partly on, bypassing, say, the patio door," Wes said as he followed Brittany back into the kitchen. "It'd be a piece of cake for someone to climb the wall, get into the yard and hang out and watch to see if a door or window is left open so they can sneak in when Amber goes out."

She stopped just short of the doors that led outside. "You know, Sherlock, if you're right about people being able to hop over the wall—and I'm not convinced you are because I sure couldn't do it—this place is big enough that your guy could have sneaked in while Amber was home. She never would've known."

"Yeah, you're right."

"Which is kind of scary, huh?"

"Kind of."

"You better go talk to her," Brittany told him. "I think it would be a good idea for her to make sure her alarm system is on all the time. No shunting. Even when her housekeeper's here."

"Aye-aye, Captain Evans," Wes said. "But you better come with me, because once I step out that door, I'm sharkbait."

Brittany laughed. "Shall I try to look enormously satisfied—like we just had a quickie in the closet?"

Wes laughed, too, as he put his arm around her waist, pulling her so that their hips were touching. "Just stay close and, you know, run your fingers through my hair every now and then as you gaze at me adoringly."

She reached up to push his hair back from his face, her fingers gentle and her eyes suddenly so soft. "How's that?" she whispered.

As he looked down at her, his heart was actually in his throat. When was the last time that had happened?

She was standing close enough to kiss and for about a half a second he was toast. He was going to kiss her. He had to kiss her—forget about all of his reservations.

But then the corner of her mouth quirked up, as if she were trying to hide a smile, and failing.

And he knew she was just pretending. This was just a game she was playing. They were playing. He was playing it, too.

"That's pretty damn perfect," he managed to say instead of kissing her. "Let's go find Amber."

Chapter 6

Amber Tierney didn't take her sister's—and Wes's—concerns very seriously.

She was even prettier up close and in person then she was on TV, all cascading red curls and bright green eyes and a face that was nearly a perfect oval. As Britt watched Amber talk to Wes, she found her self wondering about Lana. If she looked anything like Amber, was it any surprise Wes was ga-ga over her?

Lana-the-Bitch. That was how Britt had started thinking of her. Lana-the-Bitch had a husband who was nicknamed Wizard. Wizard-the-Loser. Lana-the-Bitch knew Wizard-the-Loser was unfaithful, but instead of dumping the chump, she instead boosted her self-esteem by telling another man—Wes—to jump through hoops for her.

Well, okay, maybe she should cut Lana a little slack.

Brittany knew how awful it had been to find out that That-Jerk-Quentin was cheating on her. There had definitely been a time of uncertainty, when she'd been paralyzed and unable to take action. True, with Britt it had only lasted about twenty minutes, but some women spent weeks or even months going through all the different phases of a dying relationship.

Denial. Anger. Grief. Acceptance. More anger.

Although it sure seemed as if Lana-the-Bitch had settled on acceptance a little too early in the process— like, she'd accepted her husband's philandering. And instead of the relationship dying, her own self-respect had gone belly-up.

"I remember that the door from the garage to the kitchen was locked," Amber said, her attention flitting to some new guests who'd just arrived. She stood on her tiptoes and waved. "Carrie! Bill! I'll be right with you." She turned back to Wes. "I really don't have time to talk about this right now."

"I think you might want to consider adding some kind of security team to your staff," Wes suggested. "Maybe just as a temporary thing."

"You mean bodyguards?" Amber widened her eyes and laughed. "Look, I'm at the studio, I'm on set or I'm here at home. I don't have time to go anywhere, and I really don't think I need a bodyguard to go from my bedroom to my kitchen."

"You may not need a bodyguard," Brittany said, "but you probably could use a Sherpa."

Amber didn't hear her because she'd already scurried off to air kiss Carrie and Bill, but Wes did.

He laughed, but it turned rueful very quickly as he

watched Amber head for the bar, arm in arm with her latest guests.

"I'm going to have to make another appointment to talk to her," he said. "Maybe with her manager or her agent. Someplace we can sit down and she can attempt to pay attention to me for, jeez, maybe a whole half an hour." He shook his head in exasperation. "She doesn't think anyone can climb over this wall, either."

"That's a very high wall," Brittany told him. "Once you're up there, how the heck do you get down?"

"You jump."

"And sprain your ankle," she said. "Which would put a crimp in your stalking plans. Hard to stalk when you can't walk."

Wes sighed. "I'm going to have to set up a demonstration, I guess. Maybe that's the thing to do. Set up an appointment to meet with Amber and her manager and agent, here in her house. Tell her to turn on her security system, tell her to wait in her kitchen. And then I'll just blow right past the entire setup—come in over the wall, get into the house without a single bell going off. Did you know her third-floor windows aren't even protected?" He shook his head in disgust.

Brittany shaded her eyes from the spotlights that lit the house as she looked up at the third story. "Can I watch?" she asked. "Because I've never seen a man fly before. That *is* how you're going to get up there, right?"

That got the response she was hoping for. He grinned and his eyes actually twinkled. Oh, dear, he was just too adorable when he did that. White teeth, tan skin, laughing blue eyes, those slightly reddish highlights in his hair.

"Last time I tried to fly, it didn't end so well," he

told her. "In fact, I managed to break both my nose and my wrist."

She narrowed her eyes as she looked at him. "Let me guess. You were ten and it involved climbing up onto the roof of your house with a cape with a big *S* on it."

"I was seven," he said, "and it wasn't a cape. It was a sheet from my parents' bed. I tied a corner to each of my ankles and wrists and jumped. I didn't quite get the results I'd hoped for."

Britt laughed. "What, did you think you'd float down to the ground?"

"Well, yeah," he said. "It always worked when Bugs Bunny did it."

One of the belly button women—there were so many of them in dresses designed to show off their perfect abs—was approaching, eyeing Wes like he was one of those incredibly delicious crab pastries Britt had taken from the buffet table for her dinner.

Brittany closed the gap between them, slipping her arm around his waist. She reached up with her other hand to play with the hair at the nape of his neck. He had lovely hair, so soft and thick. "How long was it after that before you were back on the roof?" Her voice sounded a little breathless—no doubt a result of the sudden heat in his eyes. Wes was really good at looking at her as if no other woman in the world interested him in the slightest when she was standing so close.

"Three days," he admitted. He used one finger to push a stray strand of hair back from her face, hooking it behind her ear. Anyone looking at them would think they were entirely, completely wrapped up in each other.

"God bless your poor mother," she said.

He played with her earring, still with only one finger. "I figured if I couldn't fly, I better get really good at keeping my balance."

She sank her own fingers more deeply into his hair. "And it never occurred to you that if you broke your wrist once—"

"And my nose," he added, closing his eyes and sighing.

"And your nose, that you could maybe slip and fall and break something else?"

"Well, that was the idea," he said. "To get so good that I'd never fall again."

"And did you?" she asked.

He laughed. "Well, let's just say I never fell unintentionally. Or without being shoved."

She pulled back from him. "Shoved. Off the roof?"

Wes put his arm around her and reeled her back in. "I got into a lot of fights as a kid—people thought they could push me around because I was short, you know? So I had to fight to prove I was a tough guy. Sometimes all I proved was that a five foot ten inch, hundred and thirty pound kid can do a lot of damage to a four foot eleven, eighty-five pound shrimp. But still, I usually won because I was like the Energizer Bunny. They'd knock me down, and I'd get back up and come at 'em again." He touched her necklace lightly, lifting the pendant with one finger. "This is very pretty."

She refused to be distracted. "Please don't tell me you really had fights up on roofs."

"I was a fight magnet," he admitted, letting the necklace drop and lightly tracing her collarbone, which was harder to ignore. "I managed to get into fights even in church."

"Oh, God, you were probably just like Andy back

when he was thirteen. If someone so much as looked at
him funny, he'd be down in the dust, fighting with them
in a matter of seconds. Your mother must've gone pre-
maturely gray." Her voice came out sounding breathless
again. She hoped he'd think it was merely part of the act.

He nestled her even closer to him, and there was no
longer any doubt about it. No one at this party would
have even the slightest doubt that they were deeply involved. It seemed kind of ironic, because out of all the
people here, Wes and Britt weren't the actors.

"Yeah, but you see, my older brother became a
priest," he told her. "He got all As in school, too, so
that kind of canceled out all the trouble I caused."

"I would've thought it would make it much harder
for you," she said. "That's a tough act for a kid to follow. A perfect older brother…? Of course it can be just
as difficult when the younger sibling is the perfect one."

"No one's perfect," he told her. "Not even Frank."

"Melody was," she countered. "She really was. Is.
She really is that sweet—it's not just an act, you know."

"You're sweet, too," he told her. "You pretend you're
not, you try to hide it, but I think you're even sweeter
than she is."

She tried to turn it into a joke. "Is that a compliment
or an insult, bub?"

Wes just smiled. "You can take it however you want.
I happen to think you're one of the sweetest, smartest,
funniest and, yeah, prettiest women I've ever met."

Talk about sweet. He was standing so close, his face
inches away from hers. Brittany really didn't think before she did it—it just seemed like such a natural thing
to do after he said something that nice.

She kissed him.

It was just a tiny little kiss, the softest press of her lips against his.

But when she pulled back, he looked stunned. He tightened his grip on her as he opened his mouth and took a deep breath, no doubt to tell her she'd crossed the line in this charade they were playing, when a scream erupted from the other side of the swimming pool.

It wasn't an "isn't this fun?" scream. It was a frightened scream. And it was taken up by even more voices.

People were moving back, fast, from a bedraggled-looking man who stood near the deep end.

Wes swore sharply. "This guy's got a knife."

Sure enough, the wind blew and the light from the bouncing Chinese lanterns strung across the yard glinted off of a dangerous-looking blade.

"Someone's hurt," Brittany said, pointing across the pool, to where a man was on the ground, cradling his arm or his chest—she couldn't tell which. His white shirt was bright red from blood.

"Someone call 9-1-1," Amber shouted.

"Stay here," Wes ordered Brittany. "Don't go over there, don't move until this guy is under control. Do you understand?"

"What are you doing?" Britt asked, but he was already gone. Heading around the pool, toward the man with the knife. Of course. "Be careful," she called after Wes, but he didn't turn around, all of his attention focused on that knife.

Oh, God.

About fifteen feet away from the man with the knife, Amber was inching closer to the wounded man.

Britt started around the other side of the pool from Wes. If he could distract the guy with the knife, she and

Amber could pull the injured man back, and start giving him medical attention. She had surgical gloves in her evening bag. Like most medical personnel in this day and age of disease, she carried them wherever she went. She opened her bag now and slipped them on.

"Put it down," Amber said, her voice ringing clearly. "Just put it down and then we'll talk. Okay?"

"No," he said. "No!"

Was the guy with the knife someone Amber knew? He was wearing a suit, but it was wrinkled and dirty and even torn—as if he'd been sleeping in it for about a week. His hair was a mess and he had several days' growth of beard on his face. He looked as if he'd been on some kind of binge. Having worked in hospital emergency rooms for years, Brittany had seen that plenty of times before—seemingly average guys looking like homeless bagmen after spending even just a few days living on the street, drinking or doing God knows what kind of drugs.

"Steven, how badly are you hurt?" Amber called to the man on the ground, but if he answered, it wasn't more than a whisper.

From the sounds he was making… "He may have a punctured lung," Brittany said. She spoke directly to the man with the knife. "I'm a nurse. This man is injured, possibly quite seriously. Please let me help him."

"No!"

Andy pushed his way out of the crowd and met her over near Amber.

"Don't go near him," she said to him in a low voice.

"Don't you, either," he countered softly. "What is Wes doing?"

Wes was still moving, slowly and calmly, as if he

were just taking a stroll, toward the man—who had just noticed him.

"Stay back!" the man said, his attention now split between Amber, Britt, and Andy—and Wes.

Wes held out both of his hands, keeping them low, at his waist. It was more of a gesture of reassurance than surrender, especially since he kept moving toward the guy. "If you don't put the knife down, someone else is going to get hurt, and I'm afraid it's going to be you."

"Let's try to distract him," Britt said in a low voice to Amber and Andy. "If he's paying attention to us, it might be easier for Wes to get the knife away from him."

Amber pulled off her shirt. "Hey!"

"Well, okay," Britt said. "That's one way to do it."

It was going to work. Wes was forgotten as the man stared at Amber's perfect body.

As Britt watched, Wes dropped his relaxed posture. He was ready to spring, as soon as he got close enough…

But two of the bouncers who'd been working the gate chose that exact moment to come running up.

One of them reached inside of his jacket and drew a gun. "Drop your weapon!"

The man with the knife barely even glanced at them. He took a step toward Amber.

"Freeze!" the guy with the guy's voice went up about an octave. "Move again, and you're a dead man!"

God, if this bozo with the gun shot at the bozo with the knife and missed, he could very well hit Wes.

The bozo with the knife took another step toward Amber, and Wes moved.

Fast.

"Hold your fire!" he shouted.

He was a blur of motion as he came at the knife, doing some kind of fancy kung fu type move that, oh God, definitely broke the guy's arm.

The knife clattered to the ground, and Wes deftly kicked it away.

Britt, Amber and Andy ran for the injured man— Steven, Amber had called him.

But the guy with the knife had to be on some kind of mind-altering substance. The pain from his arm should have taken the fight out of him. But it didn't.

Brittany had seen that in the E.R., too. Men with bullet wounds that should have made them pass out from the pain, having to be strapped down to keep them from attacking the doctors and nurses who were trying to save their lives.

He charged Wes, knocking him down and crashing them both into some lounge chairs.

Britt made herself focus on Steven. Yes, he'd been stabbed in the chest as well as the arm.

"I don't want to die," he gasped. "I was just standing there. I didn't even see the knife."

"You're going to be okay," she told him as she worked to stop the flow of blood. "I promise. You've got one lung that's still working fine. I know it feels like you can't get enough air, like someone's sitting on your chest, but you're not going to die." She could hear the sirens as an ambulance approached. "Andy, go out to the gate and tell the paramedics it's a chest wound."

He ran.

She could hear the sound of more lounge chairs crashing as behind her the fight kept going. Please God, don't let Wes get hurt, too. She had to battle her desire to look away from Steven, to make sure Wes was still all right. Trust him—she had to trust him.

But then she heard a splash as Wes and the crazy man went into the swimming pool, and she knew—just from the conversations she'd had with her brother-in-law—that that was intentional.

Wes had brought the man into a Navy SEAL's natural habitat, so to speak. Most people panicked underwater, but Wes would be right at home.

The paramedics ran up, and Brittany moved back to give them the space they needed. The police were finally here, too, thank God.

She could see Wes in the pool, still underwater. How long had they been down there?

Andy came to stand beside her. "You need to take off those gloves and wash your hands."

She nodded, letting Andy lead her back toward the cabana, where there were changing rooms and bathrooms. She needed to do more than wash her hands— she needed to get out of this bloodied dress. But her full attention was still on that swimming pool—at least until Wes broke the surface with another splash and a huge gasp of air.

Thank God.

The crazy knife man was more than half-drowned, and the police helped Wes get him out of the pool, where he lay coughing and sputtering as they handcuffed him.

Wes pushed himself out of the pool in one athletic motion. He was dripping wet and his uniform clung to him.

As Brittany watched him, he looked around and registered the fact that Steven was being taken out on a stretcher. He saw Amber, who came toward him, her shirt back on. But he kept looking, scanning the crowd until…

Bingo. He relaxed visibly as he found her and Andy.

She held up her gloved hands, and pointed to the cabana.

He nodded, then turned to listen to whatever it was Amber was saying.

"Do me a favor?" Britt asked Andy. "Go see if Amber has any clothes in my size. I doubt it because she's much smaller than me, but I'd love it if I didn't have to wear this dress home."

Andy nodded. "You were great, Mom. And Wes… Man, he's, um, he's pretty impressive." He cleared his throat. "I couldn't help but notice that you and he have, uh… Well, I just want you to know that I think it's great. Honest. I know I've teased you a lot about, you know, when are you going to get me a dad and all that, but I wasn't serious. I just… I want you to be happy, and it sure seems like this guy makes you smile, so…"

Oh, dear. "Andy, we were just pretending. He gets hit on when he wears his uniform, and believe it or not, he's not interested in mindless sex."

"He is interested in you," Andy told her. "If you want to call it pretending, that's fine. If that's how you want to deal with it, but…he's not pretending. You should see him look at you, Britt. That's not make-believe."

She sighed. "Andy…"

"Get washed up," Andy told her. "I'll check with Amber about some clothes."

Oh, dear.

Brittany took off her gloves with a snap and washed her hands and arms with lots of soap.

Andy was going to be disappointed when Wes went back to San Diego.

He wasn't the only one.

"Brittany, you still in here?" Wes called as he went into the cabana, pulling off his soggy jacket.

Amber's bathhouse was the size of a small country, and it was set up like a locker room in a really tony health club. There were big mirrors on walls that were painted in the colors of the southwest. The toilets were in individual rooms, and there were separate areas for changing, as well as a room-size closet that held bathrobes and bathing suits of all shapes and sizes.

There was a row of sinks, and inside of one, soaking in water, was Brittany's dress.

God, what a shame. It was a great dress, but in his experience, blood didn't wash out very easily.

However, if her dress was here, that meant she was wearing…?

Hmmm.

Wes could hear the sound of water running, and he unbuttoned his wet shirt as he headed toward it on shoes that squished.

This was definitely going to be interesting.

She'd kissed him. It wasn't a very big kiss, sure, but she *had* kissed him. Unfortunately—or maybe fortunately—he hadn't gotten a chance to kiss her back. He'd been about to, though. He'd been that close to covering her mouth with his and kissing the hell out of her.

There was one central shower room in this cabana, with lots of stalls. They were separated from the main part of the room by shower curtains. He stopped in the open archway. "Britt?"

"I'm in the shower," she called out. "There were bathrobes a-plenty, and my dress was worse than I thought, so…"

"Are you okay?" he asked.

"Yes, I am, thanks."

Can I come in to make absolutely sure? He clenched his teeth over the words.

"I'm a little off balance, though, and very, very grateful that Andy wasn't standing over where Steven was when this guy pulled out that knife. Can you imagine, just standing there at a party and suddenly…whammo. Stabbed in the chest." Brittany poked her head out from behind the curtain, giving him just a flash of her bare shoulder. "Are you okay?"

He must've been staring at her stupidly, because she added, "Are you hurt?"

"Uh, no," he said. "No, I'm…a little off balance, too, I guess."

"That was some fancy move you did, Jackie Chan, getting him to drop that knife," she told him with one of those million-watt smiles.

He laughed. "Yeah, well, it was actually pretty sloppy. Jackie would have been appalled. But it got the job done."

"Are you really all right?" Her eyes skimmed his body, lingering on the open front of his shirt and his bare chest beneath. She frowned. "God, you're going to get some bruise."

He looked down, and sure enough, there was a purple mark forming right beneath his ribs on his right side. And here he'd thought she'd been ogling his ripped physique.

"You didn't even know that was there, did you?" she accused him.

"It doesn't hurt."

"It's going to."

"Nah. I've had worse."

"Take off your shirt," she ordered him.

Wes laughed. "What are you going to do, give me a physical right here?"

"I want to make sure you're okay," she said. "I *am* a nurse."

"You're a naked nurse," he pointed out. He peeled his shirt off his arms. "You want to check me out? I'll come in there and you can check me out. That way I can check you out, too, make sure you're really all right."

"I'm not the one who was wrestling with a lunatic." There was a flush of pink on her cheeks. "Besides, after Amber did her little show-and-tell, I've pretty much decided that no one's ever going to see me naked again. Wait a sec," she ordered him and snapped the curtain shut.

The water ran for a few more seconds and then went off. The towel that was hanging over the curtain rod disappeared as Britt said, "Seriously though, I thought she was very brave. I've decided it's okay if you marry her."

Wes laughed as the curtain opened with a screech.

"Follow me," Brittany commanded, as if she were wearing an admiral's uniform instead of a towel that just barely managed to cover her.

"I don't want to marry her."

"Well, that's your loss, then. She's beautiful and she's courageous."

"Not to mention rich."

"There you go. And she's definitely your type. I bet

we could get her to dance on a table with very little effort. She obviously has no trouble with the naked part."

"I still think I'll pass, thanks."

Wes trailed her back to the room with the bathing suits and bathrobes hanging in it, watching water drip from her hair onto her shoulders as they went. She had incredible shoulders and gorgeous legs and…

She took a terrycloth bathrobe from one of the hooks and put it on. With her back to him, she slipped out of her towel, and fastened the front of the robe. It went all the way down to her calves and completely covered her shoulders. What a shame. Although he still could get quite a bit of mileage out of the fact that she was naked beneath that robe.

As he watched, she rummaged through the drawers and pulled out a bathing suit, tossing it to him. "Put this on, hero-man. Andy checked with Amber's housekeeper and all these suits are up for grabs. There are T-shirts in one of the drawers, too."

Wes draped his wet jacket and shirt over a bench and started to unfasten his pants. "So the good news is that I won't be needing to make any additional demonstrations about the ineffectiveness of that wall in keeping anyone out," he told her.

Obviously, she hadn't expected Wes to drop trou right there. "Oh?" she asked as she turned her back to him, looking through the women's bathing suits as if they were tremendously interesting.

"This guy got into the party by hopping the wall," he told her as he kicked off his shoes and peeled off his socks. "The police already found part of his jacket—it caught on one of the spikes and tore on his way over.

Amber is now convinced that she needs additional security."

"But at least this guy is in custody now," Brittany said. "Right? I mean, I know there's still a threat from all the other crazies out there, but—"

"This isn't the guy we were worried about," Wes told her as he stepped out of his pants.

"It's not?" In her surprise, she turned to face him, but then quickly turned around again.

Wes caught sight of himself in one of the mirrors on the wall. His boxers were white—they had to be under his uniform's white pants—and when they were wet they became pretty damn transparent. He quickly skimmed them off and pulled on the bathing suit she'd given him.

"Are you saying that this guy isn't the guy who was in Amber's garage that day?" Brittany asked.

"Apparently not. She says she's never seen tonight's guy before in her life. You can turn around now," he said. "I mean, you could've turned around before. You're a nurse, right? What haven't you seen before?"

Brittany came toward him, her eyes narrowing as she caught sight of another bruise that was forming on his left thigh. He'd hit one of those lounge chairs and was pretty sure he broke it. The chair, that is. Not his leg. It took a lot more than that to break a Skelly's leg.

But, "This one hurts," he admitted.

"Turn around."

He obeyed. "My shoulders feel a little rug burned. I landed on my back on the concrete a few times and skidded, you know? That guy was an effin' maniac, and he had a few pounds on me, so..."

He felt her hands, cool on his shoulders. "You're a

little red, but it doesn't look too bad. We can put some lotion on it when we get home."

God, he liked the sound of that *we*.

"You're sure you didn't hit your head when that happened?" she asked. She came around in front of him, exploring the back of his head with the tips of her fingers, checking for any lumps or bumps.

Jesus, that felt good. It would feel even better if she was kissing him when she did that.

He took a deep breath. "Look, Britt. About before—"

"I know," she said, stepping away from him. "I'm sorry. I shouldn't have kissed you. I just got caught up in the make-believe. It wasn't real—I know it's not real. You don't have to worry about that, and you don't have to say anything else."

Well, jeez, he sure as hell wasn't going to say anything now, especially not, *I'm dying to kiss you again.*

It wasn't real, that kiss. Okay. That made sense. It didn't make him happy, but it made sense.

"Do you think Ethan'll mind much if we leave pretty soon?" he asked her instead.

"Ethan?" she asked.

He swore. "Did I really call him Ethan? Andy. I meant Andy. God, I'm losing it."

"Who's Ethan?"

"He was my little brother," Wes told her. "There's something about Andy that reminds me of him a little, you know?"

Was. He saw from her face that she caught his use of the past tense. Of course she had. He had a feeling that Brittany caught everything.

"I'm going to go see if I can set up something with Amber for tomorrow," he told her before she could say anything or ask any more questions. "If Andy doesn't want to leave now—if *you* don't want to leave now, I could always call a cab."

"I'd like to leave, too," she said. She held up a tank suit. "I'm going to borrow a swimsuit from Amber. I feel a little funny going home in just a bathrobe. I'll be out in a sec, okay?"

She went into one of the changing rooms, and he brought his wet clothes out to the sinks and attempted to wring them out.

"Did you find everything you need?"

Wes turned to see Amber watching him. "Oh," he said. "Yeah. Although, Britt said something about T-shirts." He forced a smile as he gestured to his bare chest. "I feel a little underdressed."

"Men who are built like you shouldn't be allowed to wear shirts," she said. And damn, wasn't *that* weird. Lana's little sister was giving him a definite "Come on, baby" look. She hadn't given him a second glance before this.

She led the way back to the room with the bathing suits. "Steven's going to be all right. I just called the hospital."

"That's great." Of course, maybe he was just imagining her interest. He decided to experiment. "You know, women who look like you shouldn't be allowed to wear shirts, either," he countered.

Okay, now was she going to hit him or was she going to give him a flirtatious smile?

Ding, ding, ding. The flirtatious smile won. She gave it to him along with a T-shirt that advertised her TV series.

Well, hell. Okay, he could use her sudden interest

to his advantage. "So we need to get together and talk more about your security system," he told her as he pulled on the shirt.

"You could stick around," she suggested meaningfully. "The party's already breaking up."

Yikes. There was no way he was going to stick around and get cozy with Lana's sister. No flipping way. Now, if it had been Britt suggesting that…

Wes shook his head. "Can't do it. I'm sorry. What's tomorrow like for you?"

"I'm busy all day," she said. "But I could do dinner."

"Okay."

"Here," she said. "Seven o'clock."

"Great," Wes said. "I'm glad—and Lana will be, too—that you're taking this seriously."

"Oh, I am," she said. "I'm taking it very seriously. See you tomorrow."

And with that, she was out the door.

"Did she ever thank you for saving her life and the lives of her guests?" Brittany asked, startling him. She came into the room.

"How much of that did you hear?" he asked.

"'You could stick around,'" she imitated Amber. "I can't believe you said no. What's wrong with you? Every heterosexual man in the free world wants to stick around Amber Tierney, and you said no."

"I'm hung up on her sister," Wes said.

Brittany had no snappy comeback for that. She just smiled at him, but it was a very sad smile. "Yeah," she said quietly. "I guess you really are, huh?"

Chapter 7

When they got back to the apartment, Brittany made a point of obviously and definitely saying good-night to both Andy and Wes, and going into her bedroom—alone.

Andy rolled his eyes at Wes as they both rummaged in the kitchen, looking for a late-night snack.

"The baseball team's going to Phoenix tomorrow," Andy told him as he poured milk over a bowl of corn pops. "We'll be gone... I think it's four days."

Wes nodded as he put two slices of bread into the toaster. In other words, he and Britt would have the place to themselves. Not that that was really going to matter. He wasn't going to act on his attraction to Brittany.

Unless she came to him and told him that she knew he wasn't looking for anything serious, and that *she* wasn't looking for anything serious either and...

Yeah, like that was going to happen. And even if it

did, man, that would make an already confusing situation even more complicated. If she approached him, he'd do his damnedest to keep her at arm's length.

"I'd like to see you play some time," he said to Andy, trying to change the subject. The kid was sitting at the kitchen table, already packing away his second bowl of cereal. He was a good-looking young man, with dark hair and eyes and a face that reminded Wes a little of James Dean.

When Wes was nineteen, he'd still looked about twelve. He'd chugged powershakes and practically mainlined doughnuts in an attempt to leave his ninety-pound-weakling stage behind. God, he'd worked his butt off to get some muscles. Andy didn't have that problem. No one could ever call him *scrawny*. Lucky kid.

"Do you have any home games in the next week or so?" Wes asked.

"Yeah, I'm pretty sure we do." Andy laughed. "You know, that's one way to get on Britt's good side."

"That's not why I want to see you play."

"Well…okay. I'm just saying—"

"Your mother wants us to be just friends, so quit it with the innuendo," Wes told him as he opened the refrigerator, got out the butter and put it on the table.

Andy stopped eating his corn pops. "What about what *you* want?"

"Sometimes you just don't get what you want," Wes said evenly.

"Yeah," Andy said darkly. "Tell me about it."

Wes's toast popped, and he put the slices on a plate and carried it to the table. He sat down across from Andy. "Did you get that girl's phone number tonight? She seemed nice."

"Yeah." The kid morosely stirred his cereal. "Did I really want her phone number? No. Am I going to call her? Probably not." He sighed. "I can't stop thinking about Dani and that son of a bitch Melero." He looked up at Wes, real pain in his dark eyes. "She slept with him. She really did. I mean, I was so sure it was just Melero's crap, you know? But I talked to her room-mate this afternoon. Sharon's a friend of mine, too, she wouldn't lie to me. Not about something like this. And she said Dani told her she spent the whole night with Melero. This is after nearly six months of her telling me that she wasn't ready for that kind of a relationship." He laughed, but it wasn't because he thought it was funny. "I guess she was finally ready, huh?"

"What is it about guys who are assholes?" Wes asked as he brushed crumbs from his fingers. He was think-ing about Wizard-the-Mighty-Quinn. Wherever the Wiz went, women fell into his lap, too. "Women just flock to them. I don't get it."

"I don't either." Andy pushed his cereal bowl for-ward, his appetite apparently vanished. "I just keep pic-turing her, with him, in his bed. God, it's killing me."

"I know what you mean." And Wes certainly did. He didn't have to work very hard at all to imagine Lana with Quinn. He shook his head to get rid of the image. "You've got to stop thinking about it. It doesn't do you any good."

"Yeah, I know, but—"

"No buts. You've got to let it go. Move on. You know, just grieve and let go of her and…just move on."

Jesus, listen to him, giving this kid advice that he himself should have paid attention to years ago.

And for the first time, his own words really seemed

to resonate. What the hell was he doing, wasting his life, pining away after Lana when the world was filled with beautiful, smart, sexy women who wanted to be with him?

Brittany, for example.

Well, okay, maybe not Brittany. She'd made it more than clear that he wasn't her type, that she didn't want to be more than friends. That was a crying shame, but he refused to let himself get hung up on yet another woman who was unattainable. Wouldn't that be the ultimate irony? To push himself to get over Lana and instantly fall for a woman who didn't want him?

But Amber Tierney—damn, she was sure interested in exchanging bodily fluids with him, and that was sure a nice place to start. And Britt had been right. The woman was courageous and smart—and in possession of the most perfect pair of breasts he'd ever seen in his life. Not that he'd had time for more than a glance, but maybe, tomorrow night, he could remedy that.

So what if she was Lana's sister? Maybe that was a good thing. What better way to completely blast Lana out of his system, right?

"Give yourself a couple of days," he advised Andy. "And then, you know, when you come back from Phoenix, call that girl you met tonight. Put her phone number somewhere where you won't lose it and take her out to the movies when you get back into town."

"Yeah, I don't know," Andy said. "I just… I thought I knew her. Dani. You know?"

"Yeah," Wes said. "But sometimes people do things that don't seem to make any sense. But it makes sense to them for their own reasons. I mean, why would a woman stay with a man who was—for example—cheating on her? I mean, after she knows about it. The best I can come up with is there's something else going on that I don't know about."

Andy stood up and poured his bowl of cereal down into the garbage disposal. "Britt didn't. She kicked her husband's butt out of the house once she found out."

Wes had to smile. "Brittany wouldn't put up with anyone's crap for a second longer than she absolutely had to." Including his own. Which was why she was adamant about keeping her distance.

Andy loaded his bowl and spoon into the dishwasher and held out his hand for Wes's plate.

"Look, Andy, for what it's worth, chalk this thing with Dani up to a learning experience," Wes told him. "But don't let it turn you into one of the dickheads, all right? Women are drawn to jerks, it might be true, but the women you want to get involved with—they're the ones like your mom, who are looking for a good man, a man who'll treat 'em with the respect they deserve. Do you hear what I'm saying?"

"Yeah." Andy closed the dishwasher. "If I don't see you in the morning, have a nice weekend."

"You, too."

"And whatever happens between you and my mom—"

"Nothing's going to happen," Wes said again.

"Just make sure you treat her nicely, all right? She doesn't go out very often. Take her out. To dinner or a movie. You want to win huge points? Take her dancing."

Wes opened his mouth to speak, but Andy talked right over him. "Even if it's just as friends," he added.

"It is," Wes said.

"Yeah, right," Andy said as he headed down the hallway to his bedroom. Or maybe he said, "Good night."

* * *

Wes's car pulled into the driveway the next evening at about a quarter to ten.

Brittany sat at the kitchen table, finishing up her homework, her reading glasses perched on the end of her nose.

This was the test. This was the real, honest-to-goodness test. If Wes came in that door and she kept her glasses on, then she really, honestly didn't want to be anything more than friends with him.

And if she took the glasses off...

She could hear him whistling as he came up the stairs.

He sounded happy and relaxed. As if he'd had a good time with Amber. A good, happy, relaxing time. Except if he'd had a really good, happy, relaxing time, he'd still be there now, wouldn't he?

The screen door opened and he came into the house and then into the kitchen. "Hello, hello!"

She looked down to see her glasses in her hands. Darnit. It was impossible to tell if she took them off on purpose or if it was merely reflex and force of habit kicking in. She could put them back on, of course, but what would be the point? She set them down on the table instead.

"How was dinner?" she asked.

Wes laughed and opened the refrigerator. "I've come to the conclusion that Hollywood stars don't eat real food." He was wearing his sports jacket again, only this time over jeans and a white button-down shirt. He'd already loosened his tie, probably on the drive home.

"The spread at the party last night was lovely," she protested.

"Yeah," he scoffed. "If you like food that's ninety percent air. What was that stuff they were serving?"

"They're called pastries," she told him. "They're supposed to be light."

"Chick food," he dismissed it. "There should have been another table with cold cuts and bulky rolls."

"And pretzels and beer?" She raised her eyebrows.

"You got it, babe." He grinned at her over the top of the refrigerator door. "Tonight we had a wide array of salads. Salads. I was ready to eat my shoe."

"Well, help yourself," she said, even though he already was, taking Andy's loaf of white bread, the peanut butter and the jelly out of the fridge. "We've got plenty of other kinds of manly food here, too. You know, Twinkies and Froot Loops and Cocoa Krispies and Pop-Tarts. And currently our manly man index has dropped by one, so you can have it all for yourself. Twinkies are just too manly for lil' ol' me."

"Ha, ha," Wes said as he slathered peanut butter onto a slice of bread. "You're so funny. But that's right— Ethan's in Phoenix. Andy. Andy." He swore. "I have to stop doing that."

"He really reminds you of your brother, huh?" Brittany rested her chin in her hand as she watched him tackle the jelly. "It's funny, Andy's coloring is nothing like yours or your sister's. You've got that Irish thing going and… Colleen's got red hair and freckles, right? While Andy's biological mother was at least part Italian."

"It's not a physical thing. It's more of a spiritual resemblance." Wes slapped his forehead with the palm of his hand. "God, I can't believe I said that. I've been living in California for way too long." He put the slice of bread with the peanut butter on top of the slice with the jelly and took a bite. "Mmmm. Finally, food I can chew," he added with his mouth quite full.

"Where are you from originally?" she asked. "Not California, I guess."

He came and sat down across the table from her, waiting until he swallowed to answer. "Everywhere. Nowhere. I'm a Navy brat. You name it, we lived there. My father was regular Navy—a master chief. But right after I enlisted, the old man retired, and he moved the family to Oklahoma—that's where my mom's parents lived. These days if I go home, that's where I go, but it's weird because I never lived there with them, you know?"

"I can imagine."

"My dad did a tour in Hawaii that absolutely rocked. I loved it there. I learned how to surf and spent, you know, my formative years there, if you want to call 'em that. When I think of home, I think of Oahu. Unfortunately, I haven't been back there in years."

Brittany had to laugh. "When I was little, I loved all those old Gidget movies. I wanted to move to California or Hawaii and find my own Moondoggie."

"Oh yeah?" Wes said. "Well, here I am, babe." He wiggled his eyebrows at her. "Live and in person. Like, your own personal surfer dude."

"Do you still surf?"

"Yeah," he said. "Every now and then. I don't have a lot of extra time these days to hit the beach, but when I do, well, I can still keep up with the youngsters."

Keep up. She would bet big money that Wes would leave them in the dust. She smiled at him. "That's so cool."

He smiled back. "Jeez, I didn't realize it would take

such little effort to impress you. I also know how to ride a bike. And I can stand on my hands and—"

"Hush," she said. "Don't tell me about little effort. I've tried to surf. I know how hard it is to do."

"Nah, it's all about balance," he said.

"Yeah, and I was the kid in gym class who didn't travel more than four inches on the balance beam before falling on her head."

"I don't believe that," Wes said. "You're very graceful."

"I think I've got some kind of weird inner ear thing."

He grinned at her. "That's always a good excuse. Trip over your own feet and fall on your face—whoops, my inner ears are acting up again."

She smiled back at him. *Tell me about Ethan, who was your brother, past tense.* "Tell me about Amber," she said instead. "Have you convinced her to get a bodyguard?"

He rolled his eyes as he finished the last bite of his sandwich, and he grabbed a napkin from the holder to wipe his mouth before he spoke. "She says she'll get a bodyguard—but only if I agree to take the job."

"I-ee-eye will always love you-whoo-whoo," Brittany sang.

He snorted. "Yeah, I guess she's trying to turn this situation into a three hanky movie—which, incidentally, means something completely different for a guy."

Brittany hooted with laughter. "I never thought of it that way—and I'd rather not have to think of it that way ever again, thank you *so* very much." But she couldn't stop giggling.

"Sorry." He wasn't sorry at all, and she'd opened the door for more gross-out jokes by laughing like that.

He'd discovered her shameful secret, and now she was doomed. Thank God Andy wasn't home.

"Frankly, she seems up for making either or maybe even both versions of this particular movie," Wes told her. "You know, wacka-chicka, wacka-chicka, 'Hello, I am your bodyguard. In order to protect you more completely I must go into the bathroom with you while you shower…'" He rolled his eyes. "She was definitely all over me, all night long."

"Oh, poor baby. How you must have suffered."

Wes brought his plate to the sink and rinsed it before putting it into the dishwasher. Holy cow—a man who cleaned up after himself.

He turned to face her. "You know, I actually went there thinking, Why the hell not? Like, it occurred to me last night, you know, that I've been waiting for Lana to discover the truth about Wizard for all these years, and Christ, now it turns out she's known for a while and… So what am I waiting for? Hell's apparently not going to freeze over, is it? I can either spend the rest of my lousy life whining and miserable or snap out of it and go for the gusto. I figured it was gusto time. I mean, Amber Tierney—why the hell not, right? So I got to Amber's tonight, you know, after stopping at the drugstore to pick up…you know, a little, you know. But, Britt…" He shook his head. "Amber leaves me cold. She's beautiful, she's sexy, she's smart, and all throughout dinner I'm sneaking looks at my watch because I'm dying to get out of there. I don't know. Maybe something's wrong with me."

Lana was what was wrong with him. Brittany's heart broke for him even as she tried desperately not to be jealous. God, she was really starting to hate Lana Quinn.

She didn't want to think what that meant in terms of her feelings for Wes Skelly.

She stood up and opened the door to the refrigerator, pulling out two bottles of beer.

"Here's a news flash, genius. You can't just decide to stop loving someone." She twisted off the cap and handed one of the bottles to him, opened the other for herself. "Love doesn't work that way."

"Thanks," he said, lifting the bottle in a toast. "The perfect complement to PB and J. Besides a cigarette, that is. I don't suppose you have one of them lying around?"

"Not a chance."

"Yeah, I didn't think so."

Brittany brought the conversation back on track. "Don't get me wrong—I think it's really great that on one level you've recognized that the chance of a relationship with Lana might be something of a dead end, but you need to give yourself a little time to absorb that. To let it sink in. Allow yourself to spend some time acknowledging your loss."

Then go searching for the gusto. And try looking someplace other than Lana's sister's house. Although she'd practically pushed Amber at him last night, after thinking it through, she'd changed her mind. Amber was not the right woman for Wes Skelly. Not right now, anyway. Talk about making things complicated....

He'd drained practically half the bottle in one slug, and now he laughed. "Yeah, you know that's roughly what I told Andy last night when we talked about Dani."

"You did?" It was all Brittany could do not to grab him by the lapels and grill him. What did Andy say? What really happened with Dani? Instead, she asked,

"Is Andy okay? He seemed all right last night at the party, and then again this morning, but…"

"Yeah, it's just an act," Wes said as he took off his tie and slipped it into his jacket pocket. "He's doing a good job hiding how hurt he really is. Apparently, Dani really did get busy with that other kid, what's-his-name. The jerk from the baseball team."

"She did? The little bitch!" Brittany couldn't help herself. "Andy must be devastated." She closed her eyes and pressed the cold of the bottle against her forehead. "Oh, my God. And he had to sit on the same bus as Dustin Melero for seven hours today."

"You know that expression, what doesn't kill you makes you stronger?"

She looked at Wes. "I'm not really that worried about Andy. Dustin's the one who might get killed."

"Oh, come on. That sounds like something I might've done when I was nineteen, but not Andy." Wes took off his jacket and hung it on the back of the chair before he sat down at the table and started rolling up his sleeves. "He's smart enough to know that fighting with Melero isn't going to make the situation any better."

"He may know that intellectually, but emotionally…?" Brittany sat down across from him. "Andy still carries a lot of anger inside of him from when he was little. I'm pretty sure his biological mother used to beat the hell out of him. Whatever the case, he learned pretty early on to try to solve his problems by using his fists. You and I both know that doesn't solve anything."

Wes rolled his eyes. "Yeah, I'm still working on learning that one, myself. And my parents didn't even hit me. Well, I mean, my dad sometimes smacked us, but it was meant to startle, you know, not injure."

"I don't think kids should *ever* be hit," Britt said. "I've seen enough kids in the E.R. whose parents only meant to startle them."

"Yeah, I'm with you there, completely. But my dad was old school, so... Still, I'm sorry Andy had to deal with that."

"He's still dealing with it. He works very, very hard to control himself, but the potential for violence is always back there. I guess it is in a lot of people, but Andy—because of his past—really struggles. He'd never hit a woman, I know that for a fact, but in his mind any man who pisses him off is fair game. I know he reminds you of your brother, Wes, but he's not Ethan. He's not even close."

"Yeah." Wes drew circles on the table with the condensation from his beer bottle. "I know he's not Ethan." He looked up at Brittany, his eyes somber. "I do know that."

She wanted to reach for his hand, but she didn't dare. "When did he die?" she asked softly.

He turned his attention to his beer bottle, his fingers fidgeting with the label, peeling it off in strips. He was silent for such a long time, she thought he simply wasn't going to answer.

"It was right after I went through the first phase of BUD/S," he finally said. "You know, SEAL training." He forced himself to look at her, forced a smile. "So I guess it's been...damn—more than ten years. God." He drained the last of his beer and pushed himself out of his chair. "You probably have more homework to do, so I'll—"

"I'm done." She held up her beer. "This signifies the official end of the night's homework."

"Well, you probably have to get up early," he said as he rinsed his empty bottle in the sink.

"No earlier than usual." She stood up, too. "How did he die?"

"Car accident." He stood there, with his back to her. "He was coming home from work and apparently, there was a patch of ice. He hit a telephone pole. It was, um, pretty bad."

"I'm so sorry."

He glanced at her before putting his bottle in with the other recyclables. "Yeah, that was a lousy night. Colleen called to tell me he was, you know, dead. Jesus, it's been ten effin' years, but when I say it aloud, I still get hit with this wave of disbelief. Like, you know, it can't be true. He was just sixteen. There was nobody who met him who didn't love him. He was… He was a great kid."

"You don't get a chance to talk about him very often, do you?" she asked quietly.

He rinsed out the sponge, squeezed it out and started wiping off the kitchen counters, unable to stand still, especially talking about this.

"I never talk about him," he admitted. "I mean, I flew home for his funeral. It was, like, unreal. I flew in and flew out right away because I was in the middle of training. I was in Oklahoma for about four hours total. Bobby Taylor came with me, which was a good thing because I was numb. He pretty much moved me around—made sure I was in the right place at the right time. He got me back on the flight to California. He even got me drunk and started a fight with these marines who were hanging at one of the local bars—he knew I needed to pound the crap out of someone, you know, to start coping with…everything."

That was how he'd coped? "You did let yourself cry, right?"

Wes looked at her as if she'd suggested he should put on a pink ballet tutu and pirouette around the room. Okay, maybe crying, even over a dead brother was something to which he didn't want to admit. She hoped he had cried. Imagine holding all that grief inside for ten years…

"Did you go to grief counseling?" she asked as he dried his hands on the towel hanging on the handle of the stove door.

He laughed at that. "Yeah, right. What is it with women and group therapy? Colleen found all these counseling groups out in San Diego and tried to get me to join one of them. I think I went to one meeting and stayed for like two minutes. It was so not my style."

"So you just…never talk about Ethan. Not with anyone?"

"No. I mean, Bobby knows, of course. He was at the funeral, but…" He shook his head. "Most people don't want to hear about my dead kid brother."

"I do," Brittany said.

Wes just stood there, looking at her, with the oddest expression on his face. She would've paid six months rent to know what he was thinking.

But then he turned away, started fiddling with the controls to the toaster. "It's not something I, uh, really know how to do. You know?" He glanced at her. "I mean, do I start by telling you that he bled to death, trapped inside the car, before the rescue team even got to the accident scene?"

Oh, God. "Yes," Britt said.

He shook his head. "I'm sorry. I can't. I… It's better if I don't…"

"Was he conscious?" she asked.

Wes sat down at the table and ran his hands down his face. "Ah, Christ, you're going to make me talk about this, aren't you?" He looked up at her. "Seriously, Britt, I don't think that I can."

She opened the refrigerator and took out the rest of the six-pack of beer. She set it on the table in front of him. "Maybe you need a little more lubrication."

"What, are you going to get me drunk?"

She sat down next to him. "If that's what it takes to get you talking, yeah, maybe I am."

He pushed the beer out of his reach. "I told you before, I'm a sloppy drunk. All kinds of nasty truths come out when I drink too much. Let's just not go there, okay?"

"Maybe that's a good thing. You can say whatever you want, whatever you feel. I swear, it'll never leave this room."

He looked her in the eye, his gaze unwavering. "I'm afraid I'm an alcoholic," he said. "I have this one beer a day limit that I've imposed on myself, but I start anticipating it and planning for it by about noon. Where'm I going to go to get it. What kind of beer is it going to be? If I get a draft, the glasses are sixteen ounces, compared to a bottle which is only twelve—but both only count as one beer, so I usually always have a draft." He smiled ruefully. "See, I'm not afraid to tell you personal things. I'm just not ready to talk about Ethan."

"Fair enough," she said, putting the beer back into the fridge. "But if you ever change your mind… I'm a nurse. I've seen more than my share of accident victims. I know what a telephone pole can do to a car and the person driving it. And I've seen plenty of DOAs. Most of the time they have massive head injuries. They hit and they're unconscious and—"

"He was conscious," Wes told her. "His legs were crushed though—he had to be in godawful pain."

"Oh, God." She put her arms around him, hugging him from behind as he sat at the table, resting her cheek on the top of his head. "Oh, sweetie, I'm so sorry."

"It wouldn't have made any difference if I was living at home, you know? I've thought about it enough. He had the accident a solid twenty-minute drive from my parents' house. By the time I could have gotten there... Unless, I was in the car with him..."

"And then maybe you would have been killed, too."

"Yeah, I know," Wes said. He actually sounded disappointed that he hadn't been.

Brittany straightened up and started rubbing his shoulders and neck.

He sighed, tipping his head to the side to give her better access to his neck. "Oh, my God. Don't ever stop doing that."

His shoulder muscles were impossible tight. "You're incredibly tense."

"I'm terrified of what you're going to get me to talk about next."

"Okay. Let's talk about something nice. Tell me something good about Ethan."

Wes laughed. "You don't quit, do you?"

"You told me not to stop."

"That's not what I meant."

"Talking about someone you loved shouldn't be hard, sweetie. Tell me... Tell me what he was like when he was a little boy."

He was silent for a moment. But then he said, "He was quiet, always reading—not real good at sports, like me and Frank. He was allergic to everything—I think he had asthma. He had one of those inhaler things. But he was always smiling. Always genuinely happy."

"He sounds great."

"He was. And he was smart, too. And very sweet. You know, when he was six he saw one of those Save the Children commercials on TV? And he figured out that if we all pooled our allowances, we could afford the 14.95 a month it cost to sponsor a child. This was a six-year-old. When I was six, I could barely count to twenty. But he was relentless about it. Frank was the holdout—that's kind of ironic since he's the one who became the priest—and Ethan and I spent a lot of nights sneaking into his bedroom, trying to brainwash him into giving up his allowance while he slept. You know, 'You will wake up in the morning and give Ethan all of your money.' Frank had his own room because he was the oldest. Ethan and I bunked together even though he was a lot younger than me, and then my sisters shared a room."

"How many brothers and sisters do you have? I had no idea you came from such a large family."

"There were seven of us—four boys, three girls. Frank, Margaret, me, Colleen, Ethan, and then Lizzie and Sean. The twins. They're much younger than the rest of us. They were my father's little retirement surprise—born right about nine months after he did his last tour on a carrier, right about nine months after he started working at the base in Norfolk, and living full-time at home. I was seventeen at the time—which is a really bad age to have a hugely pregnant mother."

Brittany laughed. "I bet."

"Frank caved in eventually, by the way. No one could say no to Ethan for too long. With my parents' help we sponsored a little girl. Marguerita Monteleone, from Mexico. She's a teacher now, in Mexico City. She still sends birthday and Christmas cards to my parents every year."

Brittany couldn't stop the rush of tears to her eyes. "Oh, my God, are you serious?"

"Yeah."

"Have you ever met her?"

"No, but Frank did. He went down to Mexico about two years after Ethan died, to see her graduate from high school. I thought… Well, my parents decided to send her to college with the money they'd saved for Ethan to go to school."

"Okay," Brittany said. "That's it. Now I have to cry."

"Oh, come on." He tipped his head back to look up at her and smile, and she had to move back, away from him. She had to stop touching him because the urge to lean over and kiss him was just too strong.

And if he didn't want Amber Tierney kissing him, he surely wouldn't want Britt to try.

"Ethan sounds like he was an amazing kid," she said, taking a tissue from the box on the counter and wiping her eyes.

"He was." He turned to face her. "Are you okay? I'm sorry—"

"Your parents are pretty cool, too."

"They're all right. They're not perfect, but… They're okay."

"You should definitely go to Mexico and meet her," Britt told him with a final blow of her nose.

"I don't know about that."

"Why not?"

He was silent for a moment as if deciding how to answer that. "It seems a little creepy," he finally said.

"Like, he was an organ donor, too, but I wouldn't want to meet the person who got his eyes."

Brittany had to ask. "You really don't talk about Ethan with your parents or your brothers and sisters? When you go home and—"

"I don't go home," he admitted. "Not very often."

Oh, Wes. "So you didn't just lose your brother. You lost your whole family. And they lost you, too."

He put his head down on the table. "Okay. I surrender. I think you better get that beer back out of the refrigerator, because I need all of it, right now, immediately."

Britt didn't move. She just leaned back against the counter, a safe four feet from him. "You know, I don't think that's such a good idea anymore."

He lifted his head off the table and turned to look at her. "I was kidding," he said. "I wasn't serious. I was just... Let's not go any further with the psychoanalysis tonight, okay?"

Brittany nodded. "If you want, I won't keep any alcohol in the house while you're staying here."

"No," he said. "Seriously. You don't have to do that. I mean, unless you really want to. But I'm not going to, like, go crazy on you or something. I won't. I wouldn't. Not here."

"If you really were an alcoholic, you wouldn't be able to have just one beer a night, would you?" she asked.

"Sure," Wes said. "Not all alcoholics drink until they're blind night after night. Although to be honest, I've been thinking lately about quitting altogether. Zero beers a night. See, every now and then I have more than just one. I have a lot. Way more than what you've got in the fridge there. And I get totally out of control. It used to happen one or two times a year, but lately it's been more often. But like I said, it's not going to happen here. It's not like I turn into Mr. Hyde or something at the random drop of a hat. It's something that I let happen. Kind of intentionally. Like, to blow off steam, or something. When I was younger, I called it partying. Lately it feels kind of ugly though—more like bingeing than partying. It's just… I'm at a point in my life where I'd rather not feel the need to get totally skunked and wake up lying facedown in someone's front yard, you know?"

She nodded. "That's a pretty mature observation."

"Problem is, I don't like myself very much when I don't have even just a little bit of a buzz on," he admitted. "I don't like myself very much then, too, but at least I don't care so goddamn much."

God, what could she say to that? "I know you don't want to talk about this anymore right now," Britt said, "but whose idea was it to give Ethan's college fund to Marguerita?"

Wes shrugged and rolled his eyes. "Yeah, okay, it was mine. Good guess. But big deal. It was obvious that it was something Ethan would've wanted to do. And it wasn't like it was my money."

Brittany crossed the room and kissed him. But it was the way she kissed Andy these days, on top of the head. "I'm going to bed," she said. "I'll see you tomorrow. And—in case it's worth anything to you, I like you very much, even when I'm stone sober. I wish you could somehow get inside of me and see yourself through my eyes."

She kissed him again, then headed down the hall, for her bedroom, hoping he would follow. Or at least stop her.

But he didn't move, and he didn't speak.

"Good night," she called. "Don't smoke tonight, okay?"

"I won't." he finally answered. "Hey," he said. "It's me, sorry I'm calling so late," and she realized he'd already dialed his cell phone.

Wes was talking to Lana. Had to be.

Brittany closed and locked her bedroom door, and went into her bathroom, terribly glad that she hadn't done something stupid, like throw herself at him. Just like with Amber, he would have turned her down.

Brittany looked into the mirror above the bathroom sink. Don't fall for this guy, she admonished herself.

But as she thought of him out in her kitchen, talking to Lana-the-bitch, her stomach churned and her teeth were most definitely clenched.

Too late.

He had her at "I think I'm an alcoholic."

Why, oh, why did she do this? Even if this guy wasn't in love with the wife of a good friend, he was completely wrong for Brittany.

He was completely perfect.

No, no, no. He was imperfect. Tragically imperfect. Any woman in her right mind would run from him, screaming.

But Britt, of course, was unable to think of anything besides how badly she'd wanted him to follow her down the hall.

Maybe it was just about sex. Maybe her body instinctively recognized that Wes Skelly would make a good temporary plaything.

Or maybe, just like with her ex-husband, That-Jerk-Quentin, she naturally gravitated toward the men who could hurt her the most.

Chapter 8

I wish you could somehow get inside of me and see yourself through my eyes.

Wes sat in his car outside of Amber Tierney's castle, eating doughnuts and drinking coffee and watching for her "enthusiastic fan" or stalker, depending on who he was listening to.

I wish you could get inside of me... Brittany hadn't meant it that way, dirt brain. So stop thinking about that.

But holy God, if only she had...

If she had, he wouldn't be sitting here right now with his teeth on edge and his nerves jangling. He wouldn't have woken up this morning with a relentless ache that made him wish he'd given in to the urge last night to lock himself into the bathroom and...

Sex or a cigarette. He wanted one or the other within the next two minutes or he was going to scream.

Of course, all he'd pretty much have to do was knock on Amber Tierney's door and…

And he'd instantly go cold.

No, it was Brittany Evans who heated him up.

Man, oh, man it had taken every ounce of willpower he had not to follow her into her bedroom last night—crawling after her on his hands and knees—when she'd said, "I wish you could somehow get inside of me and see yourself through my eyes."

Ow, ow, ow! He'd nearly started bleeding from his ears and eyeballs. For about two minutes, he'd been convinced that his head was going to explode.

And it wasn't just the very innocent, very unintentional sexual innuendo that had him going. Although that was certainly part of it. No, it was the fact that she freaking meant it.

The woman actually liked him.

But how much?

Not enough, apparently.

She'd come over and kissed him on top of the head, like some kind of flipping child. But God, she'd smelled so good.

And when she massaged his shoulders and neck, her strong fingers cool against his skin…

He'd kept himself from following her by calling Lana. He'd promised to keep her updated, and he fought the temptation that was Brittany Evans by giving her a report of his dinner with Amber.

It was kind of funny, but the entire time he spoke to Lana, he was thinking about Britt. He was listening to the sounds of the water in the pipes, to the distant sounds of movement as she got ready for bed.

As she took off her clothes and slid beneath the covers.

No, there was no way she slept naked. Not with Andy in the apartment.

But Andy wasn't there last night.

Wes could have knocked on Britt's door. He could have rubbed his eyes to make them a little red, and then knocked on her door, and said, "I can't sleep," implied that he couldn't stop thinking about Ethan and added, "Can I come in and just, you know, hold on to you for a while?"

Yeah, lying scumbag that he was, that would've gotten him into Brittany's bed—where nature would have taken its course, because she liked him. Despite her "not my type" speech, she was attracted to him, too.

He knew she was.

It was starting to be this palpable thing between them. He could practically see it hanging in the air whenever they were together. If he lit a match, the entire room would explode.

Good thing he'd quit smoking.

God, he wanted a cigarette.

But what would Brittany have said if he'd been completely honest about last night's dinner with Amber?

"The entire time I was there, Britt, I was looking at my watch and wishing I was back here, with you. And when I pulled into the driveway and saw that your car was there, that you were already home, I wanted to burst into song."

Down the street, Amber's garage door went up, and Wes tried to focus his attention.

There was no one around, no one on the sidewalks, no one sitting in any of the other cars parked on the street.

But that didn't mean Amber's overly zealous fan wasn't watching.

Amber pulled out of the garage in the Spitfire. God, what a car.

God, he wanted a cigarette.

She signaled to make a left, but then changed her mind, and headed toward him.

Directly toward him.

She even freaking waved.

She pulled up alongside of his car and lowered her window.

It was just beautiful. Way to let the stalker know that, A, Wes was here and, B, she knew him well enough to stop and chat.

"Good morning," she said, giving him a smile that was quite the little invitation.

"It's probably better if you don't draw attention to the fact that I'm sitting out here," he told her.

"Oops," she said. "Sorry. I'll go. But…are you free for dinner?"

"Not tonight," he said. "Sorry. I'm having dinner with the friend I'm staying with. My fiancée. Brittany. She came with me to your party." It wasn't exactly completely a lie. He *was* having dinner with Brittany tonight. She just didn't know it yet.

"Maybe you could come by later," Amber suggested. "After."

Yeah, he didn't think so. And certainly not if he really did have a fiancée. What was Amber thinking?

"I know we have more to discuss, but maybe we could meet for lunch, maybe on Monday." He changed the subject. "You know, you left your garage door open."

She glanced back at it. "It's automatic. It'll go down

by itself in about five minutes. That way I don't have to remember to push the button."

Wes just started to laugh.

Weary to her bones and on the verge of emotional meltdown, Brittany came home from the hospital to a brightly lit house where music was playing and the most incredible smell was coming from the kitchen.

Wes was actually cooking dinner.

She stopped just outside of the kitchen doorway. He'd set the table—sort of—and as she watched, he stood at the stove stirring a pot of...

God, it smelled like some kind of exotic dish with curry. And that was definitely the fragrant aroma of Basmati rice, too.

"Are you coming in?" he asked, "or are you going to stand out in the living room all night? Dinner's ready."

The evening was warm, and he was wearing cargo shorts with a white tank undershirt. With his feet bare, that tattoo encircling his upper arm, and his hair still damp from a shower, he looked closer to Andy's age.

And then he put down the spoon and the muscles in his shoulders and arms rippled—yes, they actually rippled, darnit—and he looked every inch the full-grown man.

Brittany peeked around the corner before stepping into the kitchen. "Are you alone?"

He laughed at her. "Yeah, what do you think I'm doing? Cooking dinner for Amber? Get real. There're too many calories in just the smell of this stew."

"Stew," Britt repeated, still moving slowly, cautiously, setting her bag down on one of the kitchen chairs. "Is that what that is? It smells wonderful."

"Chicken, canned tomatoes, green beans and a hand-ful of curry," he told her. "Throw it all together, let it cook for a couple of hours and it comes out great—even if you're in the middle of…nowhere."

He'd been about to say Afghanistan. She was sure of it.

"Did you get my message?" she asked. "I didn't have your cell phone number, so I called the answering ma-chine here and—"

"I got it," he said.

She'd called to say that she'd been asked to put in another four hours at the hospital.

"I figured four hours was just long enough to run to the store, pick up some of the supplies you didn't have," Wes told her. "I used the chicken in the fridge—it was dated today. I didn't think you'd mind."

Brittany had to laugh, but it was a Mary Tyler Moore laugh—somewhat wobbly and sounding suspiciously like a sob. "Do I mind that you cooked dinner? Do I mind that something that smells incredible is ready to eat the moment I walk in the door? Although maybe you can turn down the heat for about five minutes, because I really need to shower." Her voice shook.

Wes turned to look at her, concern in his eyes. "You okay?"

"I will be," she said. "But… We had a really bad car accident come into the E.R. A minivan—a fam-ily. The five-year-old didn't make it. The mother's in a coma. I think she somehow knows and just won't let herself wake up."

"God, that must have sucked," he said. His eyes were filled with compassion and concern. But he didn't move toward her. He didn't make any attempt at all to pull her into his arms in a comforting hug.

"It still sucks," she told him. God, she wanted him to hug her. "It will still suck on Monday, too, when I'm scheduled to go back in. I really have to shower. Do you mind?"

He shook his head as he lowered the heat on his chicken stew. "Of course not." He swore softly. "Look, Britt, I understand completely if you don't want any dinner at all. I won't be offended if you—"

"Thanks, but I didn't have lunch," she said. Maybe he didn't want to hug her. Maybe he instinctively knew that she really wanted much more than a hug, and that the moment he put his arms around her, she'd melt into an emotional puddle on the floor. Maybe he was mortally afraid of that. "I'm not as hungry as I should be, but if I don't eat something soon, I'm going to keel over."

Wes nodded. "Then you better go shower."

Britt nodded, too, still watching him. If he'd moved toward her at all, even just the smallest shift in her direction, she would have thrown herself at him. But he didn't. And she couldn't, for the life of her, read the look in his eyes.

She turned and picked up her bag, and carried it with her into her bedroom, closing the door behind her.

Wes opened the refrigerator and got out another beer. He twisted off the cap and set it down on the table, in front of Brittany.

"Whoa," she said. "What about your limit?"

"It's my limit," he said. "Not yours."

"You don't mind?" She looked at him searchingly.

"No," he said. "I don't mind." There was a lot he

didn't mind tonight. Like the fact that after her shower, Brittany had slipped into a pair of cut-off jeans and a snugly-fitting T-shirt. Her shorts and her shirt didn't quite meet in the middle. Actually, they did, except when she moved her arms, or walked.

At those times, he got glimpses of her skin, of her belly button.

It was enough to drive him mad. Of course it was equally maddening at times like right now, when she was sitting still, at the kitchen table.

Her feet were bare, and she wore pink nail polish on her toes. And he found that, for some crazy reason, outrageously sexy.

Of course Wes thought even Brittany's knees and elbows were outrageously sexy.

She wasn't wearing any makeup, and her hair was down loose around her shoulders. She still looked a little tired, but not quite as emotionally fragile as she'd seemed when she'd first walked in the door.

He'd had to work overtime to keep himself from putting his arms around her. But that would've been a mistake. If he'd so much as touched her, he would've gotten himself into trouble.

He would've kissed her, and jeez, she was vulnerable, so she might've kissed him, too. And instead of sitting across from each other at dinner, they'd be in her bedroom right now, naked in her bed. He would be—

"What are you thinking about?" she asked.

Oh, no. No, no. He stood up, carrying their plates to the sink. "I was thinking how badly I want a cigarette." It wasn't a lie. His desire for a smoke was with him 24/7.

"Well, you can't have one."

Cigarettes weren't the only thing he couldn't have. "I know," he said. "I'm trying real hard to be good, here."

"You're doing great," Britt said. "I know how hard it must be for you."

Little did she realize…

"Is it really true that you and Bobby Taylor hated each other when you first met?" she continued.

Wes laughed as he took out plastic containers to hold the leftovers. "Yes, it is."

"Tell me a story, Uncle Wesley," Britt said. "Tell me *that* story. I assume it has a happy ending, right?"

"There's really not that much to tell," Wes admitted, thankful she didn't want to crawl around in the deepest darkest reaches of his head tonight. He didn't think he could stand it, two nights in a row. "Bobby and I were in the same BUD/S class. We were assigned to be swim buddies, and it was instant dislike at first sight. I think they paired us up on purpose, because physically we were so different. He's like twice as tall as me and he weighs twice as much, too."

"Yeah, I've met him," she said.

"For a big guy he can move pretty fast—his father played football for Michigan State and was heading for the NFL when he blew out his knee. Did you know that?"

She shook her head.

"Dan Taylor. He graduated and tooled around for about a year, just kind of going where the wind pushed him, you know? And it would have to be a freaking strong wind, because he was big, like Bobby. He met Bobby's mom working on a construction site in Albuquerque, I think it was. She was his boss, which I really would've liked to have seen. She's Native American and about six feet tall herself and…

"Anyway, they hooked up and had Bobby. His dad wanted him to play football, naturally. Bobby was huge as a kid, and like I said, he could really run. He probably could've played pro ball himself, but he joined the Navy, which really blew his old man's mind. But he had heard about the SEALs and he wanted to become one.

"So, okay, there he is. BUD/S day one. No one knows anyone else. All we know is that this is it. We're here. We're going to get a shot at being a SEAL. We all know that most guys don't make it through the program, that most guys ring out. They fail. But I'm there and I'm thinking, not me. I'm not going to quit. But I'm also looking around at all these guys from all over the country, and I'm thinking, *Damn, I'm the smallest, skinniest, shortest guy here.*

"And see, after being in the Navy for a few years, I'd recognized that it doesn't always pay off to be noticeably different from everyone else. So I'm a little worried about that. But I'm not too worried. Because like I said, I know I'm not going to quit.

"I might die," he told Brittany, "but I won't quit.

"So I'm looking around and I'm thinking, 'Look at him. He's going to fail. And Jesus, *he's* outta here before the week is through. And oh, holy God, would you look at *this* guy. He's a monster. He's like twice as tall as me, but he's freaking fat. How the hell did he even get into the program? He's so gone in like two minutes.'

"And I'm standing there, listening to the instructors talk about swim buddies, about how we will work in pairs, how we will not go anywhere or do anything—not even take a leak—without our swim buddies until training is over. If we're swimming, we're only swimming as fast as the slowest of the pair of us can swim. If we're running, likewise. Whatever we do, we're together.

"So I'm trying to focus on what they're saying, you know, but there's a part of me that's thinking, 'Okay, I may be small, but I'm fast and I'm tough as hell, and as long as they don't weigh me down with one of these monster loads…' And of course they pair me up with Fatty."

"Bobby Taylor isn't fat," Brittany scoffed.

"He's not now," Wes said. "But at the time he was… well, he wasn't exactly toned. He was huge, he was strong, but he had just a little bit of a sumo wrestler thing going."

She laughed. "I don't believe you. You're so full of—"

"Just ask him," Wes protested. "Next time you see him. He'll tell you. He was a kid—we both were. He still had some baby fat.

"Anyway, I'm looking at this guy—you want the rest of this story or not?"

"Yes," she said. "Definitely."

"Okay," he said. "Because if you don't—"

"I do. You're looking at this guy—Bobby, right?"

"Yeah, and he's looking at me, looking me over, and I know he doesn't like what he sees either. And he says, 'You have no body fat. Water temperature's really low this time of year. Surf torture's gonna kill you, man. You'll be gone by freaking midnight.'

"So I say, 'That's okay, I'll just crawl into your belly button for warmth, Santa Claus.'"

She laughed. "Oh, my God, you're so mean."

"Well, sh— shucks, his first words to me were *you'll be gone by freaking midnight*."

"What's surf torture?" she asked.

"It's where the instructors send all the SEAL candidates into the ocean, with our uniforms on. The water's freaking cold, and we're supposed to link arms and just sit there for hours and hours, getting pounded by the surf, freezing our balls off. It's like an endurance test."

Brittany was watching him as he moved from the counter to the refrigerator. Her chin was in her hand, a small smile playing about the corners of her lips. God, he loved it when she smiled at him that way.

"Needless to say, my Santa comment wasn't well received. But we followed the rules. I basically pushed and pulled him over the O Course—the obstacle course—and hauled him behind me whenever we had to run or swim. He can outswim me now—don't tell him that—but at the time he was pathetic. His upper body strength sucked, too."

"He, in turn, did help keep me warm when I was about to chatter my teeth clear out of my head. And he turned out to be a better student than me. He helped me quite a bit with the classroom instruction. And as far as carrying the IBS around—we were in boat teams of about eight men, and wherever we went, we lugged around this thing called an Inflatable Boat, Small. Small, my ass. That thing weighed, like, a million pounds. I kind of stood on my tiptoes and touched it with the very tips of my fingers. I was too short. Everyone else was taller than me, especially Bobby. I'm pretty sure he carried his share and my share, too."

"So you came to respect each other over time," Brittany said.

"Nah," Wes said. "It wasn't as gradual as that. We started looking at each other differently on day three of Hell Week. The instructors were riding us, trying to get us to quit. They targeted the pair of us as losers and were trying to weed us out from the real men who were going to make it to the end. So they're screaming at us, and Bobby's getting angrier and angrier, and I just kind of turn to him and say, 'Are you quitting?' And he says, 'Hell no.' And I say, 'Well, then stop listening to them. They're the losers. Just shut them out. Turn the effin' volume down in your head. Because I'm not quitting either, man. They could hold a gun to my head, and I still won't ring that bell.' There's a bell, you know, that you have to ring when you quit. It's a major deal, like there's a little 'I quit' ceremony. You really have to want to quit to go through with it. But a lot of guys do quit.

"Anyway, Bobby looked at me and I looked at him, and again, I knew he saw the same thing in my eyes that I saw in his. We weren't going to quit. I suddenly recognized that in him—the fact that he was in for the duration. And right then, all of sudden, like whoosh, I was freaking glad—like, thank you Mary mother of God—that he was my swim buddy. Because other guys' buddies were dropping out left and right, and they were suddenly on their own, or getting teamed up with someone else who'd been quit on. And quitting is contagious, you know."

"Yeah," Brittany said, finishing her second beer. "I do know."

He took the bottle from her and rinsed it in the sink. "So we made it through Hell Week and Phase One of training, but we were still kind of tiptoeing around each other when I got the call from Colleen—about Ethan.

That's when Bobby and I became real friends. He didn't need to go home with me. I didn't ask him to, but he gave me all this B.S. about how swim buddies had to stick together, yada, yada, yada, and he wouldn't let me get on that plane alone.

"I was damn glad he was there. And we've been tight ever since. You want another beer, babe?"

Brittany laughed. "Are you willing to carry me to bed?"

Wes laughed, too. Yes. Yes, he was willing. He looked at her, and she was looking back at him, still smiling. But he couldn't for the life of him figure out if she was actually flirting or just making another completely innocent suggestion. "After only three beers? What kind of wimp are you?"

"The kind of wimp who rarely drinks more than one or two beers in the course of a week." She pointed to his cargo shorts. "You're ringing."

He was, indeed. He took out his cell phone and flipped it open. "Skelly."

"Wes, it's Amber. I'm sorry to bother you so late."

He glanced at the clock above the stove. It was barely even 2200. "It's not late. What's up?"

"I've been getting these really weird phone calls all night," she told him. Her voice sounded very young and small over the phone. She was either seriously frightened. Or a good actress. Hmmm. "It's as if someone's calling and then hanging up. And I heard this scary noise from outside, like a loud thump."

"Call the police," he told her. "Do it right now."

"I did," Amber said. "They came out, but they didn't see anyone or anything and… So they left. But then I heard the noise again. I'm not going to call the police again. They already think I'm a flake."

Brittany was watching him, curiosity in her eyes.

"Will you come over?" Amber begged. "I just… I would feel much better if you came and checked out the yard and—"

"All right," he said. "I'm on my way." He'd caved, mostly so he wouldn't be tempted to stay and open that third beer for Brittany—so he wouldn't have to carry her to her bed.

God, he really wanted to carry her to her bed.

Hoo-boy.

"Thank you, thank you," Amber was saying as he shut the phone on her.

"She heard a scary noise," Wes told Brittany.

Who laughed. "Yeah, right. Twenty bucks says when you get there, she answers the door in a negligee, saying 'Save me! Save me!'"

He grinned. "Do women still wear negligees? I thought most women liked wearing big T-shirts to bed."

"I don't know about most women," Britt said. "But I happen to have a few negligees at the bottom of my lingerie drawer."

Oh, my God. "Really?" Crap, his voice actually cracked, like he was seventeen again.

"In the event of an emergency," she said, her smile widening. "That's what my mother said when I was throwing out my entire life after I split up with Quentin. 'Keep a few, Britt—in the event of an emergency.' Like what? Aliens invade, time to go put on a sexy nightgown?"

"Well, as far as I'm concerned, it sure as hell couldn't hurt."

"I should have thrown them away," Brittany said. "I'm not the planned seduction type. It's just…it's too weird."

What was she telling him?

"I mean, what does a guy think," she added, "when he comes over and a woman's wearing something like that?"

"He thinks *hooray*," Wes said.

"Yeah, but what if he's not into her? Amber's been giving you signals left and right, and because you're still hung up on Lana, you're certainly not leaping for joy."

"It's not so much that I'm still hung up on Lana," he said, desperately trying to figure out what Britt was really saying to him. "Because, you know, I've been hung up on her for years and I've had, uh…relationships with women during that time. It's more that… I don't know. I guess Amber's not my type."

Brittany blew out a burst of disbelieving laughter. "Are you kidding? She would dance naked on a table without blinking. She's exactly your type."

His mouth was dry and he had to moisten his lips before he spoke. "You know, I think I was probably wrong about what kind of woman my type really is." *You're my type.* Jesus, he was too chicken to say it.

"You better get going," she told him. "Amber's waiting."

"Come with me," he blurted.

She laughed. "Yeah, she'd like that."

"Seriously." He didn't want his evening with Brittany to end like this. And maybe his lack of interest would finally get through to Amber if she saw him again with Britt. "Every time I talk to Amber I mention my fiancée. I think maybe she needs a visual reminder."

"Or maybe she's been talking to her sister who knows you don't really have a fiancée."

That stopped him short. God, he hadn't thought that far ahead, but sure, if Amber talked to Lana, she might mention Wes's "fiancée." Would Lana even care? Maybe not. Probably not. She hadn't mentioned it last night when Wes called her. Jesus, she probably didn't care at all.

For some weird reason, that didn't make him feel desperate or frustrated or hurt—only strangely wistful.

It was weird. For so long, he'd been carrying this hope that when Lana found out about Wizard's cheating ways she'd leave him and come running into Wes's open arms. He'd had this fantasy that Lana secretly loved him, too, but that she was staying away from him because she was a good, honest woman, honoring her wedding vows.

But she'd known about Wizard for some time now. Wes's fantasy was nothing but a silly, childish fairy tale. *And they lived happily ever after.*

Yeah, sure.

"Look, just come with me," he told Brittany now. "Help me out here. Please?"

"I love a man who cooks dinner, cleans up afterwards and says please." She stood up. "Give me two minutes and I'll be ready to go."

Chapter 9

Sure enough, Amber answered her door wearing clothes that left very little to the imagination. Gauzy white pants that were nearly transparent over red thong panties. A halter top made of red silk that was so sheer, she might as well have come to the door topless.

"Thank God you're here," she said. And then she saw Brittany. "Oh."

"Hi," Britt said.

"Amber, you met Brittany at your party." Wes draped a casual arm around Britt's shoulders.

"Sure," Amber said. "The nurse. Right. Come on in. I certainly didn't mean to drag you all the way out here, Brittany."

But she did mean to drag Wes. And his giant…flashlight.

"It's no trouble," Britt lied. "We were just about to

go for a walk on the beach, you know, before going to bed." She smiled at Wes as she said that—let Amber think whatever she wanted to think. He grinned back at her, his hand warm at her waist now as they went into Amber's house. "This isn't that much of a detour."

"Well, thanks so much for coming," Amber lied, too.

"You really should think about full-time security," Brittany told her. "I'm sure there are even female bodyguards—if you don't want a bunch of guys with no necks hanging around, watching your every move."

Wes was holding her hand now and playing with her fingers, as if he couldn't bear not to touch her—as if they really were going to go home and go to bed together. As if he couldn't wait.

Brittany had to work hard to keep her pulse from racing. *This wasn't real.*

"Where were you when you first heard the noise?" he asked Amber.

"In my TV room," she said as she led the way to the back of the house, her perfect buttocks glowing like a beacon beneath those sheer pants. Brittany was tempted to take Wes's flashlight and shine it on her buns. It was hard to look anywhere else, but Wes was watching Britt and smiling. Probably at the expression on her face.

"Actually, I offered Wes a job as head of my security," Amber turned slightly to say to Britt. "Maybe you can help talk him into it. I'm sure you'd prefer it if he were in L.A. full-time, instead of down in San Diego."

He'd put his arm around Brittany again, and his fingers slipped up beneath the edge of her T-shirt, warm and slightly rough against her bare skin.

"Oh, I'd never ask him to leave the SEALs," Britt said. Her voice sounded breathless. "Absolutely not."

Wes was doing a really good job of looking at her as if he couldn't think of much else besides getting her home and into bed. He had such heat in his eyes. And his smile had vanished as he continued to stroke the curve of her waist.

Maybe he'd picked up on the hints Britt had dropped at dinner—especially that comment about him having to carry her to bed. She couldn't believe it when that came out of her mouth.

But after a day at the hospital, filled with such suffering and pain, she didn't want to spend the night alone. She wanted comfort. She wanted to lose herself in full-body contact with this man whom she'd come to like so much in such a short amount of time.

And he either wanted that, too, or he was a better actor than Amber Tierney could ever hope to be.

"You can't be a SEAL forever," Amber said. "My sister's married to a SEAL, and she's told me it's just a matter of time before he gets too old to go running around in the jungle or whatever it is that he does, saving the world. She said it's a young man's game."

"She's right," Wes said. "Eventually, I'll get too old to keep up with the new guys, but I'm not there yet."

Brittany gently extracted herself from his grasp. "When Wes retires from the Navy, he's coming back to L.A. He's quite a talented actor."

"What?" Wes said with a laugh.

"You are," Britt told him.

He was looking at her as if she were completely crazy.

"Okay, here's where I was sitting," Amber interrupted them. "Right there on the sofa. And the noise seemed to come from that direction." She pointed toward the patio. "It sounded like, I don't know, like maybe someone was throwing something against the side of the house."

"Or climbing up the outside? Did you get the windows on the third floor hooked into your alarm system yet?" Wes asked.

"No," Amber answered. "That'll happen next Thursday. Do you really think—"

"No," Wes said. "I don't. But to be absolutely safe, you should pack a bag and stay in a hotel tonight. And tomorrow get your manager working on hiring a security team. You know, it's actually pretty amazing that you've gotten by for this long without one."

Amber didn't look happy. "Are you sure I can't talk you into staying here tonight?" She looked at Brittany. "Both of you. I have plenty of room."

"There's no way one person could keep you safe in a house this size," Wes said. "I mean, sure, I could do it if we all camped out in one room, but... Britt's son is away for the weekend, and I've got to be honest—we had other plans for tonight."

Amber nodded, definitely subdued. "All right. I'll go get a bag. Make yourself comfortable. There's wine in the kitchen fridge. I'll only be about ten minutes."

"Thanks, but we'll walk you up," Wes told her. "We'll wait just outside your room. This is a big house, and I don't want to scare you unnecessarily, but until you get the third-floor windows wired, you're really not safe here. I'm sorry I didn't make that more clear to you the other day."

Amber really *had* heard a noise outside. She really *was* scared. Because if she wasn't, now was the time when she'd reassure them that she'd be fine and send them on their way. But she turned slightly pale, and her eyes got even bigger.

No, this wasn't just a ploy to get Wes over here. At least not completely.

They followed her upstairs and, after Wes checked out Amber's flowery bedroom to make sure that no one was hiding inside, they waited for her in the hall.

"I think she's finally catching on," Wes said to Britt in a low voice. "Thanks for coming out here with me."

"You're welcome," she said. "Do you really think she's in danger?"

"She's famous. And there are a lot of crazy people out there. Some of them—not all of them, but some—know how to climb and could get into a third-floor window," he said. "Do I think she's in danger tonight? No. But we could sit around and talk about it for a couple of hours. And then she could call again at 0300, after she hears another noise. At which point, I'll come back here and help her get checked into a hotel room. I figured I'd skip the drama and go directly to the thrilling conclusion— one in which it's possible for me to get a good night's sleep. Or at least to have an uninterrupted evening."

Wes was looking at her again with that molten lava look in his eyes. Except this time Amber wasn't around to see it.

He had a wonderful smile, but even when he wasn't grinning his mouth was still beautiful, with lips that were almost delicate and quite gracefully shaped.

Oh, God, Brittany was staring at his mouth, as if she wanted him to kiss her. She looked up into his eyes instead.

Oh, God, she did want him to kiss her.

He smiled very slightly. "You want to help me make sure she never hits on me again?" he murmured.

Now he was the one who was gazing at *her* mouth.

"Okay," Britt told him, hypnotized. "How?"

"Kiss me," he said. "And then when she's packed and ready, she'll come out of her room and find us in a lip-lock. That should take care of any last lingering doubts."

"She said she'd be at least ten minutes," Brittany said. It was a stupid thing to say, considering how badly she wanted him to kiss her.

Wes smiled. "I can endure it if you can."

She laughed, and he did it.

He kissed her.

Lightly at first. Gently. Sweetly. His lips were so soft and warm as he brushed them across hers.

Britt felt herself sway toward him, and then, God, he was holding her in his arms.

"Oh, man," he breathed, and kissed her again, more completely this time, covering her mouth with his.

And oh. My. God.

She melted.

It was a kiss for the world record books—Most Romantic Kiss of All Time. Or at least it would be if it had been real.

Who would've thought that rough and tough U.S. Navy SEAL Chief Wes Skelly—a man with a reputation for salty language and a total lack of tact, a man who was known for speaking before thinking, for knee-jerk reactions, for bursts of temper and lack of restraint—would be able to kiss so beautifully, so worshipfully, so utterly sensitively, and completely tenderly?

God, if he could kiss like this, making love to him would be…it would be too perfect. Her head would explode. Bang. Complete overload of all of her systems. She would simply cease to exist.

Oh, but she wanted to risk it. She wanted to try it and see.

Except, this kiss was just a show for Amber Tierney. And Amber wasn't likely to show up in Brittany's apartment. Although maybe Britt could use that as an excuse. *Hey, Wes, just in case Amber decides to come over, maybe you should sleep in my bed tonight. And just in case she happens to come into the room, we should probably make love, you know, all night long. You know, just in case, and just to make it clear that you're not interested in her.*

Uh, yeah.

"Hi, this is Amber." Wes lifted his head to glance toward the bedroom, but Amber was only talking on the telephone, and he quickly returned his attention to Brittany.

"You're completely killing me," he whispered before he lowered his head and kissed her again.

Was she really? God, she hoped so, because he was killing her, too.

Kissing Wes for these past few minutes had been better than her entire years-long sex life with her ex-husband.

She wrapped her arms around his neck, pulling him closer. She brushed her hips against him, and... oh, boy.

He stopped kissing her, pulling back to look at her, and at first she thought she'd gone too far. Yes, he was obviously aroused, but maybe he didn't want her to know that, or to acknowledge it or...

But the heat in his eyes nearly incinerated her. He didn't say a word. He just looked at her.

And then he kissed her again.

This time, it was instant combustion. A total melt-down. He was kissing her as if he, too, had been think-ing about nothing else but making love to her for the past few days. He was kissing her as if he thought he might be able to touch her very soul if he could get as much of his tongue as possible into her mouth.

Which was really great, because she wanted his tongue there. She wanted his hands on her body, too, sweeping down across her back, across the curve of her derriere, pulling her closer, even closer to him as if he were trying to absorb her completely into him.

"Whoopsie! Sorry!"

Amber.

Wes let go of Brittany so fast, she almost fell over.

"Sorry," he said, too, but it wasn't clear if he was talking to Amber or Britt. But then he definitely turned to Amber. "I just, uh, don't get leave very often and…"

"And Brittany's son is out of town," Amber finished for him. "You don't need to drive me to a hotel. I can drive myself. Just…if you don't mind, will you walk me down to the garage?"

"Sure," Wes said. He looked at Brittany again. "Sorry. I'm…sorry."

Was he apologizing for nearly knocking her over, or that incredible kiss?

"I'm the one who's sorry I interrupted your evening," Amber apologized, too, and it was possible that she ac-tually meant it.

"It's okay," Britt said. She looked at Wes. "It's really okay, you know."

He looked at her, but he didn't say anything. What could he say in front of Amber?

Silently, they trooped down to Amber's garage.

* * *

Wes drove with both hands on the steering wheel, aware of Brittany's silence, aware that his immediate apology after Amber had gotten into her car and pulled out of her garage may not have been the right thing to do.

He shouldn't have kissed her, period. He should have kept his hands to himself. He should never have gotten a taste of her sweetness and fire.

But goddamn, she'd kissed him like he'd never been kissed before.

Even now, all these long minutes later, he was still feeling shell-shocked and emotionally dizzy.

And despite his apology, despite his admission that he'd gone too far and that kissing her in the first place had been a mistake, he wanted to kiss her again. He wanted to go even farther. He wanted...

He glanced at her.

She was looking out the window, subdued, pensive, tired. Hurt?

He honestly didn't know. She'd had a long, grueling, emotionally draining day at work. She certainly had the right to be tired.

But Jesus, what if she'd actually wanted him to kiss her, and then he'd gone and called it a crazy mistake?

Except, after Amber had come out of her room and interrupted them, Brittany had stood there, looking for all the world as if she were about to cry. He'd apologized—for what he wasn't sure. Maybe for having to stop kissing her.

Maybe for being born.

And she'd said it was okay, but she was so obviously not okay.

And she was still not okay.

And he wasn't either. He felt shaken and desperate and completely turned upside down.

Wes dragged his eyes back to the road. It was late, but the street was pretty busy. Stores were closed, but some of the restaurants were open. And the bars were still hopping, their neon lights flashing.

Joe's Cantina, dead ahead on the right, with its colorful lights and Mexican decor, looked like the kind of place he and Bobby used to hang, sometimes all the way to last call. They'd drink and drink and drink, and then drink some more.

There was a parking spot open right in front, and he hit his brakes hard, skidding slightly.

The car behind him blew his horn, then went around them with a flurry of obscene gestures and a squeal of tires.

That caught Britt's attention, and she turned to look at him in surprise while he parallel parked.

"What do you say we go get a drink?" he said as he straightened the car out and pulled up the parking brake. "I could use a shot of tequila."

She looked at him, looked at Joe's Cantina, looked back at him. "I don't think that's a good—" She cut herself off. Sat very still for a moment. Took a breath. "Of course, it's up to you if you really want to go in there and—"

"I don't really want a shot of tequila," he told her. "I want, like, ten."

Silence.

Then, "What do you want me to say to that, Wes?" she said quietly. "You tell me you think you're an alcoholic. You tell me you want to stop drinking completely.

And now you tell me…" She shook her head. "I'm not going to tell you not to drink. If you think you've got a problem, you've got to stop because you want to, not because of anything I say or do."

"I do want to," he said. "I just… Right now I really, really want to get trashed." He couldn't look at her, so he looked at his hands, still holding onto the steering wheel as if it were a life preserver. "See, if I get trashed," he struggled to find the right words, "then, you know, I can say all the things I can't possibly say when I'm sober. Like…" He forced himself to look at her. "Like, I want you so freaking bad, I don't think I can spend another night on the living room couch without completely losing my mind."

She laughed—it was more of an exhale than a real laugh, but it was enough to take the edge off of the terror that came from having admitted that.

"I think you just managed to say it," she told him.

"Yeah," he agreed. "I did, didn't I?" He looked at her, and she didn't look as if she were about to run screaming from the car. She looked…glad?

"Let's skip the getting trashed part, okay?" she said, "and just go home and make love."

Her words were music to his ears. God, she was beautiful. She was only partly lit by the streetlamps, and shadows played across her face, accenting her cheekbones and that luscious mouth. Her eyes were shining, and she gave him such a smile, that for a half a second he was sure he heard a choir of angels singing.

He was either going to cry or laugh, so he laughed and reached for her, and then she was in his arms and kissing him.

And kissing him and kissing him.

He wanted to pull her across his lap, wrestle her out of those shorts and unzip his pants and...

He didn't give a damn about the fact that they were on a public thoroughfare. That wasn't what held him back.

It was that she deserved better than some kind of slam-bang joyride in the front seat of his car.

Truth was, she deserved better than him, period.

But, damn, her lips were so sweet, her body so soft. His hand was already up her shirt, his fingers sliding against the smooth perfection of her silky skin, his palm filled with the full weight of her breast.

She opened her mouth wider, inviting him in, and he kissed her more deeply. But still slowly. If she changed her mind, he wanted her to be able to pull back. To stop him at any point.

But she didn't. She made a sexy noise, deep in her throat, as her fingers found the edge of his shirt and she slipped her hand up along the bare skin of his back. Her hand was warm and soft and perfect, just like the rest of her.

"I want you naked," she stopped kissing him to whisper.

Oh, man. He kissed her again, but then had to ask, "Are you sure you really want...this? Me and you, like this? Doing this?"

"Yes." She kissed him again, harder, hotter, but then she pulled back. "Are you?"

"What, are you kidding?" he reached for her.

But she kept him at arm's length. "No, I'm not." She gazed at him searchingly, looking for...what? Reasons they shouldn't spend the night making love? Man, he hoped she didn't find them in his eyes.

He started the car. "Let's go home, because I really want you naked, too, and that could draw a crowd here."

"Seriously, Wes," she said as he pulled out into the traffic, signaling to get into the left lane. "What about Lana?"

"Lana who?" He didn't know this part of town well, but he was guessing they were about three minutes, tops, from Brittany's apartment. Three minutes to mind-blowing pleasure.

Britt laughed. "Don't be a jerk."

"I'm not," he protested. "I'm just… When I'm with you, baby, I don't even think about her."

"Okay," she said. "Be a jerk if you have to, but just don't be a liar. Please?"

"It's the truth."

"Okay, look," she said. "If you want to sleep with me—"

"I do!" *If.* She'd actually "if-ed" him. *If* was such a little word, but it wielded tremendous power. Thirty seconds ago there had been no *if,* but now there was, and his estimate of mind-blowing pleasure in three minutes was suddenly in jeopardy. One little *if* could turn a wait of three minutes into a wait of three weeks. Or three years.

"I really do," he said again. "Honest, Britt."

"Yes!" she said, grabbing his knee and squeezing it. "Honesty—that's what we need. If you want me to sleep with you, you've got to be honest. We both know this isn't going to be long term or permanent or even particularly meaningful. We're just…two people who like each other—"

"Really like each other," he added.

"Who find each other attractive—"

"Outrageously, stupendously attractive."

She laughed. "Yeah, but the bottom line is—"

Here it came.

"…that we're just two people who are tired of being alone. And for tonight and the next few nights—or however long you're going to be in town—we don't have to be."

Thank you, God. Wes pulled into her driveway. "Race you to the door."

Brittany laughed. "Do you promise—"

"Yes."

"Wes, I'm being serious."

"I am, too, babe. I want to take off your clothes with my teeth and lick every inch of your body. Slowly."

Well, that stunned her into silence. He used the opportunity to pull her to him and kiss her, long and hard.

"Please just be honest with me," Brittany said between kisses. "Please? About everything, okay?"

"I will," he said, kissing her mouth, her face, her throat, and her breasts, right through the cotton of her shirt. "I promise."

"That's all I want." She laughed. "Well, besides the licking thing."

"Let's go inside," Wes said.

He kissed Brittany on each of the stairs going up to her apartment.

And he'd unfastened and unzipped her shorts before she even got her key into the door.

As the screen slammed behind them, Wes kicked the wooden door closed with his foot as he tried to pull her T-shirt up and over her head.

Britt laughed and tried to wriggle out of his grasp, but he was persistent. "Andy?" she called.

That stopped him.

The room was dark, and she turned on the little light near the door.

"I just want to make sure he didn't come home," she told him. "Trips can sometimes get canceled and—"

"Yo, Andy," Wes called. "You here?"

Silence.

Patience not being one of his strong suits, Wes went into the kitchen and down the hall to Andy's room. Brittany followed more slowly, but he was back in a flash.

"He's definitely not here," he said, and kissed her. And this time she helped him get her shirt off, even as she kicked her sandals from her feet.

His shirt followed, although he was far more interested in unfastening her bra.

He swore. "Help me with this, will you? What does it have, a combination lock?"

Brittany laughed, stepping out of his grasp and reaching behind her to unfasten it, but then she held it on, suddenly feeling not quite shy, but not quite as bold as she had earlier, either. "You really want to get naked in my kitchen?"

"Absolutely." He laughed softly. His muscles gleamed in the moonlight coming in through the window, and he looked breathtakingly beautiful, all broad shoulders tapering down to a narrow waist and slim hips. It was amazing that there was actually moonlight to add such atmosphere to this moment. "We've spent a lot time these past few days sitting in here, talking. I've gotta confess, the entire time, I was dying to see you naked. This is kind of like fantasy fulfillment for me."

"Well, when you put it that way..." Britt took off her bra, hanging it over the back of one of the chairs.

"Oh, yeah," he breathed. He didn't reach for her, he just looked, his eyes hot.

She pushed her shorts off as he watched, then slipped her panties down her legs.

"Here I am," she said, loving that look in his eyes, knowing she'd made the right choice tonight. This may not be a forever thing, but it was going to be wonderful. It would be a memory she would cherish for the rest of her life. "Naked in my kitchen. You want some tea?"

"No."

"What? You mean, that's not part of the fantasy?"

He laughed. "Nope."

"How about hot sex on the kitchen table?"

"Yup," he said, slowly reaching out to touch her. Her hair, her cheek, her shoulder. He ran his fingers lightly down her arm, and then over to her breast. The way he was looking at her made her feel impossibly sexy. "But later. First I want to make love to you in your bedroom, in your bed. You know, I've spent a lot of time dreaming about that, too."

Brittany reached for the button that fastened his shorts, touching him the same way he was touching her—lightly, with only the tips of her fingers. The zipper didn't go down easily, and she looked up at him and smiled.

And he kissed her—one of those impossibly tender kisses that he did so well.

She melted, closing the gap between them, and he drew her in, sighing his pleasure at the sensation of her body against his, her breasts against his chest.

There was more urgency to his kisses now, or maybe

he was just responding to the way she was kissing him, holding him, touching him.

His hands were everywhere, sweeping her body, touching, exploring, as he kissed her, licked her, tasted her.

More, more, more. She wanted more. She wanted...

He knew. And he picked her up, her waist at his shoulder, his hands on her bare butt as he carried her into her bedroom.

It was so much the opposite of that first sweet kiss they'd shared, that Brittany had to laugh. It was...so Neanderthal, and almost shockingly politically incorrect. And yet it was a total turn-on.

Maybe it was because physically, Wes wasn't any kind of a real, hulking caveman, and she wasn't a lightweight in any sense of the word. Yet he carried her so effortlessly.

But the tenderness was back as he carefully lowered her to her bed, which was also a turn-on, especially when he took a moment and let himself look at her, and let her see the desire in his pretty blue eyes.

She was the one who reached for him and finally pulled off his shorts.

He had nothing on underneath.

And so much for that cruel myth about short men...

"Gee," she said, "I was so anticipating finding out whether you wore boxers or briefs."

"Laundry crisis," he told her with a grin that made her heart flop around in her chest as he joined her on the bed.

He kissed her and she kissed him, too, reaching for him, wrapping her fingers around him. He was solid and smooth and so incredibly male.

He laughed.

"What?" she asked.

He lifted his head to look down at her. "I'm having one of those 'This can't be real' moments," he said. "You really want honest?"

She nodded, her heart in her throat.

"I feel like I'm getting away with something here. I've talked more with you than any woman I've ever known, and you still want to make love to me. I mean, I didn't have to pretend to be someone I'm not to get you to sleep with me."

His honesty would have been breathtaking even if he'd stopped right there. But he kept going.

"For the first time in my life," he told her, struggling to find the right words, "I don't have to worry about, I don't know, what to say or what not to say. I can say whatever I want, you know? Because I know that you already like me enough not to run away if I say something really stupid or...wrong."

Brittany touched his face. "I don't just like you, sweetie. I think you're wonderful."

"I think you're pretty wonderful, too, babe."

And there they were, smiling at each other, like a couple of kids at the ninth grade dance.

Except they were naked and in her bed.

"I want to make you feel good tonight," he told her with a smile that made her heart do another somersault. He lowered his head to kiss her and as his mouth met hers, her heart did an entire circus act.

And oh, no. No, no. She couldn't let herself fall in love with this man. Oh God, wouldn't that be a mistake.

Too bad it was too late.

That was ridiculous. Of course it wasn't too late. She'd barely known the guy—what was it now? Four days?

And yet here she was—in bed with him. After only four days. What did she think that meant?

Nothing. It meant nothing. It meant that she was a woman with a woman's needs and desires and it had been much too long since she'd last had a sexual relationship. It meant that she was human. It meant that she liked Wes.

Liked?

Yes. And, oh man oh man, she certainly liked what he was doing to her. She heard him laugh softly as she moaned. He held her shoulders down, keeping her from pulling him on top of her as he kissed and licked his way from her breasts to her belly button.

"Please!" she gasped. "Do you have a condom?"

"I do," he said. "It's on your bedside table. But I wasn't kidding when I told you I wanted to lick every inch of your body."

"Oh," Brittany said. "God. Can we add that to the 'Later' list, you know, along with the kitchen table? Because I haven't made love since about a year before I adopted Andy, and that was a really awful relationship that lasted only about a week."

And it had only lasted that long because the sex was so great. After divorcing Quentin, she'd needed to know that their relationship hadn't failed because she was lousy in bed. And Kyle Gherard had helped her prove Quentin wrong. Of course, Kyle was also a total idiot who'd made Britt exceedingly reluctant to engage in that kind of a relationship ever again.

Yet, here she was, doing it with Wes.

Who was looking at her as if she'd just announced

her plans to launch herself into space and orbit the moon. Confusion, disbelief, shock—it was all over his expressive face. "Are you telling me you haven't had sex in, what? Nine years?"

"No," she said. "God. Not nine years." She had to count on her fingers. "Only eight."

He laughed at that. "Only?" and grabbed for the condom, tearing it open with his teeth.

It took him about two seconds to cover himself and protect them both as he kissed her, as he nudged her legs open wider, and…

He stopped. She could feel him against her, but… he stopped.

"How slow should I go?" he asked. He was serious. "I don't want to hurt you, baby. I mean, if it's been eight years…"

In less than a heartbeat, she pushed him off of her, rolled him over, onto his back and straddled him, driving him deeply inside of her.

The burst of pleasure was so intense, she heard herself cry out.

"Sorry," she gasped, moving on top of him slowly at first, loving the way he filled her. "Sorry. I didn't mean to… I just needed…"

He was laughing. "Do you hear me complaining? I don't think so."

"Oh, Wes, this feels so good."

"Yeah," he breathed. "Oh, yeah. I guess it's like riding a bicycle, huh?"

"Believe me, this is better than riding a bicycle."

He laughed. "I meant, it's something that you just don't forget how to do."

"I want to do this all night," Brittany said. "Can we do this all night?"

His smile was so beautiful as he sat up to hold her in his arms, to kiss her breasts, to draw her into his mouth and tease her with his tongue and lips. "I vote for all weekend."

"All month," she gasped.

"All year," he agreed, pulling her head down so he could kiss her mouth.

Seconds, minutes, hours—Brittany had no idea how much time passed as they moved together, touching, kissing, stroking, loving.

Loving.

She pushed his shoulders back against the bed then sat up straight, so he could fill her even more completely.

He held her gaze as she moved, faster now. She could tell from the way he was breathing that he was close to his release.

The phone rang, but neither of them made the slightest move to stop, neither so much as looked away from each other.

In the kitchen the answering machine picked up. "You've reached Britt and Andy. Leave a message at the beep."

"Hey, Britt, it's Mel," her sister's voice came through on the answering machine speaker. "I'm just calling to see how your dinner went—your date with Wes Skelly. Call me back and tell me everything, okay?"

Wes laughed at that, his eyes sparkling. "Not everything, I hope."

Britt laughed, too, and reached behind her to touch him. Oh, he liked that. Very much. Maybe a little too much.

"Whoa," he gasped. "Wait, baby. Brittany. Britt…"

She exploded with a cry, and he was right behind her, bucking beneath her as his world crashed into a million tiny pieces, too, as his life surely fragmented, as it flew apart and spun around, before slowly coming back together again, in one piece. Like her, he was irrevocably changed.

Wes pulled her down and held her tightly, her breasts against the solidness of his chest, as he kissed her.

Tenderly.

As if she'd just given him the sweetest gift he'd ever received.

"You're incredible, Britt," he whispered.

She lifted her head to smile at him, loving his eyes, the lean line of his face, even the slight stubble on his chin.

"Okay," she said, "I think I'm ready for the licking thing now. I mean, feel free to take as long a break as you need, of course, but—"

He tickled her.

She shrieked and rolled off of him, but he quickly pinned her to the bed.

Holding her gaze, he lowered his head and licked her. From her breast all the way to her ear.

Brittany shivered and he grinned.

"I don't need a break," he said. "Like I told you, I'm going to make love to you all weekend long." He kissed her mouth so sweetly. She would never get used to that. Not in a weekend, not in a lifetime. How did he manage to be so incredibly gentle? "You just tell me what you want and when you want it," he told her. "Okay?"

She nodded again, her heart going through its gymnastic routine as he gave his full attention to her collarbone.

She was such a fool. Great sex did not equal love. So this guy was good in bed, so what?

He was more than good in bed. He was smart and funny and sweet. But just because she thought that, didn't mean she was in love with him.

Yeah, right.

Hearts could pound and do flips because of attraction and lust.

And yes, she lusted after him. Definitely.

She liked him, too. A lot. An awful lot.

But it wasn't love.

She'd be a fool to fall in love with Wes Skelly, because he loved somebody else.

Chapter 10

The phone rang.

Again.

Wes turned to look at Brittany, who was sleeping amidst the rumpled sheets and blankets, her hair a cloud of gold on the pillow, one gorgeous leg thrown across him.

"You ever going to answer the phone again?" he asked her.

She opened her eyes and looked at him. And smiled. "Hello."

He smiled back at her. "Yeah, that's what you're supposed to say *after* you pick up the phone." He ran his hand from her shoulder to her tush and back up again. And down again. Her skin was so soft and smooth. He could touch her like this for hours and be completely entertained.

The answering machine clicked on, but then clicked

off as whoever was calling hung up. He'd picked up the phone a few times when Brittany was sleeping, but whoever it was had hung up as soon as he'd said hello.

"Only person I want to talk to right now is here, in bed with me," she told him, her smile getting even warmer. She stretched and snuggled closer to him. Man, she killed him. Continuously. "Did you have a nice nap?"

"I didn't nap. I ran to the store—after I finally wore you out."

She laughed. "If you honestly think you've worn me out…"

"Yeah?" Wes said. "What? I think you're going to have to prove that I haven't."

"Kind of hard for me to prove it when I've already worn you out," she countered.

Oh, he was up for that challenge. Literally. "Just say the word," he said. "I'm ready when you are." He took her hand and placed it on the fly of his shorts. "See?"

"Well, well," she said. But then she frowned. "Why are you wearing clothes?"

"I told you. I went to the store."

Brittany stopped unzipping his shorts to narrow her eyes at him. "Not to get cigarettes."

Wes snorted. "Yeah, like I'd dare smoke and then climb back into your bed." Man, the way she touched him… "I went to the store to deal with my other addiction."

She kissed him and then looked up at him, all big blue eyes and that not-so-innocent smile. "Which is…?"

"You," he somehow managed to say. "I'm completely addicted to you. I got us more condoms."

"Good," she said and kissed him again as he ran his fingers through her hair.

Yes, this was heaven.

The phone rang.

"This is getting annoying," she said. "I know it wasn't Andy calling before, because he would've left a message."

The answering machine picked up. "Hey, you've reached Britt and Andy. Leave a message at the beep."

"Mom, it's Andy."

Brittany sat up.

"Are you there? If you're there, please pick up."

She rolled across the bed, reaching for the telephone extension on the bedside table and clicking it on. "Hey, I'm here, buddy. How are you? How's Phoenix?" She looked at Wes. "Sorry," she mouthed.

He shook his head. This was not a problem. He knew she'd been hoping that Andy would call.

"I'm not in Phoenix." Wes could hear Andy's voice still coming through on the answering machine speaker. "I'm in San Diego."

"What?" Brittany said.

"San Diego," he said again. "At Dani's sister's apartment. Mom, I need you." His voice shook. "Can you come down here?"

She stood up, getting clean underwear from her drawer, and putting it on as Wes refastened his shorts. "What happened?" she said. "Are you all right?"

"Yeah," Andy said. "I'm… Mostly all right."

"Mostly? What does mostly mean? What's going on?"

"Do you know if five days is too long to wait after a sexual assault to, you know, to use a rape kit?"

"Oh, my God," Brittany said. "Andy…"

"Dani was raped, Mom. She didn't sleep with Dustin Melero voluntarily. I heard him bragging to some of the other guys, talking about Dani and some other girls, telling how he put vodka into water bottles, and…" The kid could barely speak. He was crying.

"Oh, Andy…" She stood there, her hand over her mouth, looking at Wes, like she wanted him to say or do something, like wake her up from a bad dream.

He crossed the room to her and touched her arm, hoping that might help even just a little.

"*Give 'em enough of that,* he said—I heard him say it," Andy continued, "*And no doesn't really mean no. He said that. The son of a bitch said that!*"

"I'm so sorry," Brittany said. She turned away from Wes. "To be honest, Andy, I don't think a rape kit's going to turn up much evidence at this point. Did she shower? She must've showered, right?"

"Yeah, only about a hundred times."

Wes pulled on his T-shirt as Brittany put on a pair of jeans and a shirt, and brushed her hair, tying it back with a ponytail holder.

He hovered close by, wishing there was something he could do to save the day. But there wasn't. Not in this situation.

"Did he injure her?" Britt asked.

"Obviously."

She shook her head, hand to her forehead. "No, Andy, I know that he… I'm asking if… God. If he was rough. If he injured her physically, if there are any marks of violence." She looked at Wes, tears in her eyes. "I can't believe I'm having this conversation with my son."

Wes held her gaze, wishing he could track down

Dustin Melero and tear his ass to shreds. But he knew that what Brittany needed most right now was for him just to stand here, beside her.

"I don't know," Andy said. "She won't talk to me. She locked herself in the bathroom. Mom, she's so messed up about what happened. She thinks it was her fault. I'm scared to death she's going to hurt herself. Please come down here. If anyone can get through to her, you can."

"I'm on my way, but first give me your phone number," Brittany said. She found a pen but no paper on her dresser, and searched frantically for something to write on.

Finally something he could do. Wes held out his arm. She looked at him and he nodded, and as Andy recited the number, she wrote it. On him.

"That way we won't lose it," he told her. "Let's get the address, while we're at it."

"You're coming with me?" she asked.

"Of course," he said, and her eyes welled with tears again.

But she brusquely wiped them away. "Andy, what's the address?" Britt asked, and as he told her, she wrote that, too, on Wes's arm.

"Let me talk to him," Wes said.

She handed him the phone.

"Hey, Andy, it's Wes Skelly," he said. "Look, your mom and I are going to leave right now, but it's going to take us a couple of hours to get there. We'll call you from the car to touch base, all right?"

"Yeah."

"In the meantime, I'm going to call a friend of mine who's a professional. She's a shrink—a psychologist who's actually had some experience working with rape trauma victims. If I can catch her at home—and I'm betting I can considering what time it is—she should be able to get to you in just a few minutes. Her name is Lana Quinn."

Brittany turned sharply to look at him, but then quickly looked away, as if she didn't want him to see her reaction to that news.

The news that he was going to call Lana.

Lana, whom he'd loved for years.

Lana, whom he hadn't thought about once in the past twenty-four hours.

Lana, whose name made Brittany take notice, and quite possibly feel…jealous?

Wow.

Wes had an awful lot to think about, but no time to sort any of it through right now.

"Lana will talk to Dani," he continued. "Right through the bathroom door, if she has to. She's good, Andy. She'll be able to help, okay? So when she comes over, let her in."

"Yeah," Andy said. "Thank you."

"We'll be there as soon as we can." Wes hung up the phone and looked at Britt. "Let's go. I'll call Lana from the car."

It was late, but there was still traffic on the side streets, heading over to the freeway.

Brittany sat in Wes's car, trying not to squirm with frustration. Andy needed her, and she was miles away from him. It was enough to drive her mad.

And even if it weren't enough, Wes was on his cell phone, calling Lana-the-Bitch.

God, she hated Lana more than ever now.

"Hi, it's me," he said, because of course Lana would immediately recognize his voice over the phone, even after midnight on a Saturday night.

Maybe especially after midnight on a Saturday night.

Don't be jealous. Don't be jealous. Don't be—

Well, why the hell not? Minutes ago she'd been on the verge of having more mind-blowingly hot sex with this incredible, wonderful man. And now she had to sit here and listen while his voice got all soft and gooey because he was talking to Lana.

Lana, who was going to get out of bed and rush over to Dani's sister's house, to try to help Andy's girlfriend, who'd fallen victim to date rape.

Oh, God. Poor Dani.

Poor Andy.

Poor jealous Britt.

"Sorry I woke you," Wes said into his cell phone as he signaled to get on the freeway and kicked his car up to eighty. Britt had to hang on to the handle at the top of the window. At least she didn't have to be frustrated because he didn't drive fast enough. "But we've got something of an emergency happening, not too far from where you live."

He quickly told Lana what Andy had told them. About Dustin Melero's bragging. About Dani leaving school, and then locking herself in the bathroom when Andy came to confront her with the truth.

Andy—the son of "Cowboy Jones's sister-in-law, Brittany Evans."

Boy, she didn't even rate as "my friend, Britt."

Brittany listened while Wes read the address off of his arm.

"Thanks," he said. "And we'll be there as soon as we can." He paused, listening as on the other end of the phone Lana—Lana-the-perfect—spoke. Probably in perfect, pearl-like, clear round tones. "Thanks," he said again, his voice especially warm. "I knew you'd come through for me, babe."

Babe.

Wes called Lana *babe,* too?

Oh, God. Jealous, jealous, jealous. There was no doubt about it now. If Lana were in range, Britt would have given her the evil eye. And maybe even an audible snarl.

But she had no right to feel angry or even hurt. She knew this would happen, right from the start. She went into this thing completely aware of Wes's feelings for Lana.

But hoping that after a night or two with her, Wes would forget about Lana completely...?

No. She wasn't that stupid.

Oh, yes, she was.

Well, yeah, maybe. Oh, okay, yes, darnit.

God, she was a fool.

Wes hung up the phone, but then dialed another number.

"Who are you calling now?" Brittany asked. *Your other girlfriend?* Ooh, easy there. Deep breaths. Calm blue ocean.

"Hey, babe," Wes said, and Brittany stared at him in disbelief. "It's Wes. Sorry I'm calling so late. Is your devastatingly handsome husband around?" There was a pause, then, "Hey, Lieutenant, it's Skelly. I'm sorry to bother you. Yeah, I do know what time it is, sir, but I'm here in my car with your gorgeous sister-in-law and we're heading for San Diego at warp speed. Andy's in a jam, I was hoping you could go over to his girlfriend's sister's place ASAP and provide a little extra support until we can arrive."

He was talking to Harlan Jones, the SEAL officer with the ridiculous nickname of "Cowboy" that Britt's sister Melody had married.

It was Melody that he'd *babe*-ed. Apparently *babe* wasn't as intimate a term of endearment as Britt had originally thought. Which made his *babe*-ing of Lana a little bit easier to swallow.

Just a little.

She still felt jealous, but it was accompanied by an overwhelming wave of adoration for this man who was thoughtful enough to call Harlan Jones—a man Andy knew and trusted—to provide the first wave of reinforcements.

She wouldn't have thought to do that.

Wes gave Jones the address and ended the conversation by saying, "See you in a few."

He closed his cell phone with a snap, and stuck it on the seat in front of him, between his legs.

He glanced at Britt, sending her a smile of encouragement. "Traffic's pretty light now. We'll get there as quickly as we can."

"Thanks for driving," she said. "Thanks for coming with me."

He glanced at her again. "Why is it that bad things happen to good people? Andy sure as hell doesn't deserve this. And I'd bet the bank Dani didn't, either."

"No woman, anywhere, deserves to be raped," Britt told him. "Not ever."

"Yeah, I'm with you on that," he said. "But still.

Why did this have to happen to them? I don't get it—
you know, the way the universe works."

Brittany watched him drive, knowing he was thinking about his brother Ethan, dead at age sixteen because
of a patch of ice on a wintery road.

"I don't know," she said. "Some people flirt with disaster and walk away unscathed. Others just quietly live
their lives and end up getting slammed. It's definitely
not fair, but face it, life's not fair."

He nodded. "Yeah, I'm well aware of that."

And now he was surely thinking about Lana and her
cheating husband Quinn and…

But he reached over and took her hand. "It's going
to be all right, Britt," he said. "Andy's a tough kid.
He's going to help Dani get through this." Bringing her
hand to his lips, he kissed her. "And just in case you
were wondering, I'm here for you, too. For as long as
you need me."

There was no doubt about it.

Brittany may have been a fool, but Lana Quinn was
a total idiot.

"Dani's got to go to the hospital," Lana reported
to Wes and Brittany. "The boy was rough with her. I
haven't given her any kind of medical examination, but
I think she's got a broken rib along with, well, a vari-
ety of contusions."

Britt made a soft sound of pain, and Wes took her
hand. Her fingers were icy cold.

"I've advised her to have a rape kit done, too. It's important she goes to the hospital, not just for her health,
but also to have medical records of her injuries," Lana
continued.

"I know," Brittany said. "I've worked as an Emergency Room nurse."

"Yes," Lana said. "Andy told me. He's been wonderful, Brittany. He's incredibly supportive and patient—a real solid rock. He's exactly what Dani needs right now, emotionally. He's going to go with her to the hospital."

"I'll go, too," Britt said. "Of course."

"Well, actually," Lana said.

At that moment, Andy came out of the back room, closing the door behind him.

Brittany pulled away from Wes and went toward him.

The kid reached for her, his face looking a lot like a two-year-old who was about to cry. As Wes watched, they just held each other tightly.

"She's amazing," Lana said softly. "You know, I could probably count on the fingers of one hand the number of nineteen-year-olds I've met who would call their mother for help. You've got to be a good mother to invoke that kind of trust from your kid. But good grief, she must've had him when she was twelve."

"He's adopted," Wes and Lt. Jones both said in a near unison.

"Ah," Lana said, in that shrink way she had of seeming to comment without really saying anything.

"Dani's getting dressed," Andy said. "She'll be ready to go in a few minutes."

"I'll go with you," Britt told her kid.

But Andy pulled back slightly to look down at her, shaking his head. He had what looked like was going to be one hell of a shiner on his face, along with a swollen lip. "Mom, she's mortified. We're just going to go, the two of us. We'll be okay. I know what needs to be done. Lana went over it with me."

"Sweetie, you're not going to be able to be in the examining room with her," Brittany protested. "Doesn't Dani know I'm a nurse?"

"Yeah," Andy said. "But—"

"I can stay with her while the doctor is—"

"Mom, there'll be a nurse in the E.R. who'll stay with her and, you know, hold her hand. A nurse who's not her boyfriend's mother. A nurse she doesn't have to run into in her boyfriend's kitchen."

Brittany nodded. "I understand. I just... Sweetie, who's going to hold your hand?"

"Dani will," he told her quietly.

Britt nodded. She reached up to gently touch his bruised face. "I'm so proud of you."

He touched his own lip and winced. "Yeah, well, that's the other thing we need to talk about. I think I might've lost my scholarship. I'm not sure, but I think there might be a rule or two about scholarship recipients not breaking the starting pitcher's nose."

Brittany laughed. "Thank God," she said. "I was afraid you were going to tell me you killed him."

Andy got grim. "I wanted to."

Her smile faded, too. "I know."

"He was laughing about it," he told her, and his eyes filled with tears.

Wes turned away, his heart breaking for Andy—and for Brittany, too, who would have done anything, he knew, to take away her son's pain.

Cowboy had wandered into the kitchen, but Lana was watching Wes with her hazel eyes that were so different from her half sister's.

"Love heals all wounds," she said quietly. Her hair was brown with only the slightest red highlights. Her face was more plain than Amber's, too. She wasn't even half as exotically beautiful, but she had a genuine warmth that made her lovelier than Amber would ever be.

Or so he'd always thought. But next to Brittany's fire, Amber seemed plastic and Lana seemed cool and distant and pale.

"I don't know about that," Wes told her. "It seems to me that most of the time love's the thing that makes the deadliest wounds. I mean, if you don't love someone, then they can't hurt you when they, like, die. Or when they screw around with someone else. Right?"

She blinked. Then she smiled, her perpetual calm kicking in. "You've been talking to Amber about Quinn."

Wes didn't say anything. What could he say? *No, actually, I've known Wizard-the-Mighty-Quinn's been stepping out on you for years now.*

"I spoke to her just this morning," Lana told him. "I understand congratulations are in order for your upcoming marriage." She glanced at Brittany. "She seems wonderful."

"She is," he said.

"I'm happy for you, Wes." Her smile seemed a little forced. But maybe that was just his imagination. The tired circles underneath her eyes weren't, though. "You know, it's crazy, and I probably shouldn't be saying this, but... I used to think that we would get together someday—you and me. Seeing as how Quinn's such a jerk..."

"Why do you stay with him?" Wes asked. He couldn't believe he was having this conversation with her here and now—a conversation he'd dreamed of having for years.

It was twice as surreal, because even while he was talking to Lana, he found his attention drawn back to Brittany, who, across the room, was still deep in conversation with her son.

"I love Quinn," Lana admitted. "I guess I keep hoping that he'll change. You know, both times it happened, he came to me and confessed and begged me to forgive him. Of course, after the second time, it got a little harder to think that he wouldn't do it ever again, but…"

Wes stared at her then, completely unable to respond, totally unable to utter a word.

Both times. *Both times.* She thought Wizard had only cheated on her twice.

Wes could think of seven or eight instances where the Wiz had slept with some random woman he'd scooped up in some hotel lounge. And that was just off the top of his head.

And those were just the women Wes had known about, just the tip of the iceberg, so to speak.

"It's not real," he blurted, because he had to tell her at least part of the truth. "My engagement to Brittany. It was just… Your sister was hitting on me, and… I mean, she's nice and all, but I wasn't interested in… So Brittany agreed to play my fiancée and…" He shook his head. "It's not real."

"It isn't?"

"No."

"Your entire relationship with her is complete fiction?"

"The engagement," he clarified. "Yeah."

Lana looked at him, tipping her head slightly sideways. "Do you honestly expect me to believe you're not sleeping with her?"

Wes laughed, embarrassed. "Well, I didn't exactly say that."

"Ah."

"It's, you know, casual. A fling. She was the one who made a point of setting an end date."

"And how do you feel about that?"

He laughed again, but it felt forced. "Don't try to psychoanalyze me, babe. If you must know, I'm fine with it."

"I see."

"And don't *I see* me either. Jesus."

"Dani's almost ready to go," Andy said, interrupting them. "Do you mind if we clear the living room so she doesn't have to walk through a crowd to get to the door?"

"That's a good idea," Lana said. "I think I'll just get going. I have things to do early in the morning, so..."

Chapter 11

"I'll walk you out," Wes said to Lana.

Brittany tried to hate her, but she couldn't anymore.

Not after meeting the woman. Not after seeing how genuinely, honestly, freaking nice she was, and how very kind she'd been to both Dani and Andy.

In fact, Lana made a point to take a detour in her direction on her way to the door. And she actually embraced Brittany, surrounding her with a faint cloud of a very subtle yet enticing perfume. She was beautiful, smart, kind and she smelled good, too. Wes sure knew how to pick 'em.

"It was so nice to meet you," Lana told her. "If there's anything you need, don't hesitate to give me a call. Wes has my number."

"Thank you," Brittany said. "And thanks for coming over here so quickly."

Andy had told her that Dani's sister was in Japan on business, and Dani hadn't wanted to call her father, who'd remarried and started a new family after her mother had died. She'd been alone for all those days. Thank God Andy had come looking for her. And thank God both Lana Quinn and Harlan Jones had been able to get over here so quickly.

"I'm available, too, if the police or the D.A. want to talk to me," Lana said. "I would love to help nail the guy who did this."

"That's not going to be easy," Brittany said.

"I know." Lana's gorgeous hazel eyes filled with tears. "I do know. I've seen it so many times before."

This time it was Brittany who hugged Lana.

They both had to wipe their eyes as they pulled apart.

"Don't let him get away," Lana said to Britt in a low voice. "He's a good man."

What? Weren't they still talking about that jerk Dustin Merlero? Or… "Excuse me?"

But Lana was already heading for the door.

And Melody's husband, Harlan, aka Cowboy, was at Brittany's elbow.

"Why don't you come on home with me?" he said in his cute little western accent. He'd slapped a baseball cap on over his hair, and he'd slipped his feet into his sneakers without any socks in his haste to get here. Even dressed down the way he was, with bedhead and stubble on his chin, it was easy to see how Melody hadn't been able to resist getting busy with him in an airplane bathroom—an event which had led to her first pregnancy.

Britt watched Wes follow Lana out the door, watched the way his T-shirt fit snugly across the muscles in his back, watched the way he walked, with jaunty self-confidence that was, she knew, part of his whole act. He was taut, he was tense—some might even describe him as being on edge—but she saw him as barely harnessed, limitless energy. A lightning bolt in cargo shorts.

An all-too-human man who needed a little help learning how to relax.

She could help him with that. He'd been real relaxed just a few short hours ago, in her bed.

Oh, God.

"Mel and Tyler would sure love to see you," Harlan was saying. "Of course, they're both asleep right now, but in the morning…"

Brittany laughed. "It *is* the morning. Tyler's going to be up and awake in a matter of hours." Her nephew, like most little boys, was an early riser.

"Mel ordered me to bring you home," he persisted, leading her toward the door. "So I'm not going to take no for an answer."

"You're going to have to," she said, turning back to Andy. "Sweetie, are you sure you don't want me to—"

"Mom," Andy said, giving her a hug. "I'm sure. I'll call if I need you." He shook Harlan's hand. "Thanks for coming over, sir."

"Any time you need me, Andy," Harlan said, "all you have to do is call."

"Andy?" Dani called from the bedroom.

"Thank you." And Andy was gone.

"Come on, Britt," Harlan said. "Andy's a big boy now. You've got to let him do this the way he and Dani want to do it. They're going to need some time alone, to talk, after they get back from the hospital."

"I know," she said.

"He told me he was going to try to talk Dani into

coming back to L.A. on Monday—get her to go to the school health offices for counseling. And he's going to contact some of the other girls this guy Melero mentioned, see if all together they can't find the strength to press charges. I suspect you'll get a call from him in a few days, asking for help. But right now I'm pretty sure his priority is to make Dani understand that he's not going anywhere."

"I know," Brittany said again. "I do know all that. But thank you for reminding me. And thank you for the offer of a bed, but no thanks. Tell Mel and Tyler I promise I'll come for a visit soon."

He was frowning at her. "You aren't planning to drive back to L.A. tonight, are you?"

"I'm not exactly sure what we're going to do," she told him, and watched as he processed that *we*.

Harlan laughed and uttered an expression that wasn't repeatable as he looked at Brittany, grinning at her like the devil. "Really? You and Skelly are a *we*?"

"Shh," she said. "Andy doesn't know. He may never know. It's just…temporary insanity. You know, a short-term brain disorder. Promise you won't tell Melody, okay?"

Harlan looked pained, and she loved him even more for it. "Don't make me promise that, Britt. I love you like a sister, you know that I do, but don't ask me to keep secrets from Mel."

"It's just that…if too many people know about it, it'll end," she told him. "I mean, I know it's going to end before too long anyway, but… Between you and me, Jones, I'm having a heck of a lot of fun. I'm not ready for it to be over yet."

"Maybe—"

She cut him off. "Don't say it. It's just a fling. I made that clear to him before it started. I'm not about to change the rules on the man now."

"But what if—"

"No," she said. "See, that's what Melody is going to do if she finds out. Start *what if*-ing the situation to death. And that'll be it. Way to kill it dead. She'll freak me out, and I'll start acting weird and that'll freak Wes out and... Give me another week before you tell her. Please?"

He shook his head and sighed. "I don't know..."

"Four days. Please?"

"All right. Compromise. I'll tell her, but I won't let her call you or tell anyone else for a whole week."

Yeah, like that was going to work. But it was definitely worth a try. "Fair enough. But get it in writing from her before you tell her. And if she does call, I'm hanging up."

"You know, Britt, if you really like him that much—"

"Stop," she said. "You don't think I've thought about this? Trust me, I have. I don't know how well you know him, but... Wes is... Well, let's just say that he's emotionally attached to someone else. Someone he can't have."

Someone he was out in the driveway with right now. Someone as wonderful as he was.

Jealous, jealous, jealous.

Harlan got grim. "He's attached, but he's messing around with you? The son of a bitch. I'll kill him."

"Oh, that's exactly what I want." Brittany rolled her eyes. "God save me from testosterone."

"Okay, fine. I'll talk to him."

"And the result of your little chat will be that he'll stop seeing me. Thanks a lot."

"All right, I won't talk to him. For a week."

"You can't glare at him either," she said.

"That's going to be hard."

"No, it's not. He's on leave—you won't see him for another week and a half. Just walk out this door, get in your truck and drive away—go home to your pregnant wife and son."

Harlan let Brittany pull him out the door and into the coolness of the night.

Where, out in the street, Wes was standing over by the driver's side window of Lana's car, leaning down so he could talk to her as she sat inside.

Jealous, jealous, jealous.

"I'll talk to you in a week," Harlan said as he headed straight for his truck, completely ignoring Wes, just as she'd asked.

Except now, standing there, looking at Wes talking to Lana, Brittany was hit with a wave of doubt.

As Harlan pulled off with a wave, she realized that turning down a chance to sleep at her sister's house might've been a big mistake.

It was one thing for Wes and Brittany to be together in the nonreality of Los Angeles, but back here in San Diego where Wes lived… Where Lana lived…

As Brittany watched, Wes straightened up and stepped back from Lana's car. She pulled away, and as her taillights faded into the night, he rubbed the back of his neck as if it ached.

Heartache and longing could do that to you. Make you hurt all over.

Wes sighed, a big, deep, down-to-the-pit-of-his-soul

type sigh, and shook his head in disgust or regret. Brittany wasn't sure exactly which it was, but either way, it wasn't good.

He stood there for such a long time, she was a little afraid that he'd forgotten about her.

She cleared her throat. "So, is there, like, a sofa in your apartment that I could use to catch a little sleep?"

He turned to her then, and the look on his face was one of complete confusion. "I thought… You don't want to—" He stopped himself and started over. "I do have a double bed. Is there some reason you suddenly don't want to share it with me?"

"No," she said. "I just thought that you might not want to… You know, that seeing Lana might've…"

"Might've what?" he asked. "Made me stupid? I don't think so, babe. Come on, let's get out of here so Andy can take Dani to the hospital." He started for his car.

Brittany followed. "I wish they'd let me go with them."

"I know you do," Wes said gently, opening the car door for her. "But you can't. Andy's no fool, Brittany. He's got my cell phone number. If he finds out he's in over his head, he'll call."

She got into the car, and he closed the door behind her.

"Hey, the sun's about to come up," he said as he got behind the wheel. "What do you say we go to the beach and watch it rise?"

"Sure," she told him. "That's a good idea. I probably couldn't sleep now anyway." She was thinking about way too many things. Andy. Dani.

Lana.

He started the car and, as they pulled away, she looked back to see Andy helping Dani out of the house. The girl was moving slowly, gingerly. It was hard to tell if the worst of her injuries were physical or emotional.

Either way, her road to recovery was going to be a rough one. And Andy, God help him and God bless him, would be there, for the entire bumpy ride.

It was all she could do not to cry.

"This is my favorite beach in San Diego," Wes said as he parked, and Brittany burst into tears.

"Whoa," he said. "Hey, it's not that great a beach."

"I'm sorry," she said. "I'm so sorry." She bolted out of the car.

It was a dumb move—his trying to make a joke when she was obviously not in any kind of a joking mood.

He chased after her, dashing pretty far down the beach in the spooky, foggy light of predawn. She was faster than he would have guessed just looking at her and knowing what he knew about aerodynamics, but that was typical of Brittany. She was full of surprises. He had to hustle to catch up. "Hey!"

"Leave me alone, okay?" she said. "Just for a few minutes. I have to cry now, and I don't want to make you uncomfortable."

He laughed. "So what if I'm uncomfortable? Jeez, Britt, don't you ever stop thinking about other people and focus on yourself for a change?"

She sat down in the sand and buried her face in her arms. "Please, just go away."

"No." Wes sat down next to her and pulled her into his arms. "Baby, look, it's okay if you cry. This has been one tough night."

Brittany resisted for about a half a second, and then she clung to him, her arms tight around his neck.

He just held her and stroked her back and her hair as the sky slowly grew lighter. The fog was rolling in with a vengeance now, thick and wet and cold against his face and arms.

Britt didn't seem to notice, and he just let her be—let her grieve.

"God, you must think I'm such a wimp," she finally said, wiping her eyes with the heel of her hand.

He pushed her hair back from her face. "I think you're amazing. I think Andy's the luckiest kid in the world to have you for his mother. You know what would've happened in *my* house if I had a scholarship for college and I stood a chance of losing it because of getting into a fight?"

She shook her head.

"My mother would have gotten really grim, and my father would have barely even looked up from his dinner. He would have said—and God knows I heard this often enough," he imitated his father's voice, *"The only surprise about this, Wesley, is that it took three months to happen instead of two."*

Tears filled her eyes again. "That's a terrible thing to say to your own child."

He kissed her. "Hey. Shhh. I didn't tell you that to make you cry all over again."

"You told me that your father didn't hit you," Brittany said, "but he might as well have. Telling you that he expected you to fail is tantamount to a vicious beating, in my book."

"Yeah, well," he said. "Easy with the accusations there, because, you know, I really was a screwup."

"See?" she said. "You believed him. You still believe him."

He gently changed the subject, still running his fingers through her hair. Somewhere on her dash down the beach, she'd lost her ponytail holder. "What are you going to do if he does lose his scholarship?"

She settled back against him, her head on his shoulder. "Exactly what I told Andy. We'll figure something out."

"Such as you put your nurse practitioner degree on hold?"

Brittany nodded. "I *am* going to school on the money I saved for Andy's education," she told him. "He was planning to go to Amherst—it was a pretty short drive from our house in Appleton, you know, in Massachusetts. He wanted to live at home. In fact, he was adamant about it. I kept trying to talk him into living at college. First-year dorm. Lots of fun. Roommates and parties and all that stuff, but he just laughed and told me he spent years in the foster-care system, living with strangers. Why would he want to go live with strangers again when he was just getting used to having a real home?"

"Smart kid," he said, as aware as hell of her hand on his thigh.

She smiled, playing with the zipper pull on the pocket of his cargo shorts. "Yeah, I guess so. Then when he got the full scholarship at the college in L.A.—a baseball scholarship—God, he wanted to go so badly. But he was going to turn it down. And I suddenly thought, shoot. I've been wanting to go back to school for a long time. Surely I could find a nursing school in L.A. We could move out here together. It's kind of weird, you know, Andy and his mom go to college together. Like some kind of bad teen comedy movie. But it's what he wanted and it seems to be working." She took a deep breath. "It'll work just as well without the scholarship. With the nursing shortage, I could get a full-time job at the hospital in a heartbeat."

"That would be a shame."

"No, it would be life. Life happens, you deal with it. I'll get my degree, it'll just take a little longer than I'd hoped." She noticed the fog for the first time. "Oh, my God, who turned on the dried ice machine?"

It was kind of spooky, as if they were the last two people in the universe. Spooky, but nice. They couldn't see anyone else who might've come to the beach at this early hour, but no one could see them, either. He kissed her.

"California has the weirdest weather," she said.

"I love this kind of fog," he told her. "It's good cover for black ops."

"What are black ops?" she asked, kissing him this time. Oh, yeah. The fog no longer seemed quite so cold. He pulled her back with him, so that they were both lying in the sand.

God, he couldn't remember the last time he'd made out on the beach.

Probably for good reason. Sand and sex really didn't mix too well.

"Black ops are operations—missions—that are ultra top secret," he told her eventually. "They're usually so secret your immediate superiors on your chain of command don't know what you're up to."

She smiled down at him, pressing herself intimately

against him. "I bet your immediate superiors don't know what you're up to."

He laughed. "That's for sure."

"You know, if I were wearing a skirt instead of jeans…"

"Damn you, Levi Strauss." She laughed, and he reached up to touch her face. "Britt, you know I love it when you laugh, but don't ever think I don't want you to cry in front of me, okay?"

She nodded, her eyes suddenly so soft. "The same goes for me."

He laughed. "Yeah, thanks, but…"

"But tough guys don't cry?"

"No," Wes said. "I've seen plenty of tough guys cry. I just… I try not to make a habit of it, myself. I'm a little afraid…"

She waited.

"That if I start I won't be able to stop," he admitted.

"Oh, Wes," she said softly.

The fog had soaked them both so thoroughly by now, that water beaded and ran down her face. Her T-shirt was practically transparent. Too bad she was wearing a bra.

"You should enter a wet T-shirt contest," he said. It was a stupid thing to say—he would bet big money that Britt disapproved of such blatantly sexist exhibitions. But he was desperate to change the subject.

She looked down at herself and laughed. "Yeah, right."

"I'd vote for you."

"Thanks," she said. "I think. Although I'm not sure I should thank you for suggesting I humiliate myself and all women everywhere by standing on a stage in

front of an audience of howling men and being judged
for the size and shape of my breasts."

Ding. Correct for ten points.

She narrowed her eyes at him. "How would you like
to enter a 'who's got the biggest penis' contest? Okay,
boys, drop your drawers and face the crowd!"

"Yeah, okay, at least women get to keep their T-
shirts on."

She snorted. "Like that really makes a difference
when a T-shirt is wet." She reached up under her shirt
and, like a magician, she managed to unfasten her bra
and pull it off through the sleeve of her T-shirt. "See?"

Oh, yeah. He saw. She was soaking wet and hot for
him. It was unbelievably sexy.

Or maybe she was cold from the fog. He sat up and
kissed her and she shivered. He couldn't quite tell if it
was from desire or the fact that she was freezing her
butt off.

"Want to go to my place and take a hot shower?" he
suggested as he licked her nipple into his mouth and
suckled her, right through the cotton of her T-shirt.

She moaned as she rubbed herself against him,
through his shorts and her jeans.

And then he could feel her fingers, working to unfasten his shorts. The top button was tricky, but... Ah,
she got it and the zipper was easy and...*yes*.

"Two questions," she said. "Do you have a condom
in your pocket, and when the fog's this thick, how long
does it usually take to disappear?"

He laughed but it came out sounding more like a
groan as she touched him. "Yes," he said, "and it's a
crapshoot. When it's like this it usually doesn't burn
off till midmorning or even noon. But I'd be willing to

bet the fog'll last at least five more minutes—which is about four minutes longer than I'll last if you actually do take off your jeans and—"

Brittany let go of him and unzipped her jeans. They were wet and pulling them off was a challenge. She was up for it, though, and by the time she got one leg out, he'd covered himself with the condom he was carrying.

And then she covered him, too, driving him so deeply inside of her he nearly lost it right then and there.

She moved on top of him, hard and fast, as if her need for him consumed her completely.

Obviously, it did. She wanted him so much she was willing to make love to him on a public beach.

God, what a total turn-on.

"Britt, I was serious," he gasped. "I'm so crazy for you, I'm not going to last."

Her response was her immediate release. Hard and fast and powerful as hell, it shook her and shook her as she cried out his name.

And he was undone. Game over. He couldn't have stopped himself from climaxing if his life had depended on it. He crashed into her with an explosion of pleasure that was so intense his eyes actually watered.

"Thank you," she gasped as she clung to him. "Oh, my God, thank you. You always know exactly what I need."

Wes had to laugh. *She* was thanking *him*. "Right now, I think you need a hot shower. And a cup of tea." Man, did he even have any tea? He hoped so.

If he didn't, he'd get some from somewhere.

Hell, if she wanted the moon, he'd figure out a way to get that for her, too.

Chapter 12

By Monday morning, Brittany's jeans had finally dried and they could—if they wanted to—go out.

Wes had been a little nervous when they'd first arrived at his apartment early Sunday morning. The place wasn't exactly neat and tidy. And even if it had been pristine, it completely lacked all of the warmth and cheerful personality of her apartment back in L.A.

He'd gathered up his laundry and quickly washed the dirty dishes and emptied the ashtrays while she was in the shower. He uncovered two packs of cigarettes and tossed them into the sink, getting them good and soggy before he put them in the trash.

The thought of smoking one while she was in the bathroom didn't cross his mind. At least not for longer than two or three seconds. Which was pretty damn amazing.

He'd looked around instead, wondering what to do to make the place more acceptable in Brittany's eyes. God, his apartment was ugly. And there was nothing he really could do about the science fiction movie posters taped to the walls without frames, or the worn and faded secondhand furniture—including a purple-and-green plaid chair that now seemed to scream that not only did its owner have no taste, but he had no life as well. Because, really, no one could spend any significant amount of time in that room with that chair without going insane. It announced that this apartment was really just a place Wes came to sleep now and then. It wasn't his home.

But his worries hadn't been real. They'd spent all of Sunday in his bedroom.

In his bed.

Brittany had called both work and a colleague from school to tell them what had happened with Andy, and that she wouldn't be back in L.A. for several days. So there was nothing to do but wait for Andy to give them an update.

The kid had called several times on Wes's cell phone, the latest just this morning. Dani had an appointment with her family doctor in San Diego, late this afternoon. On Tuesday, they were returning to L.A. The district attorney there wanted to meet with Dani and discuss the possibility of her pressing charges. They currently had another complaint against Dustin Melero, and Dani's testimony would make that case more solid.

Of course it was always a crapshoot in the instance of sexual assault. It tended to come down to a "he said, she said" battle. Dani's reputation and sexual history—in fact, her entire personal life—would be scrutinized by people attempting to show that she willingly consented to having sex with Melero.

Sure. She willingly consented to getting her rib broken. She must've liked that a whole lot.

The good news was that Dani didn't have any skeletons in her closet. She was, as Wes had pointed out days earlier, a "public virgin." She'd been quite vocal in her decision to wait to have a sexual relationship. And she hadn't just discussed that with other kids. She'd talked to her doctors and her college mentor about it, as well.

Because she was a "good girl," there was a chance that her testimony would help convict Dustin Melero.

Brittany, however, was pretty steamed. After she got off the phone with Andy, she vented. "So I could go back to L.A., and in a week, when your leave is over and you're gone, say I'm walking home from the hospital late one night, and I'm attacked. Say I'm pulled into an alley, and I'm raped."

Wes winced, sitting down next to her on the bed. "I don't want to say that. Why don't we say instead that you don't ever walk home alone at night?"

She sighed in exasperation. "I'm just using myself as an example, but no, you're right, it's not going to happen, because I'm careful. I get a cab if it's too late to call Andy for a ride."

"That's good to know."

"Okay, say instead that I finally agree to have dinner with Henry Jurrik—he's a pulmonary specialist at the hospital. He asks me out about once a month." She laughed. "He must put it into his calendar or something. It's like clockwork."

"He's a doctor?" Wes asked, trying not to sound jealous, and failing miserably.

Brittany kissed him. "I have a *no doctors* rule," she told him. "But just for the sake of argument, let's say I lose my mind and agree to have dinner with him. We go out, he drives me home, walks me to my door. You know. Wants to come inside, but I won't ask him, of course, because it's only a first date. He's about as perceptive as a two-by-four, and he tries to kiss me, so I turn my head—you know, I'm completely giving him all the *no sex tonight, you idiot* signals. But he persists, and I finally have to tell him flat out, no. But Andy's not home, so he pushes me inside where he forces himself on me."

"This is a really unpleasant conversation," Wes said.

"Yeah, well, it happens to women all the time," Britt told him with that stern look he'd come to recognize and love. She wanted to talk about this, so they were going to talk about it. It was hard to imagine anyone forcing anything on her when she got like this, but Wes knew too well that despite her tough attitude, he himself could overpower her with one hand tied behind his back.

"It happened to Dani," she continued. "She said no, and Melero said tough luck. She fought him hard enough to get a broken rib. It happens, Wes."

"It better never happen to you."

She kissed him again. "Don't worry. I'm careful. If I ever did go out to dinner with someone, I'd either drive myself, or I'd make sure Andy was home."

"You weren't that careful with me," he countered. "You just invited me into your house."

"Don't change the subject. My point in this is that afterwards? I could go to the police and press charges, but the D.A. might not take the case, because the doctor's scumbag defense attorney would dig up all kinds of dirt on me—including the fact that I haven't exactly lived like a nun these past few years—in particular these past few days. I slept with you willingly. And you weren't the only man I had a short-term relationship with after my divorce. They'd find out about Kyle, too. And, oh yeah, before I got married, back when I was in college, I had two different relationships. They were more intense—a few months each, but they make the list even longer. So they would try to prove that I was some kind of loose woman, sleeping around. Surely, I'd wanted Dr. Jurrik, too."

"It sucks," he agreed. "But I think the jury would look at you and see—"

"So what you're saying is that if I didn't look quite so wholesome, I'd be out of luck? That's not fair."

"You're right, it's not."

"Even if I'd had sex with every man I'd ever met," Brittany said, "even if I were a prostitute, no means no."

"You're absolutely right." He cleared his throat. "You actually had relationships in college that were more intense than, uh, what we've got going here?"

She smiled at him. "I meant in terms of length," she said. "I don't know about you, but this you and me thing is pretty different from anything I've ever done. I mean, I think in the past three days I've had more sex than I had during all the years I was married."

Wes laughed, relieved. "Good. I was a little nervous for a minute. Like I wasn't doing a good enough job or something."

"You're doing a marvelous job," she told him with a grin. "And how'm I doing, sugar pie? Am I managing to keep you from constantly thinking about how much you want a cigarette?"

"Definitely." He kissed her, and there it was again. Desire. Damn, he just could not get enough of her.

Maybe it was knowing that there was an end date to their affair, that he only had her until the end of his leave.

God, he didn't want his leave to ever end.

"Let's go out," she said. "The paper said there was some kind of celebration at something called Old Town San Diego this evening. Let's go and dance and get really hot for each other and then come back and make love on that hideous purple chair in your living room."

Wes laughed. "What? Why?"

"You need a good reason to keep it in your living room," she told him, laughing as she danced beyond his reach. "You need to have an incredibly steamy memory associated with it, so that when people come in here and see it, you can say, 'I keep that chair for a reason.' And when they look at you, you can just smile and say 'Mmmm, yeah. I know it's something of a visual assault upon the senses, but, you know, I really like that old chair.'"

The phone rang, and Britt scooped it up. "Wes Skelly's house of ugly furniture. How may we help you?" There was a pause. "Hello?" she said. She held out the phone to Wes. "I think I scared them away."

"Skelly," he said into the phone, but there was a click as whoever was on the other end hung up.

"Sorry."

"Nah," he said. "Don't worry about it. I think there's something wrong with the phone company. I was getting a lot of hangups at your place, too. If it was someone from the Team, they would've left a message. And Andy would've called on my cell. Besides, he would've recognized your voice." He kissed her. "So you want to go out?"

"Do you?"

"Yeah," he said. "Old Town San Diego isn't too far. We could take my bike."

Brittany's eyes widened. "Your motorcycle? Really?" She'd been intrigued when she saw it parked in his carport. "Do you have an extra helmet?"

"Of course." Wes found his boots in the closet and put them on.

"Do you promise to go really slowly?"

He smiled at her. "Your wish is my command."

Wes Skelly was not the world's best dancer. But what he lacked in style and creativity, he made up for in enthusiasm. Besides, some men who should forever remain nameless—Quentin—flatly refused even to try to dance.

And frankly, it didn't matter that Wes didn't have the smoothest moves on the dance floor when he smiled at her the way he was smiling right now.

He leaned closer, so he could speak directly into Brittany's ear, so she could hear him over the sound of the salsa band. "Do you want to get something to drink? Or—I know. There's a place around the corner that sells ice-cream cones."

She let him pull her from the dance floor.

The place was mobbed. Even off the dance floor, the crowd was thick. But everyone was smiling and having a good time.

As they finally moved beyond the band's loudspeakers, she said, "You know your way around here pretty well."

He glanced at her. "Yeah. I've been down here…a few times."

"Old Town San Diego?" She lifted an eyebrow. "Somehow I wouldn't have guessed that a historic museum village was quite your speed."

"Yeah, well…" Was he actually blushing? "I'm interested. You know. In history. I like going to places like this."

"Really?" She stopped walking, and someone bumped into her. "Sorry." She pulled Wes out of the stream of traffic.

"It's stupid, I know," he said.

"No, it's not," she countered.

"Yeah, no," he said. "I know it's not stupid to come here. I meant, it's stupid to keep it a secret. It's just… I have a reputation in the teams, you know? Tattoo. Motorcycle. Profanity. I've been trying really hard to keep it clean around you, you know."

"And I appreciate that," she said. "But I don't understand. You don't think you're allowed to be smart? To go places besides pool halls and bars that have wet T-shirt contests?"

He laughed. "It's not that." He searched for the right words. "Most guys who become SEALs are wicked ass smart. Like, you know, Harvard, he actually went to Harvard, right? I'm telling you, some of these guys are fuh—are brilliant. Even Bobby—he reads a lot. He's always giving me book recommendations, but… See, I read really slowly. I mean, he gets through a book in like a week, and it'll take me two months. Maybe. So I'm carrying it around for all that time, and I start to feel… I don't know."

"What?" she asked. "You start to feel what?"

He gazed at her, and she knew he was deciding how much he actually trusted her.

"Stupid," he finally admitted, and her heart went into her throat. His telling her that was almost better than his saying that he loved her. Almost. "I had to work my ass off to become a chief, Britt. Bobby, he did it without blinking. All that reading and the written crap—excuse me—it was hard for me."

"Are you dyslexic?" she asked.

"Nah," he said. He forced a smile. "I wish I had that excuse. I'm just…slow."

"Maybe when it comes to reading," she said. "But the rest of time… I don't think so, Wes. I've never met any-one who's as quick witted as you are—and that trans-lates to smart in my book. So, it's not easy for you to read. So what? That doesn't make you stupid. You just have to learn things other ways. Like by coming to a place like this and taking a guided tour. That way you can hear the history instead of having to plow through some dusty old book."

His smile was more genuine now. "Yeah, I know. I watch a lot of the History Channel. And I sometimes listen to books on tape, too."

God, he was surely telling her things he never told anyone. Probably not even his best friend, Bobby.

Now her heart wasn't just in her throat, it was ex-panding and cutting off her ability to speak.

Good thing, because if she wasn't careful, she might go ahead and tell him that she was in love with him, and falling harder every minute that they spent together.

Instead, she kissed him. She tried to kiss him even half as sweetly as he'd kissed her that first time in Amber Tierney's house.

"I can tell you anything, and you'll still like me, huh?" he said softly.

"Yeah," Brittany said. "You can tell me anything, and it won't go any further, either."

His eyes were so blue. "It feels good," he said. "That kind of trust. And it goes both ways, you know."

She nodded. "I do know." She smiled. "But I don't have any secrets."

"Honest?"

No. She was in love with him. But that was one hell of a big secret that she wasn't about to share with anyone. Still...

"Okay," she said. "You really want to hear...?"

"Only if you trust me."

She did, without hesitation. "If I won the lottery, I'd have a baby. I'd go to a sperm bank and, you know, make a withdrawal."

He smiled. "That doesn't shock or even surprise me, you know."

"Well, gee, sorry for being so transparent."

"That's not what I meant," he countered. "It's just... maybe I've gotten to know you so well these past few days... But it's kind of obvious to me that if you won the lottery you wouldn't spend it on sports cars—except maybe the ones that you'd buy for me and your sister."

She laughed.

"So, you'd really do it, huh? If you had the cash," he said. "You'd willingly be a single mother?"

"Yes. Adopting Andy made me realize how precious children are—and how much I really would've liked to have had the experience of raising one right from the moment they were born," she said. "And as for being a single mom—I've been doing it for almost seven years now. I think I'm doing okay. I mean, it seems pretty unlikely that Prince Charming's going to come along at this point in my life, so…"

Wes looked out at the crowd and nodded. "Yeah, I guess not."

Darn.

That was where he was supposed to push her hair back from her face and kiss her and tell her that he was her Prince Charming, and he was here to stay.

God, she was still hoping for the fairy tale happy ending.

And they lived happily ever after.

Fool.

"Kids scare me to death," he admitted. "I helped take care of Liz and Shaun when they were born. I'm not afraid of changing diapers—that's not what I meant. It's just…you love them so much, and…"

"And they sometimes die on you," Brittany said. "Like Ethan, right?"

"Yeah," he said. "Just like Ethan. You know, I joined the Big Brothers program a few years ago."

She laughed. "Okay, sweetie, ten minutes ago, that would have surprised me, but it doesn't anymore. I guess we're even now. What made you join?"

"It was Ethan's birthday," he told her, "and I was feeling like crap, so… I just went in and signed up. They accepted me, and matched me with this kid— Cody Anderson. I used to bring him here, and we'd always get ice cream afterwards. It was… He was a great kid. I really liked him—he was a real troublemaker— I could really relate to that. We got pretty tight pretty fast. He liked coming here. He had to pretend that the big draw was the fudge ripple, you know? But that was okay. Then his mom got remarried and they moved up to Seattle, and... I was supposed to call the office and get reassigned, but I never did. It was too..." He shook his head. "It felt a little too much like going to get a new puppy after your old puppy, you know, ran away or something."

She hugged him. "I'm sorry."

"Yeah, I'm sorry, too. I didn't mean to go all pathetic on you. I just..." He sighed. "I don't know, Britt. I don't think I'm cut out to have kids."

"Well, you have plenty of time."

Unlike a woman, whose clock ticked louder when she was approaching forty, like Brittany.

"I don't know," Wes said again. "I was thinking about getting a vasectomy. You know, make sure it never happens."

Whoa. "That's pretty drastic. Maybe you should check with Lana before you do that."

He held her gaze silently for several long seconds. And then he looked away and laughed. "You're like, the only person in the world who would dare to talk about that—about her, you know—to just say something right in my face like that."

"She seems really special," Brittany said quietly.

Wes nodded. "Yeah. But she's never going to leave Quinn, so..."

"You don't know that."

"Yeah, I do," he said. "She actually thinks he's only cheated on her two times." He swore softly. "Try two hundred and two. We talked about it a little the other night, but I couldn't tell her the truth. I just... She seemed so... I don't know, hopeful, I guess, that he was going to change."

"Maybe I should tell her," Brittany suggested.

What was she, stupid? Did she actually want Wes and Lana to live happily ever after?

Yes. Someone might as well. And she loved Wes enough to want him to be happy.

"I'll tell her," Britt said. "I'll talk to Harlan first, see if he knows Quinn—"

"He does," Wes said. "But—"

"I'll tell Lana that Harlan told me—that way she doesn't somehow blame you. You know, death to the messenger and all that. I don't mind if she gets mad at me and hates me forever."

He was shaking his head. "No. Britt, I don't want you to, okay?"

"Why not?"

He just kept on shaking his head. "Look, are we going to get ice cream, or what?"

"Think about it, sweetie," Brittany said. "Maybe you could actually get what you want."

"Right now I want ice cream—and a cigarette," he told her, tugging her back into the crowd of humanity pushing its way along the sidewalk.

Chapter 13

Trouble erupted pretty much out of nowhere.

Wes was leading the way to the ice-cream shop, thinking about how much he'd really like to take a pint home. Cones were nice to eat with eleven-year-olds. But Brittany… What he really wanted was to lick a few scoops off of her gorgeous body.

Okay, down boy. She might not be in the biggest hurry to rush back to his place—not after having that heavy duty conversation about Lana.

God, he didn't know what to think. And then he stopped thinking as two high school kids faced off right in the middle of the crowd, directly behind them.

"You looking at my girlfriend? Who told you you could look at my girlfriend?"

Idiot One pushed Idiot Two hard in the chest, and just like that sides were drawn. Every kid wearing colors in the crowd appeared out of nowhere. Real violence hadn't exploded yet, but it was just a matter of time before it did.

Wes let go of Brittany's hand. "Go down these stairs, cross the street and take the first right. I'll meet you over there. Move as fast as you can, all right?"

"Be careful," she said.

"Yeah." He started for the pair of idiots. "Hey!" But it was already too late.

Idiot One launched himself at Idiot Two.

And just like that, they were in the middle of a fricking brawl.

Crap.

He shouldn't have left Brittany to try to play hero. He pushed his way through the crowd, trying to get back to her as quickly as he could.

And saw her lose her footing and tumble down the stairs.

"Brittany!"

There were people in front of her, so she couldn't have fallen all the way, but he saw her go down. And she didn't get up again.

It took him twenty seconds longer than he wanted to get to her. Twenty terrifying seconds of icy fear.

Was she getting trampled by this crowd? Had she hit her head when she fell? Where the hell was she?

Twenty year-long seconds later, when he finally reached the stairs, she was sitting up, thank you Lord God Jesus. Someone—God bless them—had helped her move to the side of the stairs. Although, she was holding her head with one hand.

"God, baby, are you okay?"

"Yeah," she told him as someone hurrying down the

stairs past them smacked her in the back of her head with their backpack.

"Watch it!" Wes growled, turning quickly back to Britt, protecting her with his body. He wasn't big enough to block her completely from the crowd though, and he silently cursed his mother's side of the family for giving him the five foot eight gene instead of the one from his father that would've made him six-four.

"I hit my head on something," Brittany told him, "but it's really my ankle that's..."

Someone else knocked into him in their haste to get down the stairs, and Wes scooped Brittany up and swiftly carried her away from the crowd, away from the fighting idiots.

His heart was still racing and adrenaline was still surging through his system, and if he'd needed to, he could have carried her all the way back to L.A. without slowing down.

"I'm okay," she said as they rounded a corner. "My ankle's just... It's just a slight sprain. I'm sure—"

"There's a first aid station not far from here," he told her shortly. "I'm taking you over there."

"Oh, Wes, please, I just want to go home. I know what they're going to tell me. Ice and elevation. I'm going to be fine."

"Humor me," he said.

Two police cars, sirens wailing and lights spinning, passed them, heading toward the fight.

"Ouch," Brittany said. "Ow, ow, ow! Put me down, put me down!"

Hastily, he lowered her to the ground, the fear returning instantly. She'd injured her neck. She had internal bleeding. The possibilities were endless. "What hurts?"

he asked, slipping even further into Navy SEAL Chief mode. "Where? Show me." Fear was always pushed aside in favor of action and efficiency.

"Nothing," she said. "Nowhere. I just wanted you to put me down."

He shouldn't have opened his mouth, because when he did, some words came out that he'd promised himself he wouldn't ever use in front of her. But instead of recoiling in horror, she put her arms around him.

"Oh, honey, I'm okay," she said into his ear as she held him tightly. "I'm a little shaken and I'm going to have some bruises, but I'm really okay."

He held her just as close. "I saw you fall. And all I could think of were those stories about people who get trampled to death at rock concerts."

"I'm okay," she said again and kissed him.

Relief plus adrenaline plus a kiss like the one she gave him equaled a physical reaction that she couldn't miss.

"Oh, baby," she said, pulling back to look at him, amusement in her eyes. "You really do want to rescue me, don't you?"

He laughed, too. It was freaking weird. Just a few minutes ago, he couldn't have imagined laughing again—not in the near future. "Yeah," he said. "But only *after* I take you to the first aid station and have them look you over."

Brittany was shaking her head. "That place is going to be jammed," she said. "Let's just go home."

"What if you have a concussion?" he asked.

She smiled. "Maybe—as a precaution—you should make sure I don't sleep at all tonight."

Her smile and that suggestive comment went a long

way to convincing him that she really was okay—along with the fact that she was experimenting by gingerly putting her weight on her right foot.

"I think I mostly hit the funny bone," she told him, showing him that she could, indeed, walk unassisted. Like she'd said, she was merely shaken and bruised.

But head injuries could be tricky. He definitely was going to watch her like a hawk for the next day or so. There were things she shouldn't do—such as ride home behind him on his motorcycle.

He could see the ice-cream shop down the street. It was doing a brisk business despite the mayhem that had broken out just a few blocks away. There were umbrella-covered tables out in front, right on the sidewalk.

"Let me get you an ice cream," he told her. "You can sit here and eat it while I take the Harley home. I'll get the car, come back and pick you up."

"But I liked being your motorcycle chick," she said. "Shades of Gidget, you know?"

"Sorry, but I'm not taking any chances," he said.

She knew he was talking about her head. "It's just a little bump."

"Give up," he told her. "You're not going to win this one. I'll be back in…" He looked at his watch. "Twenty-eight minutes."

Brittany laughed. "Twenty-eight? Exactly? I had no idea I was having a fling with Mr. Spock."

"Very funny. I know how long it takes me to get home from here—thirteen minutes. Add a few for going inside to get the keys to the car…" He opened the door for her. "Careful, there's a step up—don't trip again."

"I didn't trip down those stairs," she told him as they went into the shop. "I was pushed. Hard."

Jesus. Probably by some six foot tall coward rushing to save his own sorry ass. "Damn it." He turned back the way they'd come, and she tugged him inside.

"Whoever it was, he or she is definitely not still there," she said. "Your thirst for revenge will have to be sated by chocolate ice cream."

"I'm a vanilla man, myself," he told her. "But I'm going to pass right now. Ice-cream cones and bikes don't mix." He slapped a five-dollar bill onto the counter and gave her a quick kiss. "I'll be back."

Brittany sat outside, in the warmth of the afternoon sun, eating ice cream and watching people pass by on the sidewalk.

Her ankle was sore, and her head had a tender spot where she'd connected with the stairs, but other than that, she was absolutely fine.

She sighed. She'd been looking forward to riding home with her arms wrapped around Wes's waist. She'd been looking forward to dancing with him some more, too.

Now he was going to watch her all night.

Well, okay. Good. He could look all he wanted. And Brittany, well, she'd give him something to watch.

She realized she'd been ignoring her cone, and she had to lick all the way around it to keep the ice cream from dripping onto her hand. When she looked up, there was a man standing slightly off to the side, watching her.

At first glance, he seemed to be a nice enough looking guy. He was hair challenged, but that didn't take away from the handsome bone structure of his face.

But then he moved closer and she saw his eyes.

After working in countless emergency rooms on both the east and west coast, Brittany recognized mental illness when she saw it. And this guy, although he dressed nicely and even normally—no mismatched plaids and stripes, no superhero cape, no protective headgear to ward off killer bee attacks—had something in his eyes that set off all of her alarms.

Not that he necessarily was dangerous. Just that he was different.

He was holding a set of car keys, so obviously he was highly functional. But he was definitely challenged.

He couldn't hold her gaze. But he spoke to her. "You made her cry."

It was pretty remarkable, actually. They always approached her. All the certifiable ones did. There could be seven nurses working the shift, and sure enough, the patients who were mentally ill would sidle their way over to Brittany.

Andy said it was because she spoke to them as if they were real people.

Britt had laughed at that. "But they are real people," she'd argued.

"My point exactly," the kid had told her.

She looked at the Hairclub for Men candidate and tried to make both her face and her voice neutral. She didn't want him coming over and sitting down next to her, but she didn't want to ignore him, either. On closer inspection, he had the look of a man who'd gone off his medication. "I'm sorry. Have we met?"

"You made her cry," he said again, and both the tone of his voice and the look in his eyes made her stand up and start backing away.

Okay, Wes, any time now. She glanced at her watch

and saw that it was at least ten minutes before his estimated return.

"I'm sorry," she said, "but I really don't know what you're talking about."

"She cried," he said. "Her heart is broken."

"I'm sorry about that," she said again.

"No you're not."

The man slowly shuffled closer, and Britt kept on backing away, just as one of the employees came out of the ice-cream shop—a kid with a rag in his hand to wipe off the outside tables.

"Is there a pay phone inside?" she asked him.

"Nope. Sorry. Nearest one is down the street. Kelley's."

"Thank you." Brittany looked the direction he pointed, and could see the shamrock green sign for Kelley's bar. Her heart sank. It was way down at the very end of the street. Her ankle wasn't seriously injured, but it would take a lot longer to heal completely if she hiked on it.

"Move along, mister," the kid said to the bald man. "Don't hassle the paying customers."

"Can't I order an ice-cream cone?" He aimed his anger at the kid as he sat down at the same table Britt had been sitting at moments earlier. He carefully took out his wallet and extracted several dollar bills. "Chocolate chip."

"You have to order from the counter," the kid said, and as they went inside, Brittany took the opportunity to slip away.

Wes made it back to the ice-cream shop in record time, only to find that Brittany was gone.

The only people sitting out front were a mother and her four young children.

Maybe Britt was inside, and he just couldn't see her through the glare on the plate glass.

Wes tried to push away thoughts of Britt having suffered from a worse head injury than he'd imagined, falling unconscious, or becoming disoriented and wandering off...

He shouldn't have left her here. He should have stayed with her and taken a cab home. Or to the hospital. But when he left her, she seemed fine. She *was* fine. He just had to take a deep breath and calm down. She was inside. She didn't see him pull up. This was not a big deal.

He pulled into a no standing zone, and jumped out of his car, leaving his flashers on.

But as he got closer to the shop, he quickly saw that she wasn't there and the fear returned.

He opened the door and called to one of the kids behind the counter. "Hey. Do you have a ladies' room?"

"No, sir," she told him, eyeing him oddly.

"There wasn't just an ambulance here, was there?" Wes asked, his heart actually in his throat. Please say no...

"No, sir," she told him.

Thank God. But where the hell was Brittany? "Do you remember seeing a blond woman, about my height? Mid-thirties? Pretty...?" Jesus, he could be describing anyone. "Kind of pointy nose. She was wearing a blue shirt...?"

"No, sir."

"I saw her." A kid who was wiping tables straightened up. "She asked if we had a pay phone, and I sent her down to Kelley's." He gestured down the street with his head.

"Thanks." Wes was back in his car in a flash. Why did Britt need to make a call? Was she feeling worse? Had she called a cab to take her to the hospital? Why hadn't she called him?

He broke about four traffic laws getting over to Kelley's as quickly as he could, and parked—again—in a tow zone.

Kelley's was a bar about the size of his living room. One glance around told him she wasn't there. Of course not—there was a big sign on the pay phone: Out of Order.

Jesus, where was she?

Everyone had looked up when he came in, and Wes used the opportunity to call to the bartender, "Hey, pal, did a pretty blonde come in here asking—"

His cell phone rang. He had it out and open in record time. Please, God... "Britt?"

"Oh, no," she sounded dismayed. "You got to the ice-cream place and I wasn't there."

The relief that flooded him at the sound of her voice nearly knocked him on his ass. "Are you all right? Where are you?" His voice actually cracked. "Jesus, Britt, you scared the crap out of me."

"I'm sorry—I'm fine. Some weird guy was hassling me outside of the ice-cream shop. So I went down the street and... I'm around the corner at a restaurant called The Toucan. I thought I'd be able to get to a phone and call you before you got back."

"I made good time," he told her, waving to the bartender as he went back out onto the sidewalk. "Who the fuh—who was hassling you?" He'd find him and break his knees.

"Just some guy who was angry at the entire world. He was hassling everyone, not just me. But he was a little scary so—"

Some angry guy scared her. God. "I shouldn't have left you alone," Wes said. "Are you really okay?"

"Please deposit thirty-five cents for another three minutes," a computer voice cut in to their call.

"I'm out of change," Brittany told him.

"I'm on my way." Wes hung up the phone and nearly ran into a man who was standing by his car, right by the front bumper. "Sorry, I didn't see you there."

"You're not supposed to park here," the man said. Something about him was slightly off-kilter, like he wasn't playing with a full deck of cards.

"It was an emergency," Wes told him. He opened the door to his car. "Better get back on the sidewalk, buddy—I'm going to pull out, okay?"

The man shuffled over to the curb. "I'm not your buddy," he said. "You made her cry."

Oo-kay.

"You should probably stay out of the street," Wes told him before he got into his car and pulled away.

Chapter 14

Wes was silent on the ride home—except when he asked a half a dozen different times if Brittany really was all right.

She finally turned to him. "Wesley. I'm fine. My ankle's a little sore and I bumped my head. What do I have to say to get you to believe me?"

The muscles jumped in his jaw. "Sorry."

He pulled into his driveway and got out of the car. He came around and closed her door for her after she got out, and then followed her to his kitchen door. He unlocked it and pushed it open for her, all without saying another word.

He was tightly wound, every muscle tense.

Brittany waited until he closed the door behind them. "Are you angry with me?"

"No."

"You're acting as if you are," she pointed out.

He closed his eyes for a moment. "Okay," he said. "Maybe I am. Maybe I'm… God, I don't know what I am, Britt. When I couldn't find you, I thought…" He shook his head. "I was scared to death. And I don't like being scared."

She nodded. "I can relate. I don't like it, either. I'm sorry I didn't call you sooner, but—"

"Can we not talk right now?" he asked. "I just… I don't want to talk, okay?"

"Maybe now's the best time to talk," she countered. "If you're really that upset, you should get it out instead of internalizing it."

"Thanks but no thanks." He took a glass from the cabinet and got himself some water, his movements tight, almost jerky. "You know, we talk too much. I thought this relationship was supposed to be based on sex. On…" He used a verb that should have made her take a step back. A verb that was meant to make her take a step back.

But Brittany knew exactly what he was doing.

Or rather, trying to do.

And she didn't even flinch. It was going to take more than a few bad words for him to push her away just because his feelings for her scared him.

"You care about me too much," she guessed—correctly from his reaction. "And realizing just how much you care has really freaked you out, hasn't it?"

He made a sound that might have been laughter, might have been pain. "I don't have room for you," he said and winced, swearing softly. "That sounds awful and I'm sorry, babe, but I—"

"No," she said. "No, Wes, I know what you mean. I

know why you said it." And she did. She knew, without a doubt, that he was thinking about Ethan. He was thinking about loss, and about how he wouldn't feel the pain of loss if he had nothing to lose. "I'm not going to die, honey. I'm not Ethan."

"Oh, perfect," he said, famous Skelly temper flaring. "Bring Ethan into it. Why the hell not? Let's make this a complete misery-fest."

"I think that everything you do comes back to Ethan's death," Brittany told him quietly. "Everything. Your love affair with Lana—the wife of a close friend. Unrequited love—how perfect is that for you? You can't lose her because she's not yours to lose. Except you can't win, either. You can never win, never be happy as long as you—"

"Look," he said. "I'm really not interested in this. I'm going to go take a nap. You want to come lie down with me, fine. You don't, that's fine, too."

But she blocked the door that led to his bedroom. "You said you were scared today. What were you afraid of, Wes?"

He didn't answer.

He didn't need to—she knew. "You were afraid I was hurt worse that I let on," she said. "You were afraid I was badly injured. And what if I had been?"

Wes shook his head. "Brittany, don't. I already spent too much time there. It was not fun."

"If I had been badly hurt," she asked instead, "whose fault would it have been?"

He said one choice word on an exhale of air.

"Mine," she answered for him. "It would have been my fault, not yours. I'm the one who tripped down those stairs—"

"You said you were pushed."

"Yeah," she said. "Okay. I was pushed. So it wasn't completely my fault, but that doesn't make it yours either."

"If I had been with you, no one would've gotten close enough to push you—you better believe that."

"Right," she said. "And if you had been with me the summer I turned twenty-two, I never would've gone out to the movies with my ex-husband that first time. So does that make my entire fiasco of a rotten marriage your fault, too?"

He grimly shook his head. "That's not the same thing."

"You weren't there when those creeps took a potshot at the president last year," she said. "So is it your fault that that Secret Service agent died?"

"No."

"So why, then, is it your fault that Ethan died?"

He was silent, just glaring at her. "You just don't know when to stop, do you?" he finally said.

"Wes, why is it your fault that Ethan died?" she asked again.

"Goddamn it. It's not. That's what you want me to say, right?"

"No," she said. "It's what I want you to believe."

"Well, I do believe it," he said harshly. "I couldn't have saved him even if I were in the car with him. I'm not a superhero—I have no delusions about myself. None at all. Some of the guys in Alpha Squad think they're one step short of immortal. They think they're goddamn invincible. But hey—remember me? I'm the family screwup. I have a long history of annoying the crap out of everyone I ever meet—"

"Not me," she said.

"Yeah," Wes said, his voice breaking. "Jesus, I can't figure that one out. You're, like, one of the nicest women I've ever met and no matter what I do or say, you still like me. I don't get it."

He actually had tears in his eyes. Brittany took a step toward him, reaching for him, but he backed away.

"Sweetie, it's because I see the real you," she told him, refusing to be daunted. "I see a wonderful, kind, compassionate, very strong and very intelligent man who is so much fun to be around, who gives so much of himself so generously. I see someone special—"

"That was Ethan." His voice got louder as he used anger to keep himself from crying. "Not me. He was the special one. I was the one who always pushed the boundaries, the annoying kid who tested everyone's patience day in and day out. I'm the troublemaker, the roof-walker, the risk-taker, the tormentor. I'm the one who should have died. If one of us had to go, it goddamn should have been me!"

Silence.

Brittany suspected Wes had surprised himself with that statement more than he'd surprised her.

"It should have been me," he whispered as he used the heels of his hands to wipe his eyes before any tears could escape. God forbid he actually cry. "It's been years and years and I'm still angry as hell that it wasn't me in that car instead of Ethan."

"Oh, honey," Brittany told him. "I for one am so glad it wasn't you. And, for what it's worth, sweet kids are nice, but I've always preferred the annoying ones. They grow up to be the most fascinating men."

Wes reached for her then. He practically lunged for her, pulling her close and kissing her almost painfully hard.

She kissed him back just as fiercely, knowing that he needed this, that even though he wasn't going to let himself cry, that right now he could use sex as an emotional outlet.

He wasn't the only one.

God, she loved him. But she didn't dare tell him, afraid he would take her words as another burden, another worry, another problem to have to deal with.

So she just kissed him.

Wes had stopped thinking.

Thinking hurt too much, and if he didn't think, then all he did was feel, and right now he was feeling Brittany.

Brittany, who thought he was a fascinating man. Brittany who just kept on liking him, who wouldn't let him scare her away.

He felt Britt's mouth on his mouth, her breasts pressed tightly to his chest, her legs locked around his waist as he buried himself inside of her again and again and again.

She was hot and slick and he couldn't remember the last time anything—anything—had felt this incredible.

"Condom," she gasped. "Wes, we need—"

A condom. He wasn't wearing a condom.

Now there was a thought that was able to cut through the haze of all that intense pleasure, and Wes froze.

He opened his eyes and realized that not only was he inside of her without protection, but he was nailing her with no finesse, his pants around his thighs, no consideration for her comfort, her back pressed hard against the living room wall.

But even though he'd stopped, she was still moving as if she liked it. No, forget liked—as if she loved what he was doing to her—as if she wanted and needed him as much as he needed her.

"Please," she said. "We need to get a condom. But I can't seem to stop. This feels too good…"

God, she was beyond sexy and he kissed her as he reached for the wallet in the back pocket of his pants.

"Please," she begged, between kissing him again. "Please, Wes—"

Oh, yeah, the sexiest woman he'd ever had the pleasure of making it with was now begging him. But for what? To pull out, or—

She gripped him with her legs, pushing him deeply inside of her, and she made a noise that was almost enough to make him drop his wallet.

He'd put a condom in there in the event that they didn't make it home from Old Town San Diego before needing to make love again.

Because that's what being with Brittany was like— it wasn't so much that he wanted her, as a "yeah that would be nice" kind of thing, but rather that he needed her, like "if you don't make love to me right now I'm going to die." God, he needed her so badly, all the time.

Maybe he should get her pregnant and marry her.

God, okay, now he went from not thinking at all, to thinking crazy thoughts. Except merely being inside her like this, with no protection, was enough to knock her up. Enough damage had already been done.

Surely she knew that. She was a nurse.

And he wanted—needed…

Brittany. In his life.

For more than just the next week.

Oh, God, what she was doing to him, despite knowing that he wasn't wearing protection.

Maybe she wanted him to get her pregnant. Maybe she wanted him to marry her, to start a family. He knew she still wanted to have a baby. How incredibly terrifying. What would he do with a baby? And yet the idea of coming home to Brittany every night was a damn appealing one.

"I want to come inside of you," he gasped, unable to form the words to really tell her all that he was feeling. Surely she would understand what he meant by that. "Britt…"

She didn't say no, but she didn't say yes, either. She just exploded around him, and just like that, it was over for him, too. He pulled out, but it was, of course, too late.

Brittany kissed him. "Tell me," she said, before he'd even had a chance to catch his breath. "Right now, right this very moment, aren't you even just a little bit glad that you weren't the one who died?"

Wes laughed and kissed her. "Yes," he said. "Whenever I'm with you, baby, definitely yes."

The phone rang just after 4:00 a.m., waking Brittany from a restless sleep.

Wes cursed like the sailor that he was as he reached across her for the cordless phone sitting in the recharger on his bedside table. "If this is another hang-up, I'm turning off the ringer."

"What if it's Andy?" Britt asked, reaching to turn on the light.

"Skelly." Wes's scowl softened when he caught sight of her face. No doubt she looked as anxious as she felt. "It's not Andy," he mouthed silently. But then whoever was on the other end of the phone had his full attention. "What?" He swore. "When?" Another pause. Whoever he was talking to, it was extremely serious. "Are they sure?" He swore again, then took a deep breath and blew it out hard.

His hand was shaking as he ran it down his face, as he swore again. "No," he said into the phone. "I know. I never thought… I mean, if anyone was indestructible… Oh, God. And they're sure it's not a mistake?"

Oh, God—indeed. Someone had died. Someone Wes cared about.

As Britt watched, he threw back the covers and got out of bed.

"Yeah," he said into the phone, pulling clean underwear and socks from his dresser, and a T-shirt from another drawer. "I'll call Bobby. He's on his honeymoon, but he'll definitely want to know. Jesus." He rubbed the back of his neck as if it ached. "Yeah. Thank you, Senior Chief. I appreciate the call, and…" Pause. "Yeah, I'll see you over there."

He hung up the phone and stood there for a moment, with his back to Brittany, taking another deep breath and exhaling hard.

"Wes," she said softly. "What happened?"

He turned toward her, his face stony in its grimness. "Matt Quinn's dead."

Matt…? For a second, Brittany didn't recognize the name. But then she did. She just hadn't heard his given name all that often. But Matt Quinn was the Mighty Quinn. Wizard the Mighty Quinn.

Lana Quinn's husband. And Wes's good friend. And he was…dead?

"Oh, my God," she breathed. "How?"

"Helicopter crash. His SeaHawk went down over the ocean, on the way back in from an op. Jesus, I have to take a shower."

Brittany followed him into the bathroom. "Was everyone on board lost?"

"No," Wes told, turning on the water and waiting for it to heat. "The rest of his squad was pulled out of the water, but Quinn and two members of the helo crew were killed on impact. The PJ's didn't get them out before it went under, though. Apparently there's some kind of storm cooking in that area right now—it's going to be a few days before they get divers in to recover the bodies—if they manage to do it at all. Which is going to make it that much harder for Lana." He looked at her, as if seeing her for the first time since he got off the phone with the senior chief. "Will you do me a favor?"

"Of course."

"I have to call Bobby. Somewhere on the desk in the kitchen is a piece of paper with the phone number of the resort where he and Colleen are staying."

"I'll find it," she told him.

"Thanks." He stepped into the shower.

"Wes." Britt stopped him from closing the shower curtain. "It's okay if you cry when you find out that a friend is dead."

But he had that stoneman look on his face again. "Just find me that number, please."

Brittany went into the kitchen via the bedroom, where she pulled on a T-shirt and a pair of Wes's boxers.

Maybe he'd just never cry. Maybe he'd go through

life using high-intensity, mindless sex as his way of expressing his emotions.

Mindless to the point of ignoring all birth control and safe sex precautions.

A chilling jolt of disbelief went through her. God, what had they done?

Having unprotected sex was stupid. There was no good reason to do it, no acceptable excuse.

And the really stupid thing was, they hadn't even talked about it yet. After, Wes had dragged her into the shower and washed them both clean. One thing had led to another and they'd ended up in his bed, communicating once again through touch.

They'd spent the whole night sleeping and waking up to make love—with proper protection each time.

All night long, every time she'd thought about getting up the nerve to say, "So. Wesley. Sex without a condom. What were we thinking?" he'd kissed her.

And lordy, lordy, how that man could kiss!

He'd sucked all the unspoken words right out of her mouth, and managed to empty her brain of all thoughts besides those of immediate gratification.

Up to a few minutes ago, when that phone call came, Brittany had played out the "what if she were pregnant" scenario right to a fairy-tale happy ending. She'd get the baby she'd always wanted, and a husband she loved—who loved her, too. Because Wes did love her. She knew that without a doubt.

The trouble was, he loved her second best.

But now, suddenly, with Quinn's untimely death, Britt was the potential obstacle that would keep Wes from finally finding true happiness with Lana.

And wouldn't that be just his luck? Lana was finally free, although not in a way that anyone had hoped for, except, whoops, Wes might well have just gotten his girlfriend—no, make that his casual sex partner—pregnant.

Oh, God.

After Wes got out of the shower, he was going to get dressed and go over to Lana's house. *I'll see you over there.* They'd all go over to Lana's house—all of Wizard's friends and teammates, and their wives and girlfriends as well. They'd sit shiva, so to speak.

Melody had once told Brittany how tight-knit the SEAL community was. Wes and his friends would take care of Lana. They'd comfort her.

Yeah, Wes was pretty good at comfort.

In the kitchen, Britt sifted through torn slips of paper that had Wes's odd, almost spidery handwriting on them. ABC Cab, here in San Diego. His brother Frank's new phone number in Oklahoma City. Aunt Maureen and Uncle George in Sarasota, Florida. The phone number of a comic book store in Escondido. The 800 number for Alamo car rental at the airport.

Gee, that might come in handy.

Aha. Bobby and Colleen. They had an entire full, untorn sheet devoted to them.

Wes had written down their new address and phone number, as well as the dates of their honeymoon—which ended last night. Yes, according to their flight information, they'd arrived in San Diego shortly after 8:00 p.m. last night.

The shower had shut off, and by the time Brittany went back into the bedroom, Wes was already dry and getting dressed.

"I want to get over there quickly," he said to her, "so if you want to shower—"

"I'm not going," she said. "You know. To Lana's. The last thing she needs is a stranger hanging around right now."

He stepped into his pants. "It's just… I'm not sure how long I'm going to be."

"That's okay," Brittany said. "Of course you'll stay as long as she wants you to stay. I know that. Don't worry about me. I'm going to call a cab. I'll rent a car and head back to L.A. Andy's doing fine—he and Dani seem to have things under control. You don't need me hanging around here, so… I'll call work, see if they need me to do a shift tonight. It's a good thing for me to do—I'll win brownie points with my supervisor."

He nodded, clearly distracted. "I wonder if anyone called Amber."

He picked up the phone and dialed.

Brittany sat on the bed and watched as he made sure the word about Matt Quinn had made it to Lana's sister in L.A. It had. Amber was already in San Diego, with Lana.

She watched as he finished dressing in a tan uniform—a chief's uniform. It was less formal than the one he'd worn to the party, yet it still managed to accentuate his broad shoulders and trim hips.

He took his cell phone from the charger and slipped it into his pocket, found his hat…

"You can stay as long as you like," he told Britt. "Go back to sleep if you can."

She shook her head. "I can't." She handed him the piece of paper with Bobby's phone number on it.

"Don't forget to call Bobby. He and Colleen got home last night."

"Thanks. I was going to call him from the car," he said, folding up the paper and putting it in his shirt pocket. "How're your head and ankle this morning?"

"They're fine," she told him. And they were. It was her heart that was breaking.

He kissed her—briefly—on the mouth. For the last time? Maybe. Probably. Oh, God.

"I'll talk to you later," he said. "I've got to go."

Of course he did. Lana needed him.

The stupid thing was, it was Wes's love for Lana that had truly made Brittany fall for him. He was an amazing man. He'd cared about Lana so deeply for so long. And yet, he'd always done what was best for Lana, regardless of his own wants and needs—even when it would have been easier to do otherwise.

And wasn't that the exact opposite of That-Jerk-Quentin, Britt's ex, who wanted everything in life to be easy, who wasn't willing to work to make their relationship last even a few short years.

God, what she wouldn't give to spend the rest of her life with Wesley Skelly.

Brittany figured that her best chance was to be patient and steadfast and become the woman he would settle for. And yeah, loser that she was, she was willing to be his second choice. He was that great, and she loved him that much.

But now she wasn't even going to have that opportunity. Because Lana was suddenly no longer unattainable.

Britt heard the door close as he left the apartment, heard his car start as he drove away.

Out of her life.

Please God, don't let me be pregnant.

It was one thing to be his second choice when his first choice wasn't an option. It was another entirely to be his burden.

No matter what happened, she wouldn't do that.

Chapter 15

Wes had to park six houses down—there were that many cars in the street outside of the little bungalow Lana had shared with Matt "Wizard" Quinn.

Bobby and Colleen were pulling up just as he was getting out of his car, and he waited for them.

Jesus, his sister was young. Every time he saw her, he couldn't believe that she was married. God, before he knew it, she was going to tell him that she and Bobby were going to have a baby. And wasn't that going to be freakin' weird.

Bobby looked…like Bobby. Like a guy who was as big and as mean as a football linebacker, like a guy who could chew you to pieces if he got mad enough. With his long black hair tied in a braid down his back, and his Native American heritage showing in his cheekbones and coloring, people stopped and stared when he walked down the street.

Wes knew they were something of a visual joke when they were together. Bobby and Wes, the inseparable team of chiefs from SEAL Team Ten. Wes and Bobby. Mutt and Jeff. Ren and Stimpy. Fleaman and Giagantor.

Wes's lack of height and girth was accentuated when he stood next to Bobby, but the truth was that there was nowhere he'd rather stand. And Bobby, God bless him, never made Wes feel lacking in any way, shape or form.

He may have looked like a bruiser, but Bobby Taylor was one of the nicest, kindest, gentlest guys Wes had ever met, a guy with a goofy smile and dark brown eyes that could see inside of Wes's head in a single glance.

Wes held out his hand for Bobby to shake, but Bobby pushed it aside and hugged him. He and Colleen were both crying. She'd never met Quinn, but that didn't matter.

He could tell just from looking that his sister was scared to death. This was her first taste of loss of life in the teams.

Well, welcome to the harsh reality of being married to a Navy SEAL during wartime, babe. She'd been so keen to marry Bobby. Now she had to face the risks and dangers, up close and personal.

"I can't believe he's gone," Bobby said.

"Have you been inside?" Colleen asked. "How's Lana?"

"I just got here myself," Wes admitted. "So I don't know. I'm sure she's emotionally wrecked."

"Last time I talked to Quinn was, man, it must have been four months ago," Bobby said.

"I got an email from him right after you guys got married. He wanted me to tell you that he wished he could've been there." Wes had to clear his throat. He swore.

Bobby hugged him again, and then Wes found himself looking into the eyes of the man who was his best friend in the whole flipping world—and wanting to tell him about Brittany. But it didn't quite line up with all this pain about Wizard.

His news was going to have to wait. Until he figured out exactly what kind of news it was.

"You okay?" Bobby asked him.

"Yeah," Wes said. "No," he added. "I'm like you— It's so fricking hard to believe. I mean, the senior chief called to tell me, and I kept asking was he sure, you know, that it was Quinn who was dead. How could he be dead?"

Bobby sighed as he shook his head. "I don't know. We should go inside though. You're probably in a rush to see Lana."

"Yeah," Wes said, although it wasn't true. He was dragging his feet, and wasn't that strange?

He followed Bobby and Colleen up the path to where Lana's front door was wide open. They all just walked in.

The little house was crowded. Most of Team Ten was there, pulled straight out of bed upon receiving the news. Crash Hawken and Blue McCoy and even the CO, Joe Catalanotto were near the fireplace. Lucky, Frisco, and the senior chief, Harvard Becker stood by the window. Harlan "Cowboy" Jones—Britt's brother-in-law— was right by the front door, talking to Mitch Shaw.

They'd all worked with Wizard at one time or another.

"Excuse me, sir. Where's Lana?" Bobby asked Lt. Jones.

"She's taking a walk on the beach with Veronica

Catalanotto," he told them, his eyes narrowing slightly at he looked at Wes.

Jesus, that kind of look meant… Did Jones know about Wes and Britt? Oh, man, look at him—he did. What had Britt told him the other night, at Dani's sister's apartment?

Knowing Britt, she'd told Jones the truth.

Oh, boy. Wes was so dead.

"There's coffee in the kitchen," Lt. Shaw told them.

Wes escaped, certain that Jones would somehow be able to tell from looking at him that Wes had quite possibly gotten Jones's sister-in-law pregnant just last night.

He poured himself a mug of coffee and took a bracing sip. It was hot as hell and burned all the way down, but that was just as good. It distracted him sufficiently. This wasn't the time or place to be thinking about what he and Britt had done last night.

Oh, but holy God, he hadn't been able to stop thinking about it, all night long. He'd even dreamed about it, while he'd slept.

If she was pregnant, he'd marry her. He didn't have to think twice about it—but that wasn't what was on his mind.

No, what he couldn't stop thinking about was how badly he wanted to make love to her like that again. With nothing between them. If she were pregnant, then hell, he couldn't exactly get her pregnant again, now could he? So they could throw away their condoms and…

And spend the rest of their lives laughing and talking and making love the way they had this past incredible week.

Yeah, some time between last night and this morning, Wes had started praying to God that Brittany was pregnant.

And wasn't that the weirdest flipping thing?

No. Actually, it wasn't so weird. It made sense in an odd sort of way. If Britt was pregnant, Wes would have no choice.

Those things she'd said to him last night had struck home. Some truths had come out—including the fact that for all these years, Wes had felt as if he should have died instead of Ethan. It was crazy. It didn't make sense—he wasn't even in the car—but that didn't matter. He was the loser in the family, so he should have been the one who died.

He'd thought about it some last night—when he wasn't losing himself in Brittany's sweet love.

This was why he didn't go home to visit. Because he couldn't face his parents and his brothers and sisters. Because surely they looked at him and shook their heads, and wondered why God had taken Ethan and left screwup Wes on earth, instead.

So yeah. Brittany had been right about a lot of things. His loving Lana. Yes, it was true that people couldn't help falling in love. But they didn't have to spend over five years pining away, for God's sake.

Unless maybe they were punishing themselves.

Losers like Wes didn't deserve to live happily ever after. They didn't deserve a beautiful, warm, caring woman who loved them fiercely and passionately.

They could, however, get a woman pregnant and have that happy ever after forced upon them.

Jesus. He clearly needed some serious therapy.

Or a whole pack of cigarettes.

Or maybe he just needed Brittany.

The back door opened, and the CO's wife, Ronnie, came into the kitchen with Amber and...

Lana.

Wes's heart twisted when he saw her, but it was a different kind of twisting than it had been in the past.

She looked exhausted, with dark circles beneath haunted eyes, and a face that was pale and pinched with grief.

It was more than obvious that all three of the women had been crying.

Lana slipped past Wes without saying anything, with only the briefest touch of her hand on his arm. He watched her head down the hall to her bedroom, feeling helpless and useless.

He wasn't what Lana needed or wanted right now.

She wanted Quinn to come through the front door, laughing and telling them all that he wasn't dead, that it had been some kind of crazy mistake.

But Wes knew that wasn't true. The senior chief had told him that Lt. Jim Slade—the SEAL known as Spaceman—had been on that op, and had seen Quinn's body.

Ronnie followed Lana, sending Wes a look filled with sympathy and compassion, but Amber stayed behind, in the kitchen.

"They won't tell her anything about the mission he was on," she said to him, her voice tight. Amber was amazing. She even managed to look beautiful right after she'd cried.

Or maybe she was just plastic.

"Yeah," Wes said. "That's the way it works. The Navy can't give out details, and for a good reason. It put other SEALs and other ops in jeopardy. But I think

Lana probably knows in her heart what Matt and his team were doing out there. It wasn't just some pleasure cruise."

The SEALs had been making the world just a little bit safer, even if it was just by eliminating one terrorist at a time.

"That doesn't make it any easier for her," Amber said.

"No," he agreed. "It doesn't."

Amber sighed. "I know it was probably hard to tell, but... Lana's glad you're here, Wes. She's told me a lot about you, just over the past couple of days—we'd been talking a lot, on the phone, before this happened. It's crazy. I just had this conversation with her where I actually asked her if Quinn died, would she hook up with you."

Wes took a step back, not sure he wanted to hear what Lana's answer had been.

But Amber didn't seem to notice his reluctance to continue this conversation. She just kept on talking. "She said she didn't really know if that was something you wanted anymore—you know, a relationship with her. I pushed her, asking what she wanted, and she finally said maybe she would, and God help me, because I like you so much better than Quinn, I said, well, then I hope he dies."

Her face crumpled like a little girl's as she started to cry again, and Wes put his arms around her.

"Come on, Amber," he said. Like Lana, she was much shorter and slighter than Britt, and it felt odd—almost as if he were embracing a child rather than a woman, as if he had to be careful, to treat her as if she were fragile and might break if he held her too tightly. "You know saying that didn't make it happen."

"He was a complete scumball," she sobbed into his shoulder, "but Lana loved him. I didn't really want him to die."

"I know that," Wes said. "And I'm sure Lana does, too."

"I just thought she deserved better."

"She deserves someone who loves her enough to be faithful," Wes said. "Everyone does."

"I'm supposed to be asking everyone to leave." Amber looked up at him through her tears. "Lana's said she was going to take one of the sleeping pills the doctor gave her, and... But maybe you should stay."

"I don't think—"

"Maybe you could make her feel better, make her start thinking about the future. Maybe—"

The future? "That's not such a good idea."

Amber pulled back slightly. "Why not?"

He sighed. "Well, for one thing, Lana doesn't need to think about the future today. She needs to grieve. And that's not about looking ahead. It's about reflecting and, well, being. Enduring these next few days and weeks."

"She needs someone to hold her," Amber countered, wiping her face with her hands and stepping more fully out of his embrace. "She needs someone who loves her."

"That's why you're here," Wes said gently. "Right?"

Amber nodded. "But—"

"I'll stay if she asks me to," Wes said. "I'd do almost anything for her—I think she knows that. But she's not going to ask." She'd barely even looked at him when she walked past him. It was beyond obvious that she didn't need him. And funny, but that realization didn't upset him the way that it would have just a few weeks ago.

A few weeks ago, he would have followed Lana out of the kitchen—no, he would have gone out onto the beach, looking for her when he first arrived. He would have fought through a crowd to get to her side to comfort her—whether she'd wanted him to or not.

"She needs you and Ronnie to stay right now," Wes continued.

Amber wouldn't let him escape out the back door. "Lana told me that she kissed you once."

Oh, man. "Yeah," Wes said. "And the key word there is once. It shouldn't have happened, and it didn't happen ever again."

"She said you were the most honorable man she's ever met."

"Yeah, I'm not so sure about that." Time to change the subject. "How's it going with the new security team?"

Amber shrugged. "Fine. My manager found a security company that specializes in guards who fade into the background. It's working well. The weird phone calls have completely stopped."

"That's good to hear."

"Yeah, maybe he's given up and is stalking Sarah Michelle Gellar instead."

Wes glanced over at the door leading to the living room, checking out an alternate escape route, only to find Lt. Jones leaning in the doorway, listening. How long had he been standing there? He turned back to Amber. "Maybe you better go let people know Lana would like us all to leave."

She nodded, giving Jones a somewhat blatant once-over before leaving the two of them alone.

Jones—tall and lean with a face like a movie star and sunbleached hair—didn't so much as glance at Amber twice. "Where's Brittany?" he asked.

"She's heading back to L.A.," Wes said. "She's renting a car—she didn't want to stick around. She said she didn't want to get in Lana's way."

Jones didn't look happy. "So you just…what? Put her on a bus to the car rental place?"

"No, sir. She said she was calling a cab. I tried to give her money, but, you know, she's a big girl, Lieutenant. I can't force her to do anything she doesn't want to do."

"She's in love with you," Jones told him.

Wes laughed—mostly because he was so surprised. It was either that or faint. "Whoa," he said. "Wait. She actually told you that?"

With Brittany, anything was possible.

"Not in so many words, no," Jones said and the accompanying disappointment that hit Wes at that news surprised him even more. God, maybe it shouldn't have, considering what he'd been thinking these past few hours. "I know her pretty well, Skelly. She's not the type of woman to have casual sex."

"She's not some kind of nun, either," Wes told him. "She's incredibly hot and—"

Jones closed his eyes and made a face. "Yeah, don't go into any details. That's already more than I want to know."

"She's great," Wes said simply.

"Yes," Jones said. "She is. So don't mess with her. I don't know what you've got going here with Lana—"

"Nothing," Wes said. And damn if it wasn't the truth in every single way. He still loved Lana—on some levels he would always love her, but it was a pale emotion compared to his crazy feelings for Brittany. Brittany—who was so much more to him than a distant and unattainable goddess. She was his friend, his lover, his partner.

His heart.

Wes took out his cell phone. "Excuse me, sir, but I have to call Brittany. There's something I forgot to ask her before she left."

Brittany parked the rental car in her driveway in Wes's spot.

Wes's spot. Listen to her. The man had only been around for about a week, and somehow this particular patch of the driveway had become his?

Yes, he'd parked there, but big deal. It was where Melody parked when she and Tyler came to visit, too.

God, she was exhausted. And yes, let's be honest. She was sad. Very, very sad.

She was in love with Wes Skelly.

Who, right now, was probably sitting with his arms around Lana Quinn, comforting her while she cried over her scumbag of a dead husband.

Britt dragged herself up the stairs to her door, unlocked it and stepped into the past. Inside her apartment it was still three days ago. Everything was carefully preserved as if it belonged in a museum devoted to late last Saturday night.

The dishes they'd used for dinner were still in the sink. The newspaper was open on the table, to the entertainment section. Yeah, like they were actually going to go out to see a movie. They'd considered it for all of four minutes before falling back into bed.

They'd left in a hurry, though, when Andy had called.

The garbage was ripe—man, it smelled awful in there. And the dishes in the sink didn't help.

She carried the garbage pail through the living room and set it down on the porch, outside the front door.

The dishes were handled quickly, too, but the room obviously needed a good airing out. Brittany pushed the air conditioning to a colder setting, and then there was no reason to procrastinate further.

She picked up the kitchen phone and dialed Wes's cell. She already knew the number by heart.

Please God, don't let him be there. Let her leave a message. It would be much easier that way. And God knows this was going to be hard enough.

She'd come up with a plan during the drive home from San Diego, and although it involved fighting for Wes, trying to make him see just how good they fit together, it had to start with her setting him free.

Completely. Like that stupid, sappy saying about the butterfly or the bird or whatever it was that she'd always rolled her eyes over in the past. Or...

If you love someone, set them free...

She had to do this.

"You have reached the voice mail for..."

"Skelly," growled a recording of Wes's voice.

"Leave a message at the beep or press one for other options."

Britt took a deep breath as the phone beeped. "Wes. Hi. It's Brittany. I'm back in L.A.—I made it here, no problem. I just wanted to..." She had to clear her throat before she said it. "I wanted to tell you that I truly enjoyed the time we spent together these past few days. I wanted to thank you for that, with all my heart." She said the words in a rush. "But I really think it would be smart if we didn't see each other again. At least not, you know, romantically." God, now she was even starting to sound like him when she talked. "And not at all for at least a few months."

She cleared her throat again. "I'm going to pack up your things—your clothes and toothbrush and whatever else... I'll send them back to you. I'll overnight the package so you'll have it right away.

"I hope you aren't too upset with me, but I really do think it's best that we make a clean break, and that we do it now. I know your leave's not up yet, but I've got school and Andy and his scholarship to handle, and this thing with Dani to help with. I don't need any distractions right now, and let's face it, you're pretty distracting. And you...well, you've got a...well, a rather full plate right now, too."

Here came the really hard part. The flat-out lie. "I know you're probably freaking out about last night, thinking that I might have gotten pregnant, but you don't have to worry about that. Everything's fine. I got my period this morning.

"So," she said, trying her best to sound breezy and upbeat. "Okay. Thank you again. It was...fun."

Hang up the phone, fool, before you say something you regret.

"Good luck, Wes," she said. "Take care of yourself."

She cut the connection.

Don't cry, don't cry, don't cry.

Have a cup of tea instead.

Brittany emptied the kettle and filled it with fresh water, then turned on the stove. Her eyes were watering merely because it still smelled so bad in here.

She rummaged under the kitchen sink for the Lysol, and sprayed the room. Too bad she couldn't erase her feelings for Wes as easily.

But okay. She'd done it. She'd survived step one.

Step two was going to be hard, too. If he called,

she'd have to refuse to talk at any length, to be polite but firm. No, she didn't think it would be smart to see him again. No, it was no problem, in fact, she already sent his stuff. Yes, she definitely wasn't pregnant.

Liar.

She hated liars. She'd worked long and hard to teach Andy that no matter what the situation, telling the truth was the only real option.

Although, at the time, she hadn't encountered the situation in which her lover might have knocked her up on the night before finding out that the husband of the woman he truly loved had been killed.

God.

With luck, she wouldn't be a liar for long. She should be getting her period in a matter of days. And if she didn't...

She didn't want to think about that. If it happened, she'd cope.

Step three in her plan was waiting. One month definitely. Probably more like two. Matt Quinn's body had to be recovered—if possible. There would be a funeral, or at least a memorial service. And then time had to pass. Weeks. Maybe months.

Enough time for Lana to begin to stop grieving.

Enough time for Wes to feel comfortable about courting Matt Quinn's widow—if that really was what he wanted to do.

Of course, this plan could backfire. Wes and Lana could very well leap into a relationship right away. And then Brittany would lose.

But if that happened, so be it. It would mean that Wes would never have been happy with Britt. It would mean that Brittany *would* have been his second choice.

And, after a great deal of thought and reflection, she had come to the realization that being someone's second choice would never really be enough to make her truly happy.

But, in a few months, if she hadn't heard about Wes's pending engagement to Lana through reports from Melody and Jones, Brittany would plan a trip to San Diego. And while she was there, she'd make sure she bumped into Wes. Heck, she'd knock on his door if she had to.

And, at that point, after giving him plenty of time to think and recover from the shock of Quinn's death, Brittany would do her darndest to make Wes see that he belonged with her. She would fight for him. She would convince him that this thing that they'd found together—friendship, passion, compatibility, laughter, love—was worth keeping. She would convince him that she was not just his best choice, but his only choice.

But first she had to wait until the confusion and grief and emotion surrounding Matt Quinn's unfortunate death began to fade.

The phone rang, and she braced herself before she picked it up. It would be just like Wes to call immediately upon receiving her message.

"Hello?"

Silence. Then, click.

Annoyed, Brittany hung up. The phone company definitely had to troubleshoot their system. This was getting ridiculous.

Brittany took a mug and a tea bag from the cabinet, aware of how quiet it was in this apartment without Andy.

Without Wes.

The answering machine light was flashing—there

were three messages—and she pushed the play button as she unwrapped the tea bag and waited for the water to finish boiling. God, it still really smelled bad in here.

The first message was from her sister, and it had come in on Sunday morning. It was uncharacteristically terse. "Britt, it's Mel. Call me the minute you get home."

Oh, perfect. So much for her brother-in-law's promise that Melody wouldn't call her until Wes's leave was up.

At least Mel hadn't called while she was at Wes's.

The second message had come in just an hour ago, while she was still on the road.

"Britt, it's Wes. We need to talk. Call me back, baby, as soon as you can, okay?"

Oh, shoot. He sounded so serious, as if he needed to break some bad news.

Like, "Gee, Britt, we had fun together, but now that Quinn's dead, I'm moving in with Lana."

She made herself breathe slowly and evenly, calmly, as she poured her cup of tea. If Wes and Lana were meant to be together, so be it. If it meant that Wes would finally be happy, she could live with it.

She could learn to live with it.

The third message had been recorded just minutes before she got home. Maybe her luck would change and it would be George Clooney. Maybe he'd gotten her number from Amber, and…

A stream of shocking obscenities came out of her innocent little answering machine.

Who the heck…?

The voice was male, but it sure wasn't Andy or Wes or any other man she knew. The words were slurred together, but they ended with two that were quite clear. "Die, bitch."

Dear God, was it…?

She pushed the repeat button and the words washed over her again. God, she'd need a shower after this. She listened hard, but the voice definitely wasn't Andy's sworn enemy, Dustin Melero, either.

And she couldn't think of anyone else in the entire world who would record any kind of a threat on her answering machine.

It was probably a wrong number.

Still it was creepy enough to make her want to call Wes.

Of course, anything that happened was going to make her want to call Wes. She was going to have to stay strong, be tough, and keep her hands off her telephone.

First thing she had to do was pack up his stuff and take it to the post office, so that when he called she could tell him that it was already taken care of. There was no reason for him to drive up to L.A. None at all.

She went down the hall. Her bedroom door was closed. And it must have been her imagination, but it sure seemed as if that funky spoiled garbage smell was getting worse.

She pushed open her bedroom door—and dropped her mug of tea.

Someone or something had been slaughtered in her bed. The stench was hideous and she gagged, but—even though it seemed impossible that whatever was in there could still be alive—her nurse's training kept her from backing away.

But no, a closer look revealed that there was no body anywhere in the room—no animal carcass even. Just blood, everywhere. Some of it dark and drying, some of it still quite garishly red. It was on the sheets, on the floor, on the walls. And entrails—the kind you might buy from a butcher shop for your pet alligator—were part of the gory mess.

It only *looked* as if someone had been murdered in her bed.

But, God, this meant that someone had been in her apartment. Someone who might still be here.

Someone who'd recorded a message on her answering machine that said, "Die, bitch."

Brittany bolted. Out of her bedroom, down the hall. She scooped up her purse and her car keys from the kitchen table and raced through the living room.

She threw open the door and—

There, standing on the other side of the screen, was the hulking shape of a man. He was smaller and wider than Andy, but bigger than Wes.

She tried to slam the door shut, but he was too quick. He opened the screen and got a foot inside the door, pushing it open with his shoulder. The force threw her back, down onto the floor.

Telephone.

She scrambled for the kitchen, screaming at the top of her lungs. But her downstairs neighbors weren't home. They were never home during the day.

And what were the chances of anyone else hearing? All her windows were closed—the AC was on.

This guy could slice her into tiny pieces while she screamed her throat raw, and no one would hear a sound.

She grabbed the phone from the kitchen table, but he was right behind her and he hit her on the back of the head with something solid, something that made her ears ring.

She dropped the telephone as she hit the kitchen floor. It skittered across the linoleum, out of reach.

God, this couldn't be happening. But it was. Oh, Wes…

Die, bitch.

Not if she could help it. Wes wouldn't just lie back and wait for some psycho to snuff out his life. He'd fight like hell.

Britt tried to clear her head as she braced herself for the next attack, turning and scrambling to face her attacker. Her wrist was on fire, but she ignored it as the least of her worries.

She'd taken self-defense training as part of a program the hospital provided for nurses who worked the late shift, and she struggled to remember something— anything—that she'd learned in the course.

Use words to defuse a situation.

"Look, I don't know what you want or why you're here, but—"

"Shut up!"

She found herself staring up—oh, God—at the barrel of a gun.

But that wasn't the only bad surprise. The man holding the gun was the same man she'd seen just yesterday, in San Diego. At the ice-cream parlor. The angry man. The mentally ill man who'd clearly gone off his meds.

"You!" she said. My God, had he followed her here?

But no. That mess in her bedroom had been there for a while.

Unless he'd followed her to San Diego on Saturday night…

He put the gun down on the counter, then picked

up the telephone from the floor and held it out to Brittany. "Call him."

His words didn't make any sense. Although once she got her hands on that phone, she was dialing 9-1-1. *Be agreeable and compliant. Go down to zero. Don't be aggressive. Wait for an opening....*

"Call who?" She pushed herself up into a sitting position and reached for the phone.

But, oh, God, he pulled it back, out of her grasp, as if he knew what she was intending to do. "I'll dial. Tell me the number."

"Whose number?" She tried to keep her voice even and calm, tried not to look at the gun on the counter even though internally she was trying to estimate how many seconds it would take her to reach it if she suddenly sprang to her feet. But her right wrist was definitely badly injured from her fall, possibly even broken. That put her at a serious disadvantage.

"Amber's boyfriend's," he told her.

What?

Amber. Holy God. This was about Amber Tierney. This guy was...

Amber's stalker. The meek little guy who—according to Amber—would never hurt anyone.

"I only met Amber twice," she said, her mind racing, trying to make sense of this. Why would Amber's stalker start stalking her? "I don't know Amber's boyfriend."

"You were just with him in San Diego. You were..." He used some incredibly foul language that wasn't quite technically accurate.

But what he was saying didn't matter, because she

knew who he was talking about. He was talking about Wes. Dear God. He thought Wes was…

"Why do you want to talk to him?" she asked, trying not to sound hostile or aggressive, but rather simply curious.

"I'm not going to," he told her. "You are." He called her a name that left no doubt about it. He'd left that foul message on her answering machine.

"Why?" she persisted. "What do you want me to tell him? I don't understand."

"Tell him to come here. Now."

Fear made her hands and feet tingle and she couldn't keep herself from glancing at that gun on the counter.

"Why?" she asked again with far more bravado than she felt. No way was she calling Wes and telling him to come here just so this crazy son of a bitch could shoot him. "What do you want with him?"

"Just tell him to come. What's his number?"

"I don't remember," she lied.

He picked up the gun and pointed it at her. "What's his number?"

Chapter 16

Brittany didn't want to see him again.

Wes listened to the message she'd left on his voice mail for a third time, even though he'd understood every word she'd said quite clearly the first time around.

It was over.

Just like that.

She was done with him.

It was fun.

No way. No freaking way.

It just didn't sit right with everything he knew about this woman.

Of course, maybe he didn't know her that well.

Bullshit. Even though it had only been a handful of days, Wes knew Brittany Evans better than he knew any other woman on earth. He knew her inside and out.

She flipping loved him. He would bet his life's savings on that.

Well, okay, so his life savings weren't all that much, making that a statement that didn't hold all too much weight.

But he would bet his pride on it.

In fact, that's what he was doing right now by driving up to Los Angeles, by forcing her to say that final-sounding goodbye to him again, face-to-face this time.

It was going to be another half hour before he arrived, despite the fact that he was breaking the speed limit.

But she sounded just a little too cheerful, a little too okay with the idea of never seeing him again.

What if he was wrong? What if these past few days had been nothing more than a fling for her? Some laughs, some high intensity sex, some fun.

Brittany was still looking for Mr. Right, for her personal Prince Charming. Sure, she wasn't actively looking, but he knew that deep down, she still wanted the whole fairy tale package. A husband who loved her. A family. A baby.

And they lived happily ever after.

She'd told him that she wasn't pregnant. That was too bad, but so what? He could get her pregnant easily enough.

Wes smiled tightly. Sure, he would step up to that task with absolutely no arm twisting needed.

Except he was no Prince Charming. He wasn't even close.

He was a guy who was fun to have around for a few days, sure, but he wouldn't blame Britt one bit if she didn't want him hanging out in her kitchen for an entire lifetime.

Crap, now he was good and scared.

And this flipping half hour before he got a chance to talk to her was lasting too freaking long.

He dialed her number on his cell phone.

It rang once. Twice.

Come on, Britt. Be home.

"Hello?"

Okay, dumbass. Say something brilliant. "Hey, Britt. It's me. Wes."

"I'm sorry," she said. "Andy's not home."

Huh?

"Yeah," he said. "I know. He's not going to be back until tomorrow—"

"Oh, hi, Mrs. Beatrice," she cut him off. "I didn't recognize your voice. Do you have a cold? No, he went to Nevada with the baseball team."

What? Andy's trip was to Phoenix, but that was besides the point since he was in San Diego right now with Dani. And who the hell was Mrs. Beatrice? "Brittany, what's—"

"I'll tell him you called," she said. Her voice sounded strained and odd. "And that his library book came in. What was that title? *From Flintlocks to Uzis: A History of Modern Warfare?* Yes, I'm writing it down."

"Brittany, Jesus, what is going on? Is there someone in your house with you?"

"Yes," she said.

Of course. He was an idiot. "Is there someone there with you?" Someone she couldn't speak openly in front of.

"Yes," she said.

From Flintlocks to… "Someone with a weapon?" he asked, dreading her answer.

"Yes."

Oh, Christ. Wes slammed his foot to the floor. This car could do 120 mph without hesitation and neither he nor the car were hesitating now.

"Oh, there's another book, too?" she said.

"How many? Who are they?"

"Just one. Okay. *Gemstones of North America.* Yes, I've got it. Thank you, Mrs. Beatrice."

Jesus, she was trying to tell him something with that second title, but what?

"Brittany, I don't get it. What are you telling me? Gemstones…?"

"Yes, that's right. Andy was particularly interested in the stones which actually have prehistoric insects trapped inside of the rock. What is it called…?"

"That's amber," he told her, then realized what he'd said. "Damn! This has to do with Amber Tierney?"

"Yes."

"Is she there, too?"

"No, he's been a rock collecting fan for a long time."

Fan. Amber's stalker. Jesus God.

"Has he hurt you?" he asked.

"Not really— Oh, I'm sorry, Mrs. Beatrice," she said. "I have to go. Someone's at the…at the door."

"I'm on my way, baby," Wes said. "I'm already about thirty minutes from you."

"No," she said, talking fast. "I'm… I'm glad to hear Andy's been using your reference desk at the library. I've often encouraged him to *get help.*"

"I will," he said. "And I'll be there as soon as I can. God, baby, I love you. Be careful."

But she'd already cut the connection.

As he damn near flew down the freeway, Wes dialed 9-1-1.

* * *

Brittany's wrist was on fire, and it hurt even more as the phone was wrenched out of her hands.

Wes was on his way.

Damn it, she didn't want him to be on his way. She wanted him to call the police from San Diego, where he was safe and well out of range of the crazy man's deadly looking little handgun.

"You talked for too long." His eyes were flat, almost dead looking. How on earth could Amber have thought this guy was harmless with eyes like that?

"It was Mrs. Beatrice from the library," she told him. "She likes to talk to me—we're friends. If I'd just hung up on her, she would've thought it was weird, and might've even stopped by after work."

It was Tuesday afternoon and the tiny local library was closed. She prayed Crazy Man was just crazy enough not to be familiar with the schedule for the local public library—and to know that a Mrs. Beatrice didn't work there.

He pointed his nasty little gun at her again. "What's his phone number?"

He was talking about Wes again.

She had to stall for time, because—please God—Wes was on the phone right now with the L.A. emergency operator.

"I honestly don't know it by heart," she told him. "I have it written down. It's in my purse." She pointed to her bag, over on one of the kitchen chairs.

He was over there in two strides, dumping the contents out onto the table.

He hadn't walked like that in San Diego. Apparently,

the shuffling gait was just an act. Part of his harmless weirdo impersonation, no doubt.

It was all starting to make sense. The repeated hang-up phone calls at both her apartment and Wes's—Amber had gotten similar calls.

The accusation at the ice-cream parlor. *You made her cry.*

He'd been talking about Amber.

"When did I make Amber cry?" she asked him now as he stepped back and gestured for her to approach the kitchen table.

Darnit, this wrist made it hard even to pull herself to her feet.

"She called her boyfriend, and he brought you with him," he informed her. "She went to stay at that hotel, but after she drove out of her garage, she pulled over to the side of the road and cried."

And Mr. Crazy here thought that had something to do with Wes and Brittany. He'd created some kind of twisted love triangle between the three of them.

"Didn't it occur to you that she might've been crying because she was scared?" she asked him. "Of you?"

Oh, so not the right thing to say. He was not a happy camper hearing that.

"I'm sorry," she said quickly. "Of course not."

"Find his number," he said.

"I'm looking," she told him, sifting through all the little bits of candy wrappers and other papers that she'd jammed into her purse over the past few months. "Give me a minute."

Or thirty...

Please God, don't let Wes come charging in here all by himself.

* * *

"I'm unarmed," Wes reported to Bobby, who was already on board the helicopter. "I've got dive gear—a knife—and a combat vest in the trunk. But as far as weapons go, I've got nothing on me except my hands and feet." Which, with the diving knife would be enough, provided he could get into the house and close enough to the guy. His hands and feet and that knife could do some serious damage.

Even though the son of a bitch had a gun.

"Mike Lee located a field a block and a half from the address you gave us for Brittany's house," Bobby reported. "We'll be there about five minutes behind your ETA."

The L.A. emergency operator had actually put Wes on hold. So he'd called Lt. Jones at the naval base. Luck was with him, because part of Alpha Squad was already in the air, heading out via helo to the firing range to get in a little practice with some nontraditional weaponry.

Jones had patched Wes through to Bobby in the helo, and put through an order directing them to head to the Los Angeles area—to practice a different type of maneuver.

Wes's call-waiting beeped and he glanced at his cell phone. "I've got a call coming in," he told Bobby. "It's Brittany. I'll get back to you ASAP."

He clicked over. "Hello?"

"Yes, hi, Wes? It's Brittany."

Crap, she still sounded like someone had a gun pointed at her head.

"You okay?" he asked. It was a stupid question. Of course she wasn't okay.

"I'm fine," she said though, obviously trying to make

the conversation sound normal from the stalker's perspective. "How are you?"

"I've just about gone completely crazy, worrying about you, baby," he said. "And I think I must be blessed, because I haven't been stopped by the highway patrol, and I'm going faster than I've ever gone on this road. I'm still about seven minutes from your exit. I've tried calling 9-1-1 a couple of times, but I'm not getting through. I turned on the radio, and apparently there's trouble, some kind of demonstration gone out of control, happening downtown. They've got the riot squads out and everything. But that's okay, I'll be at your place soon."

"No," she said hotly, but then broke off.

"Don't worry," he told her. "I'm not going to come charging in there like some kind of hotshot wild man. I've got backup. Bobby and some of the guys from Alpha Squad are meeting me just a few blocks from your apartment. This is one guy with one gun, right?"

"Yes," she said. "But Wesley—"

"No one's going to get hurt," he told her. "I promise."

"I miss you," she said in a very small voice.

Was that something she'd been told to say, or the truth? Damn, hearing her say that made his chest feel tight.

"Will you come up to L.A.?" she asked because, obviously, that was what the stalker wanted her to ask. Wasn't *that* interesting? "Today? Please?"

"We're going to do surveillance before we come in," he told her. "You're not going to hear us, we're just going to be there in about fifteen minutes. As soon as you hear anything at all, any noise of our entry, drop to the ground, okay? Or better yet... I know—in fifteen minutes exactly, tell him you have to go to the bathroom. Get inside and lock the door and stay there. Get into the tub, babe. Lie down in it, okay? I know it sounds stupid as hell, but it'll give you some protection if he starts shooting."

"Do you think you can get here tonight?" she asked, for the gunman's benefit. "By six?"

"Good," he said. "Let him think it's going to be hours before I can get there. That's smart."

"Be careful driving," she said.

"You be careful, too."

"I'll see you at six, then."

"You'll see me soon, Britt. Remember, in fifteen minutes, go into the bathroom. And don't come out until I tell you to, okay?"

"Okay," she said. "Goodbye, Wes."

The connection was cut.

Jesus, that was a final sounding goodbye. What did she know that she wasn't able to tell him?

Wes drove even faster.

Fourteen minutes.

Wes was going to be here in fourteen minutes now.

But, God, from the look in Crazy Man's eyes, Brittany was going to be dead in about two.

"He'll be here at six o'clock," she told him as he put the telephone back into its cradle, and then started opening the kitchen drawers, looking for—of course—the knife drawer.

He found it and took out her turkey carving knife, setting it on the counter next to the sink.

"Whoa," she said. "That's a big knife. Careful you don't cut yourself, there."

"I've never had to cut off someone's head before," he told her, turning to look at her with those scary, crazy eyes.

"Had to?" she said. "I don't think that's something that anyone ever really *has* to do."

"But it's what happens next," he informed her.

My God, was he following some kind of sick script? This was like something out of a bad horror movie with the blood in her bedroom and... So okay, okay. Get him talking. Thirteen and a half minutes. She could do this.

"So... I come home and find all that blood on my sheets," she said. "What happens next?"

"Your lover comes home and finds you," he told her. "Dead."

"Oh, dear," she said faintly. But it wasn't anything she hadn't expected. "How, exactly, was I killed?"

This was, without a doubt, the weirdest conversation of her life.

But this man, this crazy-assed sicko, was some mother's son. Someone loved him, despite his mental illness. Somewhere inside of him was a human soul. Maybe if they talked long enough, she could connect with him.

"You've been shot in the neck," he reported, "and your head's in the kitchen sink."

Oh, dear God. "That's not very nice," she said.

"What you did wasn't very nice, either," he countered angrily. "Stealing Amber's boyfriend and breaking Amber's heart. She cried and cried."

"Was Amber in this movie?" she asked. This terrible scenario had to be out of a movie. She'd read—somewhere—that Amber had made several truly awful B pictures before hitting it big with her TV series. This had to be one of them.

"Til Death Do Us Part," he said. "It was great. Amber's boyfriend runs off with this other woman, and she cries and cries, because she doesn't know she's got a secret admirer, who punishes them—and everyone else who ever makes her cry."

"What happens to Amber's boyfriend?" Britt asked. She had to keep him talking. Eleven minutes now before Wes got here.

"He's shot," Crazy told her. "Right in the heart. And Amber marries her secret admirer and they live happily ever after."

Oh God. Was that really what he thought was going to happen? "There was no police investigation?" she asked. "He wasn't arrested for murder?"

He looked at her blankly. "Why would he be? No one knew that he knew them."

"What about his fingerprints," she said, "all over the apartment?"

He frowned. "That wasn't in the movie."

"That's what makes it a movie, and not real life. In real life, the police find fingerprints. You don't really want to do this, do you?"

He picked up his gun. "I don't have time to waste. I don't know how long this is going to take."

Ten minutes. "I have to go to the bathroom," Brittany said quickly. It was too early, but God, it was worth a try.

"You won't have to in a minute," he said, and aimed his gun at her.

Wes called Bobby from the park near Britt's apartment.

"I'm here," he said, as he opened the trunk of his car and put on his vest. "Where are you guys?"

"We're right on schedule," Bobby said. "Five minutes from you."

"I can't wait," Wes said. "I'm going up to her apartment, take a look around."

The sound of a gunshot rang out, loud as hell in this quiet residential neighborhood, followed by another and another.

Wes swore, and ran for Brittany's.

Brittany slammed and locked the bathroom door behind her.

Thank you God for the quality construction of the 1890s, because the solid wood door didn't even quiver upon impact.

Thank you, too, for keeping Crazy away from the local firing ranges, where he might've actually learned to aim that gun, had he bothered to take a lesson or two.

Of course, a person's neck was a pretty small target. Shooting someone in the heart would be a whole heck of a lot easier to do.

Out in the hall, Crazy threw himself at the door again. "Open up!"

Yeah, right, just open the door and let him shoot her in the neck and… God!

The bathroom window was painted shut. It was too small for Brittany to squeeze out of even if it could be opened, but she didn't care. She had to break it, so she could warn Wes.

He was going to be here any minute, and Amber's psycho stalker was going to try to shoot him in the heart.

She was not—was not—going to let that happen.

Sobbing, she grabbed the lid off the toilet tank and swung it with all her strength at the window.

It hit with a dull sounding thud and bounced back, hitting her broken wrist.

Wes made himself slow down. If he just went charging in through the front door, the man with the gun would have a definite advantage.

He needed to take just a few moments and do this right.

He had to climb up to the second floor and look in through the windows.

Find out where the gunman was, find out where Britt was.

Please, God, let her still be alive.

Pain.

Brittany's world had tunneled down to pain. Pain and bitter disappointment.

Her wrist hurt so much she was retching, but the disappointment managed to cut through.

Plexiglas.

Of course.

Andy had told her that their landlord had replaced the broken bathroom window with unbreakable Plexiglas.

She wouldn't be able to break it, and she couldn't get it open.

She had no way to warn Wes.

Wes climbed as swiftly as he could, wishing with all his heart that he was armed with something other than a diving knife.

He could hear the helicopter carrying the SEALs

making its approach to the field. He heard the sound of distant sirens, too. Someone had heard the gunshots and had had better luck calling 9-1-1 than he'd had.

The blinds were mostly shut in Britt's room. That was good. They would do a good job concealing him from view while making it possible for him to look into the room between the slats and—

Jesus!

He nearly lost his handholds on the side of the house, and he had to force himself to look again.

It was a bloodbath in there. He was too late. Brittany was dead. She had to be.

No one could bleed that much and still be alive.

Even as part of Wes died, the rest of him clicked into combat mode. Brittany's murderer was there, in the room, by the bathroom door.

The bastard was going to die.

Wes drew his knife and, grabbing hold of the edge of the roof above him, he swung himself up and out and went through the window, feetfirst.

Broken wrist or not, Brittany was ready.

She heard the crash of broken glass, and yanked the bathroom door open.

Just as she'd expected, Crazy's back was to her, and she slammed the toilet tank lid hard onto him. It only grazed his head, but it hit his shoulder, knocking him forward and down.

It wasn't enough to keep him from firing two shots.

They were deafeningly loud, two sharp explosions propelling two deadly bullets that hit Wes square in the chest, driving him back, pushing him onto the ground.

But like some kind of superhuman machine, he was

back on his feet in less than a heartbeat, coming at Crazy with a savage look in his eyes.

Brittany.

She was standing there, alive and whole, next to the gunman, without any gaping wounds.

Wes's chest had to hurt like hell, but he didn't care about that. He felt nothing but euphoria.

He knew what Lazarus's mother had experienced on the day her son returned from the dead.

"Get down!" he tried to shout as he kicked the handgun from the son of a bitch's hand, but it only came out a whisper.

Of course, Britt didn't move to safety. She raised what looked to be the lid of a toilet tank over her head, and knocked the gunman unconscious with one beautiful shot.

Wes dropped to his knees, and fell forward onto his hands.

"Get the gun," he tried to tell Britt, but again she didn't listen.

She helped him lie back. God, it was hard to breathe. And the pain...

Now he felt it.

It was okay that she didn't go after the gun, because Bobby and the other guys were there, making sure the gunman wasn't going to hurt anyone else today.

"Man, what a stench," Rio Rosetti said.

"Don't die," Britt ordered him as she tried to unfasten his vest. "Don't you dare die!"

He wasn't going to die. He tried to tell her that, but he couldn't suck enough air into his lungs to make any kind of recognizable sound.

Bobby leaned over him, putting his fingers into the two holes the bullets had made in his vest. "Ouch," he said. "That's gotta hurt."

"God, Skelly," Lucky O'Donlon complained. "Why ask for support only to go through the window before we even get here?"

"Yeah, but look at what he saw," Bobby pointed out. "If this had been Colleen's apartment, and I was out there, looking in at that bed, I'd've gone through the window, too."

"Isn't somebody going to call an ambulance?" Brittany demanded.

She couldn't believe it.

Everyone was standing around, chatting, while Wes was bleeding to death.

With one hand that wasn't working right, Brittany couldn't get his vest unfastened, she couldn't even tell how badly he was wounded underneath the cumbersome thing.

"He's wearing a vest," Rio, one of the newest members of the team, informed her.

"I can see he's wearing a vest," Brittany said. "Can someone help me get it off of him?"

"Bulletproof vest," Bobby explained, and her heart started beating again.

"Oh, thank God."

"But look where he got hit." Bobby pointed to the two holes. "Possible broken rib, probable broken collarbone. Man, that's got to hurt."

"I'm okay," Wes whispered. He reached up to touch Britt's cheek. "In fact, I can't remember the last time I felt better."

"Police are here," Rio announced.

And indeed they were. Paramedics had arrived, too, and they swarmed around Wes, taking his blood pressure and listening to his lungs.

A broken rib could puncture a lung, but his were okay. He'd just had the wind knocked out of him in a very major way.

A temporary splint was put on Britt's wrist, and the Crazy Guy was treated, too. He was carried out on a stretcher as Brittany gave a statement to the police detectives.

It was over—but now her apartment was a crime scene. A messy, foul-smelling crime scene.

Brittany was allowed back inside to pack a bag so she could stay at a hotel until the police photographers had finished taking pictures of her bedroom. Until she got that mess cleaned up.

She gathered up all of Wes's things, too, stuffing them into his duffel and awkwardly carrying it outside, both bags in her good hand.

Wes sat on the steps leading up to Brittany's apartment, with both his side and shoulder on fire. The paramedics had tried to take him to the hospital for X-rays, but there was no screaming rush. His collarbone was definitely broken—he knew because he'd broken it before—and there was really nothing they could do for him. It wasn't the kind of break that got put into a cast.

It just hurt like hell for a few weeks. And then it hurt like heck for a few weeks more.

He needed to get the X-ray, but he wasn't going to the hospital without Brittany.

She came down the stairs and...

"What happened to your wrist?" he asked.

"He hit me and I fell on it the wrong way."

Goddamn it. "I should have killed him when I had the chance. I heard most of your statement to the police. Brittany, God, this is all my fault. If I hadn't come to L.A.—"

She wasn't going to let him take the blame. "Then maybe he would've gone after Amber. Or others of her friends who wouldn't have been able to keep him from hurting them."

"He hurt you badly enough." Just the thought of him hitting her was enough to make Wes feel faint. He didn't want to think about all that Amber's stalker—his name, apparently, was John Cagle—had had in mind for Brittany.

She looked down at the splint on her wrist. "Believe me, it could have been worse."

"I know. Britt, I really am sorry."

"I'm sorry, too." She set something down next to him, and he realized that it was his bag. She'd packed his stuff, just as she'd told him she would in that message she'd left on his voice mail.

What if she had been serious? Jesus, was this really it?

"I'm sorry I had to drag you away from one crisis to a completely different crisis," she said. "How's Lana doing?"

"I don't know," he said. "I didn't stay at her place too long. Ronnie Catalanotto and Amber were going to stay with her while she tried to get some sleep."

"Oh," Brittany said.

What the hell did that oh mean?

"Britt, do you like me?" he asked.

She didn't hesitate. "Of course."

He laughed because her response was so typical Brittany, so definite with a hint of challenge to it. Of course she liked him. Why wouldn't she like him? But laughing made his side and shoulder hurt like hell, so he swore. "Sorry."

"That must really hurt," she said, now all sympathy and warm concern.

And Wes couldn't take it a second longer. "Will you marry me?" he asked.

Well, okay, he'd surprised the hell out of her.

"Please?" he added. Although it was a little late to try to win points for being polite.

She sat down on the steps, next to him. "Are you serious?"

"Yes, I am. Very."

"You did get my message, right?" she asked, looking at him searchingly. "About me not being pregnant?"

"I know," he said. "I don't want to marry you because I think you're pregnant. Although that would be okay with me, too, you know. It's not about that, though. I want to marry you because, well…" Just say it. "Because I'm in love with you."

She made a sound that was half-exhale, half-laughter. Was that a good sign or a bad sign? He didn't know. All he could do was try to explain the way he felt when he was with her.

"You were right about me," he told her. "Ever since Ethan died, I've been, I don't know, punishing myself, I guess, just for being alive. I could never let myself enjoy anything too much, I couldn't let myself get too happy. And you were right—I found one hell of a way to make myself properly miserable by falling in love with someone that I couldn't ever have."

The stupid thing was, he didn't realize he was doing that until he met Brittany. Brittany, who liked him.

"And you know, as time went on, I think I probably stopped loving Lana and started loving the idea of Lana. You know, the fact that she was unattainable made her even more attractive, since my goal, you know, was to be miserable. There was one time—I was really drunk, and I think she probably was, too—I kissed her. It scared the crap out of me. I think I was more in love with not being able to have Lana, than I was with Lana.

"And as for Lana, well, what she really wanted was for Quinn to have my kind of, I don't know, devotion, I guess. She didn't ever want me."

He looked at Brittany. "But you do. You want me." He laughed, and it hurt and he swore. "I don't get it, but you seem to like me—you know, even the dark, scary parts of me that I'm afraid to let most people see. There's no part of me that I'm afraid to show you, Britt. There's no part of me that's too intense, too extreme for you. You're just…you're okay with it. You're okay with me.

"When I'm with you, baby, even just sitting here like this, there's absolutely no doubt about it—I'm very glad to be alive. And when I'm with you, you know, I'm not so angry at the world, and I'm not so angry at myself anymore, either. When I'm with you, I actually kind of like myself, too. And if that's not freaking amazing…"

Brittany, sweet Brittany, had tears in her eyes.

"I want to be that guy," he told her, "the one that I like, the one I see reflected in your eyes—for the rest of my life. So marry me, all right? Put me out of my misery and tell me you love me, too."

"I love you, too," she said. "Oh, Wes, I'd love to marry you."

And it was everything he'd hoped for, this knowing she'd be at his side until the end of time.

But God, the best part of her answer was the warmth of Brittany's smile, the love in Brittany's eyes.

If he'd been the kind of guy who cried, he would have been sobbing right now. As it was, his eyes were feeling dangerously moist.

Wes kissed her.

"You know," Brittany said after she'd kissed him again—carefully so as not to jar his shoulder. "My sister and Jones are never going to let us forget they were the ones who set us up on a blind date."

"That's okay, baby," Wes said, kissing her again. "Because I'm never going to stop thanking them."

Epilogue

"What would you say if I told you I was thinking about taking a year off from school?" Brittany asked.

Wes looked up from his computer, spinning in his chair to face her.

She was standing in the bedroom doorway, leaning against the jamb.

He measured his words before answering her. "I guess I'd ask you why you're thinking about doing that. And I'd tell you I hope it's not on my account."

"It's not," she said.

"Honest?" he asked. It hadn't been easy—living and working in two different cities, but it wasn't awful. "If I've complained too much lately just tell me to zip it, babe. It's not going to be forever, and besides, we have Andy to think about."

Andy needed Britt around more than ever now. Dani

was back in school, but Dustin Melero's trial date was approaching. There were no guarantees, rape trials always came down to "he said, she said," but four other girls had come forward, with stories identical to Dani's. Together, they were working to lock that bastard up.

Yeah, maybe Dustin could share a jail cell with John Cagle, Amber's crazy-assed stalker.

Amber had beefed up her security, and Wes and Britt had put an alarm system in both of their apartments, too.

Not that they were worried about him getting out of jail any time in the near future. But the security system made Wes breathe a little easier when he and Britt were apart.

"That was Andy on the phone just now," Britt told him.

"How'd the team do?" They were in Sacramento this weekend.

Andy hadn't lost his scholarship, and with the new baseball season starting, there was already talk that he was going to be the college team's MVP. The scouts were swarming. It was just a matter of time before the kid went pro.

"He called to say he's made up his mind. He's signing with the Dodgers, can you believe it? He'll start playing on their Triple A team in May."

Wes searched her face. "You okay with that?"

"Very much so." Brittany smiled. "Of course, I made him promise that someday he'd go back and finish getting his degree. Even if he plays baseball until he's forty-five. First thing he does after retiring—go back to school."

Wes reached for her, and she came and sat on his lap. "Wow. So what are you thinking? With Andy playing pro, out on the road, traveling all the time, you're going to come live with me in San Diego?" He tried not to sound too hopeful and failed.

"Yeah," she said. "You got a problem with that?"

"Not even close." He kissed her, but then stopped her from kissing him again. "I do have a problem with this leaving nursing school thing. Becoming a nurse practitioner has been your dream for a long time. I don't like the idea of you giving it up just to be with me more days a week. I'm out of town a lot, too, Britt."

"I know. I thought I could look into transferring to a school in San Diego," she told him. "But not for a few years." She smiled at him. It was the kind of smile he'd learned to watch out for. The kind that said, *Duck and cover! Incoming!* "Not until after the baby turns two or three."

Wes heard the words, but they didn't make sense. And then they made a crapload of sense. He laughed his shock and surprise. "Are you telling me...?"

"Remember about two weeks ago when we weren't really careful?" she asked.

He laughed again. "Uh, yeah, but I seem to remember a lot of times since we've been married, Mrs. Skelly, that we haven't been particularly careful." And he'd loved every minute of it. But a baby. Jesus.

"Well, I just did a test, and... It's definite." She laughed. "Sweetie, you look scared to death."

"I am scared to death. I'm thrilled, of course, you know I am but... I'm also scared to death. A baby. Holy Mother of God."

Brittany was glowing. He'd heard that word used to describe pregnant women, but he'd never believed anyone could actually glow. But Brittany sure as hell was doing it.

And he knew why putting her career aspirations on hold wasn't such a big deal for her.

Because even though getting this degree had been a dream of hers for a long time, she'd had another dream, too.

To have a baby.

And even though it had happened accidentally, Wes had helped make that particular dream come true.

"I love you," he told her. "More than you'll ever know."

Her eyes shone with unshed tears. "Oh, but I do know," she whispered. She kissed him.

Good thing he wasn't the crying kind, because if he were, he'd be in a puddle on the floor.

"If it's a girl, let's name her—"

"Whoa," Wes said. "Whoa, whoa, wait. I can't have a girl. Girls grow up and become guy magnets, and I'm telling you right now that I absolutely won't be able to deal with that."

"Well, I guess there's a fifty-fifty chance it'll be a boy—"

"Yeah, but, Jesus, having a boy would be even worse. I don't know anything about being a father to a son— look who I had for a role model. My father sucked— you've said so yourself. No, there's no way I can have a son."

Brittany was laughing at him. "Breathe," she said. "Sweetie, just breathe. You're going to be a great father." She put his hand on her stomach, over her womb, where her baby—their baby—was growing right as they spoke. "All you have to do is love this little baby half as much as you love me. And I have a feeling after you see his little face, you're going to love him even more."

"I think I might throw up," Wes said.

Britt laughed. "That's my job for the next few months."

"God," he said, "are you feeling okay? Do you have morning sickness? Are you—"

"Actually, I feel great. Melody had terrible morning sickness, but that doesn't mean I will."

"No more riding horses," he told her. "Until the baby's born. I heard that somewhere."

"Well that should be easy, since I've never been on a horse in my life." She laughed. "You're going to go completely neurotic on me, aren't you?"

Wes closed his eyes. "I'm sorry. It's just…"

"It's going to take some time to get used to," she told him. "I know. Especially the part about not needing to use birth control for the next nine months. That's going to be really rough."

He opened his eyes at that to see her smiling at him. She wiggled her eyebrows. "In fact, maybe we should go practice."

"Oh, baby," he said, and kissed her.

And they lived happily—with lots of loud discussions and plenty of laughter—ever after.

* * * * *

USA TODAY bestselling author **Barb Han** lives in north Texas with her very own hero-worthy husband, three beautiful children, a spunky golden retriever/standard poodle mix and too many books in her to-read pile. In her downtime, she plays video games and spends much of her time on or around a basketball court. She loves interacting with readers and is grateful for their support. You can reach her at barbhan.com.

Books by Barb Han

Harlequin Intrigue

An O'Connor Family Mystery

Texas Kidnapping
Texas Target

Rushing Creek Crime Spree

What She Did
What She Knew
What She Saw

Crisis: Cattle Barge

Kidnapped at Christmas
Murder and Mistletoe
Bulletproof Christmas

Visit the Author Profile page at Harlequin.com for more titles.

HARD
TARGET

Barb Han

This book is dedicated to the amazing and strong people in my life. Allison Lyons, you continue to amaze me with your insight and passion. Jill Marsal, you are brilliant and I'm grateful to work with you.

Brandon, Jacob and Tori, you bring out the best in me every day—I love all three of you more than you can know. John, none of this would be *this* amazing and fun without you—my best friend and the great love of my life.

Liz Lipperman, a huge thank-you for answering my many medical questions and offering brainstorming support. You really are the bomb!

Chapter 1

Emily Baker pulled her legs into her chest and hugged her knees. Waves of fear and anger rolled through her.

A hammer pounded the inside of her head, a residual effect from the beatings. Her busted bottom lip was dry and cracked from dehydration.

"Move," one of the men commanded, forcing her to her feet.

A crack across her back nearly caused her to fall again.

The whole experience of the past few days had been surreal. One minute she'd been kayaking in a tropical paradise, enjoying all the rich sounds of the dense forest. The next she was being dragged through the jungle by guerrillas. She'd been blindfolded for what had to be hours, although she'd completely lost track of time, and had been led through pure hell.

Vegetation thickened the longer she'd walked. Thorns pierced her feet. The sun had blistered her skin. Ant bites covered her ankles.

A man they called Dueño had ordered the men to change her appearance. They'd chopped her hair and poured something on it that smelled like bleach. She assumed they did it to ensure she no longer matched the description of the woman the resort would report as missing. Oh, God, the word *missing* roiled her stomach.

She'd read about American tourists being snatched while on vacation, but didn't those things happen to other people? Rich people?

Not data entry clerks with no family who'd scrimped and saved for three years to take the trip in the first place.

Men in front of her fanned out, and she saw the small encampment ahead. The instant a calloused hand made contact with her shoulder, she shuddered.

"Get down!" He pushed her down on all fours.

The leader, Dueño, stood over her. He was slightly taller than the others and well dressed. His face was covered, so she couldn't pick him out of a lineup if she'd wanted to. "You want to go home, Ms. Baker?"

"Yes." How'd he know her name?

"Then tell me what I want to know. Give me the password to SourceCon." Anger laced his words.

How did he know where she worked? All thoughts of this being a random kidnapping fizzled and died.

"I can't. I don't have them." The night before she'd left for vacation, she changed them as a precaution. Her new passwords were taped to the underside of her desk at home.

"Fine. Have it your way." He turned his back. "Starve her until she talks."

Twenty-four hours tied up with no food or water had left her weak, but she couldn't give him what she didn't know.

He returned the next morning. "Do you remember them now?"

"No. I already told you I don't have them." Anger and fear engulfed her like a raging forest fire.

He backhanded her and repeated the question. When another blow didn't produce his desired result, he ordered one of the men to beat her, and another to dig a hole.

Fear gripped her as she was shoved inside the dark cramped space.

After dark, there were only three guards keeping watch. One drank until he passed out. She'd been working on loosening her bindings all day and had made progress. Maybe she could make a move to escape.

"I need to go to the bathroom."

One of the guards hauled her out of the hole, removed the rope from her ankles and then shoved her into a thicket. He looked at her with black eyes. "Two minutes."

He hadn't noticed the ropes on her arms were loose. Hope filled her chest for the first time since her capture. Immediately, she shucked the bindings from her arms, and then took off.

For two days, she'd carved her way through the dense vegetation, fearful. Any minute she'd expected the men to catch up, to stick her in another hole. Her punishment this time surely would be death.

Exhausted, feet bleeding, she made it to the edge

of the jungle. In the clearing ahead, she spotted ships. Her heartbeat amplified as her excitement grew. She'd rummage around for something to eat, and then wait until dark.

Time stilled and the hours ticked by. The few berries she'd eaten kept her stomach from cramping.

When all commotion on the dock stopped, she checked manifests until she located one in English. The ship was heading to Galveston, Texas. She buried herself inside a small compartment in one of the crates. No matter how weak she was, she didn't dare sleep.

By sunrise, voices drew closer and the ship moved. The boat swayed, and she battled waves of nausea. Her stomach rumbled and churned, protesting the amount of time that had gone by without a meal.

How long had it been since she'd eaten real food? Five days? Six?

Hours had gone by and the air was becoming thicker. Her breathing labored. She swiped away a stray tear, praying she was nearing shore. All she had to do was survive a little while longer. The panels of the wooden freight box she'd jammed herself into seconds before the ship had left the dock were closing in on her, making it hard to move, or breathe. She couldn't afford another panic attack, or allow her mind to go to the place where she was in that dark hole being starved and beaten. A sob escaped before she could suppress it.

The ship had to be closing in on its destination by now. She was so close to the States she could almost taste her freedom.

Or was she?

All her hopes were riding on a journey across the Gulf of Mexico, but the truth was she could be anywhere. She reminded herself that she'd read the manifest, and prayed she'd understood it correctly.

Emily bit out a curse at the men who'd made her feel helpless and kicked at the walls of the crate, withdrawing her foot when she blistered it with another splinter. Her soles were already raw. She'd need to make sure she cleaned them up and found antibiotic ointment when she got off this horrible boat.

She'd already collected splinters in her elbows and thighs. Escaping the compound in a swimsuit wouldn't have been her first choice, but she'd grasped her first opportunity to run. There'd been no time for debate. Her chance had presented itself and she'd seized it, not stopping until long after the men's voices had faded.

She repositioned herself in the crate, grateful she could almost stretch her legs. She'd survived so far by doing mental math calculations, flexing and releasing her stomach muscles, and tightening her abs.

No food left her weak.

The minutes seemed to drip by, and her body cramped from being in such a small space. She had no watch, no cell phone and no purse.

None of which she cared about as much as her freedom.

She could get the rest once she got out of the crate and off this boat.

The resort area had been paradise when she'd first arrived, but nothing sounded better to Emily than home, a hot bath and her own bed.

Holy hell. She couldn't go home. If they knew her name and where she worked, they had to know where she lived, too. A ripple of fear skittered across already taut nerves.

She pressed her face against a crack in the crate.

Darkness. Nothing but darkness behind her and darkness in front of her.

The man who'd helped her onto her kayak had told her to stay close to the ocean side and not the jungle because of the risk of running into alligators. Now she wondered if maybe they'd known about the rebel groups scouring the edges all along. They hadn't warned her about men with massive guns, and bandannas covering their faces, leaving only black eyes staring at her, coming to take her. She would've listened to that. She wouldn't have ventured off, following a monkey in the canopy. And where had the monkey gone?

Onto one of her kidnappers' shoulders.

She'd initially hoped the resort would send security once it discovered she hadn't returned to her room. She'd held on to the hope for two days in the jungle. With no shoes, her feet had been bitten, cut and aching after the daylong walks and nights of camping. And hope had retreated faster than the sun before a thunderstorm.

There'd been shouting, too. It had scared her nearly to death. At first she feared they would rape her, but no one had touched her.

Extortion? Drugs? Ransom?

Nope. None.

He'd asked for her passwords.

A sense of relief had washed over her. If she'd had to rely on her family, she'd be dead for sure. Her family wasn't exactly reliable, and they were broke. Even skilled trackers like these would have trouble locating her mother. The Bakers had split faster than an atom, and left similar devastation in their wake. At least the ones she knew.

Emily had always been the black sheep. She'd moved away, worked hard and put herself through college. Her mom had refused to allow her to take the SAT, saying it would only train her to be some corporation's slave, so she'd researched a grandfather clause in a North Texas school, did two years at a community college, and after another three years, graduated from the small university.

She'd come to North Texas solely on the promise of affordable living and an abundant job market, figuring she could build the rest of her life from there. And she had. She'd gotten a job as a data entry clerk at a computer company and was working her way up. Her boss was due a promotion and she'd been promised his job.

There were rare occasions when she heard from her mother, although it was mostly when she needed money. Turns out free love didn't pay all that much. Watching her mom wither away after her dad walked out, Emily had made a vow. No one would take away her power. Ever.

Being resourceful had gotten her through college, and landed her first real job. She'd pulled on every bit of her quick wit to escape her captors. Once back in the States, she could locate a church or soup kitchen, and get help. No way could she find a police station. Not after overhearing her abductors talk about bribing American border police. Her body trembled. They'd hand her right back to Dueño. She'd be dead in five minutes. Not happening.

Once she was on dry land, she could figure out a way to sneak into her town house. She needed ID and clothes. There was a little money in her bank account. She could use it to disappear for a year or two. Wait it out until this whole thing blew over. Dread settled over her at the thought of leaving the only place that felt like home.

She thought about the threat Dueño had made, the underlying promise in his tone that he had every intention of delivering on his word. The way he'd said her name had caused an icy chill to grip her spine.

The ship pitched forward then stopped. Had it docked?

Emily repeated a silent protection prayer she'd learned when she was a little girl as her pulse kicked up a notch. She had no idea what she'd find on the other side of the crate.

Her skin was clammy and salty. She was starving and dehydrating. But she was alive, dammit, and she could build from there.

There were male voices. Please, let them be American.

She listened intently.

At least two men shouted orders. Feet shuffled. She couldn't tell how many others there were, but at least they spoke English. Her first thought was to beat on the walls of the crate, let them find her and beg to be taken home. But then, she was in a shipment, beaten and bruised, illegally entering the country with no ID.

Would the men call police? Immigration?

There were other, worse things they could do to her when they found her, too. A full-body shiver roared through her.

She couldn't afford to risk her safety.

Besides, the man who'd had her kidnapped had been clear. She'd been his target. If she surfaced now, she'd most likely be recaptured or killed. Neither was an acceptable prospect.

Could she figure out a way to slip off the boat while the deckhands unloaded the other boxes?

If she wriggled out of the crate now, she might be seen. The only choice was to wait it out, be patient until the right opportunity presented itself. This shipment had to be loaded onto something, right? A semi? Please, not another boat.

Painful heartbeats stabbed her ribs. She tensed, coiled and prepared to spring at whatever came next.

A voice cut through the noise, and everything else went dead silent.

The rich timbre shot straight through her, causing her body to shiver in the most inappropriate way under the circumstances.

She listened more closely. There were other sounds. Feet padding and heavy breathing.

Oh, no.

Police dogs.

Their agitated barks shot through the crate like rapid gunfire, inches from Emily's face. In the small compartment, she had nowhere to hide. The dogs' heated breaths blasted through the cracks. If her odor wasn't bad enough, this certainly wouldn't help matters. Now she'd smell like dirt, sweat and bad animal breath.

Emily's heart palpitated. She prayed an officer would stop the dogs. From the sounds of them, they'd rip her to shreds.

"Hier. Komm!" another voice commanded.

Emily made out the fact the officer spoke in another language. Dutch? German?

Damn.

She was about to be exposed. Her heart clutched. She had no idea how powerful the man who'd kidnapped her was. One thing was certain. He had enough money to buy off American border police. Was she about to come face-to-face with men he had in his pocket?

She shuddered at the thought of being sent back to Dueño, to that hell.

Her left eye still burned from the crack he'd fired across her cheek when she'd told him she didn't know the codes.

Maybe she could tell the officers the truth, beg them to let her go.

If they were for real, maybe she had a chance.

Voices surrounded her. Male. Stern.

She coiled tighter, praying she'd have enough energy to fight back or run. She'd have about a half second to decide if they would send her back to that hellhole, but she wouldn't go willingly.

A side panel burst open and Emily rolled out. She popped to her feet.

The officer in front of her was tall, had to be at least six-two. His hair was almost dark enough to be black. He had intense brown eyes, and he wore a white cowboy hat. He was built long and lean with ripples of muscles. Under normal circumstances, she'd be attracted to him. But now, all she could think about was her freedom.

He had a strong jawline, and when he smiled, his cheeks were dimpled. His eyes might be intense, but they were honest, too.

She held her hands up in the universal sign of surrender. "Help me. Please. I'm American."

"You're a US citizen?" Reed Campbell had taken one look at the curled-up little ball when he opened the crate and felt an unfamiliar tug at his heart. He pushed it aside as she shot to her feet. Her face was bruised. She had a busted lip. Even though her hair was overly bleached and tangled, and she could use a shower, her hazel eyes had immense depth—the kind that drew him in, which was ridiculous under the circumstances. It had to be her vulnerability that stirred the kind of emotions that had no place at work.

"Yes." She spoke in perfect English, but American citizens didn't normally travel home in a crate from Mexico. It looked as if standing took effort. "You can sit down if you'd like."

She nodded and he helped her to a smaller crate where she eased down. He asked an agent to grab a bottled water out of his Jeep. A few seconds later, one of his colleagues produced one.

The cap was on too tight, and she seemed too weak to fight with it.

"I can do that for you." He easily twisted off the lid.

She thanked him, downed three-quarters of the bottle and then poured the rest over her face.

"What's your name?"

She stalled as though debating her answer. "Emily Baker."

"I need to see ID, ma'am. Driver's license. Passport." He looked her up and down. No way did she have a wallet tucked into her two-piece swimsuit. The material fit like an extra layer of skin, highlighting full breasts and round hips. Neither of which needed to go in his report. He forced his gaze away from the soft curves on an otherwise firm body.

He cleared his throat. Damn, dry weather.

"I don't have any with me." The words came out sharp, but the tone sounded weary and drained. The crate she was in was huge and there were several compartments. More illegals? Human trafficking? Reed had seen it all in the past six years as a Border Patrol agent.

"Let's see what else we find in here," Agent Pete Sanders said.

She seemed to realize she stood in front of them wearing next to nothing when she crossed her arms over her chest and her cheeks flushed pink. She suddenly looked even more vulnerable and small. Her embarrassment tugged at his heart. More descriptions that wouldn't go in his Homeland Security report.

She shivered, glanced down and to the right. She was about to lie. "Look. I can explain everything."

"I'm all ears."

Agents hauled over two crew members and told them to stay put.

She looked up at Reed again, and her hazel eyes were wide and fearful. Her hands shook. The men seemed to make her want to jump out of her skin even more. She was frightened, but not a flight risk. Cuffing her would most likely scare her even more. Besides, pulling her sunburned and blistered arms behind her back would hurt more than her pride. She also looked starved and dehydrated. One bottle of water would barely scratch the surface.

Getting her to talk under these circumstances might prove even more difficult. As it was, she looked too frightened to speak. Reed needed to thin her audience. He glanced at the K-9 officer. "I got this one under control. The other agents will see if there are more stashed in there. She's a quick run up to immigration."

The officer nodded before giving the command for his dog to keep searching. As soon as the two disappeared around the corner, the blonde dropped to her knees. Tears filled her eyes, a perfect combination of brown, gray and blue.

"I know how this must look. I'm not stupid. But I can explain."

"You already said that."

"Okay. Let's see. Where do I start?" Even through her fear, she radiated a sense of inner strength and independence.

Hell, he could respect that. Even admired her for it. But allowing a suspected illegal alien, or whatever she was, entry into the country wasn't his call. "At the beginning. How'd you end up in the crate?"

"I, uh, I…"

This was going nowhere. He wanted to reach out to her, help her, but she had to be willing to save herself. "We have some folks you can talk to. They can help."

"No. Please don't take me anywhere else. Just let me go. I'll show up to whatever court date. I won't disappear. I promise. I have a good job. One that I can't afford to lose."

Reed knew desperation. Hell, most drug runners were just as desperate. They'd offer bribes, their women, pretty much anything to manipulate the system.

His sixth sense told him this was different. There was an innocence and purity to her eyes that drew him in. Victim?

He pressed his lips into a frown. "Let's not get ahead of ourselves."

"Am I under arrest?"

"No."

"Then I'm free to go?" The flash of hope in her eyes seared his heart.

"I didn't say that." With her perfect English, he knew she wasn't illegal. But what else would she be doing tucked in a crate headed for the States, looking like a punching bag? Human trafficking? She was battered and bruised. If someone was trying to sell her, she'd fought back. But that explanation didn't exactly add up. Most traffickers didn't risk damaging the "product."

The officers moved to another wall on the other side of the crate. Twenty people could've been stuffed in there. He hoped like hell they weren't about to open up the other side and find more in the same shape as her. Seeing a woman beaten up didn't do good things to Reed. He fisted his hands.

"What happened to you?" Even bruised and dirty, she was pretty damn hot. The tan two-piece she wore stretched taut against full breasts. Reed refocused on her heart-shaped face. Was someone trying to sell her into the sex trade? One look at her curves and long silky legs told him men would pay serious money for her. His protective instincts flared at the thought.

"I was on vacation and was robbed. They stole my passport. Said if I told authorities, they'd find me and kill me. I spent a night in the jungle trying to find my way back to the resort. I walked for an eternity, saw this ship and hopped on board praying no one would follow, find or catch me."

The bruises on her face and body outlined the fact she wasn't being honest. He shot her a sideways glance. "What happened to your face?"

"One of the men hit me?" Yeah, she was digging— digging a hole she might not be able to climb out of. It would take more than that to cause the bruising she had.

"I hope I don't have to remind you it's not in your best interest to lie to the law."

Her gaze darted around before settling on him.

"So, the story you're sticking with is that they jumped you on the beach?"

"No. I went into town."

"In just your swimsuit?"

A red rash crawled up her neck. Hell, he hadn't meant to embarrass her. She already seemed uncomfortable as hell in his presence. He had an extra shirt in his vehicle he could give her.

"Oh, right. I, uh, I already said I got lost."

"Enough to jump inside a random cargo ship and go wherever it took you? Sounds like someone trying to get away from something." Or someone. Yet another truth that hit him like a sucker punch.

She fixed her gaze on the cement. Was she about to lie again?

"You want to explain what really happened?" he pre-empted, pulling a notebook and pen from his pocket. She was beautiful. An inappropriate attraction surged through him. He shouldn't have passed on the offer of sex from Deanna the other night. And yet, the thrill of sex for sex's sake had never appealed to Reed.

"I've been through a lot in the past couple of days. Like I said, I got disoriented or something." She blinked against the bright sun. "Where am I?"

"Galveston, Texas."

Relief washed over her desperate expression. "Oh, thank God. That's perfect. I'm from Plano, a Dallas suburb."

"I'm familiar with the area. Have family there." He

looked up from his pad. "What are you really doing here?"

"I work for a company called SourceCon. You can call and check. They'll tell you I'm on vacation. My boss has my itinerary."

Finally, he was getting somewhere. She was still lying about getting lost in Mexico, and she was a bad liar, too. That was a good sign. Meant she didn't normally lie her way out of situations. She didn't have the convictions of a pathological liar. But now he had something to work with. It wouldn't take much to make a quick call to verify her employment. He could do that for her, at least.

The sound of one of the crate's other walls smacking the pavement split the air.

"Hey, Campbell," Pete said.

"Yeah. Right here."

"You're gonna want to see this." He rounded the corner, hoisting an AR-15 in the air. "Looks like your friend here is involved in running guns."

Reed deadpanned her. "You just bought yourself a ride to Homeland Security."

Chapter 2

The trouble Emily was in hit with the force of a tsunami. "I'm broke. I'm exhausted. And they promised to hunt me down and kill me if I crossed them."

A strong hand pulled her to her feet.

"You can lean on me," he said before turning his head and shouting for someone to bring water.

The agent's gaze skimmed her face one more time, pausing at her busted lip. His brilliant brown eyes searched for the truth. A thousand butterflies released in her stomach with him so close.

Emily hadn't seen a mirror, but based on her amount of pain she had to be a total mess. The only good news was that he seemed to be considering what she was saying. *Please. Please. Please. Believe me.*

Another bottle of water arrived. The agent twisted off the cap and handed it to her. His broad cheekbones and rich timbre set off a sparkler inside her.

The glorious water cooled her still-parched throat. She downed most of the contents, using the leftovers to splash more water on her face. "Thank you."

Her stomach growled. "Any chance you have a hamburger hidden somewhere?"

He shot her a look full of pity. Something else flashed behind his brown eyes when he said, "We can stop and pick something up on the way."

"Please don't turn me in. I can prove I'm American if I can get to my belongings." She took a step forward, and her knees buckled.

The agent caught her before she hit the ground. "Let's get something in your stomach first."

He helped her across the loading dock to his Jeep parked in the lot.

She eased onto the passenger seat.

"You're welcome to my extra shirt." He produced a white button-down from the back. "And I have a couple extra bottles of water and a towel."

A spark of hope lit inside her. Was he going to help? She thanked him for the supplies, pouring the opened bottle of water onto the towel first. The wet cloth felt cool on her skin. She dabbed her face before wiping her neck, chest and arms.

Pulling on the shirt required a little more finesse. She winced as she stretched out her arms. The agent immediately made a move to help. He eased one of her hands in the sleeve, and then the other. She managed the buttons on her own. Taking in a breath, the smell of his shirt reminded her of campfires lit outdoors and clean spring air.

"I have a power bar. Keep a few in a cooler in back for those long stretches of nothingness when I'm patrolling fence." He held out the wrapped bar and another water.

She took both, placed the water in her lap and tried to steady her hands enough to open the wrapper.

The protein bar tasted better than steak. She drained the water bottle in less than a minute. "I've already thanked you, but I'd like to repay you somehow."

His gaze locked onto hers. "Tell me the truth about what happened to you. I can't stop these men from hurting other women without information."

Was he saying what she thought? The men who'd abducted her belonged to a kidnapping ring? Of course they did. She hadn't even considered it before, she'd been too concerned about her own life, but they seemed practiced and professional. If she could stop them, she had to try.

She nodded.

He climbed into the driver's side, put the key in the ignition and then waited.

"At first, I couldn't believe what was happening to me. I just kept thinking this couldn't be real." She looked over at him, hating that she was trembling with fear. "I was dragged through the jungle for hours, starved and then stuck in a hole with no food or water." Tears welled. She would hold back the information about knowing she'd been a target until she was certain she could trust him. As it was, maybe he'd let her go.

"Do you know how long you were there?"

"What day is it?"

He glanced at his watch. "Monday."

"My flight arrived in Mexico last Monday."

"A week ago."

"The sky was clear blue, the most beautiful shade

I've ever seen. I'd stayed up late at a welcome party, so I didn't get outside until noon or so the next day. Took a kayak out, and that's when they grabbed me."

Compassion warmed his stern features. "Now we're getting somewhere. How many men were there?"

"Half a dozen."

"Can you give a description?"

"They wore bandannas to cover their faces. Other than that, they were a little taller than me." She was five foot seven. "They had to be five-eight or five-nine. Black hair and eyes."

His face muscles tensed.

"I just described half of the country, didn't I?"

He nodded, his expression radiating a sense of calm. "Dark skin or light?"

"Dark. Definitely dark."

"Can you describe their clothing?"

"Most of them wore old jeans and faded T-shirts. Looked like secondhand stuff. They were dirty."

"Some guerrilla groups live in the jungle," he agreed.

Did he believe her? He'd stopped looking at her as if she belonged in the mental ward, so that had to be a good sign.

"If they abducted you for extortion, they would've contacted your family. Can I call someone? A spouse?"

"I'm not married." An emotion she couldn't identify flashed behind the agent's brown eyes. "As for the rest of my family... There's not really... It's complicated."

"Mother? Father?"

"I don't know where he is. My mom isn't reachable. She's sick." Why was she suddenly embarrassed by her dysfunctional family?

The better question might be when had she not been?

Emily remembered being scared to death she wouldn't pass the background check required to work in her job for a major computer company. She'd had to get clearance since she entered data for various banks, some of which came from foreign interests. With a mom living in basically a cult and a dad who was MIA, Emily had feared she wouldn't get through the first round with her prospective employer. Emily had always been responsible. She hadn't even sampled marijuana in college as so many of her friends had. While all her classmates were "experimenting" and partying, she'd been working two jobs to pay tuition and make rent. Not that she was a saint. She just didn't have spare time or energy to do anything besides work, study and sleep.

She had to keep a decent GPA, which didn't leave a lot of time for anything else.

Heck, her college boyfriend had left her because she'd been too serious. He'd walked out, saying he wanted to be with someone more fun.

What was that?

Life hadn't handed Emily "fun." It had given her a deserter for a dad and a mom who was as sweet as she was lost.

Fun?

Emily clamped down a bitter laugh.

She'd had fun about as often as she'd had sex in the past year. And that really was a sad statement. Getting away, going to the beach, was supposed to represent a big step toward claiming her future and starting a new life.

"There's no one we can call?" The agent's voice brought her back to the present.

She shook her head. There was one name she could

give him, her boss. She hated to do it. The last thing she wanted to do was jeopardize her job, but Jared could corroborate her story and then the agent would believe her. Possibly even let her go?

With the information she'd given the agent so far, she had a feeling she was going to need all the help she could get. "My boss."

Agent Campbell pulled his cell from his pocket.

She gave him Jared's number and took a deep breath.

Reed punched in the number the witness had given while he kept one eye on her.

She was still desperate, and there was an off chance she'd do something stupid, like run. He didn't feel like chasing after her. He'd catch her. And then they'd be having a whole different conversation about her immediate future.

As it was, he figured a quick trip to Homeland Security would be all that was required. Minimal paperwork. Let them sort out the rest.

His years on the job told him she wasn't a hard-core criminal. There was something about her situation, her, that ate at his insides. God help him.

"This is Jared," came through the cell. His voice was crisp, and he sounded young. Early thirties.

Reed identified himself as a Border Patrol agent. "I'm calling to verify employment."

"Then you'll want to speak to HR."

"I'd rather talk to you if it's possible," Reed interjected.

"That's against policy—"

"I wouldn't ask if it wasn't a matter of national security. You can clear something up for me. Save me a lot of time going through rigmarole, sir." Reed listened for the telltale signs he'd convinced Jared.

A deep sigh came across the line.

Bingo. "Does Emily Baker work for you?"

"Yes, she does. Why? Is she all right?"

Reed picked up on the uncomfortable note in Jared's voice. Was it curiosity or something more? "Is she there today?"

"No. She's on vacation. Mexico, I think."

Part of her story matched up. The woman sitting beside him could be anyone, though. He'd already caught her glimpsing his gun. Logic told him she was debating whether or not to make a run for it.

"Can you give me a description of Miss Baker?"

"Why? Did something happen to her?" Panic raised his tone an octave. Something told Reed the guy on the phone was interested in more than her work performance. Wasn't he the caring boss? A twinge of jealousy shot through him. What was that all about?

She was vulnerable. Reed's protective instincts jumped into overdrive. He was reacting as he would if this was one of his sisters, he told himself.

"No. Nothing to worry about, sir. Routine questions." Reed hadn't exactly lied. She was a witness.

"Okay. Good. Um, let's see. She's medium height, thin, light brown hair. She's a runner, so, um, she has the build for it, if you know what I mean."

"Yeah. I get the reference." How nice that her boss paid attention to her workout routine. Clearly, there was more to this story. An office affair? Disappointment settled over Reed for reasons he couldn't explain. Why did he care whom she dated?

He reminded himself to focus on the case. This

woman fit two-thirds of the description. It was obvious her hair had been bleached. The dye job was bad, and so was the cut. Her hair had been chopped off. Even so, she was beautiful.

And her legs were long and toned. She could be a runner. He made a mental note of the fact, in case she decided to bolt. It was easy to see she was in good physical condition, aside from events of the past few days.

She glanced around, antsy. Her expression set, determined, as she skimmed the docks. Was she working with someone? For someone?

Or was she just a few grains of sand short of a castle?

The tougher job was to assess her mental fitness. If she wasn't involved in bringing guns into the country, and, really and truly, she would've been smart enough to have one loaded at the ready if she was, he had to consider the possibility she might be a danger to herself or others.

He'd witnessed all kinds of crazy.

In fact, in six years with Border Patrol, he'd seen just about everything. And a whole lot of nothing, too, especially when he was a rookie.

"Eye color?"

"Green, I think."

They were hazel, but lots of people confused hazel with green or blue. The description was close enough. "Thank you, sir. That clears everything up."

"She'll be back to work next Monday, right?"

Reed figured the boss wanted the answer to his question more for personal reasons than anything else. "I don't see why not."

"And she's okay? You're sure?"

Another sprig of jealousy sprouted. "She is. That's all the information I need. Have a nice—"

"I don't want to ask anything inappropriate, but our job requires a certain level of security clearance. She hasn't gone and done anything that might jeopardize her position at work, has she?"

"Why would she do that?" Reed knew she wasn't telling him something, but he doubted she was involved in criminal activity. Couldn't rule it out yet. Even though his instincts never lied, he preferred logic and evidence. Did this whole episode have to do with her job? What would she have to gain?

A relieved sigh came across the line. "She wouldn't. At least, I don't think she would. I guess you can never really tell about people, but I don't have to tell you that. Not in your line of work."

The man finally said something smart. "Desperate people can do all kinds of interesting things."

"I'm sure. I already asked, but she's okay, right?"

"Yeah. She'll be back to work next week, and I'm sure she'll explain everything then." Reed ended the call.

"I lost my job, didn't I?" She sounded defeated. "It doesn't matter."

"You didn't tell me everything," he hedged.

She repositioned in her seat.

"You're tired and hungry, so I'm afraid you're going to make a bad choice. Whatever you're running from, I can help you."

She deadpanned him. "No. You can't."

"Not if you don't tell me what it is."

"I won't run. Please don't take me in." Her wide hazel eyes pleaded.

"There's protocol for situations like these. You came into the country in a shipment full of guns. Who do they belong to?"

"I'd tell you if I knew." Tears welled in her eyes.

"I need a name. They'll take it easy on you if you cooperate."

"Are you arresting me?" She glanced toward the field to her right.

Was she getting ready to make her move?

He started the engine, determined to keep her from making another mistake she'd regret. "Buckle up. We can finish this conversation over a burger."

"You didn't answer my question. Are you going to arrest me?" she repeated slowly, as if he was dim.

"No. Why? Do you plan on giving me a reason to?"

The drive to the nearest fast-food burger place was quiet. His passenger closed her eyes and laid her head back.

She didn't open them when he pulled into the drive-through lane and ordered two burgers, two fries and two milkshakes at the speaker box.

Reed gripped the steering wheel tighter, thinking about what she'd been through in the past few days. He also realized she was keeping secrets. Professional curiosity had him wanting to find out what they were. Or was it something else?

He dismissed the idea as standing in the sun too long back at the docks. His interest in Emily Baker was purely professional.

At this point, he'd classify her as a witness. However, she was walking a fine line of being moved into another category—suspect—and she didn't want to be there. He should probably haul her up to Homeland Security and be done.

But he couldn't.

Something in those hazel eyes told him there was a bigger story, one that frightened her to the point of almost becoming mute.

If she talked, he might be able to track down gun runners, or get the connection he needed to stop another coyote from dumping illegals across the border. Heck, most died of dehydration before they ever reached their desired location. She was weak. No way was she illegal, but they used the same paths for everything from human trafficking to gun running. Besides, maybe she had information that could help him make a bust. The innocence and desperation in her voice had drawn him in. He needed to make sure she'd be okay.

He couldn't turn his back on her any more than he could walk away from one of his sisters. Something about Emily brought out a similar protective instinct, but that's where the similarities ended. Nothing else about her reminded him of his siblings.

After paying at the window, he accepted the food. There was a shady spot in the parking lot across the street. He pulled into it and parked.

She blinked her eyes open when he cut off the engine.

He unwrapped a burger and handed it to her. "It's not steak, but it should help with your hunger."

Her eyes lit up as she took the offering. "That smells nothing short of amazing."

A few bites into her meal, she set her burger down. "I don't understand. I'm famished but I can't finish it."

Poor thing was starving. Another fact in this case that made Reed want to punch something.

It was one thing for traffickers and drug pushers to maim and kill each other, but to drag women and children into their web made his fists clench and his jaw muscle tick. Five minutes alone with any one of them, and he'd leave his badge and gun outside the door.

"That was the best food I've ever had," she said, wiping her mouth with a napkin. "Ouch. Sorry. I'm bleeding again." She searched the empty food bag and seemed to fight back tears. "You've been really nice to me and I don't want to get blood on your clean white shirt."

"Nothing to worry about." Reed handed her his napkin. "It's an old shirt. A little blood won't hurt anything."

Her back was ramrod. He wasn't any closer to getting her to trust him.

Maybe softening his approach would work. "Believe me when I say I've had to clean up worse than that. The shirt's yours. Keep it."

She apologized again. Her bottom lip quivered, indicating she was probably on the brink of losing it. Who could blame her? She'd been amazingly strong so far.

For now, the person of interest in his passenger seat was safe and calm. She'd had a few minutes to think about where she might end up if she didn't give him something to work with. "Why'd they really hit you?"

She searched nearby shrubs and buildings as if expecting the men who'd hurt her to jump out from behind one.

Fear was a powerful tool.

Whoever hurt her did a good job of making her believe he'd come back for more if she gave him up. "I know this is tough. Believe me. But it's the only way I can help you."

She brought her hands up to rub her temples and trained her gaze on the patch of cement in front of the Jeep. She was teetering on the edge.

He was getting close to a breakthrough. "They shouldn't be allowed to get away with this. I don't care what they threatened. The US government is bigger than whoever did this to you."

A few tears fell, streaking her cheeks.

"Whatever they said, don't believe them."

She dropped her hands to her lap, and then turned toward him. Her hazel eyes pierced right through him. "You give me your personal promise to protect me?"

Chapter 3

If Agent Campbell made one wrong blink, Emily had already decided she'd bolt. She'd put it out there and asked him to make a commitment. Now it was his turn to make a move.

"It's my job to—"

"I want to know if you promise to protect me. And not just because of your badge." Even though he was a stranger, everything about the agent next to her said he was a man of his word. If he made a personal pledge, she'd trust him a little.

He finished chewing his bite of hamburger and swallowed before he set his food on the wrapper and used a napkin to clean his hands.

"My name is Reed, and you have my word." He stuck his hand out between them.

She took it, knowing she shouldn't. There was no

way he could guarantee her safety. The instant they'd made contact, a spark ran between them. She didn't withdraw her hand. Neither did he.

Their eyes locked, and she felt another jolt. An underlying sexual current simmered between them, which was shocking given what she'd been through. He was the first person in ages who'd expressed interest in helping and protecting her, she reasoned, and it felt nice to have that.

Under different circumstances, she might enjoy the spark. Not now. All she could think about was getting out of this mess and going into hiding.

Another thing was certain. By the set of his jaw, she could tell that Reed Campbell meant what he said. No doubt about it. Could he deliver against a rebel faction that could have law enforcement officers bought and paid for?

He looked like the kind of man who, once he gave his word, would die trying to deliver on his commitments. And something about the depths of his eyes had her wanting to move a little closer toward his strength, his light.

All her danger signals flared.

Getting too close to a man who could have her locked up was a bad idea, no matter how much honesty radiated from his brown eyes.

His cell buzzed, and she pulled her hand back, breaking their grasp.

A half-eaten burger sat on his knee on top of the wrapper. He answered the call, keeping his gaze on her.

Was he afraid she'd take off? He had to know she'd scatter like a squirrel at one loud noise.

At six-two with muscles for days, he must realize

he could be physically intimidating. Was that why he seemed to make so much of an effort to keep her calm?

Against her better judgment, it was working. She felt a sense of being protected with him near. A luxury she couldn't afford.

"Uh-huh, I have her right here," he said. His gaze narrowed.

Trouble?

"Thanks, but I've got this one."

Was someone offering to take her off his hands? This seemed out of the blue. No way could it be standard procedure.

A shudder of fear roared through her. She folded her arms to stave off the chill skittering across her skin.

"No, I'm sure." He shook his head as if for emphasis. "We're heading northbound on I-45. Why?"

Emily's chest squeezed, and she knew something was wrong. Agent Campbell gave the person on the phone the wrong location. Why would he do that?

"Will do." Agent Campbell ended his call.

"Who was that?"

He sat looking dumbfounded for a second. "That was odd. Agent Stephen Taylor volunteered to meet me and take you off my hands. Said he was headed in and it wouldn't be any trouble to take you along with him."

"I don't know this area at all, but we're sitting in a parking lot, and you told him we were on the highway. Why?"

Using the paper wrap, he wadded up the few bites of hamburger he had left and tossed it in the bag. "That call doesn't sit right. Something's off."

Emily gasped. "That can't be normal."

"Nope. Never happened to me before in six years of service." He checked his rearview mirror.

The last thing Emily wanted to do was tell the agent more about what had happened to her. In fact, she'd like to be able to forget it altogether. But both of their lives were in danger now, and he deserved to know the risk he was taking. "There was a man back in Mexico. They called him Dueño. He promised to…"

Saying the words out loud proved harder than she expected. Tears pricked the backs of her eyes.

Gray clouds rolled in from the coast as the winds picked up speed.

The agent sat quietly, hands resting on the steering wheel, giving her the space she needed to find the courage to tell him the rest.

"To find me no matter what. I know he has law enforcement on his payroll. I overheard them talking about it."

Agent Campbell started the ignition, and eased the Jeep into traffic. "They give any names?"

His rich timbre was laced with anger. She could imagine how an honest man like him would take it personally if one of his own was on the take. "No. All I knew was that once I got away from him, I had to disappear. I couldn't trust law enforcement or anyone else. That's why I can't let you take me in. I'm begging you to let me go."

Thunder rumbled in the distance.

"Hate to believe agents are on the take." He looked to be searching his memory as he narrowed his gaze onto the stretch of road in front of them. He muttered a string of curse words. "There have been a few articles in the paper hinting at the possibility. The department issued a warning. We'd picked up a few bad eggs during a hiring surge, but we've been assured they were weeded out."

"You take me in and he'll get to me. He has people on the inside. I can identify him and testify. They'll kill me."

"Slow down. I'm not going to let that happen. We can figure this out."

"They won't stop until they find me."

"Which is why it's a bad idea for me to let you go. At least while you're with me, I can protect you."

"Can't you tell your department you let me go?"

"Why would I do that?"

"Because you have to. I know what they wanted when they targeted me. There's a fortune on the line."

"Hold on a sec. You led me to believe this was random," he said. His eyes flashed anger.

"I'm sorry. I lied. I wasn't sure if I could trust you before." She had to now.

His grip on the steering wheel tightened. His gaze intensified. "What else?"

"They wanted my passwords. I work at a computer company. We keep account information secure for big banking institutions. I'm sure they planned on moving money."

"Cybercrime can be harder to track if they know what they're doing. Why didn't you just give them the passwords and save yourself?"

She deadpanned him. "I figured they'd kill me either way. Even so, I couldn't give them passwords if I'd wanted to. I always change them before I leave for vacation. I didn't have my new ones memorized."

"He beat you because he didn't believe you."

"Not for a second."

"I'm assuming you have your codes written down somewhere?"

She nodded. A thought struck her. "What if they get to my place and find them? I'm sure they knew where I lived."

Agent Campbell's cell buzzed again. He put on his turn signal, moved into the left turn lane and then shot a glance at her before answering. He turned on his hazard lights, even though there were no cars coming.

Thunder rumbled louder. A storm was coming.

"Yes, sir, I heard from the agent."

There was a long pause.

"No, I didn't turn over the witness. I can run her in to make a statement."

Emily slipped her hand as close to the seat belt release button as she could without drawing attention. Her pulse kicked up a notch.

A light rain started, nothing more than a spring shower. The glorious liquid spotted the windshield.

She had enough sustenance in her to manage a good sprint. Would it be enough to get away? Her feet still ached and her head pounded. A good night of sleep, some medicine, and she'd recover. But would her body give her what she needed to get away now?

Possibilities clicked through her mind.

If she made a run for it, could she disappear in the neighboring subdivision? Maybe hide in a parked car?

The capable agent in the seat next to her would catch her. His muscled thighs said he could outrun her if he needed to. One look at the ripple of muscles underneath his shirtsleeve said he was much stronger than she.

Might be a risk she'd have to take.

Stay there and she'd be dead in an hour if he followed through with his plans to take her to Homeland Security. One of the men in Dueño's pocket would alert him to her whereabouts, and they'd be ready for her when she walked outside.

The best chance she had would be to make a move right now while Agent Campbell was distracted by his phone call. If she were smart, she'd unbuckle and run like hell.

"I didn't say she was a suspect, sir."

Her heart jackhammered in her chest. Should she bolt?

Reed glanced over at Emily. Her back was stiff, her breathing rapid and shallow. He covered her hand with his, and she relaxed a little. A smile quirked the corner of his lip.

"I can take this one, sir. Not a problem."

Confident he'd convinced his boss, Reed ended the call. A rogue agent was a dangerous thing. Reed could personally attest to that.

This one had involved his boss, who was being played. The agent who'd tried to get his hands on Emily wouldn't be allowed to have his way.

"Your boss wanted you to hand me over to someone else, didn't he?"

Reed nodded.

"Could going against your boss cost your job?"

He wasn't sure why he chuckled. "Yeah."

"You're willing to take that risk to help me?"

"It's my duty." "Honor First" was more than words on a page to Reed.

Emily leaned against the seat and pinched the bridge of her nose. "Then, what do we do next?"

"Good question."

Reed checked the rearview and saw a truck screaming toward them.

He banked a U-turn in time to see a metal shotgun barrel aimed at them.

Emily must've seen it, too, because she yelped.

"Get down on the floorboard. Now."

A *boom* split the air.

Reed gunned the gas pedal, made a U-turn and then hooked a right, blazing through the empty parking lot. For a split second, time warped and the memory of being shot and left for dead blitzed him.

A walk down Memory Lane would have to wait. He battled against the heavy thoughts, blocking them out. If he lived, *correction*, when he got them out of this mess, he'd deal with those. *Yeah, right, like that's going to happen.*

The reality was that he'd had plenty of time since returning to work to rationalize his feelings. Doing that ranked about as high on his list as shoveling cow manure out of the barn at Gran's place. He took that back. Shoveling cow manure was far more appealing.

Reed glanced at Emily, who was not more than a ball in the floorboard. Her face scrunched in pain from being forced to move. The thought of doubling her agony lanced his chest. "Hang tight. I'll get us to safety soon."

She glanced at him through fearful hazel eyes. "Maybe we should break up. I can hide on my own. Might be better now that they know we're together."

Was she still worried he'd run her in? Handing her

over to his agency would only put her in more jeopardy. "Not a chance."

Anxiety and fear played across her features.

A need to protect Emily surged, catching Reed off guard, because it ran deeper than his professional oath. He knew exactly what it was like to be in her position—to be the target of someone who had a dirty agent in their pocket. Reed had a bullet hole in his back to prove it.

"I'm your best option right now. And I'm not ready to let you out of my sight."

Chapter 4

Pain rippled through Emily's bruised and battered body as she crouched low and hugged her knees into her chest, making herself as small as possible in the floorboard. One of her ribs had to be cracked. The sharp pain in her chest sliced through her thoughts. Being run through a cheese grater would hurt less than the bruises on her face and body.

The agent, Reed, had said she could trust him. He'd said the magic words—he wasn't hauling her butt in to Homeland Security. And yet, her internal alarm system was still set to red alert. Why? What was it about him that had her wanting to run? Was it the alarming comfort his presence brought?

Sporadic turns and the sound of another shotgun blast said they still had company. Emily didn't dare try to peek even though her tightly coiled nerves might break at any moment if she didn't know what was happening. Even so, she doubted her body would be able to respond to her brain's command to get up.

Reed swerved the car left and then made a hard right. "Wish I'd been alone when I found you. That would make things less complicated."

"Would you have believed me?"

His compressed frown said it all. No, he wouldn't have. "I owe you an apology for that."

"I don't blame you. I'm sure you deal with all kinds of crazy people in your work."

"Most have nothing to lose when they run into me. And I've learned logic is a better resource than instinct."

He was used to being shot at? That revelation shouldn't reassure her. Oddly enough, that's exactly what it did. Maybe because she had no clues how to escape armed men or dodge bullets and there was no way she'd still be alive without his expertise. Her world had been catapulted into a whole new stratosphere of danger. Having a man around who knew how to use a gun and was on her side didn't seem like the worst thing that could happen.

Yet, depending on anyone was foreign to her. Thoughts of too many hours of her childhood spent crouched low in the corner behind her bed while her mother experienced "free love" in the next room assaulted Emily. She'd been old enough to remember what it was like to live in a suburb with a normal family and a father whom she believed loved her. Her fairy-tale world had ended the day he left. Emily squeezed her eyes tighter, trying to block out the memory.

Emily slowly counted to a hundred to keep her mind busy, refusing to let fear seize her when more bullets came at them. They pinged by her head tat-tat-tat style, and she knew by the sound difference that whoever was chasing them had changed weapons.

"I can lose them around this bend or when I get on this highway. This turn is going to get hairy, so hang on."

Chancing a glance at Reed, seeing someone who wasn't afraid, held her nerves a notch below panic. However, the contents of her stomach retaliated at the high rate of speed combined with sharp turns. She'd probably eaten too fast because the burger and milkshake churned. "Are they still back there?"

"Get back in the seat belt. The threat has tripled, and we're going to sustain a hit." The authority in his voice sent a trill of worry through her.

"Okay." She struggled to move, wincing as she planted one hand on the glove compartment and the other on the seat, praying she could gain enough leverage to push herself up from her awkward position on the floorboard. Her arms gave out and she landed hard, racking up another bruise on her hip.

A glance at Reed said they were almost out of time.

"Brace yourself for impact." He tapped the brake and swerved.

Emily lurched forward, her head caught by Reed's right hand moments before it hit the dash. Pushing through the pain, she pressed up to the seat and quickly fastened the belt over her shoulder.

Large SUVs pulled on each side of them as the truck she recognized from earlier roared up from behind.

The quick look Reed shot her next said whatever was about to happen wasn't going to be good. He floored the gas pedal, shooting out front. Temporarily.

On the right, the SUV hit the brakes. The one on the left barreled beside them, keeping pace.

The window of opportunity to hop onto the freeway and lose these guys was closing with the SUV on the left blocking the on-ramp.

A bumper crunched against the back of the Jeep. Emily's head whipped forward.

Dueño's reach had long arms. Just as he had promised. Could Emily envision a life on the run? No. She'd fought too hard to put down roots. She'd found a new city, bought a town house and worked her butt off to be next in line for her boss's job. Dueño was forcing her into a different direction. Anger burned through her.

Another hard jerk of the steering wheel and Emily felt herself tumbling, spinning.

Reed's rich timbre penetrated the out-of-control Ferris wheel. "Relax as much as you can."

Time temporarily suspended. Emily drifted out of her own body as the spinning slowed, and then stopped.

Everything went black, but she still could hear shouting. Someone was yelling at her. A deeply masculine voice called. She coughed and blinked her eyes open.

Smoke was everywhere.

Everything burned. Her nose. Her eyes. Her throat.

Her body might've stopped spinning, but her head hadn't.

"Emily. Stay with me." The voice came from a tunnel filled with light.

Or did it?

There was something comforting about the large physical presence near her.

"Emily. I need you to try to move." A sense of urgency tinged the apologetic tone.

Her response came out as a croak. She tried harder to open her eyes and gain her bearings.

Sirens sounded in the distance a few moments after she heard another pop of gunfire. The men. Oh, no. All at once she remembered being on the run. Their car had been forced off the road, while speeding, and thrown into a dangerous spin. The Jeep had rolled. And that voice calling her belonged to Border Patrol Agent Reed Campbell.

Her eyes shot open.

Heat from a fire blazed toward her. Flames licked at her skin. Thick smoke filled her lungs.

She was trapped in a burning car while men shot at her. It took another few precious seconds for her to realize she was upside down. At least the inferno kept the men at bay, except for Reed. He was right by her side. An unfamiliar feeling stuck in her chest at the thought someone actually had her back for a change. Emily wanted to gravitate toward the pleasant emotion, except she couldn't move. She wiggled her hips, hoping to break free. No luck.

The seat belt must be stuck.

There was no feeling in her legs. She tamped down panic, knowing full well that couldn't be good. Even if she could work the belt free, which she was trying with both hands, how would she run?

She'd have to solve that puzzle when she came to it.

"Take this." A shiny metal object was being thrust at her through the thick wall of smoke separating her from the agent.

Reed's face was covered in ashes and worry lines. Blood dripped down his cheek from a cut on his forehead. There was compassion in his clear brown eyes and what appeared to be fear.

She took the offering, a knife.

"Cut yourself free." His arms cradled her shoulders.

"Okay." She shot him a scared look.

"I'll catch you. I won't let you get hurt."

Her gaze widened at the figure moving toward them. "Behind you."

The agent turned and fired his weapon.

She worked the knife against the fabric, wanting to be ready, knowing they were out of time.

Sirens split the air.

Reed turned his attention back to her as soon as the man disappeared. "I'm ready. Go."

The last patch of thread cut easily. Emily didn't want to think about how good his hands felt on her as he pulled her from the burning Jeep across the hard, unforgiving earth. Or how nice it was to have someone in her corner.

The head of the House believed placing labels on people degraded them, so he simply called her girl. Her mom soon followed his lead.

Growing up in a house full of free love and short on anything meaningful, like her mother's laughter, had made Emily wary and distrustful of people. Watching her mom adopt the long hair and threadbare clothes everyone in the House wore made Emily feel even more distanced from everything familiar.

In the twelve years Emily had lived there, her mom had six children by various housemates. It had been like living in a time warp. Apparently, the label "Father" was also degrading because no one stepped up to help care for the little ones, save for Emily. She'd taken care of the children until one of the men had decided that at seventeen she was old enough to learn about free love. She'd fought back, escaped and then ran.

Emily had learned quickly the outside world could be harsh, too.

With no friends on the streets, she'd had to fight off men who confused her homelessness for prostitution. Her first stroke of luck had come when she found a flier for a shelter that handed out free breakfast. A worker there had told her about the nearby shelter for teens. For the first time since leaving Texas as a child, Emily had her own room.

All her life savings, money she'd made from her job at the local movie theater, was hidden in the House. Emily had saved every penny. Needing a fresh start, she'd slipped into the House, took her life savings and then bought a bus ticket to Dallas, where she could return home and put down roots.

By the time she'd finished a few college courses and gotten a decent job, her half siblings had scattered across the country, and she heard from her mother mostly when she needed something.

No matter how honest and pure the agent looked, Emily knew not to get too comfortable.

Feeling vulnerable out in the open, she searched for the men. Where were they?

She glanced around, half expecting more gunfire. Instead, EMTs ran toward them and all she could hear was the glorious thunder of their footsteps.

But, where was Reed?

Then she saw him. He lay flat on his back and her chest squeezed when she saw how much blood soaked his shirt. One set of EMTs rushed to him, blocking her view. Another went to work on her as firemen put out the blaze.

The cavalry had arrived.

But how long before Dueño's men returned to finish the job?

Emily needed a plan.

Heaven knew she could never rely on her mother. The woman had shattered when Emily's father left. Even then, Emily knew she needed to help her mother. The woman couldn't do much for herself in the broken state she was in. When she'd finally forced herself out of bed, a neighbor introduced her to "a new way of thinking."

It wasn't long before Emily's mom packed the pair of them up and moved to California to live in the House. Emily had been excited about the promise of perpetual sunshine, but her enthusiasm was short-lived when she figured out no one ever left the grounds except in groups to shop for food.

Which was why she couldn't afford to rely on the agent much longer. Especially not the way he stirred confusing feelings inside her that had no business surfacing. She knew where that would end up.

Reed stripped off the oxygen mask covering his face. "I'm fine."

"Can you tell me what day it is?" the young EMT asked.

"Monday. And I know I've been in an accident. I was forced off the road by another vehicle. I have to call local police to file a report." He reached for his phone, needing an excuse to step away and make eye contact with Emily. He wanted to know she'd be okay. Men were huddled around her, working on her. Reed tamped down the unexpected jolt of anxiety tensing his shoulders. "What's going on with my witness? She'll be okay, right?"

"We'll know in a few minutes."

Not good enough. Reed had to know now. He pushed off the back of the truck.

The EMT stepped in front of Reed. "Sir, that's not a good idea."

"Why not? Is she hurt badly?" The young guy was big, worked out, but Reed had no doubts he could take the guy down if necessary. Reed's hands fisted. His jaw muscle twitched.

"The others are working on her. I'm talking about you. I'd like to finish my exam, if that's okay."

The guy seemed to know Reed could take him down in a heartbeat. He reminded himself to stay cool. The EMT was only doing his job. No point in making it any harder for him.

Reed fished his wallet out of his pocket and produced his identification. "Name's Reed Campbell. I'm a Border Patrol agent. I have two brothers and two sisters. It's Monday at…" He checked his watch. "Four o'clock."

"Good. I think it's safe to say you didn't suffer a concussion. Will you let me patch up your forehead before you go, and let me take a look at what's causing all that blood on your shirt?" the young guy asked, resigned.

"Can't hurt." He sat still long enough for his gashes to be cleaned and bandaged.

"I still think it's a good idea for you to go to the hospital."

"I plan to." His gaze fixed on the team working on Emily.

"As a patient."

"I promise to get checked out if I take a turn for the worse."

"No changing your mind?"

"I appreciate all you're doing for me, but I'm more worried about her."

Reluctantly, the EMT produced papers. "Then I need your autograph on these. They say you received basic treatment at the scene and refused to be taken in for further medical evaluation."

Reed took them and signed off, uneasy that Emily was still surrounded by a busy team of workers. If someone on the inside of his agency was helping Dueño, Reed couldn't chance his phone being hacked. His best bet was to play it cool with the EMT and pretend his had taken a hit. "Any chance I can borrow your phone? Mine's a casualty of the wreck, and I need to check in with my boss."

The worker nodded, handing over his cell.

They needed transportation, and Reed trusted a handful of people right now—most of whom shared his last name. His brothers were in North Texas, too far to catch a ride. His boss was his best bet. After being shot in the line of duty, Reed knew he could trust Gil. And with any luck, no one would be listening in on his boss's phone, either. Reed would play it cool just in case.

Gil picked up on the second ring.

"It's Reed. I had to borrow a phone. I don't have time to explain, but I need a car." There'd be a mountain of paperwork to deal with when this was settled.

"Where are you?"

"My Jeep's been totaled. I was chased off the road. This is big, Gil. Fingers are reaching out from over the border." Reed kept the name to himself to be on the safe side.

Gil muttered a curse.

"We need to be careful here," Reed warned. "We might have another Cal situation on our hands."

Gil grunted. "I'll have transportation waiting for you… Wait, let me think."

"How about the little place you like to visit on special Thursdays?" The Pelican restaurant in Galveston was Gil's wife's favorite seafood spot. He took her there every anniversary and occasionally on Thursday nights for their catfish special. Gil didn't go out on Fridays. Said it was too crowded. Few people knew Gil's habits the way Reed did. He'd learned a lot about his boss during the man's visits to the hospital after Reed was shot.

"Got it."

"Leave the keys so I can find them. The usual spot."

"Okay."

Keys would be under the sink in the bathroom. Reed glanced at Emily. The EMTs were still surrounding her. They'd want to take her to the hospital. With the amount of smoke she'd inhaled and the possible swelling, it was probably a good idea. "Can you get ahold of the local police chief? I'd like a fresh set of eyes on us at the hospital."

"I'll make the call myself from Vickie's personal cell."

His admin's number should be safe. "Appreciate it."

"You need a place to stay in the meantime?"

"I'll figure it out. Besides, the less I involve the department, the better. Probably best if I branch out on my own for this one." And he had no intention of leaving Emily for a second. These guys were relentless and she was scared. Not a good combination. If she made one mistake it'd be game over. The thought sent a lead fireball swirling down Reed's chest. Didn't need to get inside his head about why his reaction to the thought of anything happening to her was so strong. Reed passed it off as needing to keep his promises.

Gil paused. "Be careful."

"You know it." Reed ended the call. Now all he had to figure out was how to get to the bank and withdraw enough money to get by for a while. Then he'd need transportation from the hospital to The Pelican. No way could Emily walk in her current condition. She'd need time to rest and heal.

They didn't have the luxury of either.

Whoever was after her meant business.

The EMTs loaded her into the ambulance. Reed pushed through and took the step in an easy stride.

He was instantly pulled back.

"Sorry. It's policy. No one rides in back except us," one of the men said. He was older than the guy who'd worked on Reed.

"No exceptions?"

"Afraid not. How about you take a seat up front? We've already called a tow truck for your vehicle."

Reed nodded, not really liking the thought of being separated from Emily. Anything could happen to her in the back if those men were waiting, or worse yet, ambushed the ambulance.

Climbing into the cab, he told himself he cared only for professional reasons. The chance to nab a jerk who would do this to a woman fueled his need to protect her. And that it had nothing at all to do with the fact those hazel eyes of hers would haunt him in his sleep if he walked away.

Now that he knew her story had merit, he wanted to know more about her. It had everything to do with arming himself with knowledge that might just save both of their lives and nothing to do with the place in his heart she stirred, he lied.

Chapter 5

The long stretch of country road ahead provided too many opportunities for ambush. Reed reloaded his weapon, his gaze vacillating between looking ahead, to the sides and behind. "How much longer?"

"Fifteen minutes at the most."

"And the woman in back? How's she doing?" Reed glanced out the side-view mirror.

"My guys don't look as busy as they did on-site. That's a good sign in our line of work." He paused a beat. "They've been treating her for smoke inhalation. All I can tell you so far is that they're giving her oxygen, and she can expect to have a sore throat for a few days. Depending on the swelling in her throat, she might need to be intubated."

Reed didn't realize he'd cursed out loud until he saw the surprised look on the driver's face.

"She must be important to your case to get a reaction like that."

"I don't have one without her." Reed didn't appreciate women being beaten up, and especially not by men. His sister Lucy had received injuries as a teenager from an obsessed boyfriend. Reed chalked his current defensive feelings toward Emily up to bad memories.

"I notified my boss of the situation. He's calling ahead so the hospital will be ready with security."

"Thank you."

"She has a lot of other injuries and those might be of concern. Says she sustained them before the crash?"

Reed nodded.

"She needs a chest X-ray to ensure nothing's broken."

The way she'd been hugging her arms across her chest earlier now made more sense. He hadn't considered the possibility of cracked ribs. Anger bubbled to the surface. Reed muttered a string of curse words.

The EMT paused before continuing. "From the looks of it, she's been through hell and back. Those injuries could be far worse than the ones she sustained in the crash, but my guess is the doctor in charge is going to want to keep her for a while based on her pulse oximetry numbers."

"What's that?"

"Shows the amount of oxygen in the blood. Normal is one hundred and hers are ninety. She's experiencing some difficulty breathing, which leads me to believe her respiratory tract has some swelling."

"But she'll be okay?" In a matter of a few days she'd been beaten, starved and denied water. Reed's training and experience had taught him not to assume an injured person was telling the truth. In fact, most of the time

they weren't. It was logic backed by years of experience. So why did he feel so damn awful about his earlier suspicions about her now? Was it the vulnerability
in her eyes that hit him faster than a bullet and cut a
similar hole in his chest? This case was different. Hell's
bells, that statement didn't begin to scratch the surface.

"How long was she trapped in the Jeep?"

"Not more than eight or nine minutes."

"Less than ten minutes is good. That and the Jeep
being open is a big help. With her oxygen levels being
on the low side, best-case scenario is the damage to her
airway and lungs is minimal. If there's no real swelling, she can expect a full recovery. We're almost there,
by the way. The hospital is only a few minutes out. The
doctor can tell you more after his exam. Her vital signs
looked good."

"May I borrow your phone? I need to call work, and
my cell didn't make it out of the Jeep," he lied. It was
easier than explaining the whole situation.

The EMT glanced down at his cell, which was on
the seat between them. "Be my guest."

Reed hoped his brother Luke would pick up.

"Hello?" The word was more accusation than greet-
ing. Being in law enforcement made them suspicious
of everything unfamiliar, and Luke wouldn't have recognized this number.

"It's Reed."

"What's up, baby bro?" Luke's stiff voice relaxed.
"Leave your phone at a girl's house again?"

Reed ignored the joke. "I need help. I'm headed
to ClearPond Regional Medical Hospital southeast of
Houston with a hot package. I got a lot of eyes on me
and fingers reaching from across the border."

"On my way." Bustling sounds of movement came through the line.

"Thanks." Reed would breathe a little easier when he had backup he could trust.

"I need to get anyone else involved?" Luke asked.

"Nah. I'm good with just you."

"Be there as fast as I can." More shuffling noises indicated Luke was already heading to his truck. "How can I reach you when I get close? I'm guessing your phone is toast."

"Yeah, that reminds me. Can you bring me Mom's old phone?" The saying was code for a burn phone, which couldn't be traced.

"Sure. Anything else?"

"Let Nick know what's going on."

"He's going to want to come." The Campbell boys had learned early in life to count on each other after their father had ditched the family and left their mother to bring up five kids on her own. Nick, the oldest, had taken over as a father figure.

"Tell him to stay put for now. I'll call when I need him."

"He may not listen."

"I can use any information he can dig up about a man they call Dueño. He's most likely running guns, trafficking women, but see if he can find anything else we can use to get to know this guy better."

"That should keep our brother busy. He still might want to come." Sounds of the truck door closing came through the line.

"Understood. I'll figure out what to do if he shows up. For now, try to discourage him." Reed totally understood his brother's need to be there. Reed would do the same thing if he were in Nick's shoes. "Let him know I can use him more on the sidelines right now. Plus, I'll have you to watch my back."

"Will do, baby bro."

Reed ended the call, thanked the driver and set his phone on the seat between them.

As promised, Reed saw the large white building ahead. He surveyed the parking lot as they pulled inside the Emergency bay.

A Hispanic male stood by the corner of the building, smoking. He wore jeans, boots and a cowboy hat. The loose shirt he wore could easily hide a weapon. His head was tipped down, so Reed couldn't get a clear visual of the man's face.

The hospital was regional, so it was decent in size. There were a few dozen cars scattered around the parking lot, the heaviest concentration located closest to the main hospital entrance.

For a few seconds, Emily would be completely exposed while being wheeled inside. She'd be easy pickings for a trained sniper. Heck, any experienced gunman would be able to take her out faster than Reed could blink.

Luckily, there were no tall buildings nearby to gain a tactical advantage. A local hamburger joint, a taco-based fast-food chain restaurant and a gas station were located across the street. Those buildings weren't tall enough to matter.

Only an idiot would blitz them with a head-on attack. If this guy was smart and powerful enough to have a US presence, he didn't employ stupid people.

Reed's main concern was a bullet fired from in between the cars in the lot.

The gurney rolled through the sliding glass doors, where they were met by an officer. A sigh of relief passed Reed's lips once Emily was safely inside the building, but he wasn't ready to let his guard down.

The gurney was wheeled past an officer, and then disappeared inside a room. Reed paused at the door. "Your help is appreciated."

"I'll keep an officer here at all times and another at the elevator. The stairs are located at the end of the hall, so he'll be able to watch both exits from his vantage point." Reed had already counted the possible entry points and memorized the layout. Having someone centrally located was a good idea. Didn't hurt to have another officer right outside the door, as well.

"Hopefully, whoever is doing this will have enough sense to leave her alone for now. If not, your men should be a good deterrent." Reed couldn't be certain the officers appointed to watch over her could be trusted, but he was short on options.

Even if this one was honest, there was no way to know if the others were.

Cal had seemed honest and as if he was with the department for the right reasons. First impressions could be deceiving. Not only had Reed been ambushed and shot, his fiancée had been sleeping with Cal. The double deception had left him leery of trusting anyone whose last name wasn't Campbell.

Reed had doubted Gil for a while, too. But, his boss's true colors had come through when he'd maintained a bedside vigil next to Reed until he was out of the woods. Neither had stopped searching for Cal.

Letting Reed's guard down wasn't an option. He'd

stay alert in Emily's room. He could rest when Luke arrived.

And Reed hoped like hell there wouldn't be any more surprises between now and then.

Stepping inside the bleached-white hospital room caused phantom pain to pierce his left shoulder—the exact spot where he'd taken a bullet. His attempt to take a step forward shut down midstride. *Shake it off.*

Forcing his boot to meet the white tile floor, he couldn't suppress the shudder that ran through him after he pulled back the curtain and got a good look at Emily. Tubes stuck out of her from seemingly every direction. Monitors beeped.

With an uncomfortable smile on his lips, he moved closer.

As soon as she made eye contact, her face lit up. The tension in Reed's neck dissolved and warmth filled him. What was he supposed to do with that?

She lifted the oxygen mask off her face and quickly reined in her excitement, compressing her lips together instead. She could've been a poker player for the facade she put up now. Her even gaze dropped to the blanket covering her. "Thought maybe I'd scared you off."

"It takes more than a woman in trouble to make me run," he shot back, trying to get another smile from her. She didn't need to see the worry lines on his face. It would only make her panic.

A nurse fussed at Emily for lifting her mask. "I'll help you change into a gown." She turned to Reed. "You, sit. Or you'll have to go even though my boss gave me the rundown of the situation and you are law enforcement."

"Yes, ma'am." He took the chair closest to the bed,

ignoring the uncomfortable feeling in his chest at seeing Emily look vulnerable and detached again. For her
to have escaped the kind of man who could reach her
from across a border, she had to be one tough cookie.
Reed admired her for it. Hell, respected her even. Under
different circumstances, she was the kind of woman he
could see himself spending time getting to know better. Experience had taught him to keep his business and
private lives separate.

Reed had no plans to break his rule no matter how
much the scared little thing in the bed next to him
tugged at his heart strings. *Scared? Little?* He almost
cracked a smile. From what he could tell so far, she
wouldn't like being referred to as either.

Compared with his six-foot-two frame, most people
would be considered small. Besides, it was normal to
feel something for a woman in her circumstances. He
wouldn't be human if his protective instincts didn't flare
every time he saw the bruising on what would otherwise be considered silky, delicate skin. A woman like
her should be cherished, not beaten.

The thought of the men in the parking lot waiting
to make sure those hazel eyes closed permanently so-
bered Reed's thoughts. "How are you really feeling?"

A small woman in a white coat pushed past the nurse
and introduced herself to Emily before she answered.

Reed sat patiently by as the doctor performed her
exam. Based on how much attention Emily had received
on the scene and when she'd first arrived at the hospital, he figured they wouldn't be letting her go tonight.

Reed had mixed feelings about her release. He
couldn't be certain they were secure here at the facil-
ity—hell, in this town. And yet, she'd been in pretty

bad shape when he found her. He couldn't deny her the medical attention she needed. The crash had made her physical condition even worse. Even if he had wanted to run her in for questioning, he doubted she would've made it through the interrogation without collapsing from exhaustion.

Then again, he knew better than to underestimate the power of fear. And *scared* didn't begin to describe the woman he'd found on the docks.

The doctor scribbled notes on the chart as she examined Emily.

He recognized the bag of saline. Good. She needed hydration, and that would be the quickest way. She'd already gone through a bag during the ambulance ride, according to the EMT. Her skin already looked pinker, livelier.

A nurse gently washed Emily's face and then blotted ointment. "Your sunburn is healing. This'll speed up the process."

Keeping her alive wasn't the only problem Reed had. He needed to see if Dueño's men had broken into Emily's town house and found the passwords.

The doctor abruptly turned on Reed. "I understand you were driving the vehicle before it crashed?"

Reed introduced himself, producing his badge. "That's correct, ma'am. How is she?"

"So far, so good. We won't know the extent of the swelling for another couple of hours." The doctor gently pinched the skin on Emily's forearm. "She's severely dehydrated."

"She went without water for several days."

A look of sympathy crossed the doctor's features. "Then we'll want to keep her on the IVs, slowly introduce her to solid food." She turned to the nurse. "Start with a clear liquid diet, advance to full liquids, soft and then regular."

"She managed to eat half a hamburger earlier."

"That's encouraging."

"How soon will she recover?"

"Good question. A lot depends on her. But because of the smoke inhalation, I'm apprehensive. She's been having some difficulty breathing due to a swollen respiratory tract. Since she's getting to the ER so late, I'll want to keep her overnight at a minimum to ensure the swelling subsides. We need to keep a read on her arterial blood gases, too."

Reed's lips compressed in a frown. He leaned closer to the doctor when he said, "Doesn't sound good."

"My inspection of her airway is encouraging. Edema is minimal—"

Reed must've given her a look without realizing it because the doctor stopped midsentence.

"The swelling isn't bad. Of course, with any smoke inhalation I'm concerned about the swelling increasing in twenty-four to forty-eight hours. I'm holding off on intubation for now. I'll be keeping a close eye on her, though. Any movement there and I'll have no choice. I've already given her a dose of steroids, and the nurse will give her a bronchodilator treatment."

The thought she needed help to keep her throat from swelling shut didn't encourage Reed. "What about her other injuries?"

"We won't know until we dig a little deeper. I'll send in a tech to take her for X-rays after her breathing treatment."

"I'm responsible for her safety. Any chance I can tag along?"

"Shouldn't be a problem. I'll make a note on her file." The doctor's gaze intensified on Reed. "How about you? Mind if I take a look while you're here?"

"Me? Nah. I'm fine."

"Looks like your forehead took impact and you have substantial bleeding on your shirt. I'd feel a lot better if you'd let me take a look."

"It's just a scratch."

The doctor held her ground. "Even so, I'd like to examine you while the nurse administers treatment."

Reed focused on Emily, who was being told to inhale medicine from a tube.

The doctor kept her gaze on him. "My brother-in-law is a firefighter. His job is to help everyone else, but he's the last person to ask when he needs it."

"A job hazard," Reed joked, trying to redirect the seriousness of the conversation. "If it'll make you feel better, go ahead."

The doctor examined him, cleaned his cuts and brought in another nurse, instructing her to bandage his wounds.

"I'll check in on you both later," she said before making a move toward the door.

"Can those treatments stop the swelling?" Reed inclined his head toward Emily.

"That's the hope," the doctor said. "Like I said, we'll have to keep her overnight for observation to be sure."

Reed hoped they had that long. He didn't like feeling this exposed, and he couldn't be sure he could trust local police. Aches and pains from the day hit hard and fast. His brother would arrive in a few hours and then Reed could get some rest.

Until then, he didn't plan to take his eyes off Emily.

* * *

Whatever the doctor had ordered was working wonders on Emily. Her head had stopped pounding, and her body didn't feel as if she'd been run through a cheese grater any longer. News about the results from the X-rays had been promised.

A glance at the clock said she'd been in the hospital for two hours already. Had she dozed off?

She didn't dare move for fear she'd wake the agent slumped in the chair next to her bed. He needed rest.

Other than a bandage on his forehead and chest, he'd refused medical treatment. He'd taken the nurse up on her offer of soap, a washcloth and dental supplies. He'd washed in the bathroom and stripped down to a basic white T-shirt he'd borrowed from one of the orderlies before leaning back in the lounge chair and closing his eyes. His T was the only thing basic about him. His job would require a toned body. One glance at the muscled agent said he took his profession seriously.

His rock-hard abs moved up and down with every even breath he took. The rest of him was just as solid and in control.

Emily reached for the water he'd placed near her head on the cart next to her.

"How was your nap?"

She suppressed a yelp. "You startled me."

"Sorry."

"I thought you were out." She took a sip.

"I'm a light sleeper."

Of course he was. A man who was always prepared for the worst-case scenario wouldn't zone out completely. "How long have you been in your job?"

"Six years."

Emily had been in her job half that time. She worried the only steady thing in her life would be gone by the time she returned to Plano.

But a man who looked like Reed Campbell must have a wife waiting for him. "The hours have to be difficult on your family."

"You might be surprised. One of my brothers is a US marshal, the other is FBI." He cracked a smile, and her heart skipped a beat. "My sisters aren't much better. One's a police officer in Plano and the other's a victims' rights advocate for the sheriff. Guess you could say law enforcement runs in our blood."

"Wow. That's impressive. I was actually thinking about your wife and kids."

He shook his head. "No wife. No kids."

"A committed bachelor?"

"No time."

She almost believed him, until the corner of his full lip curled. Surely, a tough and strong man who looked like him attracted plenty of women. "Are you teasing?"

"It's been a tough day." He scrubbed a hand over the scruff on his face. Lightness left his expression. "How are you holding up, really?"

"They seem to be patching me up okay." Why couldn't she admit how much pain she was actually in or how scared she was about her future? A part of her wanted to believe the agent cared how she was actually doing, and not just making polite conversation, or ensuring his witness could testify. Besides, she couldn't remember the last time she'd opened up to someone. Heck, she'd made herself a loner at the House when she wasn't feeding or bathing one of her half siblings. She'd skillfully hidden behind attending to them. "I took a few bumps. I'll be good as new by morning."

He shot her a look. "Okay, tough guy. I'm not buying that."

Most likely, he needed to assess her condition to see if she was stable enough to travel or go on the run. Duh. What a dummy. She'd almost convinced herself the hunky agent actually cared about her. Wow, she must've taken more damage to the head than she realized. "He'll come for me here, won't he?"

He eyed her for a long moment without speaking. "Suspicious men are already stationed outside."

Was he trying to figure out if he could trust her? "I know my story sounds crazy."

"I've heard worse."

Of course he had in his line of work. "Maybe it just sounds bizarre in my head."

"It's normal to need a minute to let this sink in. Your world was just turned on its head. It'll take a bit to absorb. Don't be hard on yourself. I've seen grown men buckle under lesser circumstances."

Was that a hint of pride in his brilliant brown eyes? Or was she seeing something she wanted to see instead of reality? This was most likely the speech he gave to all the victims he came across. *Victim?* The word sat bitterly on her tongue. She may have had a rough childhood and she might be in sticky circumstances now, but no way was she a helpless victim. "This might sound weird. I mean, we've only just met. But, I feel like I *know* you."

"We've been through hell and back. It forms a bond." A wide smile broke across white teeth, shattering his serious persona.

Emily forced her gaze from his lips.

Chapter 6

Experience had taught Emily the best way to dispel the mystery of someone was the reality of getting to know them. And the last thing she needed was for the agent to realize she was attracted to him. Heck, she'd wanted to crawl under the bed and hide earlier when he walked in the room and she grinned like an idiot. Hopefully, she'd reined it in before she'd made a complete fool out of herself. "You said earlier that you came from a big family?"

"You'll meet one of my brothers in an hour. Luke's the one who works for the FBI." Reed popped to his feet and walked to the window, his thigh muscles pressing against his jeans as they stretched. He had the power and athletic grace of a predator closing in on its meal. His gaze narrowed as he peered out the window.

"Maybe the doctor will let me go tomorrow." She

glanced at the door and back to Reed. "It doesn't seem safe for us here."

"All I need for you to do is rest and get as strong as you can." He didn't say because they might need to bolt at any moment, although the tension radiating from his body told her exactly what he was thinking.

"What about you? You ever sleep?"

"Not much when I'm working on a case. Speaking of which, we should talk about yours." He moved back to his seat, but positioned himself on the edge and rested his elbows on his knees.

"You already know I work at a computer company. That pretty much sums up my life. I'm in line for a promotion, so I've been working nonstop for months. It's part of why I panicked when you called my boss." Telling the handsome agent work was all she had, made her life sound incredibly small and empty. Speaking of which, what would Jared think when she showed up to work Monday looking as if she'd been the warm-up punching bag for an MMA fighter? Her boss was a climber, and she knew he used her to do much of his own work under the guise of training her. Was there any way to finagle more time off without jeopardizing her position?

A lump of dread sat in her stomach. How could she go back at all now? With a man like Dueño chasing her, would she even be able to pick up her old life where she'd left off? She focused on the agent. "How do we keep me alive?"

"I could talk to my brother Nick about witness protection. He's a US marshal."

And leave behind everything she'd worked for? It was sad that her first thought was dreading having to start all over with a new job, and not that she'd be leaving her friends and family behind. A bitter stab of loneliness pierced the center of Emily's chest.

Her reaction must've been written all over her face because Reed was on his feet, his gaze locked on hers. "It's just an option. I'm not saying we have to go through with it. I wouldn't be able to leave my family behind, either."

At least he couldn't read her mind. A man like him with more family around than he could count wouldn't understand her desperation at leaving behind the only thing she'd ever been able to count on. Work. The sadness in that thought weighted her limbs. Emily refused to give in, crossing her arms.

"It's okay. It's a reasonable option. I should definitely give it some serious consideration." She hoped the agent didn't pick up on the fact there was no emotion in those last words.

"I just thought we should explore every possibility of keeping you safe until we can put this jerk behind bars." Whereas her words might've lacked emotion, the venom in his when he said the word *jerk* was its own presence in the room.

Emily had always believed that she was making the best out of the situation she'd been handed. Being successful at work was so much less complicated than dealing with people and especially family. She'd never minded being alone before. In fact, she'd preferred it. So why did it suddenly feel like a death sentence?

Wasn't getting the chance for a new identity, a fresh start in life, the ideal solution to many of her problems? As much as she didn't want to leave the life she'd built in Plano, the option had to be considered. "How does witness protection work exactly?"

"We could talk to my brother to get all the facts, but you'd be assigned to a US marshal who'd become responsible for giving you a new identity, a place to live and a job somewhere no one would know to look for you."

"And contact with my family?"

His gaze dropped to the floor. "I'm afraid that's not possible."

Even though she spoke to her mother only a few times a year, Emily couldn't imagine cutting off that last little connection to her past, to her. "And what if that's not possible?"

"Do you remember anything about the person who did this to you?"

"No. I didn't see him at all. They were careful about protecting him. All I heard was his voice. I'd know that sound if I heard it again." She paused a beat. "Which isn't much to go on, is it?"

"It's something," he said encouragingly.

"Not enough for an arrest, though, let alone a conviction."

He didn't make eye contact when he said, "No. But maybe you can lead us to his hideout. We've already been able to pinpoint the area of abduction, and these guys tend to be territorial."

She told him the name of the resort where she'd stayed, and everything else she could remember about her abduction, which was precious little since she'd been blindfolded most of the time. "That's where it gets even worse. I mean, I wish I could give you more to work with. I was blindfolded for much of the walk, which felt like it took forever."

"These guys are professionals. It's not your fault. We have the location of your abduction. They didn't take you anywhere by plane, right?"

"No. We walked the entire time."

"That gives us a starting point."

"Except that we could've been walking in circles for all I knew."

"Believe it or not, you've narrowed down the possibilities with what you've told me so far. It's a start." Reed stabbed his fingers through his thick dark hair. "Anyone have a spare key to your town house?"

Like a friend? Emily almost choked on her own laughter—laughter that she held deep inside because if it came out, so would the onslaught of tears. "No."

His dark brow arched. "Not even a neighbor or your landlord?"

"I own it." Emily didn't address the bit about the neighbor. She didn't want to admit she didn't know the people who lived around her. A casualty of working too many long nights and weekends, she decided. Her life had never seemed empty to her before, so why did it now? Without her job, her career, it would be.

She'd worked too hard to let it all be taken away by some crazed criminal. What if she told her boss about the car crash? Maybe she could convince Jared to give her an extended leave of absence and save her job. It wasn't as if she took days off. With her rollover vacation days, she could take off two months. That might give the agent a chance to catch Dueño, and she could restore her life. She might have invested a lot of time in her work, but it was all she had. And if Jared asked too many questions or figured out her half-truth, she might not have that anymore. Maybe she could tell him what had happened. On second thought, there was no gray area with Jared. How many times had he fired someone for a slight infraction? Even though she hadn't broken any company rules, he would assume she'd done something to bring this on herself. He'd start viewing her as a threat to the company and find a reason to get rid of her.

The thought of giving up everything she'd worked for sucked all the air out of her lungs. Hadn't she fought long and hard to put down roots? Her place in Texas was home. "It seems like witness protection is my only option, but what if I don't want it?"

Reed ran a hand over the scruff on his chin. "We catch this guy and you're home free. Otherwise, we wait it out and keep you safe. My experience with men like these is that they have a short memory. If I can get you safely through a few weeks, you should be in the clear."

Was returning to her life in a few weeks really an option? Surely, she could get that much time off. The first real spark of hope in days lit inside her. Maybe she wouldn't have to give up the only life that felt like hers. "What if these people are different and don't mind waiting it out? How will we know for sure?"

The intensity in his brown eyes increased. "My brother Nick is digging deeper to find out their story. He'll be able to tell us what we're facing. My plan is to catch them and put them in jail where they belong."

"I could make up a story for my boss. Take time off."

Reed gave her a look as if he understood. Did he? No way could he get that she wasn't staying because of family or friends. He probably had more of those than he could count, too. How did she tell someone who had so many relationships worth living for the real reason she wanted to keep her life was because of her work? Or maybe she needed to dig in and fight for the small life she had. There wasn't much else she could be sure of right now except that she couldn't bear the thought of losing everything again as she had when she was a little girl and the only life she'd ever known had been stripped away from her. "Things get too intense, can I change my mind?"

"WitSec will always be an option."

"And what about you? What will happen to you if I go in?" She hadn't considered the agent before. Wouldn't her going into the program take him out of the line of fire? "I don't want to put you in any more danger."

"This is my job. Besides, I want to catch this son of a bitch as much as you."

Whether Emily went into WitSec or not, Reed had every intention of seeing this case through to the end. A bad agent had infected the agency. Reed needed to find out who before someone else got shot, or worse, killed.

At least Emily's story had checked out with her boss. Reed had almost asked his brother to investigate her background. He was still scratching his head as to why he hadn't. The only people he didn't run background checks on were the women he dated, which put him in unfamiliar territory with his witness. He'd have to gain her trust and actually have a conversation with her to find out what he wanted to know. And then, he'd have to trust she'd told the truth.

Trust? Interesting word. Other than his boss, Reed hadn't trusted anyone who didn't share his last name in the past year. He was bad at it. And yet, gaining hers might be the key to unlocking who in his agency was involved in this. He'd always suspected Cal wasn't the only bad crop in the garden.

Reed could give up a little about himself if it meant advancing his case. There were other reasons compelling him to open up a little to this witness, too. None of which he wanted to explore. The image of her smile— the one like when he'd first walked in—stamped his thoughts. She'd suppressed it faster than a squirrel hides its supper, but for the second it was there, her whole face shone. "Someone in my agency is corrupt. I have every intention of finding out who they are and bringing them to justice."

Her gaze intensified. "That part of your code of honor?"

"It's more than that." Uneasy and unsure if he was about to do the right thing, he pulled up his T-shirt and turned to let her see the scar on his left shoulder.

"Ohmygosh. What happened to you?" The warmth in her voice would melt an iceberg.

It drew him in and made him want to connect with it. He lowered the hem of his shirt and returned to his spot on the edge of the chair, making sure he maintained visual contact with the door in his peripheral. The thought of discussing what had happened to him a year ago parked an RV on his chest.

He took a breath and shoved past the feeling. "While on a case a year ago, I got a hot tip on a kidnapping ring. Young girls were being snatched, shuffled across the border and sold before their parents even knew they were missing. Heard a few were holed up and drugged in a house near the border. I'd been tracking a coyote for two years." He paused when her eyebrow shot up. "Human trafficker. Seemed like he knew every time I got close. He'd up and relocate his business. Goes without saying how badly I wanted to put this guy away and toss the key for what he was doing to those young girls. And yet, I was careful not to make a mistake. I was so close I could almost taste it."

"So what happened?"

"This guy had big connections on both sides of the border. He was under the protection of a rebel leader. And that guy had a border patrol agent on his payroll. He discovered I was about to bust the coyote, so… Let's just say I was set up. Wasn't supposed to walk out of the hot spot they'd sent me to. Thought I was close to this guy. Turns out, he was closer to my fiancée."

"Oh." The flash in her eyes went from sympathy to indignant. "Two people you trusted betrayed you? That must make it hard to believe in anyone else."

She had no idea. Or, did she?

There was a subtle lilt to her tone, an unspoken kinship that said she might know exactly what he was talking about. Had someone she'd trusted turned on her? "I spent a little time in a room just like this one. Gave me a lot of time to think. Figure a man should be left alone with his thoughts for about two minutes before he turns against the world."

She didn't laugh at his joke meant to lighten the mood.

"What happened to the people who did that to you?" There was an all-too-familiar anger in her voice now.

"He disappeared across the border before he could be arrested. Someone has him tucked away nicely because not one of our informants has seen him."

"And the woman?"

"Could be with him for all we know." He paused. "She didn't exactly break the law."

"I'm so sorry. Having people you trust turn on you is one thing, but then never having him brought to justice adds a whole new level of unfairness."

The depths of her eyes said she knew about unfair. What had happened in her life for her to be able to sympathize? More questions he didn't have answers to.

A knock at the door brought Reed to his feet, his weapon drawn and leading the way as he stalked toward the entrance to the room.

"There's someone here to see you, Agent Campbell." Reed recognized the voice as belonging to the officer. "His ID says he's Special Agent Luke Campbell."

The past few hours had soared by. What was it about talking to Emily that made time disappear and the ache in his chest lighter?

"My brother's here," Luke said to ease the tension he felt coming from Emily. Her compassion had melted a little of the ice encasing his heart. Relieved for the break, Reed wasn't ready to let anyone inside. And yet, talking to her had come easier than he'd expected. Even more surprising was the fact that he wanted to tell her more.

"Send him in." Reed kept his weapon drawn on the off chance someone other than his brother walked through that door, refusing to be caught off guard again. It was unlikely anyone would know he'd called his brother, but taking chances was for gamblers—and Reed didn't bet on odds.

"It's me." His brother seemed to understand Reed's

apprehension as he walked through the door with his hands up in the universal sign for surrender.

Reed lowered his weapon and returned it to his holster. He greeted his brother with a bear hug and introduced him to Emily, surprised to see a tear roll down her cheek.

"Nice to meet you," she said quickly. Her unreadable expression returned so fast Reed almost thought he'd imagined her brief show of emotion.

Reed caught a glimpse of his brother's reaction to seeing the bruising on her face as Luke handed over the burn phone he'd brought. No Campbell man would take lightly to a woman being beaten, even though they saw it far too often in their lines of work.

"We have a lot of company outside." Luke leaned against the wall near the big window facing the door, and crossed his ankles. Another habit formed on the job—they never put their backs to the door.

"I saw a couple when we came in."

"There's half a dozen now, covering all entrances. One looked twice at me even though I kept my head down." He wore a ball cap, T-shirt and jeans. "I'm guessing they saw the resemblance."

"You two do look a lot alike," Emily agreed.

Reed couldn't argue. So, the men might just think it was Luke leaving when Reed ducked out later. Now that Luke was there, Reed could risk leaving Emily's side without fearing for her safety. "I have to run out in a bit. Mind if we switch hats?"

Luke shook his head and pulled off his ball cap. "Make sure you pull it down low, over your bandage. Looks like you took a pretty good hit."

"I'm fine."

Emily coughed loudly enough to let everyone know she'd done it on purpose. "Um, he pulled me out of a burning car while fighting off men shooting at us. He has to be exhausted. I don't think he should be going anywhere."

Reed had to fist his hands to stop from wiping the smile off his brother's face.

"What did I say?" Emily's gaze bounced from one to the other.

They stood, staring, daring the other to speak first.

"Nothing," Reed said too quickly. He didn't want to share the fact that both of his brothers had fallen in love with women they were protecting. "My brother just has a twisted sense of humor."

Luke turned to her. "I want the same thing you do for my brother."

"Rest?" she asked, puzzled.

"Peace."

When no one explained what Luke meant, Emily shrugged.

Reed handed over his Stetson.

"I think I'm getting the better deal out of this exchange," Luke joked, replacing his ball cap with the white cowboy hat.

"We'd better trade shirts, too," Reed said.

"Can I see you for a second, Reed?" Emily asked. "Privately?"

Luke's gaze locked onto Reed's. He nodded.

His brother excused himself to the bathroom.

"Everything okay?" The fear Emily's condition was getting worse gripped Reed faster than if he'd walked into an intersection and had been hit by a bus.

"Come closer?"

Reed moved to the side of her bed.

She patted the sheets, and he took her cue to sit down next to her. The nurse had helped her shower, and Emily looked even more beautiful. This close, she smelled clean and flowery.

"I'm scared." The words came out in a whisper.

Those fearful hazel eyes were back, the ones threatening to crack more of the ice encasing his heart, and his pulse raced.

For lack of a better way to offer reassurance, he bent down and gently kissed her forehead. "My brother's the best. You'll be safe."

She shook her head, her gaze locked onto his the whole time. "I know. I'm afraid for you."

The warmth of a thousand campfires flooded his chest. Hell's bells. What was he supposed to do with that?

He opened his mouth to speak, but her hands were already tunneled into his hair, urging him closer. Last thing he wanted to do was hurt her, so he stopped the second their lips touched, waiting for a sign from her she was still okay.

Her tongue darted inside his mouth, and he had to remind himself not to take control. She knew what she could handle, what hurt, so he momentarily surrendered to her judgment, careful not to apply any more pressure than she could handle.

Those soft pink lips of hers nearly did him in. Every muscle in his body was strung so tight he thought they might snap. He wanted more.

For her, he would hold back.

As her tongue searched inside his mouth, he brought his hands up to cup her face.

A noise from the bathroom caused Reed to pull back first.

Emily brought her hand up to her lips, her nervous "tell." "I'm sorry. I probably shouldn't have done that."

"It's a good thing you did."

She smiled and those thousand campfires burst into flames.

"I know you're going to search down the agent who called before everything went crazy."

He didn't deny it.

"Just be careful. And come back." The sincerity in her eyes nearly knocked him back. Her concern was outlined in the wrinkles in her forehead.

He bent down and kissed them. Then he feathered kisses on the tip of her nose, her eyelids.

Not a lot made sense to him right now except this moment happening between them. Underneath the bruises and the bad bleach job, there was a beautiful woman.

And he was a man.

Their lives had been in danger and they'd both nearly been killed today.

Reed couldn't be sure if this was the beginning of real sparks between the two of them or if the attraction was down to basic primal urges and they both needed proof of life, but for a split second, his defenses lowered and she inched inside his heart.

Chapter 7

The faucet turned on in the bathroom, and Reed heard the rush of water in the sink. He figured it was Luke's polite way of saying he was done hiding.

Reed needed to get moving, anyway. He stood. "All clear."

Emily blinked up at him. "Remember what I said."

"Try to get some rest." He grazed the soft skin of her arm with the tip of his finger. He needed to catch these guys and give Emily her life back.

She closed her eyes and smiled.

"Here's what you need to know before you head out." Luke quietly reentered the room. "Dueño is believed to be a ghost. No one's seen him. Some people aren't even sure if he exists, but if something's illegal and it touches South America, his name shows up every time."

Emily blinked her eyes open. "I've seen him. He's real."

"Our lowlife owns those distribution channels?" Reed asked.

"The guy can get any product moved for a price." Luke's gaze moved from Emily to Reed. "Makes a lot of money on women and children."

Reed muttered a curse. "What else?"

"Like I mentioned, he stays out of the spotlight. No one's seen him. He's like a damn phantom."

"So he likes to hide. Makes it easier to stay under the radar that way."

"And harder to convict," Luke agreed. "He has several high-ranking lieutenants. Marco Delgado, Julian Escado and Jesus Ramirez are at the top."

"I've heard of Ramirez, but not the others. His name was associated with Cal's, but I thought he worked alone."

"I remember. Dueño set up the teams in supercells, so they'd be harder to trace back to him. This group plays their cards close to their vest. Nick found out they have a meeting once a year at Dueño's compound to discuss business. Other than that, there's no communication."

"Makes it hard to track their activity back to him."

"And that's one of the biggest benefits. Has its risks, too."

Reed rocked his head. "Any one of them could go rogue and Dueño wouldn't know about it for a while."

"The lieutenants know each other, obviously, but the men in the ranks don't know they all work in the same organization. Word on the street is that these three are heads of their own groups. Members view each other as competition."

"A misunderstanding and they could end up killing

one of their own without knowing it." Reed rubbed the scruff on his chin.

"True."

"If they think they're turning in a rival, we might get them to talk about each other." Reed pinched the bridge of his nose to stem the dull ache forming. This was bigger than he'd imagined. Emily was in grave danger. "Do the low-ranking guys know about the summit?"

"Some do. They think the guys are meeting next week to agree on territory."

"We might be able to get one of our informants to speak. Any idea where this compound is located?"

"Unfortunately, no. It's impossible to get anyone to talk. They're afraid of repercussion. The organization is well run."

"We might know a link. An agent phoned after I pulled away from the docks, asking if he could take her in for me." Reed stopped long enough to pace. "Besides, men who run things for others get greedy. They end up asking why they should do all the work for someone else's gain. Maybe we can figure out a way to pit them against each other."

"Your guy might be the connection we're looking for." Luke grabbed his keys and tossed them to Reed with a grin. "Bring it back in one piece. You know how I love that truck."

"We'll see." Reed glanced at Emily, again thankful her eyes were closed and her breath even. "Take care of her. She's been through a lot."

"You know I will, baby bro."

Reed hugged his brother, the manly kind of hug with backslaps.

Keeping his head low, he tucked his hands in his

front jeans pockets and strolled down the hall. Dueño's men would have all the exits covered. The trick would be getting to Luke's truck without being noticed.

It was long past midnight. The darkness should help. Although, it also meant there'd be fewer people coming in and out of the hospital.

Reed took the stairs to the bottom floor and, by memory, located the ER. There was no one in the long hallway leading to the parking lot where he'd initially entered the building. An eerie quiet settled over him.

The click of his boots was the only sound as he entered the sterile white passage.

Going outside without a cover was a bad idea. Last thing he needed was someone following him. Maybe he could grab some coffee in the waiting room, bide his time until someone left.

An agonizing forty-three minutes later, he got his chance as a family left with their teenager. His arm was heavily bandaged, and his washed-out expression said he'd most likely been drinking and had done something stupid to get hurt. The young man had to be six foot and close to two hundred pounds. He took after his father. The pair should offer plenty of cover.

Reed shadowed the family, breaking off in the parking lot as he ducked in between two cars. He located his brother's truck, which was exactly where he'd said it would be. Reed kept his head down as he climbed in the cab. His thoughts focused on Agent Stephen Taylor—get to him and find the answers.

He located the family's car as they pulled out of the parking lot and followed.

A quick call to his boss on the burn phone Luke had provided and Reed had Gil updated and working on finding Agent Taylor's home address inside of ten minutes. Double that, and Luke was on the expressway, blending in to his surroundings. His tail had given up fifteen minutes ago, figuring, as Reed had hoped, that he was part of the family leaving and not a person of interest. It most likely hadn't hurt that Luke had come in twenty minutes before Reed left.

No matter how quickly he returned to the hospital, his sense of unease about leaving would still produce a lump in his gut. Even though Luke was capable of handling any situation he encountered, he was one man and these guys had brought an army.

Emily's bruised face and vulnerable eyes pierced his thoughts.

His cell buzzed and he realized how tightly he'd been gripping the steering wheel. The text came. Stephen Taylor's address. Reed pulled off the highway and plugged in the location to Luke's GPS.

Another fifteen minutes and Reed was in the neighborhood.

Taylor's street was dark, save for a streetlight next to his house. Reed crept past the front of the one-story ranch house and then rounded the block. There could be a fortress inside and Taylor could be waiting. No doubt, he'd be on edge if he was close to Dueño.

Reed shut off his lights and parked down the street. He put on the Kevlar vest in the backseat of the cab, and then palmed his weapon.

With his Glock leveled and leading the way, he moved along the shrubbery, saying a little prayer no dogs would bark.

The home was a simple brick ranch. More details about Taylor came through via text. Turned out, Taylor had a wife and a baby. He was the last person Reed would suspect to be dirty but then again he had no idea what the guy's personal situation was, and greed was a powerful motivator. Cases like these had a color. Green.

None of this place fit. This was a nice middle-class neighborhood. Wouldn't a dirty agent live in a nicer house? There was nothing wrong with this one, but it was definitely something Taylor could afford on his own. He didn't need a side income for this. If an agent was dirty, there were clues. They'd live in a house clearly above their pay grade or have expensive hobbies, such as collecting sports cars.

Maybe the guy was in debt. He could have a sick kid or a gambling problem. If he was really smart, he'd give the appearance of living off his means and sock the money away for the future. Men who planned for the long-term usually had more sense than to get involved with criminals.

Blackmail? There were other possibilities Reed considered as he surveyed the perimeter, allowing his eyes the chance to adjust to the dark. The curtains in the living room had been left open. The slats in the two-inch wood blinds provided enough of a gap to get a clear view into the living room. Nothing stood out. The furnishings were simple and had a woman's touch. A baby swing, playpen and toys crowded the place. Not one thing looked out of the ordinary for a young family of three.

Reed could plainly see through to the back door into the kitchen. No keypad for an alarm system. He changed his vantage point. No sign of one near the front door, either.

No alarm system. No dog. No real security.

He'd expected the guy to be paranoid.

Another piece of the puzzle that didn't fit.

Reed ran his hand along the windowsills, looking for a good place to enter the home. He didn't care how careful this guy was. Reed had every intention of getting answers tonight.

The windows and doors were all locked. Twelve windows and two doors were possible exit points. Reed peeked in each, memorizing the layout before returning to his spot. The front door was made of solid wood, which made it difficult to breach without making too much noise. Reed's best bet would be to enter through the kitchen. The top half of the door was glass. He shucked the vest, and took off his T-shirt and wrapped it around his hand like tape on a boxer's fist.

A dog barked. Reed bit out a curse and worked faster. No way was he leaving without questioning Taylor. This guy was the ticket to putting the puzzle pieces together. Memories of the night Reed was shot flooded him. Reed battled to force them away and stay focused.

He punched through the glass and then unlocked the door. A few seconds later, his T-shirt and Kevlar was on. He wasn't taking another chance with a dirty agent.

The house was quiet save for the ticking clock hanging on the wall in the kitchen. Reed cleared the room and rounded the corner toward the bedrooms, his weapon leading the way, and froze. From three feet away, the business end of a Glock was aimed at his face, most likely right between his eyes.

"What are you doing here, Agent Campbell?" Stephen asked.

"Put your gun down and I'll explain." Reed intentionally kept his voice calm and low.

"Not until you tell me what's going on." Stephen's hands shook and he didn't lower his weapon.

Reed leveled his, aiming for the chest. Stephen wore pajama pants and a T-shirt. He hadn't had time to put on his Kevlar. One shot and his chest would have a hole. Reed said a silent prayer he'd get his shot off first. Kevlar didn't help with a bullet in the head. Both were trained shooters, a requirement of the job. "We need to talk."

"In the middle of the night? What the hell could be this important?"

Neither made a move to put down his weapon.

"It's about the woman." Reed took a step back, inching toward the corner, anything that could be a barrier or slow down a bullet. If this guy was in league with a man like Dueño, he'd have no problem doing away with anyone or anything that got in his way. And yet, nothing about his house said he was on the take. There were signs with Cal. He'd driven a fifty-thousand-dollar car. Lived in a neighborhood a little too pricey for his pay grade. He'd chalked it all up to rich parents and a partial trust fund. If anyone had bothered to take a closer look or check his file, they'd have realized his parents were blue-collar workers from Brownsville. But then, it wasn't as if Cal had invited anyone from the department over to his place for backyard barbecues. And he'd been smart about it. He lived in a nice house but not so expensive it would draw attention.

None of those signs was present here at Stephen's. His place looked as if he lived on the paycheck provided by the agency. Then again, looks could be deceiving. He'd also believed his fiancée when she'd said there was nothing going on between Cal and her.

Stephen stepped forward. "What are you talking about?"

"You called me earlier this afternoon. Asked to run in my witness for me."

"Yeah. So what? Thought I was doing you a favor."

Right. Reed wasn't about to let Stephen off with that pat answer. "Since when would anyone want to take on filling out someone else's paperwork?"

Stephen didn't respond. Reed was pretty certain if he could peel back the guy's skull Reed would see fireworks going off in there.

"You plan to shoot me?" he hedged.

"Not unless you fire first."

"Then why don't we both put our weapons down and talk?" In a show of good faith, Reed lowered his first. He was close enough to the corner to make a fast break if this didn't go as planned.

Stephen lowered his weapon at the same time a baby wailed in the next room. On edge, he bit out a curse and shot a stern look to Reed. "Wait here. And don't you move."

"I'm not going anywhere until I get answers." Reed tucked his gun in his holster, and then crossed his arms over his chest.

"Good." He moved to the end of the hall where the master bedroom was located. "Kiera, the baby's up. I'm in the kitchen with a work friend, and we need to finish our business."

Reed didn't hear her response, but she must've agreed because Stephen turned his attention back to Reed and urged him into the kitchen.

"What the hell's going on?" Stephen asked. Confusion mixed with the daggers being shot from his glare.

"You tell me."

"Tell you what?" he parroted.

"Why'd you feel the need to relieve me of my passenger?" Reed followed Stephen's gaze to the broken glass on the kitchen floor.

"Great." He moved to the pantry, retrieved a broom and started sweeping up the shards. "My baby plays on this floor. And, my wife is going to be pissed when she sees this. You know, you could've knocked."

Well, hell in a handbasket, Reed really was mixed up now. "Stop sweeping and fill me in."

"My wife'll be in to get a bottle, so I can't stop sweeping. She's going to be pissed enough as it is."

Nothing about Stephen's actions said he was anything but a family man. Reed sighed sharply. "If you didn't want my witness, why'd you call and ask for her?"

The sound of crying intensified. Stephen glanced toward the hall. "Grab a bottle from the fridge, and put it in the microwave for a minute and a half."

Reed did as he was told, sticking the glass bottle in the microwave.

"Take the lid off first. Don't you know anything about babies?" Stephen's pleading look would've been funny under different circumstances. Even a tough guy like him seemed to know better than to anger his wife.

"Okay." When his task was finished, he handed the offering to Stephen. "Done. Now talk."

Stephen's wife walked in, baby on hip, wearing a robe. She'd be all of five foot two if she had heels on. She was pretty, blonde. Her gaze bounced from the floor to Reed, and then to her husband. "What's going on? Why is he here in the middle of the night?"

This was all wrong. The house. The wife. The baby. What in hell's kitchen was going on?

"Here you go, honey." Stephen handed her the bottle. "It involves an active case, so I can't talk about it. But I'll be in bed before you put the baby down."

She took the bottle. The crying baby immediately settled the second he tasted milk. Warmth flooded Reed and his heart stirred.

He shook off the momentary weakness, attributing it to the fact that yesterday had been the anniversary of his planned wedding with Leslie. Her betrayal had come the month before. Infidelity had a way of changing people's courses.

Kiera eyed her husband for a long moment then, on her tiptoes, kissed his cheek. "Don't be too long."

He bent down and kissed her forehead before planting another on his baby's cheek.

Her gaze narrowed when it landed on Reed. "I suspect you know how to use a door to get out?"

"Yes, ma'am." A moment of embarrassment hit. He'd acted on facts. He refused to wallow in guilt if he'd been wrong. Too many lives were at stake.

When she was safely out of earshot, Stephen continued, "Shane put me up to calling you. Said he needed your help on a case he was working, and that I should call you to see if I could take over for you. Said you were working on a routine immigration case."

"Shane Knox? He sure didn't let me in on it."

"Why would he do that?" Stephen's gaze was full of accusation now.

The weight of the conversation sat heavy on Reed's chest. "Because he's dirty."

"Hold on. That's a serious accusation. What makes you think that's the case?"

"I know."

"Then you need to fill me in."

Reed lifted the ball cap to reveal the bandage on his forehead. "Minutes after you made that call I was shot at before being run off the road. My Jeep caught fire."

More fireworks had to be going off in Stephen's brain based on the intensity of his eyes. "What happened to your witness?"

"She's in the hospital, but she'll be okay. The wreck was bad, but she'd been beaten up pretty badly before then."

"And Knox is connected to the initial incident?"

"As far as I know." Reed studied Stephen. "You called. I was run off the road."

"If they were coming after you, why have me call?" He snaked his fingers through his hair. "Never mind. I know. He was hoping to have her handed over to me. But why? I wouldn't have turned her over to him."

"He must've planned to follow you to the handoff so he could find us. He'd already sent men hunting for me, I'm sure of that."

"We traded vehicles a couple of weeks ago. He still has a few things in there. Must've left something in there he can track. Or he figured I wouldn't be suspicious if he stopped me somewhere along the way. You'd be leery after what you've been through. Or, maybe he planned to run me off the road instead."

"They want her alive. She has passwords to a computer. Or at least they think she does, which no longer matters because whether she produces them or not, they'll kill her." Reed rubbed the scruff on his chin.

Dueño had gone to great lengths to hide his identity. Emily was the only person on the outside who'd heard his voice or could prove his existence. There was no doubt in his mind she'd been marked for death. The phone in his pocket vibrated. He fished it out and checked the text. As he made a run for the door, he said, "Something's going down at the hospital."

"Which one?" Stephen opened a drawer and pulled out an AR-15.

"ClearPond Hospital on I-45." Reed bolted out the door.

Stephen followed. "Then you're going to need backup."

"I appreciate it." Luke's message said the lights had gone out on the sixth floor, Emily's floor. Luke was smart enough to see it for what it was. But was Emily strong enough to move?

Without selling his brother short, Reed figured it'd be difficult to haul her away and fight off whoever had decided to breach the building.

He cursed Knox as he hopped into his brother's truck and fired up the engine, grateful for the help loading into the passenger's side.

Reed couldn't allow himself to consider the possibility that he wouldn't make it back to the hospital in time.

Chapter 8

The door opened to Emily's room. Blackness surrounded her. Even with her hand stuck out flat, directly in front of her face, she couldn't see it.

"I'm to your right," Luke whispered, touching her arm.

An officer identified himself, flashing a light on his face. "Hospital security wants to move her to another room. They've established a safe route for us."

Luke squeezed her arm, but said nothing.

"Okay," she agreed.

"We'll unhook you from these machines to make it easier to transport you, okay?" the nurse said as she brushed against Emily's other side.

The beam of light transferred to her, and Emily saw fearful eyes.

"Sounds good. Do I have time to get dressed?"

"I'm afraid n—"

"She does," Luke interrupted, handing her a folded stack. "I brought fresh clothes."

As the tubes were unhooked, one by one, Emily pulled on a pair of jeans that fit perfectly and a V-neck cotton shirt. Thankfully, they'd let her keep her bra and underwear on earlier, and the dark had shielded her.

"You're good to go. Be careful. Those first few steps can be tricky," the nurse said.

"I will. Thank you."

"I'll try to find you later," the nurse whispered so quietly Emily barely heard.

Something hard, made of metal, was pressed to her hand. It had to be a weapon of some sort from the nurse.

The door opened again and footsteps grew distant.

Standing, Emily leaned against Luke for support and took a few tentative steps.

"I gotcha. Don't worry. I won't let you fall," he said.

She wanted to warn Luke. The nurse wouldn't have given her a weapon unless she'd wanted Emily to be able to defend herself. The hospital had been informed about the need for tight security. This instrument was more than a warning.

"Ready, ma'am?" the officer asked.

"Yes." How could she get the message to Luke without broadcasting it?

"Then, follow me."

An occasional beam of light could be seen in front of them as they followed behind the officer.

Emily tugged at Luke's sleeve. He squeezed her arm in response. Good, he knew she wanted to communicate something to him. She placed the metal object in his hand. He took it, squeezed again.

The floor was calm. Too quiet. Where were the other

patients? Nurses? How would Reed know where they'd been moved? She remembered Luke had sent a text to his brother earlier.

Fear of not knowing where Reed was or when he'd return sent icy chills down her back. And where did these guys plan to take her? Hadn't she overhead Reed telling his brother that they couldn't trust anyone?

At least she'd had a chance to rest. Her knees were less wobbly with every step. She was gaining her bearings. She'd be ready to fight. *Might have to be.*

The officer turned right, his flashlight illuminating a long hallway.

Luke urged her to veer left. Almost the second he dropped her hand, she heard a shuffle. Then a quiet thud. She couldn't yell for help or she'd alert everyone. She said a silent protection prayer instead.

When a hand gripped her arm, she bit down a yelp.

"It's me," Luke whispered, guiding her through the hallway in the dark.

Walking proved challenging, let alone navigating through the blackness all around them.

A little piece of her feared she'd never see Reed again. But now, all she could focus on was getting out of the building alive.

What if they didn't make it? Outside had more men, more danger, more risk. Even if they hid, and gave Reed a road map to find them, how would he get through?

A wave of hopelessness washed over her as pain ripped through her thighs. Moving hurt.

Commotion from behind caused her heart to skip a beat. She heard at least three voices firing words in Spanish.

"I don't know what happened. They were behind me

one second, the next I was on the floor." The voice was familiar, the police officer.

If Dueño had locals in his pocket, how would she and Luke make it out of this building alive? The irony of being killed in a hospital where people were brought back from the jaws of death on a daily basis hit her hard. Who would take care of her mother when she needed help? What about her other siblings? Would anyone other than her boss even know she'd died? Would anyone care?

Jared would notice only if she didn't show for work Monday. Her mortgage company would figure out she wasn't keeping up with her payments after a month or two. Eventually, they'd foreclose. At least she existed on paper.

But would anyone *really* know she was gone? Would anyone miss her?

Suddenly, for the first time in her life, she felt an overwhelming urge to be with someone who cared, with Reed.

The probability he would be able to find them was low. Sure, they could text their location, but that didn't mean he'd get through the militia waiting in the parking lot or the hallway.

Luke stopped and turned, pausing for a moment. Then a door opened and he guided her inside to a corner where she eased down. Pain shot through her thighs. The room had to be small because she'd taken only a couple of steps. A supply room?

The door closed.

"We can hide here for a little while," Luke said. His phone appeared. He covered the screen with one hand, allowing enough light to figure out where they were and thumbed a text with the other.

"Where are we? Don't they lock these doors?" Her guess of being in a supply room was dead-on.

"Supply closet. The nurse handed me the key. I'm guessing she knew what was going on."

"Explains why she gave me the piece of metal, whatever that was."

"She tipped me off that the officer wasn't there to help. Came in handy when I subdued him."

"How so? I didn't see a thing."

"She whispered when she walked past me."

"I heard the officer's voice back there. I'm guessing he'll live."

"A bullet would've made too much noise." The calm practicality in his voice when talking about killing someone was a stark reminder she wasn't remotely connected to the world she knew or understood anymore.

The snick of a lock cut through the quiet. Luke squeezed her arm and then let go, presumably to ready his weapon.

"Don't shoot. It's me. I was your floor nurse."

"How did you get in? I thought you gave Luke your key," Emily said.

"I'm the floor supervisor. I have a spare. Besides, when I noticed the men talking to the officer, I knew something was suspicious."

"Ever think about changing professions?" Luke asked. "You'd make a great cop."

"I'm addicted to all those crime shows on TV." She snickered quietly then suppressed it. "Figured you might need some help."

"Believe me, it's appreciated. And, believe me, I'm glad you're on my side."

"I hoped I'd find you in here. An officer pulled me away as soon as you left the room. I barely got away. Since I know the floor plan of the hospital, I had an advantage."

"I'm good there, too. Memorized it on the way in." His low voice didn't rumble the way his brother's did. Nor did it have the same effect on Emily.

There was something special about Reed Campbell. Being with him made her feel different in ways she couldn't begin to explain, let alone understand.

Would she live long enough to find out where it might go?

Reed grabbed an extra Kevlar vest and told Stephen to take it. "My brother has the witness in a supply room on the sixth floor. He thinks they're safe. For now."

"No one knows what I look like. I can go first. Blaze a trail."

"On my last count, there were half a dozen men on the perimeter. That number could be double by now," Reed said flatly.

"How long have you been gone?"

"Hour and a half, max."

"Hopefully, the numbers haven't changed much."

The picture of Stephen's wife holding his baby popped into Reed's thoughts. All he had to worry about was himself. He didn't have a wife and child depending on him to come home every night. If anything happened to Reed, of course his family would miss him, but that wasn't the same thing by a long shot. Leslie had begged him to think about changing professions once they were married. And Reed had been dumb enough to consider it. "On second thought, this might be too dangerous. You stay here. I'll call if I need backup."

Stephen muttered the same curse word Reed had thought a second earlier. "This is my job. I do this for a living. What's the big deal?"

"I can think of two reasons not to send you into what might be a death trap."

"Kiera knows who I am," he said, indignant.

"I don't know. It's risky. Even if I can breach the building, I have no idea what's waiting for me once I make it to the sixth floor. These guys are no joke, either. They probably have more guns than we do."

"Are you saying this mission is too dangerous for me, but the jobs we go out and do every single day aren't? That working for Border Patrol is a walk in the park?" Stephen issued a disgusted grunt as he shot daggers with his glare.

"It does seem ridiculous when you put it like that. You ever think about quitting? About getting a nine-to-five so you can watch your kid grow up?" Reed ran through a few best-case scenarios in his mind as they talked.

"My son is fine. I have every plan to be right there alongside my wife to see him off to college and beyond, but this is what I do. It's who I am. If my wife doesn't have a problem with it, then you sure as hell shouldn't."

Good point. "She never asks you to quit?"

"Why would she? She knew who I was when she married me." The look of disgust widened with his eyes.

Shock didn't begin to cover Reed's reaction. Everything Stephen had said was absolute truth, but Leslie had seen things very differently. She'd begged Reed to reconsider his line of work. Even said she didn't think they could have children as long as he was an agent. Her internet search hadn't done him any favors, either.

Yes, Border Patrol agents had the most dangerous jobs in law enforcement. Reed had calculated the risk when he took the job and had decided he could live with the odds. If he'd gone into Special Forces operations, the danger would've been greater. He figured most women would react the way Leslie had, so he gave up on getting serious for a while.

Good thing most women weren't like Leslie. They probably didn't cheat, either.

Reed put his hands up in the universal sign of surrender. "Sorry. I got no problem standing behind you, next to you, in front of you, whatever. I just don't want to go to sleep at night for the rest of my life with your kid's face being the last thing I remember."

Stephen issued a grunt. "You have a better chance of getting shot than I do. These ass-hats aren't even looking for me."

"True. If you're good with the risk, then I am, too. Besides, I need your help." Reed pulled into the gas station across the street from the hospital and cut his lights. He studied the building. It was the middle of the night, so it was unlikely there would be a shift change. The cafeteria wouldn't be open, either. No way to slip in unnoticed there. Security would be tight, as well. Then there were corrupt local police to deal with if he and Stephen got inside. The sixth floor would be crawling with Dueño's men. "You got any binoculars in your pack?"

"Yeah. Night vision." He pulled his gym bag from the backseat, dug around in it and produced a pair.

Reed surveyed the parking lot. Dueño's men had to be swarmed inside because there were only two left outside. From the looks of things, getting inside the building wasn't going to be the problem. Once there, Reed figured they'd be up against a wall. Almost all of Dueño's men were most likely on the sixth floor—which was the same place Luke and Emily were.

The need to see Emily, to make sure she was okay, seeded deep in the pit of his stomach. A primal instinct to protect her gripped him. Strange that they'd only just met.

After his relationship with Leslie, Reed Campbell didn't *do* feelings while working this job. Leslie had taught him not to expect more than a casual relationship. He'd convinced himself that one day the adrenaline would no longer be enough to satisfy him and he'd get tired of the job or burned out on the demands. When that happened, he could change careers and could settle down. Having both at the same time seemed as out of reach as finding Cal and bringing him to justice.

Even more surprising was a woman who got it, who supported her husband and his career. Surely, Kiera was one of a kind.

Either way, Emily's case was about to get a lot more interesting. "You have a pen and paper in the bag?"

"Sure. Hang on." Stephen produced the items.

Reed sketched the hospital's layout. It was shaped like a T, the front doors being at the intersection. "Emily's room is here on the sixth so the supply closet must be nearby." He circled a spot on the map he'd drawn to the left of where the letter T most intersected. "So, there are two out here that we know of. No big deal there. Inside, there are at least four armed men, plus whoever else has joined the party that we don't know about. Another pair of local officers who might be dirty round out the guest list. Did I forget anyone?"

"That about sums it up based on what you've said so far. On our side, we have the two of us and your brother who's in the FBI, and he's with the witness?"

"You good with that?"

"I've worked in worse situations," Stephen said honestly.

Having backup was nice. Different. In their line of work, they didn't get that luxury most of the time. Only problem was they hadn't worked together before. Teams required teamwork, and that required people who knew the ins and outs of how each other worked. "No matter what we find in there, I'll always go right."

"Good. I like taking the left side. It's natural for me." Stephen pulled a Kevlar vest from his pack. "Looks like I'll need this."

"Ready?" Reed looked into Stephen's eyes, really looked, for any signs of hesitation.

The slightest delay in judgment and they'd both be dead. And that was most likely why Reed didn't choose a job in law enforcement working with a partner. He'd stand side by side with either of his brothers any day. But his future in another man's hands? *Not his warm-and-fuzzy.*

The black sky was dotted with tiny bursts of light. Highway noise pierced the otherwise quiet night.

Pitch-black covered the sixth floor. The rest of the hospital had lights.

Head down, gun palmed, Reed stalked toward the white building. He stopped at the edge of the parking lot, near the ER. A distraction would be nice right now, but Reed had never been able to rely on luck. Figured it was the reason he'd learned to work hard instead.

Tightening his grip on the butt of his Glock, he tucked his chin to his chest and quickened his stride toward the entrance. Stephen stayed back until Reed reached the glass doors. He took a position inside the building, and surveyed the lot. His buddy easily made it inside. It was all too easy. Then again, these guys were focused on Emily and they must believe they had her right where they wanted her. Plus, Luke could pass for Reed to the untrained eye.

The fact security was loose in the lot most likely meant these jerks figured they had who they wanted trapped upstairs. It also indicated the closer Reed got to Emily and Luke, the more men there'd be to get past.

"Which way?" Stephen asked, inclining his chin toward the elevator, then the stairs.

"Both make too much noise. Plus, the light will give us away."

Out of better options, Reed pitched toward the stairs with Stephen close behind.

Reed stopped on the fifth floor. The only distraction he could count on would be one he created himself. The nurses' station was quiet save for the click of fingers on a keyboard. The young nurse glanced up. "Can I help you?"

Reed pointed to the badge clipped to his waistband.

She nodded. "I need to talk to my supervisor."

"Understood." He located a fire extinguisher and slammed it into the glass, sounding the alarm.

"Sir, you can't do that." The nurse burst from her chair, shouting over the wail of alarms.

Reed and Stephen made a play for the stairs. Within

two steps of freedom, the door blasted open and two men in security uniforms blocked the entry.

"Step aside. We work for Border Patrol and we need to gain access to the stairwell." He motioned toward his badge.

The sound of feet shuffling in the stairwell broke through the noise as security stepped aside and allowed Reed through.

A gunshot split the air.

Must have come from behind.

"You good?" Reed asked.

"Yeah. You?"

A quick scan revealed Reed had not been hit. "Fine."

He took the stairs three at a clip. The stairwell would be full of people in another few seconds. Doors already opened and closed on lower levels. Panicked voices echoed.

If Reed were lucky, the men would scatter, too. He almost laughed out loud. *Luck?* Right. Go with that, he thought wryly. His best-case scenario? The commotion would give Luke a chance to escape with Emily.

Reed trusted his brother. So, why did he want to be the one to take Emily to safety?

Chapter 9

Alarms pierced through the supply closet. Emily didn't dare cover her ears for fear she'd miss out on critical instructions.

"We need to move. Can you stand up?" Luke offered a hand.

"I'm good." She wouldn't tell him how much her body ached already.

"She needs to take it easy," the nurse said. "Think you can get us off this floor?"

"I have to," Luke said.

"Then I can get us out of here safely."

"How do we know Reed's okay?" Thirty minutes had passed since Emily had watched Luke text his brother with no response.

"Because of that sound." He motioned toward the air.

Reed had set off the fire alarm? She didn't want to

acknowledge the relief flooding her, giving her the extra will to push forward.

"I'll go first. Squeeze my arm if you get in trouble," Luke whispered over the noise.

"Okay."

The door creaked open. Emily's breath caught in her throat. She eased a few steps forward, one hand on the nurse and the other on Luke.

Even in the dark, she could see the silhouette of two men moving toward them. Her eyes had somewhat adjusted. She squeezed Luke's shoulder.

As the pair neared, she could make out a face. Reed's.

Ignoring the shivers running up her arms, she reached for him.

"We managed to scatter them, but not for long," he said. The rich timbre of his voice settled over her as he wrapped an arm around her waist for support.

He nodded toward his brother and took more of her weight as the nurse led them through a couple of back rooms and into a staff elevator.

"You're bleeding. What happened?" Emily touched the soaked spot on his sleeve.

"It's not from me." Reed double-checked himself as though unsure.

"Then who?" Emily asked.

Reed's gaze shot straight to the friend he'd brought with him. "They got you?"

"It's nothing." He lifted his shirt on his left side. "Just a flesh wound."

"Dammit, it's more than that." In a razor-sharp tone, he muttered the same curse Emily thought.

"Don't worry. I can take care of him. You two need

to get out of here." The nurse pulled off her scrubs and handed her top to Emily. "Put this on."

"I can't leave my buddy." The anguish in his voice softened the earlier tension.

"You don't have a choice. Take her with you. I'll stay with him," Luke said.

"I—"

"When that door opens, I want both of you the hell out of here. We'll catch up as soon as…" His gaze searched Reed's friend.

"Stephen—"

"I'll catch up as soon as he's square," Luke finished. "I won't let anything else happen to him, I swear."

Emily eased the scrubs over her head with Reed's help. The tenderness in his touch warmed her. She tried her best to ignore it, considering they were about to face a parking lot full of Dueño's men—men who were trying to kill her.

"They'll be watching for her. All the exits will be covered," Reed said.

"Exactly why I'll pretend to be her. I'll hold on to these two and fake a limp," the nurse said.

Emily didn't want to put others in jeopardy for her sake. She remembered the nurse talking about her younger brother on his freshman spring break trip to Matamoros, Mexico, being ritualistically killed and buried. The emotion had still been raw in her voice after three years. Was that the reason she was intent on helping? "I still don't think this is a good idea."

The statement was met with nods of agreement from the men in the elevator.

"I understand why you have hesitations. I do. Seems like I'm putting myself out there for strangers. But I

need to do this for Brian. I don't expect you to understand. Please don't stop me." The determination in her
tone caused Emily to cave.

"These aren't the same men," Emily protested, but
she already knew she'd lost the battle. Because she did
understand the need to make things right for something in the past.

"They are in a sense. Those men are cut from the
same cloth. They hurt innocent people and destroy
lives." She paused a beat. "It's too late for me to help
my brother, but I can help you. Don't take that away
from me."

The moment of silence in the elevator said no one
would argue.

Reed slipped off his Kevlar vest and placed it on
the nurse before turning to Emily. The brilliance in his
brown eyes pierced through her. "Think you can walk
on your own through the parking lot?"

"I'll make it." She ignored the shivers trailing up
her spine.

Reed bear-hugged his brother and then Stephen before turning to the nurse. "I'd be even more in your debt
if you'll promise to take good care of this guy once you
get out of here."

If the nurse didn't, Emily knew without a doubt that
Reed wouldn't be willing to walk away. He'd take Stephen with him.

An emotion Emily couldn't quite pinpoint hit her
fast and hard. She'd never known that kind of loyalty
before. At the House, people would drop in and out
based on their own needs. No one seemed concerned
with the children other than making sure they had food

and clothing. Schedules made people slaves, the guy in charge had said, so there was no routine.

Homeschooling had been inconsistent, too. In addition to a couple of workbooks, the children had been given homemade pamphlets on the importance of peace and love. Emily appreciated both and yet there was no real love at the House. No one had been there at the end of the day to tuck her into bed and make her feel secure as her father had when she was little. No one had taken her to the playground to be with other kids, since leaving the compound was forbidden. No one had nursed her cuts and bruises or held her while she cried herself to sleep. All of which had happened too often in the House, and especially in the early years when she was trying to adjust to her new life.

Busying herself with the little kids had been a much-needed de-stressor. Work had a way of providing a welcomed distraction. Was she still hiding behind hers?

The elevator dinged, indicating they'd reached the bottom floor. Tension billowed out as the doors opened.

Reed took Emily's hand, palm to palm, as they stepped out of the elevator. "Ready?"

"I hope." Contact with Reed seemed to shrink the world to the two of them. Emily prayed she'd be prepared for whatever waited ahead, in her immediate future and beyond.

Scrubs made quite a difference in helping Emily blend in. They did nothing to help her walk faster. She had to be in severe pain to stand straight, let alone move. Frustration nipped at Reed.

He had two choices if he wanted to move faster: leave Emily alone for a few minutes in the parking lot to bring

the truck to her, or carry her. Leaving her unguarded
even for a second wasn't a real consideration, which
left carrying her. There was no doubt he could easily
hoist her over his shoulder. But could he pick her up and
get her to the truck without drawing attention? At least
the false alarm had brought people out of the hospital.
Standing around in small groups, they provided a buf-
fer between Emily and him and Dueño's men.

Stephen had a bullet scrape to prove how far they'd
go to stop them.

A fresh wave of guilt followed by red-hot anger
pulsed through him at letting his buddy get shot. Reed
would have to face Kiera and her baby to explain and
apologize for what had happed. No way would he sleep
at night otherwise.

Worrying about a wife and child, even Stephen's,
was a distraction Reed couldn't afford when his mind
needed to be sharp. Maybe Leslie had been right. A man
in this job had no right to put his wife and child through
the pain of not knowing if he'd be coming home. Or, if
he did, what kind of shape he'd be in. And yet, a little
piece of him wanted to believe things would be different if Emily was the one he'd be coming home to.

Small crowds stood, facing the building. Others
walked slowly to their vehicles, checking back often.
They'd hide Emily's pace as long as Reed mimicked
them. He did.

"Slow and steady. Take your time." The feel of her
hand in his warmed him in places he shouldn't allow.
And yet, it felt so natural to touch her.

The kiss they'd shared earlier wasn't helping his concentration, either.

Distractions he couldn't afford fired all around him

when she was this close. Being away from her was even worse.

They made it to the edge of the lot without drawing attention.

He and Emily were safe for now. Part of him was relieved beyond measure. The other part didn't like putting his friend and brother in harm's way.

Once clear of the lot, he'd check in with his brother while he located a decent hotel. Emily needed a good night of sleep.

Reed wrapped his arm around her waist and took most of her weight. "I can carry you if it'll help."

"We made it this far. I can go a few more yards. I just hope they're all right."

"As soon as they realize they're after the wrong people, they'll circle back to the hospital." He helped her into the truck.

"I hope we're long gone before that happens," she said through a yawn, the medicine obviously doing its job.

"I plan to be. Try to get some rest." He nodded toward his shoulder.

"I doubt I can after all that." She slid across the seat as he belted himself, and leaned against him.

"Close your eyes. You might be surprised at how tired you are." He started the engine and eased the truck onto the highway.

"How far away is the place we're staying?"

"About twenty minutes up the road."

"Now that you mention it, I could use a bed to stretch out on even if I don't sleep."

Sleep was about the last thing Reed could imagine with Emily curled up next to him. He was in dangerous emotional territory with her because he could imagine sleeping next to her, or better yet not sleeping, for the foreseeable future. "You're brave. I'm proud of what you did back there."

She smiled one of her light-the-sky-with-brilliance smiles.

Not five minutes into the drive she drifted off to sleep, her soft, even breathing not more than a whisper in his ear.

Her being with him was the only thing that made sense.

And yet, what did he really know about her?

They'd barely met, he reminded himself for the twentieth time as he looked out at the long stretch of highway in front of him. And yet, he couldn't deny the familiarity she'd talked about earlier—closeness he felt just as strongly as she did even if he wasn't quite ready to acknowledge it as special.

It was special.

The sign for his exit came up. Reed put on his blinker and changed lanes. The movement caused Emily to stir. He stilled as he took the off-ramp, afraid to move too much so he wouldn't hurt her. She burrowed into his side and mewled softly.

Damn, that sound was the sexiest thing he'd heard in a very long time, which pretty much proved the well had been bone-dry for him. What did it say about him that every time she was near his thoughts were inappropriate?

She sat up straight and rubbed her eyes, blinking against the sudden light from the highway. "Are we there?"

"Yes." He heard how thick and raspy his own voice

had become. A ride in a truck shouldn't qualify as the sexiest moment of his year. So far, it did.

Reed vowed to change that once this case was over.

"A bed sounds amazing right now."

"Stay here while I grab a key from the hotel desk."

Within minutes, he returned and helped her inside.

Standing in front of the door, he jammed the key-card inside the slip. His effort was met with a red light. He muttered a curse, and then an apology. A couple of more tries yielded the same result.

"I think you have to pull out faster."

Reed wasn't about to touch that statement. "Would you like to try? I don't seem to have the right touch."

"Sure," she said with a coy smile.

He moved to the side and allowed her access. The damn thing lit green before she slid the card out.

"See how it's done?"

Suppressing a grin, he helped her inside, where a plush king-size bed filled the room.

"What's that smile all about?"

"Not going there." He chuckled about all the other things he'd like her to show him. Joking was his way of easing the tension from what had happened earlier.

He immediately texted Luke to get a read on Stephen's condition.

With Luke behind the wheel, they'd gotten rid of the men who'd chased them. Stephen was doing fine.

Relief flooded Reed. He turned to Emily, who was studying his expression.

"Did you get good news?"

"Stephen's grumbling about not needing a nurse, but he's cooperating. And he'll be fine. He and Luke are going to bunk at the nurse's place tonight."

"She's a good woman. We wouldn't have survived without her."

"Agreed. On both counts." He stopped in front of the bathroom door. "You want me to run a bath for you?"

"The nurse helped me shower at the hospital. I'm all clean."

There was an image Reed didn't need in his head. Plus, the smell of flowery soap was still all over her. He tried to shake it off. Didn't help. He settled her onto the bed, trying to suppress the smirk stuck to his lips.

"Okay, what's going on?"

"Nothing I can talk about."

"Why not?" Her gaze moved from his eyes to his lips, where it lingered, then down his body.

Scratch what he'd thought a little while ago. That was the sexiest thing to happen to him in the past year. "I need a shower."

"Want some help?" she teased.

"Normally I'd take you up on that." He stalked across the room, pausing at the door to the bathroom.

"I was kidding. No man on earth would want to shower with me the way I must look."

He moved to the bed and leaned over her, stopping a fraction of an inch before their lips touched. "Why not? Most men I know appreciate a beautiful woman."

Those stunning hazel eyes of hers darkened. Being this close was probably a bad idea. Even if she wasn't his witness, she was injured. No way could they do anything in her condition.

Autopilot had kicked in, and Reed couldn't stop himself from reaching out to touch her face. He ran his finger gently along the line of her jaw, and then her lips.

Her hands came up around his neck, and her fingers tunneled into his hair.

Kissing her would be another bad idea, but that knowledge didn't stop him, either.

Softly, he pressed his lips to hers, careful not to hurt her. She tasted sweet and hot, and a little like peppermint, most likely a remnant of brushing her teeth at the hospital. But mostly, she tasted forbidden. A random thought breezed through that he shouldn't be doing this. His sense of right and wrong should have him pulling away. Where was his self-discipline?

Tell that to his stiff length.

Better judgment finally won out when he realized this was about as smart as jabbing his hand into a pot of hot oil. Even if she wasn't his witness, they couldn't finish.

Reed pulled back. The look of surprise in her eyes caused his resolve to falter. "I can't keep going. Not comfortably."

"Oh." She sounded confused.

"Believe me. I want to." How should he put this? It wasn't his nature to be delicate.

"Oh?"

"I don't want to risk anything with your injuries."

The look in her eyes, the hurt, almost had him changing his mind. She looked away. "I understand. It's probably for the best."

"Can I take a rain check?"

"You don't have to say that to make me feel better. I kissed you in the hospital. Not the other way around. I understand that you're not attracted to me."

That's what she thought? "Do you want to know what you do to me?"

She didn't respond.

"I'm going in the other room to take a shower and quite possibly take matters into my own hands because I want you so badly right now, it's painful." He glanced down at his straining zipper.

She did, too.

"Oh. Sorry about that." Her cheeks flushed six shades past red, causing his heart to stir and bringing an amber glow to her already bright face.

"Don't be embarrassed. I'm not. One thing you can count on from me is honesty. If we're going to spend time together, I expect the same."

He was rewarded with a warm smile. Emily was outdoors, warmth and open skies with a sexual twist. And as long as she was willing, he had every intention of showing her just how desirable she was when he could be absolutely sure he wouldn't be hurting her in the process.

"Honesty is a good thing," she finally said. She winked, and it made her eyes glitter. "And as long as we're being honest, I can help you with that little problem in the shower."

"One time won't be enough for me." He stood and walked toward the bathroom, stopping at the door. "And it's not little."

Chapter 10

Reed finished drying himself, brushed his teeth and slipped into a clean pair of boxers. He climbed under the covers on the opposite side of the bed so he wouldn't wake Emily. She'd left one of the bedside table lamps on, and it cast a warm glow over the room. He doubted he'd be able to grab any shut-eye for himself, but she needed her rest.

As he settled in for a night of nonsleep, she shifted and threw her leg over his. His pulse kicked up a notch or two. Heck, it raised more than he wanted to admit.

Yeah, he definitely wouldn't be getting any sleep now. Not with her silky warm skin pressed to his. How could his thigh touching hers be so damn sexy?

She reached across his bare chest, only a thin piece of cotton stopping her firm breast from touching his bare skin. He groaned. It was going to be a long night.

He was aroused. She was fast asleep. Even if she was wide awake, it didn't change the fact that she was badly injured.

That she'd taken off everything but a T-shirt and underwear brought his erection back to life with a vengeance.

His whole body stiffened. He didn't want to move for fear he'd hurt her.

And then he felt her hands moving over his chest.

"You can't break me," she whispered, and her voice slid over him, warming him. Her hands moved across his chest, stopping at the dark patch of hair in the center.

He was afraid he'd do just that. Hurt her. So he wouldn't force anything. Her mouth found his, and her tongue slid inside.

His hands moved, too, with gentle caresses as he smoothed his palm across the silken skin of her stomach.

She moaned as he cupped her breast. She carefully repositioned, a reminder they needed to take it slow, and his sex pressed to her stomach.

Last thing Reed needed to think about just now was her light purple panties. He already knew they were silk. With an image like that and her curled against him, things would end before they even started. She seemed to want this every bit as much as he did. Used to being in charge in bed, he'd have to remember to let her be in control.

Lying side by side, Reed slowly lifted her shirt as he bent down then slicked his tongue over her nipple. It hardened to a peak. The soft mewling sound she made stiffened his length. Much more of this and he'd be done right then and there. Her back arched then the sound she made next stopped him in his tracks.

"Are you okay?"

"Y-es." The way she drew out the word told him she wasn't convinced.

There was a point of no return when it came to foreplay, and a breast in his mouth had always been the line for him. They'd careened sideways and beyond as far as Reed was concerned, so stopping now would prove even more difficult. Except when it came to pain. No way could he feel good about having sex if it hurt his partner in any way. And the painful groan that had just passed her lips had the effect of a bucket of cold water being poured over him.

"We can't do this." He gently extracted himself from in between her thighs because one wriggle of those taut hips and he'd be in trouble again.

She didn't put up an argument this time.

Reed settled onto his back as she curled around his left side. "Tell me where it hurts."

"This position is good. The other way only hurt when I moved." She laughed. It was the kind of laugh that promised bright sunshine and blue skies.

He leaned over and pressed a kiss to her forehead.

"You make me happy," she said in a sexy, sleepy voice.

Reed should be coming up with a strategy for how they were going to catch the guys chasing them instead of feeling perfectly contended to lie in bed with Emily in his arms. But that's exactly what was happening. And he wished they could stay there for a while. Except that wasn't an option. They'd have to leave first thing in the morning. "Me, too, sweetheart. Think you can get some rest? We have a long day ahead tomorrow."

She blinked up at him with those pure, honest hazel eyes. "What will you do if I go to sleep?"

"Come up with a plan."

"I want to help."

"The best thing you can do for either of us is rest."

It didn't take fifteen minutes for the medicine to overtake her willpower and for her to fall asleep again.

Reed wasn't so lucky. He ran through several scenarios, none of which gave him a warm-and-fuzzy feeling. Then there was the thought of visiting Stephen's wife. Why did it weigh so heavily on Reed's conscience?

A text message from Luke had confirmed that Stephen was fine. His injury wasn't more than a big scrape, a flesh wound. The trio had made it out of the parking lot without too much trouble as had Reed and Emily. His assumption that the men who'd followed them would give up after they realized they were following the wrong people had turned out to be true.

Then there was the issue of Emily to think about. Her warmth as she pressed against him while she slept. He could get used to this.

Emily stretched and blinked her eyes open to a quiet room and an empty bed. The mattress was cold where Reed used to be.

Where was he?

Climbing out of the bed brought a few aches and stiff muscles to life. Surprisingly, some of her pain had subsided. She moved to the bathroom, brushed her teeth and dressed.

Back in the room, she noticed his keys and cell phone

were missing. She prayed nothing had happened in the middle of the night to make him leave, such as getting a hot lead.

The thought of Reed being out there, alone, with Dueño's men surrounding him tightened a coil in her chest. Surely, he wouldn't go anywhere near them without someone to back him up.

Moving to the window to peek outside, she heard the snick of the lock and froze.

Reed shuffled in with company. She recognized his brother, who was following closely behind. He glanced at the bed with a raised eyebrow.

Emily let out the breath she'd been holding.

"I brought breakfast," Reed said with a forced smile. "How are you this morning?"

"Much better." She took the brown bag and inhaled the scent of breakfast tacos. "Smells amazing."

Reed slid his arm around her waist as he moved beside her. With his touch, heat fizzed through her body. Too bad they had company.

He helped her to the desk.

"Is something wrong? What happened?" Emily tried to brace herself for more bad news. "Is Stephen okay?"

"Yeah. He'll be fine. The nurse bandaged him up at her place last night."

"That where you two spent the night?" She picked a breakfast taco out of the bag and unwrapped it, keeping one eye on Reed.

"Yeah. Her house isn't far from here. She gave Stephen a ride home this morning, so I asked Reed to pick me up."

She set her breakfast taco down and turned to Reed. "Then what's going on?"

"Luke has to get back to North Texas for a case he's working on. He'll take us to a car my boss has stashed for us and then you and I will have to take it from there." Reed took a breakfast taco and then handed the bag to his brother.

The thought of leaving the relative safety and comfort of the hotel held little appeal. However, staying meant they couldn't follow leads. Besides, wasn't there a saying about sitting ducks? It was probably better to keep on the move. "When do we head out?"

"After we eat," Reed said, taking a seat next to her.

Emily finished her food and then excused herself to the bathroom, stopping in front of the mirror. Even as a teenager, she'd resisted the urge to go blonde. Now she was living proof it was a bad idea. With her hazel eyes, the lighter shade washed her out. Grateful to have real clothing and a rubber band, she pulled her hair up in a ponytail and washed her face. Some of the swelling had gone down, and her bruises were already yellowing. The sunburn had improved dramatically. The peeling was easing up, too.

Her eyes had seen better days, and she wished she had makeup, but other than that she figured nothing had happened that would leave a permanent mark so far.

Circumstances weren't good. Thinking about being broke and totally dependent on someone else didn't sit well. Even though Reed had proved he could be trusted. He'd kept by her side and put his own life on the line to save her, which wasn't the same as needing him more than she needed air.

If men hadn't started shooting at them, would Reed have hauled her in and walked away, though?

None of that mattered now. Second-guessing the situation wouldn't help. Reed Campbell was a good man who was doing what he believed to be the right thing. She respected him for it.

Even so, Emily wanted her own money, her own car and her own clothes. The only way to get those things was to convince Reed to take her to her town house, which was risky.

Looking at her reflection, it was readily apparent she wouldn't get by on her good looks. She almost laughed out loud. How could anyone get past her current condition? And hadn't Reed seemed to look past all that and see her from the inside?

Hadn't he said that they felt close because they'd survived a near-death experience? And that was most likely true because she'd never believed in love at first sight.

Even if she did, no way would she trust it. Relationships grew by getting to know someone. Sure, what she felt for him was different. Special, even. But real love? Her heart said it was possible, but her mind shut down the thought.

Rather than jump into that sinkhole feetfirst, Emily decided to hold whatever else she felt at bay. Yes, she was physically attracted to Reed. There was no denying it, especially with how right she felt in his arms. Crazier still, he seemed to return the sentiment.

She'd be smart to exercise caution, and not get too caught up in emotions that could change in an instant.

Her mom had loved her dad with everything inside her. Look what had happened there. Emily had trusted her father. Look where that had gotten her. She'd tried to save her mother with similar results.

And the last serious relationship she'd gotten involved in? The jerk turned out to be married with kids.

Emily had spent last year's vacation curled in a ball on her bed, crying. She'd pretty much acquiesced to the idea that even though her heart wanted things normal people had—white-picket fence, a husband, children— those "things" most likely weren't in the cards for her. She'd settled into the routine of work, free from distractions. With no real attachments, her weekends were free for overtime.

Even though it had been a year ago, being put in the role of other woman had been like a knife wound to her chest. Jack had said he respected her space and wanted to take it slow, for her sake. He was actually busy at his kids' soccer games and then date nights with his wife on the weekends.

Knowing Emily had done that to another woman, even if unintentionally, had left behind an invisible gash across her chest—a scar that might never heal.

Love hurt. Love was unfair. Love had consequences.

Was she falling in love with Reed? Whatever was happening, she'd never felt such an initial impact when she'd met someone before. It was like reentering the earth's atmosphere from space.

Since her heart wanted to plow full speed ahead, she would force some logic into the situation. When it came to Reed, caution was Emily's new best friend.

"Ready?" Reed called from the other room, forcing her attention out of her heavy thoughts.

"Might as well be." She took a last look in the mirror and followed them out the door.

They walked to the car with Reed in front and Luke behind her.

Luke took the driver's seat. Emily squeezed in the middle. Reed was to her right.

She reached for the seat belt and winced, pain shooting across her chest. Her bruised ribs had something to say about the movement.

"Here. Let me get that for you." Reed made a move to help.

"No, thanks. I can manage by myself." And she had every intention of keeping it that way.

Chapter 11

By the time they reached The Pelican, the doors had just opened for lunch. Reed shifted in his seat to get a better view, scanning the surrounding area on the two-lane highway. Palm trees lined the streets. Their relatively thin stalks made it difficult to hide behind, giving Reed a decent view of the scattered buildings next to open fields.

The lot to the restaurant was empty. Reed cracked the truck's window. The air outside had that heavy, middle-of-summer, salty-beach smell. They weren't close enough to the water to benefit from a cool ocean breeze. "The car should be parked around back if it hasn't been towed."

Gravel crunched underneath the tires as the truck eased through the parking lot and toward the twin Dumpsters behind the restaurant where a few cars were parked.

"I'll have to run inside to pick up the keys."

Luke backed the truck into a spot positioned in the corner so that they could see anyone coming from around the building. He shifted gears to Park, leaving the engine idling. "You want us to go in with you?"

"Nah. It's better if I go in alone. Fewer people will notice that way. You keep watch from here." Reed slid out of the truck and secured his cowboy hat. He fished his cell out of his pocket and held it up. "Let me know if anything looks suspicious."

"I'm on it."

Reed stuffed the cell in his front pocket, lowered the tip of his Stetson and tucked his gun in his holster. He took Emily's hand and squeezed. "You've been quiet for most of the ride. Are you hurting?"

"A little. Nothing I can't handle." She smiled but it didn't make her eyes sparkle like before when she'd looked at him.

He made a mental note to ask about that later, and turned to his brother. "I'm not out in two minutes, don't hesitate to come after me."

Luke nodded. "Grab that key and get your butt back here."

Reed's boots kicked up dust as he walked.

The hostess looked young, as if she might be home on summer break from college. She greeted him. "Table for one?"

"Men's room first?" He smiled, not really answering her question.

She pointed to where he already knew it was. He'd been in the restaurant once before with Gil.

This early, there were no other patrons. His boots scuffed along the sawdust-covered floors. Metal buck-

ets filled with peanuts were being placed on the tables.
A waiter was hovering next to a waitress as she filled
an ice pail from the soda machine. Both were laughing. Judging by the way she flipped her hair and smiled,
both were flirting, too.

Not much else was going on other than bottles of
salt and pepper being filled and placed on tables. The
usual prelunch-crowd preparations were being made.

Reed located the men's room and slipped inside,
moving straight to the sink farthest from the urinals.
He slid his hand under the porcelain rim and felt around
for the key. There was nothing. He bent his knees and
leaned back on his heels so he could visually scan underneath. Bingo. There it was. Reed palmed it, and
headed out of the bathroom.

As he neared the front door, the hostess smiled.
"Your table's ready."

"Change of plans." He smiled, and she blushed.
Guess she was doing a little flirting herself. Normally,
he'd enjoy the attention. It was barely a blip on his radar
now, leaving him wondering if his lack of interest had
something to do with his stress meter, or his growing
attraction to Emily.

He fished his cell out of his pocket and hit Gil's name
in the contacts. The call rolled into voice mail. Reed
muttered a curse as he fired off a text, and moved toward his brother. Reed shrugged.

Luke kept visually sweeping the area as Emily slid
out of the passenger side.

"Got it," Reed said.

Emily took the arm he offered.

Thoughts about her, how warm she felt curled up
next to him last night, had no place distracting him. He

helped her lean against the hood of the vehicle. He'd just pressed the unlock button when his phone rang.

Reed gripped the handle at the same time he heard a click from underneath the car. What would they have done? The car was there, so they must've wanted him to get inside.

Dropping to the dirt, he climbed around on all fours until he saw it. Wires and metal were taped together to the underbelly of the car. A bomb. He'd most likely detonated it by lifting the handle. He needed to get Emily off the hood. "Get back in the truck."

"What's under there?" Her gaze widened.

"It's wired!" he shouted to Luke. Reed was to his feet and by Emily's side in two seconds, urging her forward. Not wanting to hurt her was outweighed by his fear of the bomb going off with both of them right there.

His brother said the same curse word Reed was thinking. As he rounded the side of the truck, time seemed to still. The explosion nearly burst his eardrums. The earth shook underneath his boots. The truck had shielded much of his body from shrapnel. He dropped to his knees, managing to maintain his hold on Emily. Her arms tightened around his neck and her head buried where his neck and shoulder met.

Luke was out of the truck, moving toward them. Reed had dropped his cell and so the connection with Gil had been lost. Without a doubt his boss would do everything in his power to protect Reed, so who the hell figured out where the car and key were? The only other person from the agency Reed had been in contact with was Stephen. No way could this have been Stephen's doing. He was clean. Besides, he didn't even know about the stashed car. Someone else had figured it out. But who?

Between Reed and Luke, they hoisted Emily onto the bench seat of the truck. If they'd been parked any closer to the car, Reed didn't want to think about what would've happened to them. Before he could finish asking Emily if she was okay, Luke had pulled a fire extinguisher from the back of his truck and blasted the cool foam toward the blaze.

"I'm okay. Just a little freaked out," Emily said. Her bravery shouldn't make him proud. It did.

"I've already notified the police. We'll need to stick around long enough to give a statement. Then we'll head back to Dallas." Luke maneuvered his jaw as though he were trying to pop the pressure in his ears, and tossed the empty canister into the Dumpster.

Ringing noises blocked most of Reed's hearing. "Can you set us up with a place to stay?"

"Sure thing. How about Gran's?"

"Thought about Creek Bend. Might be a good option given the circumstances."

"We can use my car if you'll take us to my town house," Emily said. Her vacant expression indicated she was in shock.

Luke glanced from Emily to Reed. He nodded. "Might be a good idea to see if they've already been there."

"I guess we'll find out, won't we?" Reed shrugged.

"Want to send Nick over to check it out while we're on the way?"

"Good idea. I'd hate to lose more time, and these guys seem to be a step ahead so far." The tide needed to turn. Reed was getting a little tired of being on the wrong end of the wave.

"How will he get inside without a key?" Emily asked. The answer seemed to dawn on her when her eyes lit up and she said, "Oh. Right. Guess he doesn't exactly need to use the door. Tell him my alarm code is six-one-five-three. There's a small window in the laundry room toward the back. It'll be easy to break in and slip through it. There's a huge shrub in front of it. That window is the reason I put in an alarm in the first place."

Luke's cell was already out before she finished her sentence.

A squad car roared into the lot, kicking up dust and gravel.

Another cop on Dueño's payroll? The thought crossed Reed's mind. Luke's clenched jaw said he feared the same. But they both knew logic dictated only one or two cops would be dirty on any given police force, so the odds were in Luke and Reed's favor. On the off chance the guy didn't walk on the right side of the law, the crowd that had gathered would deter him from doing anything stupid.

Cell phones were out recording the damage, which could bring on more trouble for him and Emily. Social media would soon light up with the account, and the chances of Dueño's men pinpointing Emily at this location grew by the second. Reed turned to where Emily sat in the truck. "Lie down and stay low until we get out of here."

That was the first thing on his agenda.

Luke instinctively moved in between the gathering crowd and Emily, blocking everyone's line of sight and therefore their ability to snap a picture of her.

Reed, keeping his hands out in the open in plain sight, stopped midway between the truck and the officer. The cops around here didn't see much gunfire, which made them itchy, a threat. They constantly prepared for the one-off chance something could go wrong. The nervous twitch this guy had was his biggest tell.

"My name's Reed Campbell and I work for Homeland Security in the US Border Patrol Division."

"Keep your hands where I can see them." The guy inched forward.

Reed kept his high, visible. "My badge is attached to my belt on my left hip."

"Stay right there. Whoever's in the truck, put your hands up and come out." The high pitch wasn't good.

Emily raised her hands and kept her head low.

"Sir, if you make her come out of that truck, you'll be putting her life in danger." Reed motioned toward the sea of cell phones recording the event.

The officer shouted at the crowd to put their phones away or be arrested.

"Your boss should have gotten a call from mine," Reed said.

The cop's radio squawked. He leaned his chin to the left side and spoke quietly. His tense shoulders relaxed, and he lowered his weapon. "My supervisor confirmed your identity, Agent Campbell. Sorry about before."

Reed shook the outstretched hand in front of him. "Not a problem. The woman in the truck is my witness. This is my brother Luke. He's FBI."

The officer's eyes lit up as he shook Luke's hand. Reed choked down a laugh. He'd be hearing about how the FBI was better than Border Patrol on the way to Plano for sure because of that one.

Firemen had arrived and were checking the scene. Luke had already pulled a fire extinguisher from the truck and put out the fire. Reed finished giving the officer his statement. He shook Luke's hand rather enthusiastically one more time before clearing a path for them so they could leave.

When they settled into the truck, Emily leaned her head on Reed's shoulder and closed her eyes.

They hadn't gone five miles before Luke fired the first barb. "Told you the FBI is better. Take the cop, for instance. Did you see his reaction—"

"We both know more agents are killed in my line of work than yours," Reed shot back, grateful for a light-hearted distraction to ease the tension in the cab. "And I think we also know the officer had a professional crush on you."

"I can't help it if I'm good-looking, too," Luke said with his usual flicker of a smile. "And you're still there because?"

The circumstances might not be ideal, but Luke cracking jokes and smiling was a good thing. He'd gone far too long after his stint in the military in solitude, refusing to talk to anyone. Since reuniting with his ex-wife, signs of the old Luke were coming back. "We both know Julie's going to make you quit after the wedding."

"Look, baby bro, there's something I've been meaning to tell you." Luke's serious expression jumped Reed's heart rate up a few notches.

"Don't leave me hanging. Get on with it."

"Julie and I, well, since this wasn't our first time, we decided not to wait. We got married last weekend."

"And you didn't tell me?" Reed feigned disgust. In truth, he couldn't be happier for his brother.

"We didn't let anyone in on it. Headed over to the justice of the peace's office after thinking about everything. It's not like it was our first go, so we didn't want to make a big production. Seemed to make more sense to keep it about us."

Reed belted out a laugh.

"What's so funny about me getting married to my wife?"

"Well, that for starters."

Luke shook his head and chuckled. "Okay, you got me. That sounds messed up."

"You think?"

His brother's laugh rolled out a little harder this time. "Yeah, it's a lot screwed up. But we never should've divorced in the first place."

"That's the smartest thing you've said today." Reed thought for a second. Oh, this was about to get really good. "Holy crap. You said you haven't told anyone else yet?"

"No." The problem with that word seemed to occur to Luke a second after it left his mouth. "That's not going to go down well, is it?"

"Gran will not be amused."

"Maybe you should tell her. You know, soften the initial impact."

"Oh, hell no. I'm not risking my ears."

"You think there'll be a lot of yelling?"

"Yeah. There'll be a lot of that. Then, she'll tell you that you're not too old for a butt-whooping. This is going to be dramatic."

"You gotta help me out here. Tell her for me," Luke pleaded.

"I plan to be there when she's told. But I have no

plans to step into that fire barefoot. Your best bet is to bring Julie with you."

"Good idea. Surely, Gran won't want to scare her off."

"No, that's a great idea. And you owe me one for that."

"Fine. Then, I'll help you tell everyone about your friend here."

Reed glanced at Emily, thankful she was sound asleep. Besides, how'd this turn into a discussion about her? "What's that supposed to mean?"

"I'm not stupid. I can see you have feelings for her."

"And?" Reed wasn't ready to talk about what he had with Emily, if anything. Hell, he hadn't figured it out for himself, yet.

"I'm only saying she's a sweet person. You could do a lot worse."

"She's my witness. This is an investigation." The finality in his words most likely wouldn't sell Luke on the idea, but Reed had to try.

"You sure that's all?" His brow was arched as he leaned his wrist on top of the steering wheel, relaxing to his casual posture again.

Was it? Hell if Reed knew.

"Whatever is or isn't happening between the two of you, I think you need to have a conversation with her about federal protection."

"What? You think I haven't already?" Reed sounded offended to his own ears. His shoulder muscles bunched up, tense. A weekend-long massage wouldn't untangle that mess.

"Oh. Sorry. I just assumed since she was still here that you hadn't brought it up."

"If it makes you feel any better, it was the first thing I mentioned to her. She doesn't want it."

"And you don't, either."

"Here we go again." This conversation didn't need to happen.

"You may have been the quiet one, but nothing's ever gotten in your way once you set your mind to it."

"I gave her the options. She turned them down. End of story. What else was I supposed to do?"

"Persuade her," Luke said without blinking. "You have to have considered the fact it may be the only way to guarantee her safety."

"Believe me, I have."

"So, why didn't you convince her of that?"

What was with the riot act? "I did what I could. In case you haven't noticed, she's a grown woman capable of thinking for herself."

"I noticed. Half the men in the country would notice her, too. The other half would be afraid their wives would catch them staring with their mouths open. She's a knockout even in the condition she's in. The fact hasn't been lost on you."

"I'm neither blind nor an idiot. Get to your point." Of course he'd noticed how her full breasts fit perfectly in his hands. Her round hips and soft curves hadn't gotten past him, either. The imprint of her body pressed to his still burned where they'd made contact. He'd become rock-hard when she'd thrown her leg over his last night. Did he want to sleep with her? Yeah. Was it more than that? Had to be since Reed hadn't done casual sex since he'd been old enough to buy a lottery ticket. Didn't mean he had to think with his hormones.

Luke hesitated, as if he was choosing his next words

carefully. "I know you're too smart to jeopardize a mission or a witness, so I won't insult you. Deciding to keep her with you might not be in her best interest. It's up to you to make her see that."

"I don't care where she is as long as she's safe," he lied. Reed didn't make a habit of deceiving his brothers, so part of him was surprised to hear the words coming out of his mouth. The truth was he did care. And Luke was right. Probably too much. Reed's agitation had more to do with the fact that his brother was forcing Reed to think about his feelings for Emily, which was not something he wanted to do. Not with cars exploding and danger around every corner. His mind needed to stay sharp, so he wouldn't miss a connection when the other guys made a mistake. Given enough time, they would screw up.

His cell pumped out his ringtone. He glanced at the screen, grateful for the distraction. "It's Nick."

"Hey, baby bro," Nick said.

"What'd you find?"

"The place is in good shape but someone's been here. Thankfully the codes are still taped under her desk, like she said."

"Have you contacted SourceCon's security team?"

"Yeah. They're cooperating. Of course, they want to handle their own investigation, but they've agreed to give us full access to their people."

"Good point. Maybe someone on the inside knows something."

The line beeped. Reed checked the screen. "My boss is calling, so I'll have to catch up with you later. Keep me posted on anything you find."

"Will do. Be safe, baby bro."

Reed said goodbye and switched to his other call. "What's the word, boss?"

"I got a rundown on what happened from the chief of police. I tried to call you earlier when we got cut off but my call went straight to voice mail. Didn't do good things to my blood pressure."

"I must've been out of range for cell service. There are a lot of dead spots out this way."

"At least you're all right."

That was the second time someone said that in the past two minutes. "So far, so good. Someone wants this witness pretty badly."

"Clearly, they want you, too. I believe this case is also connected to yours."

"I know Stephen Taylor was set up by Shane Knox, but what does he have to do with me?"

"He was in the room when I spoke to you yesterday. He must've decoded our conversation and located the car." Anguish lowered Gil's baritone. "It's my fault this happened. I'm sorry that I trusted him."

"What's the connection, though? I don't remember Knox and Cal working together."

"I have their files right here in my hands. Turns out, they went to the same high school. Grew up in Brownsville, Texas, together. Played football. To say they knew each other well is an understatement. As my teenage daughter would say, 'they were besties.'"

"That town is right on the border. Most people have family on both sides of the fence."

"It's certainly true of Cal Phillips. He has relatives in both countries on his mother's side. Her maiden name is Herrera."

"Any chance she's related to the man they call Dueño?"

"There's no immediate connection that I can find, but it's possible he's a distant relative. I'm still mapping out all the possibilities. All I know about Dueño so far is that he's big over there. And well protected. I'm not just talking about his men. Government officials won't give up any information on him, either. There's no paperwork on him. It's almost as if the guy doesn't exist."

Went without saying the man had help. "Except we both know he does. What are we going to do to stop him?"

"I have guys working round-the-clock to uncover the location of his compound, but it's risky to mention his name. Just knowing he exists is enough to get a bullet through the skull. My investigators have to move slowly on this one."

Reed didn't have a lot of time. "I'll involve my brothers' agencies. See if we can move any faster that way."

"We need all the help we can get on this. I'll let you know as soon as I hear anything else."

"I appreciate it. What about Knox? Where is he now? Should be easy enough to detain him for questioning. Maybe we can get answers out of him."

"I'd like nothing more than to have that SOB in custody. Only problem is, he's gone missing."

Damn. "You think he's lying low or permanently off the grid?"

"Could be either. Or dead. The minute I started asking questions about him in connection to Dueño put his life in danger. If Dueño's inner circle didn't get to Knox, then government officials might. They'll do anything to cover their tracks."

Reed didn't like any of this new information. It meant that Emily might never be safe. And now that he was knee-deep in mud with her, they could be digging two graves. He informed his boss about the upcoming summit.

"I have a guy who's been able to climb fairly high in Delgado's organization. I'll see if he can get information for us."

"Sounds good. Keep me posted."

"Be careful out there. I don't want to visit you in the hospital again. Or worse."

"I have people I can trust watching my back this time. But I won't take anything for granted."

Reed ended the call.

"Did I hear that right? This is related to what happened to you before?" Luke clenched his back teeth.

"Yeah. It's the same group." Reed had every intention of locating that compound and finding a way in.

"I can take some time off work. The FBI will understand. Nick will want to be involved, too."

Normally, Reed would argue against it. He knew better than to turn down an offer for help when the odds were stacked this high against him. "Okay."

"I know what you're thinking. Don't be stupid," Luke warned.

"No, you don't."

Emily stretched and yawned. "Don't be stupid about what?"

"Nothing," Reed lied. His brother knew Reed had every intention of locating that compound and doing whatever it took to breach it.

Because anger boiled through his veins that the same son of a bitch who'd gotten to him wanted to hurt Emily.

Chapter 12

Reed opened his eyes the second the truck door opened. He glanced at the clock on the dashboard. He'd caught an hour of sleep.

"Relax, just filling the tank. You need anything from inside?" Luke asked, motioning toward the building.

"I'm good. Thanks."

Emily was already awake, sitting ramrod straight. The sober look on her face said Luke had filled her in. Reed hoped she hadn't overhead their conversation, especially the part where his brother was pressing about her. Reed might not've come across the right way, and he didn't want to jeopardize whatever was going on between them by a misunderstanding. He almost laughed out loud. What *was* going on between them? If someone could fill him in, then they'd both know.

All he knew was the thought of spending more time

with her appealed to him. He actually *wanted* to talk to her, and he wasn't much for long conversations otherwise. And the way her body had fit his when they were lying in bed last night was as close to heaven as this cowboy had ever been.

And yet, there was a lot he didn't know about her, and her family.

He made a mental note to talk to her about what he'd said to Luke when the two of them were alone again, which a part of him hoped would be soon. Based on the look on her face, she'd heard something, and he hated that he'd hurt her.

The chance to bring up the subject came when Luke finally quit fidgeting in the backseat and shut the door to pump gas. Thankfully, the large tank would give Reed a few uninterrupted minutes.

"Did my brother tell you about the conversations I had with our older brother and my boss?"

She nodded, keeping her gaze trained out the opposite window.

He couldn't read her expression from his vantage point but knew it wasn't good that she couldn't look him in the face anymore. Bringing up what he really wanted to talk about was tricky, so he took the easy way out. "Did you get any rest?"

Did he really just ask that? Reed was even worse at this than he'd expected to be. Most of the time, he sat back and observed life. That was his nature. He'd never been much of a "wear his feelings on his sleeve" kind of person. This was hard.

If he'd blinked, he'd have missed her second nod.

This was going well. Like hell.

"Emily, would you mind looking at me?"

Slowly, she brought her face around until he could see the tears brimming in her eyes.

"Did I say something to hurt you?" Stupid question. Of course he had.

"No." A tear got loose and streaked her cheek.

He reached up and thumbed it away, half expecting her to slap his hand. She didn't. So, he took that as a good sign and forged another step ahead. "My brother was asking questions I wasn't prepared to answer about us."

"Is there an 'us,' Reed?" Her lip quivered when she said his name.

"It's too soon to tell. If we met under different circumstances, there's no doubt I'd want to ask you out. We'd take our time and get to know each other. Figure it out as we went, like normal people. Start by dating and see where it went from there."

"But now?"

"Everything feels like it's on steroids. Plus, to be honest, I'm not looking to be in anything serious right now. I'm not ready to make a change in my career."

"Why would you have to change jobs? It's only dating, right?" The bite to her tone said he'd struck a nerve.

Damn. Trying to make things better was only making it worse.

Luke had finished pumping gas and disappeared inside the store. He'd be back any second, and Reed would never be able to dig himself out of this hole in time if he didn't do something drastic. Did she need to know how he felt about her? Since he was no good with words, he figured showing her was his best course of action.

Gently, slowly, he placed his hand around Emily's neck and guided her lips to his. That she didn't resist

told him he hadn't completely screwed things up between them. Besides, he'd been wanting—check that—
he'd been needing to kiss her again the whole damn day.

And that was confusing until his lips met hers and,
for a split second, he felt as if he was right where he
belonged. Did she feel the same? A sprig of doubt had
him thinking she might slap him or push him away.

Instead, she deepened the kiss. With all the restraint
he had inside, he held steady, ever mindful of not hurting her. Control wasn't normally something he battled.
With Emily, he had to fight it on every level, mind and
body. Let emotions rule and he'd want to get lost with
her. His body craved to bury himself in the sweet vee
of her legs. With those runner's thighs wrapped around
his midsection, he had no doubt he'd find home.

But that wouldn't be fair to her.

He had nothing to offer. He wasn't ready to leave his
profession behind, and a woman like Emily deserved
more.

She pulled back first. "Who said I was looking for a
serious relationship? I have my career to think about,
and that takes up most of my time."

Reed was stunned silent. She'd pulled the "my work
comes first" card? Okay. He needed to slow down for
a minute and think. "Where do you see yourself in the
future?"

"Independent."

What did that mean? From what he'd seen of her so
far, she was too stubborn to let men with guns scare her.
Reed respected her for it. Did she mean alone? She'd
also just turned the tables on him. "Why can't you have
a job and a boyfriend?"

"That what you're asking for?"

"What if I was?"

She stared impassively at him. "I don't do relationships, so I'm not asking for one with you if that's the impression you're under."

Wait a damn minute. "Why not? Is there something wrong with me?"

"Not that I can see. I don't have time. I work a lot of hours. If I haven't lost my job, I plan to throw myself back into my work when this whole ordeal is over." Her expression was dead serious.

"And what if I wanted to see you sometime?"

"I live in Plano. You live south…somewhere… I'm not exactly sure where."

"I live in a suburb of Houston. Rapid Rock."

"At least that's one thing I know about you." She paused, and a weary look overtook her once bright eyes. "How far away is that from Plano?"

"Three hours. Four if traffic's bad."

"See. Too far."

"People date long distance, you know. It wouldn't be the end of the world."

"I don't."

Luke opened the door, and reclaimed his seat before shutting the door.

The conversation stalled. No way was he finishing this with his brother in the vehicle. Reed was butchering it all by himself. He didn't need an audience to tell him what he already knew. He was bad at relationships.

"Your brother and I spoke about federal protection," she said stiffly.

That's what this was all about? Had Luke encouraged her to go into WitSec? Why did Reed feel betrayed?

"And? What did you decide?"

"I want to discuss my options with your older brother."

"Fine."

That one word was loaded with so much hurt, an invisible band tightened around Emily's chest. She didn't want to upset Reed, but what else could she say? The truth was that she might need to go into the program, just as Luke had suggested. His thoughts made perfect sense, and she'd be a fool to put herself or Reed in further danger.

Besides, Reed was determined to bring the man who'd shot him to justice. And she couldn't blame him. If the shoe were on the other foot, she wouldn't rest until the person was behind bars, either.

And Dueño? That was a man who needed to be locked up forever along with a pair of former Border Patrol agents.

She'd talked to Reed about work, but the reality was she most likely would have to get a new identity if she wanted to live, let alone have a family of her own someday, which was what she wanted. Wasn't it?

The idea had held little appeal after her last relationship. She'd all but closed herself off to the possibility of a real life, or a family of her own. Being with Reed stirred those feelings again, and she couldn't ignore them with him around. Not that he'd be there for long.

The minute he went after Dueño, she feared Reed would be hurt. If she showed up to visit him in the hospital, she'd be dead. From the looks of it so far, she'd be running the rest of her life. And the worst part was she'd almost be willing to risk everything for a man like Reed.

How crazy was that?

Especially when he'd made it seem as if he didn't

share the same feelings. She'd overheard his conversation with his brother earlier. Her chest had deflated knowing he didn't feel the same way she did.

Which was what exactly?

Were her feelings for Reed real? Could they last? How could anyone figure out anything with bullets flying and cars exploding?

Maybe it would be best to separate emotions from logic in the coming days in order to stay alive. They could figure out the rest later.

That she felt Reed's presence next to her, bigger than life, wouldn't make it easy as long as they were around each other. But difficult was something Emily had a lot of experience with. And challenging relationships were her specialty.

"We heading to my place?"

"It seems safe enough to stop in and let you grab a few of your things." Reed looked at her intensely before turning his head to stare out the window. A storm brewed behind those brilliant brown eyes. "We'll have to be careful, though."

"That would be nice. I'd love to wear my own clothes again. Can't even imagine what it would feel like to have my own makeup."

"After we make a pit stop, we'll head to my gran's ranch outside in Creek Bend."

Luke cleared his throat. "It'll be easier to connect with Nick and talk about options there."

The tension between brothers heated the air for the rest of the ride.

Emily was grateful to step outside and stretch her legs when they arrived.

Luke had parked a block away, explaining that he

wanted to walk the perimeter before they approached her town house. Seemed like a good idea to her. Not to Reed. He grumbled at pretty much everything his brother had said, and she knew it had to do with him talking to her about federal protection.

She wasn't sure what she wanted to do. The promise of a clean slate offered by the program wasn't the worst thing she could think of at the moment. But then, what about her mother?

The woman barely hung on as it was. What would she do if the only daughter she could depend on disappeared altogether? Emily was the only one holding the family together. And she barely did that. Heck, she didn't even know where a couple of her siblings had disappeared to in the past few years. As soon as they'd reached legal age, they'd bolted and hadn't looked back. Emily most likely would've done the same thing, except that she remembered what her mother had been like before. She'd had the same fragile smile, but it had been filled with love.

And now? Everything in Emily's life was unraveling.

She took a deep breath and stepped out of the truck. The thought of having a few comforts from home gave Emily's somber mood a much-needed lift. It was amazing how the little things became so important in times of disaster. Something such as having her own toothbrush and toothpaste put a smile on her face.

Once Luke gave the all-clear sign, she and Reed moved to her town house. She packed an overnight bag as the men watched the front and back doors.

Reed's oldest brother had done a great job patching the hole he'd put in her window. The board should hold nicely until she could get a glass person out next week. Next week? Those few comforts had relaxed her brain a little too much. Clean pajamas wouldn't take away the dangers lurking or give her back her life.

Just to be sure no one could steal her pass codes, she pulled them out from underneath her desk where they were taped and tucked them inside her spare purse. Luckily, she'd taken only her driver's license, passport and one credit card to Mexico. Everything else had been tucked into an extra handbag she kept in the closet.

She checked her messages. The resort had called concerned that she hadn't been back to her room since Tuesday. She made a mental note to reach out to the manager and have her things shipped back to the States. Everything wasn't a total loss. She'd get her IDs and credit card back.

Except if she took up the offer for federal protection, she wouldn't need any of those things again, would she?

Her pulse kicked up a notch. No amount of deep breathing could halt the panic tightening her chest at the thought of leaving everything behind. She prayed it wouldn't come to that.

For now, she was safe with Reed and Luke. She'd have to cross the other bridge when she came to it. Surely, the right answer would come to her. As it was, she was torn between both options.

A good night of sleep might make it easier to think. No good decision was ever made while she was hungry and tired.

She took one last look around her place—the only place that had felt like home since she was a little girl—and walked downstairs. "I'm ready to go."

Reed stood at the window, transfixed.

"Everything okay?"

"They must've been watching for you. Someone's coming. Go get my brother. Tell him we have company."

Chapter 13

Reed crouched behind the sofa near the window as his brother entered the room. "I saw two men heading this way."

"The back is clear," Luke said, standing at the door.

"Then take her out that way." Reed's weapon was drawn and aimed at the front. Anyone who walked through the door wouldn't make it far. He had no intention of being shot and left for dead again.

"I'm not leaving you." The finality in Luke's tone wasn't a good sign.

Reed needed his brother to get Emily to safety. "They get her and it's game over. And I might never be able to find Phillips. Get her out of here, and I'll meet you at the truck in ten minutes. I need to make these guys talk."

Luke hesitated. "I'm not sure that's a good—"

"Go. I'll be right there. If you don't leave now, it'll be too late."

His brother stared for a moment then helped Emily out the back. Good. Last thing Reed needed was someone getting to her. He had no doubt that he and Luke could handle whatever walked through that door, but Emily was weak from her injuries, and Reed didn't want to take any chances when it came to her. Besides, he'd already hurt her enough for one day.

Crouched low, he leaned forward on the balls of his feet, ready to pounce.

The doorknob turned. Clicked.

A loud crack sounded, and the door flew open. These guys were bold. Didn't mind walking through the front door or making noise to do it. Also meant they were probably armed to the hilt.

"Stop right there, and get those hands in the air where I can see them. I'm a federal agent." Reed paused a beat and peered from the top of the sofa. "I said get those hands in the air where I can see them."

The first bullet pinged past his ear as the men split up.

Reed fired a warning shot and retreated into the kitchen. The sofa wouldn't exactly stop a bullet.

His boot barely hit tile when the next shots fired, *ta-ta-ta-ta*.

Reed leveled his Glock and fired as bullets pinged around him. Hit, the Hispanic male kept coming a few steps until his brain registered he'd been gravely wounded. Blood poured from his chest, and he put his right hand on it, trying to block the sieve.

As Reed wheeled around toward the back door, a second man entered. Reed was close enough to knock the weapon out of the taller Hispanic's hand. Tall Guy caught Reed's hand and twisted his arm.

Instead of resisting, Reed twisted, using the force of a spin to gain momentum until he broke Tall Guy's grasp. Reed pivoted, losing his grip on his gun in the process, and thrust his knee into Tall Guy's crotch. He folded forward with a grunt.

About that time, he must've seen his partner because he let out a wild scream and threw a thundering punch at Reed's midsection, then grabbed his shoulders and pushed until he was pinned against the granite-topped island.

Reed's first thought was that he prayed these guys didn't bring reinforcements. His second was that he hoped like hell Emily and Luke had made it to the truck. With Emily's injuries, Luke wouldn't be able to take care of her and fight off several men. It wouldn't be possible. Not even with his gun, although Reed knew his brother would do whatever he had to in order to protect Emily.

Another blow followed by blunt force to the gut and Reed dropped to his knees, the wind knocked out of him. He battled for oxygen as he pushed up, trying to get back to his feet. His gun was too far to reach. Tall Guy must not've seen it slide across the room and under the counter.

Reed, fighting against the hands pushing him down, reared up and punched Tall Guy so hard his nose split open. Blood spurted.

That's when he saw the glint of light hitting metal. The sharp blade of a kitchen knife stabbed down at him. Reed shoved Tall Guy, ducked and rolled to the left. The knife missed Reed's head a second before it made contact with the tile.

What Reed needed was to restore the balance of power. And he could do that only on his feet.

Tall Guy dived at Reed, landing on top of him. Even though Reed rolled, Tall Guy caught Reed on his side. The knife came down again, fast.

Reed rolled again, catching Tall Guy's arm. The knife stopped two inches from Reed's face. Testing every muscle in his arm, Reed held the knife at bay. Another roll and Reed might be able to reach his Glock. With a heave, he managed to roll and stretch his hand close enough to get to his gun.

He fired and fought Tall Guy. Problem with shooting a guy was that it still took a few moments for his brain to catch up. Reed struggled against the knife being thrust at him for the third time.

The tip ripped his shirt at his chest. Blood oozed all over Reed.

As if the guy finally realized he was shot, he relaxed his grip on the knife. It dropped, clanking against the tile.

Reed couldn't afford to wait for more men to show. He pushed Tall Guy off and managed to get to his feet. His boot slicked across the bloody floor. He wobbled, and then regained his balance, stepping lightly in the river of blood. Before he left, he fished out his cell and took a picture of each man.

All he could think about was Emily's safety. He broke into a full run as soon as he closed her back door.

Maybe Luke could get the FBI to clean up the mess Reed had left behind. As soon as he knew Emily was safe, he'd blast the pictures of his attackers to all the agencies and see if he got a hit.

His heart hammered his ribs. Not knowing if she was okay twisted his gut in knots.

Rounding the corner, he pushed his burning legs until the outline of the truck came into view. Where was she? Where was Luke?

He didn't slow down until he neared the empty vehicle. Sirens already sounded in the distance. If Luke had made it out safely, surely he would've called one of his contacts. Or had a neighbor heard gunfire and called the police?

His heart pounded at a frantic pitch now as he surveyed the area, looking for any signs of Emily and Luke, or worse yet, indications of a struggle.

Was the truck locked?

He moved to the driver's side and tried the door. It opened. That couldn't be a good sign.

The town house-lined street was quiet, still.

Motion caught the corner of his eye.

"Get in the truck," Luke shouted.

A shotgun blasted.

"Get inside and get down." Luke carried Emily in a dead run. By the time he reached the truck, sweat dripped down his face. He tossed Reed the keys.

Reed hopped into the driver's side and cranked the ignition, thankful the two people who mattered to him most right now were safe. The truck started on the first try.

Luke hauled Emily inside and hopped in behind her. He pulled an AR-15 from the backseat. "Drive."

"Buckle up." Reed stomped the gas pedal. He didn't want to admit how relieved he was to see that Emily was okay. He didn't want to consider the possibility anything could happen to her. Exactly the reason he needed to talk her into WitSec. That might be the only way to keep her safe.

"Bastards brought reinforcements. I couldn't get to you in time," Luke said, in between gasps of air.

"You should've kept Emily in the truck."

"And let them kill you? They had three more on the way."

"I could handle myself." He kept his gaze trained out the front window, but he could see from his peripheral that Emily was assessing his injuries. "I got cut with a knife. Most of this blood belongs to someone else."

"Oh, thank God." She let out a deep breath. "I thought…"

He took her hand—it was shaking—and squeezed. "I'm okay."

"Cut right and we'll lose them," Luke said. "They're on foot."

Reed brought his hand back to the wheel and turned. "They must've been watching to see if she'd show up since they didn't find the pass codes."

Luke picked up his cell phone, studied it and held it out. "We're done dealing with these jerks on our own. I'll call in the guys."

No way would Reed refuse the help. Dueño was closing in and Reed still had no idea who the guy really was or in which region of Mexico he lived. Not to mention he remembered what both of his brothers had gone through in the past couple of years. A determined criminal was a bad thing to have on his radar.

"I have a few pics we need to circulate." He fished out his cell and handed it to his brother.

"Good. We can blast these out to all federal agencies."

"Gil's number is on the log. Make sure he gets copies."

"Will do, baby bro." Luke made a move to set the phone down. It pinged. "Looks like we got a hit already."

Reed tightened his grip on the steering wheel.

Luke studied the screen. "Both of these guys are wanted for trafficking. One's name is Antonio Herrera."

"Looks like we found our family connection. That's Cal's mother's last name."

"Tell me about it." Luke cursed. "We have an ID on the other one, too. Name's Carlos Ruiz."

"Guess I don't know him."

It took a little extra time to reach Gran's place in traffic, but Reed couldn't think of a better sight than Creek Bend as the ranch-style house came into view.

In order to protect them and the ranch, men had been stationed along the road and Luke had been reassured there'd be more in the brush, as well. He'd had to call ahead to let Gran know in case she spotted one and panicked. She'd been prepped on what to expect upon their arrival, too. Mainly, so she wouldn't be surprised when she saw Emily's condition. Even though she was improving, she still had the bumps and bruises to prove she'd been through the ringer. Seeing it was another story altogether.

Potholes had been filled on the gravel road, making for an easy trip up the drive. Good that Emily wouldn't be bounced around. The last time she repositioned in her seat, she'd sucked in a burst of air, and her arm came across her ribs. She'd caught herself and immediately sat up.

The fact she'd been silent for the journey didn't reassure Reed. Eyes forward, she hadn't slighted a glance toward him. He needed to make things right. But first, she needed to heal.

The front door flew open before they'd even made it out of the truck.

Nick and Sadie rushed out first, followed by Gran, their sister Lucy, and Julie.

The tension in Reed's neck eased a notch. There was something about having Emily here at the ranch with his family that made sense in this mixed-up world.

Reed offered his arm for Emily to use as leverage to get out of the truck. She sat there, stone-faced.

Damn that he couldn't tell what she was thinking. Did the whole clan overwhelm her?

He hoped not. He hoped she could get used to them being around.

She took his arm, but as soon as she raised hers, she flinched.

"You're hurting worse than you want to let on, aren't you?"

"I'm sure I'll be better after a little more rest."

Why did she always have to armor up when he got close? Reed had never met someone so strong on the outside. Or someone who'd erected an almost impenetrable fort on the inside.

The pain medication she'd been given at the hospital had worn off. "The nurse gave me a few pills. I'll bring them to you as soon as you get settled."

His sister and sister-in-law took over with Emily, and he was left standing, holding the door open.

Nick waited for the women to take Emily inside before he motioned for Luke and Reed to stay out.

"I've got men everywhere. No way can anyone get

through the woods or down that lane unnoticed. Now, I know you want to go after these guys, and we will. All three agencies have men on this."

"Good. We'll need all the help we can get." Reed shuffled his boots on the pavement. Dueño's men were smart. If there was a way inside the ranch, they'd find it. But with all the agencies sending men, it would be a lot harder.

"In the meantime, we wait for good intel," Nick said. "Oh, and Gran lifted the ban on guns in the house. Said she figured rules had to be bent when it made sense. She's still on me for not warning her beforehand when I brought Sadie there to protect her."

Reed thanked his brothers. They bear-hugged before splitting up. "Luke here has some news for her."

"Gran already saw Julie wearing a wedding ring." Nick glanced from Reed to Luke.

"And?" The way his face twisted up Reed would think his brother was waiting to hear about another serial killer on the loose.

"You know Gran. There were hugs and tears."

Luke blew out his breath. "Thank heaven for small miracles."

"You're another story, I'm afraid."

"In the hot seat?"

"Guess you didn't see the way she looked at you when you first pulled up."

"I'm hoping Emily will keep Gran distracted and this one can slide past," Luke joked.

It was nice to laugh with his brothers. Maybe Reed should take Luke up on his offer to start a PI business together when this whole mess cleared up. And it would get straightened out. Reed had the chance to right two wrongs in this case. He had no other thought but to bring justice to the men who'd hurt Emily and put his life in danger. Five minutes alone with the bastard and a shallow grave would suit Reed better at this point, but he'd settle for a life behind bars.

"Good luck with that. She might give Julie a break, but you're a different story," Reed teased.

"Yeah. As long as she doesn't bring out the switch, I'll be okay." Luke cracked a smile.

"We knew she'd never really use it on us, but the threat of it was a powerful tool. Even if she had, it wouldn't have hurt more than letting her down."

"We could be trouble," Nick added.

"And we still are," Reed agreed.

"I better go face the music. Get this over with," Luke conceded.

"Better you than me, dude," Reed gibed.

"Where's my backup when I need it?"

"Nick here is your man. I'm planning to take a look and see what needs to be done in the barn. Been sitting too long and need to stretch my legs." Not ready to go inside, he headed to the barn instead.

There was nothing like hard work to clear his mind—a mind that kept circling back to the woman inside. Because having her at Gran's felt more natural than it should.

Chapter 14

When all the outside chores were done and the sun kissed the horizon, Reed took off his hat and walked inside.

Concentrating on work when Emily was in the house took far more effort than he'd expected. The need to check on her almost won out a dozen times. He wanted to be with her, and especially right now, but that's about as far as he'd allowed his thoughts to wander.

Gran stood in the kitchen. "I fixed biscuits and sausage gravy. Your favorites. You want a plate?"

"No, ma'am. I'm not hungry yet. Thank you, though. I'll make those disappear later," he said with a wink. "How's Luke?"

"He's resting. She is, too. In case you were wondering," Gran said, returning the gesture.

Not her, too. Luke had already read him the riot act

about Emily. Reed didn't need to hear it from Gran, too. "If anyone needs me, I'll be out checking the perimeter. I'll ask the men on duty if they want any biscuits."

"Here. Take this with you. I already packed sandwiches for them." She motioned toward a box on the table.

Reed kissed her on top of the head before hoisting the box on his shoulder, and grimaced. "Keep mine warm."

He wouldn't eat before he made sure the men outside had food.

Gran opened the door and Reed nodded as he left for the barn. He pulled out a four-wheeler and loaded the box of food on it, using a spring to hold it on the back.

Riding the fence took another half hour. It was dark by the time Reed returned the four-wheeler to the barn and moved inside again. He showered and ate before heading down the hall to Emily's room.

Standing at the door, he listened for any signs she was awake. He hated to disturb her if she was asleep.

Instead of knocking, he cracked the door open and waited. The need to see her, to make sure she was okay, overrode his caution about entering a sleeping woman's room.

Warning bells sounded off in his head all right. And not the ones he'd expected. These screamed of falling for someone he barely knew. Reed prided himself on his logical approach to life. He'd always been the one to watch and wait. Emily made him want to act on things he shouldn't, against his better judgment. Exactly the reason he didn't get all wound up when it came to feelings. Then again, he'd never met someone who'd made him want to before, not even his fiancée. Had he pushed her away? Not given her a reason to stay? The obvious answer was yes. Reed was realistic. Even so, when it came to Emily, he needed to force caution to the surface.

"Hi." Her voice was sleepy and soft.

Reed was in trouble all right. He sat on the edge of the bed and touched her flushed cheek with the backs of his fingers. "How are you, sweetheart?"

"Ibuprofen does a world of good." She moved back to give him more room, froze and flinched.

"Don't hurt yourself."

"I'm okay." She inched over and patted the bed.

"Can I ask you a question?" he asked softly.

"Sure." There was plenty of light in the room. Enough to see her beautiful hazel eyes.

"Why do you always have to put up such a brave front?"

"I don't."

"Honesty. Remember? We promised not to lie to each other."

Her lips pressed together and her face was unreadable. "I just don't know how to be another way."

What did she mean by that?

Tears welled in her eyes.

"Why not?"

"Because it's always been me being the strong one. I don't expect you to understand. You have all this family around, helping, ready to lay their lives on the line for you." She paused and her shoulders racked as she released a sob. "I have me."

Reed couldn't begin to imagine how lonely that must feel. "Can I ask what happened to your parents?"

"Doesn't matter. It was a long time ago."

"It does to me."

"Why?"

"I want to know more about you. It'll help me figure out how to help you." Why couldn't he tell her that he wanted to know more for reasons he didn't want to explore? What was so hard about telling her he might be falling for her? Maybe it would break down some of that facade she so often wore.

Then again, move too fast and she might scurry up a tree like a frightened squirrel. She deserved to know how he felt about her. And he had every plan to tell her as soon as he figured it out himself. Right now, he didn't need the complication.

But that still didn't stop him from reaching out and touching her. He moved his finger across her swollen lip, lightly, so he wouldn't hurt her.

Those big hazel eyes of hers looked into his. "When my father left, my mother was devastated."

"Did he leave before or after he found out she was sick?" Reed's fists clenched. He knew exactly how it felt to have a father walk away. Except that Reed had had so much love in his life, it didn't affect him as much as it had his brothers.

"I wasn't completely honest with you before. I was too ashamed. She isn't sick in the traditional sense."

"Alcohol?" Lots of people turned to the bottle in hard times. Not everyone had the strength to battle their demons.

"No. Not exactly." She looked away.

"You can tell me anything. I won't judge you for it."

"How could you not? You have this big family around you, supporting you. I don't even know where to start."

He cupped her face and turned it until she was looking at him again. "Right here. Right now. This is where you start. Tell me what happened."

Tears fell and she released a sob that nearly broke Reed's heart. "It's okay. I'm right here."

She buried herself in his chest. "She drank at first. On a date with a man she barely knew, she was raped. After that, she just lost it. She joined a religious cult and moved us to California. Then she started popping out babies. She said that the men at the House cared about her, at least. Everything was up-front and honest. No one lied to her."

"At least there were people around to help. Your mother must've needed that."

"Except that they didn't. I did the best I could raising them. I'm used to living alone, being alone. Helping everyone else. But, it's not entirely her fault. I think she's sick or something. Underneath it all, my mother is very sweet. I mean, I know everything she did sounds bad, but she loved me. She kept me with her. Not like my father, who just walked away after pretending to care for us."

And Emily never wanted to be that vulnerable. It was starting to make sense why her work was so important to her. "It's okay to love your mother. Sounds like she was all you had growing up."

"It's screwed up, though, right?"

"Not really. I mean, all families are messed up in some way."

"She tried when I was little, but after all that, my mother was just...lost."

Also explained why Emily didn't want to be dependent on a man.

More sobs broke through, even though she was already struggling to contain them.

"It's okay to cry, sweetheart."

A few more tears fell that she quickly swiped away. "I just can't afford to let my guard down."

"Crying doesn't make you weak. But holding all that in for too long will break you down from the inside out one day. You don't have to put up a brave front all the time."

"I can't afford to fall apart. I'm all I've got."

"Right now, I'm here. Let me take some of the burden." Sure, Reed's father turned out to be a class-A disappointment, but he'd been one person. Reed couldn't imagine what it would feel like if everyone in his life had let him down.

"You are so lucky to have all this. To have such an amazing family...this beautiful ranch."

"We're a close-knit bunch. But then, we've always had to be. What about you and your father? He left your mother, but did he ever contact you?"

"I found him once. It was the week before college graduation. An internet search gave me his phone number, address. I thought I'd hit the jackpot. Guess as a child I'd convinced myself that even though he left Mom, he still loved me. I decided that he must not have known where I was after we moved. And that's why he never called on my birthday or had me to his house for Christmas."

"Kids make up fantasies when one of their parents is gone."

"Did you?"

"I didn't need a father. I had two older brothers constantly looking out for me. The whole situation was harder on them, and especially Nick being the oldest. He stepped inside a father's shoes and filled them out. I was damn lucky to have him."

"That must've been hard on your mother, too."

"She's an amazing woman for taking care of us the way she did."

"Did you ever look for your father?"

"Guess I never felt the need to find the man with all these jokers around trying to tell me what to do." He tried to lighten the mood, and was grateful when she smiled even though it didn't last.

"Some of my younger siblings were sent to live with other relatives when people found out about what went on at the House."

Reed had heard stories, too. Read reports about places like those, none specifically about the place where she grew up, but there were others. He'd had to raid a few since some on the border were known to harbor criminals. All kinds of marginalized people lived there. The thought Emily had endured a place like that made his heart fist in his chest.

Her bottom lip quivered.

He leaned forward and pressed a light kiss to her mouth. He kept his lips within an inch of hers. Her breath smelled like the peppermint toothpaste Gran kept on hand. "You're one of the bravest people I've ever met to go through all this alone and still be this normal."

She blinked. He imagined it was a defensive move to hold back more tears from flowing.

"Thank you, but—"

He pressed his lips to hers again to stop her from speaking. Her fingers came up and tunneled into his hair.

She pulled back and kept her gaze trained to his. "I'm not sure if throwing myself into my work or at you makes me brave, but I appreciate what you're saying."

"You survived. You carved out a normal life. You did that. And with no one there to support you. You are an amazing woman. And I'm one lucky bastard."

This time she pulled his lips to hers, deepening the kiss.

That moment was the second most intimate of his life. And both had to do with Emily. Both had similar effects on his body. He was growing rock hard again. No way would he risk hurting her. Both made him want to get lost in her.

She needed sleep, not complications.

"Think you can get some rest? I can come back to check on you in the morning."

She opened the covers. "Stay with me tonight?"

All his alarm bells warned him not to climb into those covers with this beautiful and strong woman. The more he learned about her, the more he respected her courage, her strength.

He thought about the women he'd dated in the past, and not one measured up. Not even the one he'd intended to marry.

Reed slipped under the sheets and took to his back.

Emily curled around his left side and he wrapped his arm around her. The perfect fit.

"Fair warning. You get any closer, and I can't be held responsible for my actions. Keep in mind the other bedrooms are at the opposite end of the house."

A laugh rolled up from her throat. It was low and sexy. "That makes two of us."

Getting stiff when Emily was around wasn't the problem. He had no doubt the sex would blow his mind. But then where would that leave them after?

Why should he risk getting closer to her when he

knew the second he found Dueño's location and arrested him, their professional need to be together would
be over?

With enough people working on the case, the information could take a little time to track down, but they'd
find it…find him.

Emily deserved to have her life back. And, just
maybe, she'd find a little room for him in her day-to-
day life, too.

"Good morning," Reed said as he brought a fresh cup
of coffee to Emily. He'd made it a habit in the couple of
weeks she'd been staying in Creek Bend.

She pushed up and then rubbed her eyes.

"You want me to come back later?"

"No. I'm awake. Besides, you brought coffee. That
just about makes you my favorite person right now."

"Then I won't keep you waiting." He handed her the
cup, smiling.

"You're up early. Any news?"

"We have three government agencies with men on
this case and no new information. They've interviewed
everyone linked to Knox and Phillips. Nothing there.
All our hopes were riding on the summit, and that
turned out to be a disappointment. Luke said one of
his contacts in the FBI thinks he might be getting close
to a breakthrough."

"It's only been two weeks."

Reed glanced at the clock. "Your boss will expect
you online soon."

"Thanks for helping me figure out how to handle
this whole mess with Jared. I'm still surprised he didn't
want to come see me personally at the hospital to make

sure I wasn't lying. But then, I've never heard him so worried."

Her boss was being a little too concerned, which didn't sit well.

"The part about you being in a wreck is true. We just fudged the rest." The only good news that had come out of the past couple of weeks was that Emily was up and moving. Her injuries were healing nicely. The bruises on her face were gone, and she was even more beautiful than before. Reed could see her light brown hair starting to show through, and he could only imagine how much more beautiful she'd look when it was restored to its natural color.

However, being landlocked was about to drive Reed to drink. Plus, he was getting used to waking up to Emily every morning. A dangerous side effect.

"Caffeine and ibuprofen are my two best friends right now." She hesitated. "Aside from you."

"Good to know I rate right up there with your favorite drugs," he teased. "Speaking of which, I have a couple right here."

"I don't know if I've said this nearly enough, but thank you." Her playful expression turned serious as she took the pills from his outstretched hand. "Seriously, I don't know what I would've done without you."

The band that had been squeezing his chest for the past two weeks eased. Warmth and light flooded him. How had she become so important to him in such a short time? And maybe the better question was: what did he plan to do about it? "I have a feeling you would have figured out a way to get through this on your own."

And he already knew the answer to his question. He

didn't plan to do anything about it. Their lives were in limbo until he found Dueño and put him behind bars.

"I'm not so sure." She tugged at his arm, pulling him toward her.

Happy to oblige, he leaned in for a kiss. The taste of coffee lingered on her lips. "Keep that up and I won't let you out of bed."

"Promises, promises."

"You let me know when I wouldn't be hurting you and I have every intention of living up to that promise."

They both knew sex wasn't an option while she was healing. They'd pushed it a time or two with bad results. He wouldn't take another risk of hurting her until he could be sure.

Reed chuckled. Restraint wasn't normally a problem for him, but with Emily his normal rules of engagement had been obliterated. Holding back had become damn painful, especially when her warm body fit his so well.

"What? Why are you laughing?"

"No reason. You just focus on getting better. We'll take the rest one step at a time." Going slow would be better for the both of them. They both crashed into this—whatever *this* was—like a motorcycle into a barricade. They hit a brick wall wearing nothing but jeans and a T-shirt. No helmet. No protective gear. Being forced to cool their heels wasn't the worst thing that could happen as his heart careened out of control.

Reed Campbell didn't do out of control.

The pull toward Emily was stronger than anything he'd felt for Leslie, and he'd almost made the grave mistake of spending the rest of his life with her. Thinking back, had he even really wanted to marry Leslie? Or had the idea just seemed logical at the time?

They'd been dating for two years. She'd dropped every hint she possibly could they were ready. Even then, Reed had been cautious.

When she'd given him the ultimatum to move their relationship forward or she'd walk, he'd thought about it logically and decided to take the next step. She had a point. They'd been together long enough. She'd moved in, even though he hadn't remembered asking her to. Slowly, more and more of her stuff had ended up at his place. First, the toothbrush and makeup appeared in his bathroom. She'd been sleeping over a lot, so he figured it made sense. Then, she left a few clothes in his closet. Again, given the amount of time she spent at his place, a logical move.

When she'd approached him with the idea they could both save money if she didn't renew her apartment lease, he'd thought about it and agreed. He'd gotten used to Leslie being there. Didn't especially want her to leave. So, he figured that was proof enough he must want her to be there. He didn't think much about it when she spent Saturdays watching shows about wedding dresses. Or when she'd started asking his opinion about what she'd called "way in the future" wedding locations. Bridal magazines had stacked fairly high on the bar between the living room and kitchen when she finally forced his hand.

Reed knew he wasn't ready for marriage. He figured most men who'd come from his background would have a hard time popping that question of their own free will.

When he'd really thought about it, he decided that he might never be ready. But it had made sense to marry the person he'd spent the past two years with, so he'd asked.

With Leslie, he didn't have to stress out about picking a ring because she'd already torn out a picture of what she wanted from one of those bridal magazines and left it in his work bag the day before.

She'd thought of everything.

Had he really ever been crazy in love with Leslie?

Being with Emily was totally different.

Sitting there now, enjoying a cup of coffee with her, gave him a contented feeling he'd never known. And made him want to jump in the water, feetfirst, consequences be damned.

And it was most likely because they couldn't, but he'd never wanted to have sex with a woman as badly as with her, either.

If absence made the heart grow fonder, then abstinence made a certain body part grow stiffer. Painfully stiff.

"I better hit the shower." And make it a very cold one at that.

"You sure I can't convince you to climb under the covers where it's warm?"

He stood and shook his head. The naked image of her just made him certain he'd need to dial the cold up even more.

Besides, he was going stir-crazy being holed up at the ranch for two solid weeks. He itched to get out today, figuring he'd be fine on a motorcycle.

Reed kissed Emily's forehead, ignoring the tug at his heart, and then strolled to the shower to cool his jets. And a few other body parts, too.

Drying afterward, he slipped on boxers, a pair of jeans and T-shirt. He didn't stop to eat breakfast, heading out the back door while everyone was busy instead.

He grabbed a helmet and pulled his motorcycle out of the barn. Anyone watching the house wouldn't know who was leaving since he and his brothers looked alike from a distance. Plus, he knew a back way off the land and onto the street.

The men watching were used to Reed checking the perimeter every morning by now, so he kept his helmet tied to the back so they could see it was him.

Before he hit the main road, he stopped long enough to slip on the helmet. A pair of shades would disguise him further.

On the road, he expected to feel free.

He slipped past the inconspicuous car parked behind an oak tree. There were two others he spotted and, most likely, one or two he didn't. The Feds were keeping an eye on movement outside the ranch. Since no laws were being broken, there wasn't much they could do about Dueño's men being there.

Getting out proved easier than he'd expected. Then again, they wanted her, not him. It would be clear to anyone that he was a man.

Winding around the roads, pushing the engine, should feed his need for adrenaline and feeling of being out of control while completely in control. The speed, the knowledge that he could go faster than anything on the road with him, made it almost feel as if he became one with the bike and was in total control. Gran had always said that Reed had a need for controlled chaos, which was a lot like how he felt with Emily. Instead, the more distance he put between himself and the ranch gave him an uneasy feeling in the pit of his stomach and an ache in his chest.

What if Dueño's men made a move while Reed was

gone and they were one man down? Reed might have unwittingly just played right into their hands. Logic told him it didn't matter. The ranch had almost as much coverage as the president. Even so, being away from Emily left him with an unsettled feeling.

Reed needed to turn around and get back to the ranch. Except when he did, he noticed two cars heading toward him in the distance. They were coming fast, side by side on a two-lane road. Isolating him was the best way to get rid of him.

Run the other way and they'd chase him. The farther he got from the ranch, the more vulnerable he became.

Reed clenched his back teeth and opened the throttle. Looked as if he was about to be forced into a game of chicken.

Chapter 15

Since Reed had left, Emily had a hard time concentrating. She'd eaten and logged on for work. An uneasy feeling had consumed her when she saw him take off on his motorcycle.

Being here with his family had brought a strange sense of rightness to her world.

Maybe it was just the thought of family that made her all warm and fuzzy on the inside. With a deserter for a dad and a sweet-but-lost mom, Emily had never known a life like this.

And how adorable was Gran?

No doubt, she was the one in charge of these grown men.

The house itself was well kept and had a feeling of ordered chaos. The rooms were cozy, and keepsakes were everywhere.

Emily dressed, ate and stepped outside. Life abounded. A small vegetable garden was next to the raised beds of planted herbs. Flowers grew in pots on the back porch complete with a couple of chairs around a fire pit. Birds nested in the trees.

But her favorite place was the barn and being with the horses.

No wonder the Campbell boys had grown up to be caring men. A place like this would do that.

After two weeks of big family meals, great conversation and being with people who genuinely cared about each other, Emily was surprised at how much this place felt like home to her.

And yet, it was like a home that had existed only in her imagination before. How many nights as a child had she fantasized her life could be more like this?

Hers had been filled with dry cereal and people who talked a whole lot about love without it ever feeling sincere.

Love, to Emily, was making a real breakfast for others. Love was kissing good-night and being tucked into bed. Love was being brought coffee in the morning.

Reed?

Did she love Reed?

Would she even know love if it smacked her in the forehead?

Emily hadn't known this kind of love existed. It was fairy tales and happily-ever-after. She had no idea it could happen in the real world. Even when she'd dated Jack, she hadn't felt like this. She had needed her space, and that's most likely why he'd been able to get away with being married while he told her she was the only one.

She cursed herself for not recognizing the signs. He

hadn't worn a wedding ring. There was no tan line on his left hand.

But then, he hadn't had to be very deceiving when she let him come around only once a week and had insisted he go home every night.

Guess she was an easy target.

Then there was the guy she'd dated before him, who after six months had told her three was a crowd in a relationship. She thought he was accusing her of seeing someone else. When she told him she wasn't, he laughed bitterly and said he knew she wasn't seeing another man. He was talking about her job.

Being with Reed was different. It felt completely normal to wake up in his arms every day.

And that thought scared the hell out of her.

Reed aimed dead center at the car on his left. A split second before his wheel made contact with the bumper, he swerved to the center line, narrowly avoiding both cars.

If that wasn't enough to kick his heart rate into full speed, a near miss with a shell casing was. The blast had come from behind.

Soon, the cars would turn around, but they'd have a hell of a time trying to catch him. The curvy road would make him a harder target to see and, therefore, shoot.

Getting back inside the ranch would be tricky. If he could get a message to Luke, he could alert the men.

Reed had to take a chance and stop. He pulled over and eased his motorcycle into the brush for cover.

The text that came back clued Reed in to just how pissed off his brother was. In retrospect, his brother was right. Going for a ride this morning was a bone-headed move.

Not two minutes later, a pickup truck roared to a stop followed by two unmarked vehicles.

Reed expected a lecture when Luke hopped out of the driver's seat.

"You take the truck. I'll bring in the motorcycle." His brother had been too focused on the mission of bringing Reed home safely.

He understood. There was no room for feelings during an op.

Reed nodded and thanked Luke before taking a seat behind the wheel. Knowing that he came from a place of love humbled Reed. After spending time with Emily and hearing about her childhood and lack of family, he'd grown to appreciate his even more.

As he wound down the twisty road home, he thought about what it must've been like for her. To grow up surrounded by so many people in a communal house, but so very alone at the same time.

He hoped having her at the ranch had helped her see real families, though not perfect, existed. For his, Gran had provided the foundation. She'd given them a roof over their heads when their father had taken off.

Reed's mother was one of the strongest people he knew, but bringing up five kids alone was a lot for anyone. He wished Emily had had a mother who sacrificed for her the way his mother had for them. Her life wasn't about date nights or spa appointments. She'd given hers to her children. And yet, she didn't resent them. Loving them seemed to feed a place inside her soul and make her even stronger.

Emily was strong, too. And his chest puffed with

pride every time he thought of her, of what she'd survived. Yeah, she had bruises. But hers were on the inside, and even with them she'd opened her heart a little to him.

Pulling up the drive, seeing her leave the barn stirred a deep place inside him. A spot deeply embedded in his heart that was normally reserved for people with the last name Campbell.

His circle might be small, but the relationships in it weren't. And they had a name. He needed to remind himself that Emily's last name was Baker. Leslie had pretty much destroyed the chance of anyone else finding their way inside permanently when he'd caught her in bed with Cal.

When he'd been shot later that day, she hadn't visited him in the hospital. For the week he'd been ordered on bed rest, she'd stopped by all of once.

The moment he'd broken consciousness, he'd waited for her. For an excuse. For an apology. Something.

She'd texted him that she was moving out of their apartment. Said that he wasn't there for her in the way Cal had been. Reed wondered if Cal was still there for her. If they were together somewhere in the hot, unforgiving jungle. It would serve her right.

Reed parked the truck as Emily came toward him.

"I thought you left on a motorcycle."

"That was a bad idea."

Luke didn't speak when he passed them. Reed understood why. They didn't need words to know his brother was frustrated. Inside the perimeter, the ranch had sufficient protection to keep out a militia. Reed was angry with himself. No one could punish him for his mistakes more than he could. Wasn't that exactly what he'd been doing since Leslie?

Not letting another woman get close to him?

Emily reached for his hand. "Come on. I want to show you something in the barn."

He had some explaining to do when Luke cooled off. In the meantime, staying out of his way wasn't such a bad idea. "What did you find in there?"

"Come on. You'll see." She tugged at his hand.

With her palm touching his, he could feel her pulse, her racing heartbeat. "Fine. But shouldn't you be working?"

"I'm on lunch break. Besides, Jared called. Said he didn't like me trying to work so much while I'm trying to heal."

Reed would bet her boss was concerned for more than just her general well-being. Was he just a little too worried? "I'll bet he is."

"Said he wanted to come see me."

A bolt of anger split through Reed's chest, spreading to his limbs. Logic said she wasn't interested in the guy. So, where was reasoning at a time like this? As it was, Reed's brain didn't seem to care a hill of beans about being rational with his body pulsing from anger and something else when she was this close—something far more primal.

He pushed those thoughts aside. "So what did you want to show me in the barn?" A few things came to mind. Her naked topped the list. So much for leaving those high-school-boy hormones behind. Her being vulnerable, with him putting her in that position, must be weighing on his mind and his body was trying to compensate. Otherwise, if those pink lips curled one more time he'd have no choice but to cover her mouth with his and show her just how much of a problem she was creating for his control.

Once again, his logical mind had failed.

Thinking back, didn't most of his ex-girlfriends accuse him of thinking too much in their relationships?

And now Emily had come along and seemed to be doing her darnedest to turn everything that made sense to him upside down.

And he didn't like one bit that her boss seemed to want more than nine-to-five from her. He'd ask Nick to run a background check on the guy just to see what Reed was dealing with. "I don't think you ever told me Jared's last name."

"Why do you need it?" she teased.

"I like to know everything I can about my competition," he teased.

"Sanchez. His name is Jared Sanchez."

"Has he always kept such a tight leash on his employees? Or just you?"

"He's the worst. I can't go to the bathroom at work without him knowing my schedule."

Reed remembered his conversation with Jared. The man had acted as if he was guessing where she'd gone on vacation. A background check sounded like a better idea all the time. "So, what did you end up telling Mr. Sanchez?"

"That I was resting at a friend's place, and it was too far for him to drive."

Reed would've felt better if she'd said she was at her boyfriend's. "Feel free to use me as an excuse. I don't mind."

"What? And tell him we're in a relationship?" She

snorted. "The only people you'll ever really trust have the last name Campbell."

It wasn't that funny.

She stopped at the closed barn doors and covered his eyes with her free hand. "No peeking."

In the dark with his eyes shut, he resigned himself to be surprised and let her lead him inside.

"Don't open yet." She closed the barn door.

Even at midday, it would be fairly dark inside unless she'd turned on the lights.

"Okay."

She hadn't. He glanced around. Nothing looked out of place. No big surprises lurked anywhere. "Yep, it's a barn."

"Uh-huh."

"What did you want me to see exactly?"

She steeled herself with a deep breath, pushed up on her tiptoes and kissed him.

His arms around her waist felt like the most natural thing to him. He splayed his hand low on her back, springing to life more than a deep need to be inside her.

Her hands came around his neck, her body flush with his, and his body immediately took over—his hands moved down to her sweet bottom and caressed.

The little mewling sound that sprang from her lips heightened his anticipation.

The kiss ended far too fast for his liking. She looked him deep in the eye.

"You can't break me." She took his hand again, smiled a sexy little smile that caused his heart to stutter, and led him upstairs to the loft.

A thick blanket had been spread on the floor. There

was a soft glow lighting the room by one of those battery-powered lamps.

Logic told him to turn around and walk out before he couldn't.

Practical thinking said he shouldn't let his relationship with a witness be muddied by sex. Even though he had no doubt it would be mind-blowing sex.

Reasoning said as soon as this case was over he'd be back in South Texas and her life would continue in Plano.

All of which made sense. Not to mention he'd be breaking agency rules.

Reed knew he should say something to stop her. If things ended badly between them, it could jeopardize his career, his future with the agency and his future employability.

"I wanted to show you this." Emily stopped in the center of the room, locked gazes and slowly unbuttoned her shirt.

One peek of that lacy pink bra did him in. To hell with logic.

He crossed to her before the blouse hit the floor.

This close, he could see hunger in her eyes that he was certain matched his own. His lips came down hard on hers, claiming her mouth, as his tongue thrust inside searching for her sweet honey.

The sound she released was pure pleasure.

He cupped her breast and then pressed his erection to her midsection, rocking his hips. "You sure about this?"

She nibbled his bottom lip. "I've never been more certain about anything in my life."

Emily took a step away from him and shimmied out

of her jeans. He almost lost it right there when he saw her matching panties. Pink was his new favorite color.

Her hands went to the button fly of his jeans, but his made it there first. He toed off his boots, and his jeans hit the floor shortly after. She'd already made a move for his T-shirt, so he helped the rest of the way. "That's better. We've both had on way too many clothes."

Her musical laugh, a deep sexy note, urged him to continue.

Looking at her, her soft curves and full breasts, her gaze intent on his, was perfection. She was perfection. "You're beautiful."

That she blushed made her even sexier.

"Nothing hurts, right?" he asked, needing reassurance. This time he was already lost in her, and stopping would take heroic effort. He hoped like hell he'd be up to the challenge if he needed to be because looking at her in the low lamplight was the most erotic moment of his life.

"Fine. You first, then." He guided her onto the blanket, watching for any signs of pain.

There were none, so he made his next move. Her panties needed to go. If she could handle him pleasuring her with his tongue, he could think about filling her with something else.

He started at her feet and peppered kisses up the insides of her calves, her thighs.

Placing his hands gently on her silken thighs, he slowly opened her legs, checking to make sure she didn't grimace. Nope, he was good to go.

Her uneven breathing spiked as he bent down to roll his tongue on the inside of her thigh, moving closer to her sweet heat.

Using his finger, he delved inside her. A guttural groan released when he felt how hot and wet she was for him. His tongue couldn't get there fast enough. He needed to taste her. Now.

Her hands tunneled into his hair.

There were no signs of pain, just the low mewling of pleasure intensifying as he increased pressure, rubbing, pulsing his tongue inside her as she moved her hips with him.

Using his thumb, he moved in circles on her mound, and his tongue delved deeply, moving with her, tasting her, until her body quivered and she gasped and then fell apart around him.

He shouldn't be this satisfied with himself. He couldn't help it. Pleasuring her made another list he didn't know he had until meeting Emily. This one involved his favorite moments.

Taking a spot next to her, giving her a chance to catch her breath, he couldn't hold back a smile.

"That was… You are…amazing." She managed to get out in between breaths.

He turned on his side, needing to see her beautiful face. The compliment sure didn't hurt his ego. Truth was he wanted to hear her scream his name. And only his name.

Setting the thought aside when she rolled over to face him and gripped his straining erection, he took a second to really look at her. Perfection. She was that rare combination of beauty and strength. He wanted to bury himself inside her and get lost. Her mouth found his and he took the first step on the journey to bliss.

His heart hammered against his ribs, and for a split second he was nervous about his performance. He opened his eyes and chuckled against her lips. The vibration trailed down his neck, through his chest and arms.

Hers did the same. She smiled, too.

And his heart took a nosedive. He was in trouble, which had nothing to do with how great the sex was about to be.

Careful not to put too much weight on her, he rolled until he was on top of her. Her legs twined around his hips.

"Hold on." He tried not to move much while he wrangled a condom out of his wallet, grateful his jeans were within arm's reach. He ripped it open with his mouth, his hand shaking as he rolled it over the tip.

"Let me help with that." Her touch was firm but gentle as she rolled the condom down his shaft, lighting a fire trail coursing through his body, electrifying him.

When she gripped him and guided him inside her, he nearly exploded. His body shook with anticipation as he eased deeper.

"You won't hurt me." Her gravelly voice was pure sex.

Reed needed to think about something else if he wanted this to last. And he did. Until her hips bucked, forcing him to let go of control and get lost in the moment, the sensation of her around him, her innermost muscles tightening around his erection.

Looking into those gorgeous hazel eyes, he thrust deeper, needing to reach her core.

There was no hint of pain, only need.

They moved in a rhythm that belonged only to them. He battled his own release until she shattered around him, begging him not to stop. She breathed his name as she exploded, her muscles tightening and contracting.

When her spasms slowed, he pumped faster and harder until his own sweet release pulsed through him.

Exhausted, he pulled out and disposed of the condom before collapsing beside her.

"That was amazing," she said.

"Yeah. We're pretty damn good together, aren't we?"

"Best sex of my life."

"I couldn't argue that." His, too. He hauled her close to him.

She settled into the crook of his arm.

"And you're okay?"

"Never felt better."

"You tired? You want to go back to bed and rest?"

"I want to go back to bed all right. But not to rest." Her smile lit up her eyes.

He could get used to looking into those eyes every day. His erection had already resurrected. "Good. Because I'm going to need to do that a lot more to you today."

She reached for his wallet, which was still splayed on the floor, and retrieved another condom.

He didn't need to worry about whether or not he would be able to accommodate her. He was already stiff again. "I want this, too. Believe me. But should we wait a little while?"

"Still worried about hurting me?" She opened the package and rolled the condom down his shaft.

"I'm always going to want to protect you. But, yeah, I don't want to cause you any pain. You've been through enough and you're just now healing."

"Then, cowboy, you better lie back and let me show you what I can and can't do." She mounted him, still wet, and he groaned as she eased onto him.

"Better watch out. I could get used to this."

The corners of her mouth tugged when she bent down to kiss him. "Good. Because I'm counting on it."

Chapter 16

After taking a break from work to get fresh air, Emily walked into a house full of Campbells, and one very special little bundle in one of the women's arms. Reed introduced her to his sister Meg and her husband, Riley, the proud parents of baby Hitch.

"His name is Henry, but we call him Hitch for the way he 'hitched' a ride into our hearts," Reed explained.

Emily's heart skipped a beat at the proud twinkle in his eyes when he looked at the baby. And a place deep inside her stirred. She wanted a baby someday. But now? She'd kept herself so busy with work, it had been easy to avoid thinking about it. Maybe she'd been afraid to want something that seemed so far out of reach, something she had no idea how to attain given her screwed-up past. Seriously, her mom lived as if it were the sixties, probably a throwback to her youth. Although Emily could appreciate the Beatles, she believed the present was far more interesting than the past. And yet, hadn't she been stuck there in some ways, too?

Meg leaned toward Emily, who couldn't help but smile at the baby. "Do you want to hold him?"

"I would like that very much." Emily sat in a chair and took the sweet boy, who was bundled in a blue blanket with a brown horse stitched on it. "I love this."

"Gran made it." Meg beamed and Emily figured the look of pride had more to do with Hitch than his wrap.

"It's beautiful. And he's a gorgeous baby."

Emily expected to be overwhelmed by the group, but everyone stood around and chatted easily. Their level of comfort with each other was contagious. Instead of wanting to blend in with the wallpaper, as she usually did in groups of people she barely knew, she enjoyed joining in conversation. Laughing. There was real laughter and connection, and love.

Reed stood next to her, smiling down during breaks in bantering with his brothers, and her heart skipped a beat every time.

When was the last time she was so at ease in a room full of strangers? Heck, in any room?

Emily couldn't remember if she'd ever felt this relaxed, normal, as if she belonged. She credited it to the Campbells' easy and inclusive nature. They had enough love for each other, and everyone else around them. Images of Christmas mornings spent huddled around a tree in this room came to mind. Warmth and happiness blanketed her like a summer sunrise.

Hot cocoa and a blazing fire in the fireplace would be more than enough heat to keep them warm as they exchanged gifts.

There'd be laughter and Reed by her side. The realization Emily wanted all those things startled her. Because she was a guest there. And no matter how comfortable they made her feel, she didn't belong. Had never belonged anywhere or to anyone.

The thought sat heavy on her chest as she cradled the baby closer, trying to edge out the pain.

She glanced at the clock. It was time to set her fantasies aside and retreat to her room to work.

Glancing down at the sweet, sleeping baby, the earth shifted underneath her feet. Good thing she was already sitting or she feared she'd lose her balance. Because holding this little Campbell was nice. Better than nice. Amazing. And Emily could only imagine how much more fantastic it would be to hold her own child someday. One created with the man she loved.

Realization hit her in a thunderclap, ringing in her ears. She did want to have a baby. *Someday.*

For now, she had more pressing needs. To stay alive, for one. To keep her job, for another. Maybe once she got back on her feet, she'd be in a position to open herself up to other possibilities, as well.

"I better get back to work." She stood and reluctantly handed the little bundle over to his mother. "Thank you for letting me hold him. He's a sweet baby, and it was gracious of him not to cry." The only babies she'd ever held before had wailed. Of course, she'd been stiff as a board when their mothers had placed them in her arms. The babies most likely picked up on her emotions. And now she realized she'd also been afraid—afraid that by holding them, she'd realize she wanted one of her own. Maybe, when her life was straight and she met the right man, she'd be ready to think about a future.

Meg rewarded Emily with a genuine smile. "He's especially good when he's sleeping, which isn't much these days since he started teething."

Reed followed her into her room, took off his shoes and made himself comfortable on top of the bedspread. Seeing him there, fingers linked behind his head, made her almost wish she could start on her future now.

Silly idea.

But then great sex had a way of clouding judgment. And theirs had been beyond anything she'd ever experienced before. She couldn't help but crack a smile. Until reality dawned and she realized her time in paradise had a limit.

As soon as the right call came in, Reed would be out of there, tracking the most deadly man in Mexico. If this was anyone else other than Reed, she'd consider going into WitSec and asking him to come with her. She knew in her heart a man like him wouldn't give up his family or go into hiding for the rest of his life. He was honest, strong and capable. Injustice would hit him harder than a nail. And he wouldn't sleep until he'd made it right.

Her worry was probably written all over her face, but she couldn't help it. She'd grown to care for Reed in the past few weeks, and she didn't want to think about him leaving. She'd also overheard conversations where she knew they were getting close to pinpointing a location.

"What's wrong?" His dark brow lifted.

"Nothing. I was just thinking how cute Hitch is," she lied.

He patted the bed next to him. "Come here."

She sat on folded knees, facing him.

"I can't help if I don't know what's really bothering

you. Is it my family? They can be a bit much for people when they're all together."

"Not at all. I like being with them very much."

He leaned forward and kissed her. "That's nice because they love you."

She couldn't hold back her smile. Love? Being near Reed had a way of calming all her fears. But the last thing she needed to do was learn to depend on him. His family might love her, but did he?

"What is it really?" He kissed her again. "I hope you know you can tell me anything."

Except the part where she'd lost the battle against the slippery slope and was falling for him. Hard.

She had no doubt Reed could solve any problem, aside from that one.

"I'm just thinking about a work issue. It's nothing."

"Why don't I believe that?" Reed surprised himself at just how important Emily had become to him in the past couple of weeks.

She leaned forward and kissed him.

"Keep that up and we're not leaving this room for a long time," he teased, but he was only half joking.

"Who said I'd mind?" She laughed against his lips.

Before she could get too comfortable with that thought, he flipped her onto her back and pressed his midsection into the open vee of her legs. "I have no problem rallying for that cause."

Reed cursed as he heard his name being called from down the hall. "Ignore it."

"Not happening, cowboy. Not in broad daylight with your family in the next room shouting for you."

"I was afraid you'd say that. Hold that thought. I'll

get rid of them and be right back." He kissed her again and then hauled himself out of the bed. He sat on the edge for a long moment, needing to get control over his body before he headed out of the room. "This is your fault, you know."

"What did I do?"

"Made it where I can't get enough of you."

Luke shouted again.

With a sharp sigh, Reed pushed off the bed and headed down the hall. He followed the voice to the kitchen, where Nick and Luke were seated at the table. They were staring intently at someone's laptop.

"What did you guys find?"

"Turns out that name you wanted us to check out the other day is involved," Nick said.

"Jared Sanchez?"

"Yeah. His mother's maiden name is Ruiz."

Reed cursed and fisted his hands. So much of Jared's behavior made sense now. No wonder he'd been so forgiving. He was keeping tabs on Emily. "So, he's related to the guy at the town house."

"That's not all. He's up to his eyeballs involved," Luke said.

"I'll kill that SOB myself," Reed ground out. "What else did you find?"

"Sent in a couple of boys to 'talk' to him and once he started, they couldn't shut him up. Turns out his cousin—your friend from the town house—realized what a cash cow Jared could be with his job at Source-Con."

Reed's jaw twitched. He didn't like where this conversation was going. "Go on."

"Jared swears he didn't want Emily to get hurt. Says

he made his cousin promise nothing would happen to her. Jared's the one who gave up her location at the resort. She was supposed to be returned once she gave the codes. No harm. No foul. Jared wouldn't be connected to the crime and he'd make sure she kept her job."

"Except she didn't have her passwords."

"With her access to accounts in major banking institutions, Dueño must've also realized the kind of money on the line because he doesn't normally get personally involved. When she wouldn't give him what he wanted…well…you know what happened next."

Anger burned a raging fire inside Reed. "Tell me Sanchez is in a cell."

"Of course," Nick said quickly. "And there's a silver lining. Ruiz feared for his life when the job went sour and turned state's evidence. He gave up the location of Dueño's compound. We had it checked out and our guys confirmed it. Dueño's compound is in Sierra Madre del Sur, midway between Acapulco and Santa Cruz."

"And they're sure it's him?"

"Ninety-six percent certainty." Luke repositioned his laptop so Reed could see the screen. "That's our guy."

"Dueño?"

"That's him."

Reed took a minute to study the dark features and black eyes. "I need a plane."

"You need to check your messages. Your boss wants you to stand down on this one," Luke said.

"No way. I'm not letting someone else risk their lives for this."

"That's exactly what we thought you'd say. We stalled your boss. A chopper's on its way to take us to the airport."

"What do you mean *us*?"

"We're going with you."

"It's too dangerous."

The look on both of his brothers' faces would've stopped anyone else dead in their tracks. But Reed was immune. "Look, I'm not saying you're not the best at what you do, but you have families now. I can't let you take that risk for me."

"What the hell is it with you and families?" Nick asked, disgusted. "I know how to do my job."

Reed wouldn't argue the point.

"And if my baby brother is going anywhere near that compound, I'm going with him. This isn't just your fight. They messed with a Campbell. We stand together."

"Goes without saying."

"Then stop being a jerk and let us help you," Nick said flatly.

Luke added, "I don't trust anyone else to watch your back."

Reed couldn't argue that point, either. He felt the exact same way. "Okay, then. Whose resources are we using for this? Because it doesn't sound like my boss is going to pony up."

Luke raised his hand. "FBI wants this guy, so they said they'd back the mission. However, anything goes wrong, and we're on our own to explain it. We can do whatever we want with the jerk who shot you if we find him. He's a bonus."

"Or collateral damage," Nick interjected.

"I'd like to see him spend a long time behind bars. Dying is too easy for him." Reed paused and then clapped his hands together. "Sounds like a party. So when do we leave?"

"About half an hour. We'll get close to the suspected location and then wait it out until the middle of the night."

"Sounds like you have it all figured out." Reed needed to tell Emily about the plan. He felt a lot better about his odds with his brothers backing him. "What coverage do we have here in Creek Bend?"

"Enough to ensure the safety of a dignitary in a red zone. When this is over, we have to talk about setting up our own company. Just us brothers," Luke said, but the deep set to his eyes said he wasn't joking around this time.

Reed glanced at Nick. "What do you think about the idea of us going into business together?"

"After what happened to me, heck, I'm the one who suggested it."

"Did not," Luke interrupted. "You know this was my original idea from way back."

Reed smiled. Working with his brothers wasn't a half-bad idea. His job at Border Patrol had gone sour the day he'd realized he couldn't trust some of his own. As it turned out, his shooting wasn't as uncommon as it should be. But then, one should be enough. "First things first. Let's go pick up a couple of hot tamales across the border, and then we'll talk business."

He couldn't ignore the possibility that forming an agency with his brothers would bring him back to North Texas and closer to Emily. Would she be open to exploring the idea of them as a couple when he returned? For now, he had to figure out a way to tell her he was about to leave. For a split second, he considered taking her with him. Having her by his side was the only way he could be certain she'd be safe. But bringing her to Dueño's door wasn't a bright idea. There were enough federal men crawling through Creek Bend and around the ranch to keep an eye on her and his family.

The right way to tell her he was leaving didn't come to him on his walk down the hall. He stopped at her doorway and asked if he could enter.

One look at his serious expression and her smile faded, disappearing faster than a deer in the woods at the scent of man.

"What did your brother say?"

He kissed her, mostly to reassure himself, because he suddenly wasn't sure how she'd react to the news.

Tension bunched the muscles in his shoulders worse than a Dallas traffic jam as he prepared himself for the worst.

When she realized how dangerous his job was, she might not want to see him anymore. Especially once he gave her back her life, which he had every intention of doing by morning. He also had every intention of living to see it…but he couldn't make promises on that one.

The right words to tell her still eluded him, so he just came out with it. "We found him."

Reed studied her expression, surprised at how much he needed her reassurance. But she was completely unreadable. Should he tell her about her boss? On second thought, maybe he should wait. He could explain everything once this ordeal was over.

"When do you leave?"

"Soon. A chopper's on its way."

She drew in a deep breath. "And you're sure it's him?"

"You can never be one hundred percent, but this is about as close as it gets." He took her hand, relieved she didn't draw away from him.

Staring at the wall, as if she was reading a book, she took another deep breath. "Okay. We should get you ready to go."

She wasn't upset? No begging him to stay? "You're all right with this?"

"'This' is what you do, right?" Her honest hazel eyes were so clear he could almost see right through them.

"Yeah. It is." No way could she be okay.

"And 'this' is what you love. It's part of who you are, right?" There was no hesitation in her voice.

Was it possible she understood? "Yes."

"I'm falling hard for you, Reed Campbell. I wouldn't change a thing about you." She smiled, leaned forward and kissed him. "Who am I to complain about your job?"

Did she really mean that? He studied her for a long moment then squeezed her hand. He didn't like the idea of leaving her, especially since Dueño's men were never far. The best way to protect her was by putting Dueño in jail. "You are someone who has become very special to me."

"Good. Because I happen to like who you are, Mr. Campbell. You're kind of dangerous." She peppered a kiss on his lower lip. "And mysterious."

She captured his mouth this time then pulled back just enough to speak. "And I happen to think that's very hot."

Chapter 17

Reed gathered his pack, loaded it onto the chopper and climbed aboard. The loud *whop, whop, whop* couldn't drown out the sweet sound of Emily's last words. It was still foreign to him that someone could become so special in such a short amount of time. His feelings defied logic, which confused the hell out of him. And he didn't need to be thinking about it when he should be focused on his mission.

To make this day more complicated, he didn't like being away from her, or not being there to protect her. Even though the ranch was under lockdown by the FBI.

Finding and arresting Dueño was the best way to keep his family safe. Throw in the bonus of possibly locating the man who'd betrayed Reed, and he'd be doubling down on this mission.

No matter what happened, Reed would be ready. He

and his brothers had gone over the operation's details a half dozen times at the kitchen table. Reed had memorized the map. No one needed to be reminded that although the FBI funded the detail, it wasn't sanctioned by the US government. Meaning, if things went sour, they'd be on their own.

But he and his brothers would be in constant communication. Plus, they had the added bonus of knowing each other inside out. Most teams trained for years to get that kind of chemistry.

The chopper took them to DFW airport, where they climbed aboard a cargo plane that would take them to Oaxaca, Mexico.

All joking stopped during the three-hour flight the moment they crossed the border into Mexico. From there, they'd board a smaller aircraft headed to a military airstrip in the foothills of Sierra Madre del Sur, and it'd be a quick half-hour drive from there.

Flights had left on time and they were on schedule as the second plane landed. Every mission had its quiet time so that the men could gather their thoughts.

They were all business as they met the driver. He'd take them to the base of the mountains then leave. They'd be on foot for the rest of the journey.

From the airport to camp took another half hour. The camp had been set up at the base of the mountains. It wasn't much more than a tent and the makings for a fire. There was wood and a circle of rocks. Since both Nick and Reed had learned the hard way that not everyone could be trusted, Reed suggested they relocate as soon as the driver returned to his vehicle.

His brothers nodded.

As soon as the vintage Jeep disappeared, Reed pulled

up the tent stakes. "I say we camp an hour from the compound at the most."

"Good idea," Nick said.

They'd walked a mile in silence when Luke finally spoke up. "She'll be all right, you know."

"I hope."

"They couldn't protect her any better than if she'd been placed in WitSec," Luke continued.

That Reed didn't know the men she was with personally didn't sit well on his chest. Especially after what Nick had gone through a year ago when a US marshal supervisor had gone bad. Reed knew all about working with the unpredictable as a Border Patrol agent. All it took for a dozen bad seeds to be planted was a piece of legislation mandating his agency double up on personnel in order to stem the flow of illegals. Reed didn't mind the legislation; the idea was in the right place. But mandating all the hires happen in a month wasn't realistic. Detailed background checks took longer than that to execute and return.

The current system made it way too easy for criminals to make it into the system as agents. His grip tightened around his pack. Phillips and Knox were prime examples.

But it was rare for a US marshal to turn.

"I hope you're right." Being separated made him jumpy. Fine if it kept him that much more alert while on his mission. Not so good if it distracted him. "How do you guys deal with it?"

"What?" Luke asked.

"The job. Having someone back home."

"I know what Leslie did, but it should never have

been that way," Luke said. "Julie has never asked me to quit my job."

Nick rocked his head back and forth in agreement. "Sadie, either. Why? You think Leslie had a point?"

When Reed really thought about it, no. He didn't think she had a valid point. He'd been on the job when they met, so she knew what she was getting into from the get-go. "I can't blame her for not wanting to sign on to this."

"Then she shouldn't have from the beginning," Luke said emphatically as he eased through the brush.

"There should be a clearing with a water source over this next hill," Reed said, changing the subject. "We can camp there."

"I think I can speak for Nick when I say being in a relationship in this job is a good thing as long as it's with the right woman." Luke wasn't ready to let it go.

"How so?" Reed knew all about being in relationships with the wrong ones.

Luke didn't hesitate. "Training gives you the skill set to handle any mission. A family gives you the mental edge to make sure you make it out alive. I have so much more to come home to now. I can only imagine what it'll be like when we have kids."

There was something different about Luke's voice when he said the last word. If there was a pregnancy, his quickie wedding made more sense. "Do you have something else you want to tell us?"

"Yeah."

"And you waited until we were out in the jungle before giving us a hint?"

"If Gran freaked about the wedding, what will she say about this?"

"She'll be as happy for you as we are," Nick interjected.

The image of Emily holding Hitch edged into Reed's thoughts. Something deep and possessive overtook him at the memory. He shoved it away. Because it looked a little too right in his mind. And since he'd known her for all of two weeks, it didn't make any sense to start thinking about how beautiful she'd look pregnant with his child.

He climbed to the top of the hill and looked out at the lake in front of him. The ground was level enough to make a good campsite. "There it is. Let's settle down here for a few hours."

The climb to their new location had the added benefit of giving their bodies a chance to get used to the altitude. They would need to be at their absolute physical peak when they breached the compound later.

Every step closer to that complex and Reed's determination to put an end to all this craziness grew. Whether or not he spent another day with Emily, she deserved to have her life back. "Luke, you serious about starting an agency?"

His brother's surprised smile said it all. "Yeah. Why? You interested?"

"I might be." Options were a good thing, right?

Once this case was over and Cal was behind bars where he belonged, Reed could think about doing something else for a living.

"Then, let's talk about this tomorrow morning."

Reed knew what his brother was doing. It helped with nerves to start talking about the future. Knowing they'd have one gave the mind a mental boost. "Deal."

For the rest of this day, they'd settle around their camp and wait.

* * *

Emily wrung her hands as she paced. Focusing on work was a no-go. Reading a magazine didn't provide the distraction she needed. So, she resigned herself to worry.

What if something happened to Gran? It would be all Emily's fault.

And Reed? The thought of anything happening to him was worse than a knife through the chest.

With all the FBI crawling around, a cockroach couldn't slip past unseen. She wasn't worried about herself, anyway. Reed was the one running into danger, when most people ran the opposite direction.

He was brave and strong, and everything she admired in a man. It didn't hurt that he was drop-dead hotness under his Stetson.

The thought of anything happening to the man she loved seared her. *Love?*

Did she love Reed Campbell?

Oh, yeah, her heart said. And she figured there was no use arguing. The heart knew what it wanted, and hers wanted him.

Sleep was about as close as Christmas to the month of June. Hours had passed since her usual bedtime, but it didn't matter. Hot tea did little to calm her nerves. Warm milk had similar success.

She curled under the covers and tried to remember how she'd survived the many stresses of her childhood. Easy. She'd pictured her future exactly how she wanted it to be and then worked toward it with everything in her power. There was something incredibly powerful about making a decision and then holding it strong in her mind's eye.

Maybe she could use that same approach now.

It would be a heck of a lot better than wearing a hole in the carpet.

Determined to see his face again, she took a deep breath and pictured Reed holding Hitch at the family barbecue Gran had scheduled next month to celebrate Luke and Julie's marriage.

Closing her eyes tightly, she held that image in her mind as she drifted off to sleep.

The air was still, the monkeys quiet.

Reed looked from one brother to another. "Give me a minute?"

They nodded and walked away, each in a separate direction. Apparently, he wasn't the only one with a ritual for when he intentionally put himself into harm's way.

This was the time he went into his private zone where he took a moment to think about his loved ones and recommitted himself to getting back to them safely. No way would he allow the only fathers he'd ever known, Nick and Luke, to be without their brother. Emily's face invaded his thoughts, too. He had every intention of seeing her again…the way her face flushed pink with desire when he kissed her. The feel of her soft skin underneath his rough hands. Her strength under adversity. And her smile. Those were things to get home to.

Reed moved back to the edge of the lake. Anything happened and they had a place to stay the night. They could carry an injured man this far without too much effort.

Every mission had to have a backup plan. With only three of them on an unsanctioned assignment, they had only each other to depend on. There'd be no Blackhawk if this thing went south.

First Luke returned, then Nick.

Reed performed a final check of their emergency supplies, shouldered his pack and put on his night-vision goggles. His cell was on vibrate, but communication back home was pretty much dead for now.

The compound was an hour's hike. They'd given themselves plenty of time to adjust to the altitude and hydrate for the trip. The mission had been timed to perfection. It was three o'clock in the morning. They'd reach the compound around four. They had roughly twenty minutes to locate the target and then drag his butt out of there.

A Jeep would pick them up at the original campsite at five thirty to take them to a waiting plane, which would be fueled and ready to go.

Dueño's actual place would be more difficult to reach. He'd built the small mansion in a valley that was flat, affording tall mountain views on all sides. Nature's perfect barrier. So, Reed would have to climb up and down to reach the place.

Based on intel, there were enough men with guns surrounding the nine-foot-high concrete fence to guard the president, all of whom were inside. Under the cover of night, Reed was confident they could make it down the side of the mountain undetected. Getting inside the gates would be a different story.

The hike was quiet, save for the soft steps behind him. Anyone else would have to strain to hear them. Reed could sense his brothers' movements. Years of playing in the trees long past dark on the ranch had honed their skills.

Luke was probably the most quiet of the trio. His military training had most likely kicked in at this point, and Reed hoped it didn't bring back bad memories.

At the peak of the last incline, a breeze carried voices from below. Reed made a mental note of how easily sounds traveled, and forged ahead.

The compound came into view as soon as he peaked. To say it was huge was an understatement. They'd seen it from a satellite picture, and yet the photo didn't do it justice.

Clearly, someone important lived here. A man like Dueño, someone with his power, would make his home in something like this. Crazy that a jerk like him made money hurting women.

The image of Emily when Reed had found her stamped his thoughts. She was beaten and vulnerable but not defeated. Dueño might have hurt her physically, but she'd made it clear that's all he could do.

From what Reed could see, coming in from the south, as they were, was still the best option. He'd wait for Luke's signal to continue.

Two thumbs-up, the sign to descend, came a minute later from Luke.

With each step down, Reed's temper flared. He'd become a master at controlling his emotions, and yet, getting closer to the man who'd hurt Emily, who had her running for her life, kept his mood just below boiling.

He'd enjoy hauling this guy's butt to the States, where he could be properly arrested.

Twenty more steps and they'd be at the concrete fence.

Luke popped over first. Then came the signal. Reed followed next, then Nick.

Crouched low, Reed moved behind the first guard.

With one quick jab, the guy was knocked unconscious. Reed pulled a rope from his bag and then tied and gagged the guy to his post just in case he woke before they'd finished.

They didn't have a lot of time.

It took another five minutes to locate the window of the room where the target was believed to be sleeping. A curtain blew in and out with the breeze. With all this security around, the guy didn't feel the need to close his windows. That was the first lucky thing Reed had encountered so far.

In his experience, a man got two, maybe three lucky breaks on a mission. The op had to be planned to a T. Reed pulled on his face mask, giving the signal for the others to follow. When their masks were secure, he opened the tear gas canister and placed it on the sill. The gas wouldn't hurt anyone inside in case there were children, but it would disorient and confuse anyone who breathed it.

Reed pulled himself up and slipped inside. He rolled the canister toward the center of the room. Plumes of gray smoke expanded and filled the room. Before he could signal his brothers, a fist came out of nowhere. He took a hit to the face, dislodging his mask. He spun around and repositioned it. As soon as he got a visual on the guard, Reed kicked the guy. The blow was so hard, he took two steps back and began coughing as the gas shrouded him. He dropped to the floor and disappeared into the haze of smoke, giving Reed enough time to motion for his brothers to join him.

As they cleared the window, the light flipped on.

The room was dense with smoke. Sounds of coughing were followed by footsteps.

Reed identified three distinct voices. Luckily, none belonged to children. He moved to the bed and handcuffed the biggest body. Luke had already dispatched the guard and Nick was subduing a screaming female.

When the guy spun around to face Reed, he got a good look at him. He released a string of curse words. This wasn't Dueño.

The door burst open and several men pushed through, choking and gagging as they breached the room. Reed studied their faces. Disappointment edged in when he realized neither Cal nor Knox was there.

Were they with Dueño? On their way to find Emily? In fact, there wasn't nearly enough security at the compound. Had they mobilized most of their men to get to her?

Reed cleared the bed and yelled to Nick that the guy wasn't there. By the time they got to Luke, bullets were flying. Whoever was shooting couldn't see clearly, either. Not exactly the ideal scenario.

They needed to get out of there. Fast.

If Dueño wasn't here, he could be anywhere in Mexico, or Texas. And where was Cal? All hopes of finding him fizzled and died. An overwhelming urge to get back to Emily hit Reed faster than a car on the expressway.

"Abort!" he shouted, but his brothers were already to the window.

Fear gripped Reed. Had they just played right into Dueño's hands?

Chapter 18

Emily jolted awake to the sound of glass being cut. Oh, God. She heard movement in the other room. She threw her covers off, hopped out of bed and grabbed the lamp on the bedside table. Her mind clicked through possibilities as she reached for her phone and shouted for help.

"Who's there? Somebody help." A shaky finger managed to touch the name of the supervisor she'd been given to call in an emergency on her phone.

Three men stormed her bedroom. Three guns pointed at her. Three voices shouted orders at her.

Adrenaline pumped through her. She could lie down and let them take her, or go out fighting. If she could stall long enough, maybe someone would hear her. She shouted again. Why wasn't he coming through that door?

Let the men with bandannas covering their faces take her and she might as well already be dead.

The first one rushed toward her, and the others followed suit. For a split second, she thought they looked like a bird formation. Emily reared back, grabbed the lamp and swung it toward the first man with everything inside her.

He took a hit hard enough for blood to spurt from his nose. Except the other two men were already there, grabbing her, before she could wind up and swing again. One jerked the lamp out of her hands.

The first man cursed bitterly, and she knew there'd be a consequence for her actions later. That didn't stop her from kicking another one in the groin. He bent forward but didn't loosen his grip.

With one man on each side of her and another behind, she was forced into the living room at the same time the front door burst open.

At least six men wearing vests marked SWAT surged inside the door, stopping the moment they saw the gun pointed at her temple.

"Stop or she's dead," one of the men said in broken English. "And we already took care of him."

The SWAT team didn't lower their weapons, but they didn't move, either.

A little piece of her heart wished it had been Reed storming through that door. Another broke for the officer they'd disposed of because of her. It would be too late because the men already had her. They'd torture and kill her once they got her to a secure location. But she wished she could see him one last time. She shut her eyes and tried to conjure up the details of his face, his intense and beautiful brown eyes. The sharp curve of his jaw. Hair so dark it was almost black.

If she concentrated, maybe his face would be the last thing she remembered.

Emily didn't open her eyes again until she was outside, being shoved toward a white van. By this time, officers were everywhere and she could imagine how helpless they felt. They'd sworn to protect, and the ones she'd met so far took that oath seriously.

It wasn't their fault. Not one had a shot with the way they'd used her as cover.

Dueño was powerful enough that if he got her to the border, it would be over. American law enforcement had no jurisdiction in Mexico. Without cooperation from the Mexican government, she'd be left defenseless.

Emily kicked the man in front of her. He spun around and smacked her so hard she thought her eyeball might pop out. Could she move out of the way enough for one of the SWAT officers to get a clean shot? It'd take more than that since one of the other two could shoot her.

No way would the officers risk her life.

Dread settled heavy on her shoulders as they forced her to move.

The van was only a few steps away, blocking the view of officers surrounding the ranch.

Let these men get her inside the vehicle… Game over. There'd be no cavalry.

She reared her right foot back again ready to deliver another blow, but it was caught this time. Twisting her body left to right like a washing machine, she struggled to break their grasps, to do anything that might give officers a line of sight to get off a shot and take down her captors.

The barrel of a gun pressed to her head. "Keep at it, bitch, and we'll shoot."

Why hadn't they already? Dueño must want her alive.

She could only imagine the tortures he had planned for her. A shudder ran through her.

Even so, she'd pushed it as far as she could. Hopelessness pressed heavy on her chest as she was thrown into the back of the van. Her head slammed against the seat and something wet trickled down her forehead.

Pain roared through her body. Her injuries had been healing nicely until now. Being thrown around and kicked awakened her aches. But none of the physical pain was worse than the hole in her heart.

One of the men sat on top of her, his weight an anchor being tossed to the depths of the ocean.

"There. Now she won't move." His laugh was like fingers on a chalkboard, scraping down her spine.

He bounced, pressing her body against the seat so hard she thought her ribs might crack. She cried out in pain.

"Don't hurt her. Dueño wants her alive," the driver, a white man, said as he gunned the engine.

"I'm not killing her. But she deserves a little pain after breaking my nose." His words came out through gritted teeth, slow and laced with anger.

The emptiness of her life caused the first tears to roll down her cheeks as a stark realization hit her. She didn't fear death. She was only sorry for the life she'd led. Too many times she'd let her demons stop her from pushing herself out of her comfort zone. Her fear of ending up broke and needing some man to save her pushed her to spend too much time at work and too little with people she cared about. And whom did she really care about?

Of course, she loved her mom and siblings. But who else had she let inside her life?

Sobs racked her shoulders.

"Make her shut up," the driver said.

Chapter 19

"What the hell do you mean they got her?" Reed fisted his hands as he glared at Luke. Their plane wouldn't land for another hour. "Have all airports and security checkpoints at the border been sealed?"

"Yes. And for what it's worth, I'm sorry, little bro." Anguish darkened Luke's eyes. "As you know, there are only a few places they can cross the border—"

"Legally. But this guy has more channels than cable TV." Whatever they'd done to Emily before would be nothing compared with the torture they'd dish out now. Reed cursed.

"I just spoke to the pilot. Our flight has been diverted to Laredo. There are only so many routes they can take to get to the border."

"That's true." Reed thought about it long and hard. Which highway in Texas would they take? Or was that too easy? "He expects everyone to be watching for him in Texas, so he won't risk it. Can you talk to the pilot, have him take us to El Paso instead?"

"I'm on it," Luke said as he made a move toward the cabin.

Reed leaned back in his seat and tried to stem the onset of a raging headache.

"We'll find her." The determination in Nick's eyes almost convinced Reed.

Emily had no idea how long they'd been driving when she heard a harsh word grunted and the screech of a hard brake. The van careened out of control and into a dangerous spin.

The next thing she knew, the van was in a death roll. The man who'd been sitting on top of her acted as a cushion, sparing her head from slamming against the ceiling now beneath them.

Emily braced herself as the van stopped. If she could get to the door while everyone was disoriented, maybe she could get away and make a run for it. She doubted there'd be anyone around to help since she hadn't heard a car pass by in hours.

She made a move to grab the handle. The Hispanic man caught her arm.

"Where do you think you're going?" he asked.

The door flew open, anyway, and there he stood. Reed. His gun was aimed at a spot on the Hispanic guy's head. Six other officers stood to each side of him.

"She's coming with me, Cal. And you're going to jail." Satisfaction lightened Reed's intense features.

Cal? The man who'd shot Reed?

Emily leaned toward him, unable to get her bearings enough to make her legs move. Or maybe they were broken because they didn't seem to want to move.

Dozens of officers moved on the men in the van, subduing them while Emily was being hauled into Reed's arms.

"I thought I lost you." The anguish in his voice nearly ripped out her heart.

"You can't get rid of me that easily, Campbell." She wrapped her arms around his neck.

He tightened his arms around her. "How badly are you hurt?"

"I'm shaken up, but I'll be okay." She tested her legs. Much to her relief, they worked fine. Adrenaline was fading, causing her to shake harder. Glancing around, all she could see was barren land. "Where am I?"

"In New Mexico. About five minutes from the Mexican border."

Reed held her so close she could hear his heart beat as wildly as her own. Relief flooded her.

"And that's the guy who shot you?" She motioned toward Cal.

"Yeah."

"I understand if you want to be the one to cuff him."

"I'm exactly where I want to be."

"And your brothers?"

"They're following a car we believe Dueño is in. We've been watching the caravan for an hour, waiting for it to split up so we could make a move. I knew Dueño wouldn't risk drawing too much attention so close to the border. He spread his men out and we made our move." His cell buzzed. He fished it from his pocket, keeping one arm secure around her waist, and then glanced from the screen to her. "It's Luke."

Reed said a few uh-huhs into the phone before ending the call. "Dueño got away. And they can't find him. Knox was driving. He's under arrest."

A helicopter roared toward them, hovering over him. If the officers shot it down, innocent lives would be lost. Reed tucked Emily behind him and moved to cover.

The chopper landed in a field, kicking up a tornado of dust.

"I have to distract him or he'll get away."

Reed caught Emily's elbow as she tried to pass him. His anger nearly scorched her skin. "I won't let you do this."

"It's the only way. If I can get him out in the open, maybe one of the guys can get a shot."

"A man who hides behind women and children won't risk being exposed." Reed stepped in between Emily and the chopper, weapon leveled and ready.

Movement to her left caught Emily's eye. She made a move to let Reed know, but his gun had already been redirected.

"Stop moving and put your hands where I can see them," Reed demanded.

"Put down your weapon and I'll consider it," Dueño said. The sound of his voice sent an icy chill down Emily's back.

"Always looking for the advantage, aren't you?"

"What would you do if you were in my position?"

"That's where you're wrong. I'm nothing like you. I'd never be in your position."

Dueño spun toward them, a flash of metal in his hand.

Fire exploded from Reed's gun first. Dueño took a

few steps toward them, and then dropped to the ground. SWAT had already mobilized, taking down the pilot.

"We did it," Emily said. Relief and joy filled her soul as Reed's arms wrapped around her, pulling her body flush with his.

"You're safe now."

"When they abducted me, my worst fear wasn't dying. It was that I'd never see you again. I love you, Reed. I want to be with you, even though I know you'll never fully trust anyone who isn't a Campbell." She'd said it, and the heaviness on her chest released. Like a butterfly breaking free from its cocoon, flapping its wings for the very first time. He didn't have to say it back for happiness to engulf her. She loved him. And she wanted him to know.

His intense gaze pierced her for a long moment. "We can change that, you know."

"Change what?" she parroted.

"Your last name." Holding her gaze, right there, he bent down on one knee.

"I've always been a logical man, believing everything had a place and a time, and had to make sense. Until the day I met you. From that moment, I knew there was something different about you. I was in love. I love you. And the only thing that makes sense to me now is to grab hold with both hands, and hang on with everything I have. Will you do me the honor of becoming my wife?"

Tears of joy streamed down Emily's face as she said the one word she knew Reed needed to hear. "Yes."

"I've been talking about it with my brothers and we've decided to open a P.I. business together in Creek Bend. I want to be around for you. And I promise to

love and protect you for the rest of my life." He rose
to his feet, never breaking eye contact, and pulled her
into a warm embrace.

In his arms, Emily had found her permanent family,
she'd found exactly where she belonged. She'd found
home.

* * * * *

Five years of memories didn't compare an ounce to the man
they'd been made about. Not when he seemingly materialized
out of midair, wrapped in a uniform that fit nicely, topped
with a cowboy hat his daddy had given him and carrying
some emotions behind clear blue eyes.

Eyes that, once they found Mel during her attempt to flee
the hospital, never strayed.

Not that she'd expected anything but full attention when
Sterling Costner found out she was back in town.

Though, silly ol' Mel had been hoping that she'd have more
time before she had this face-to-face.

Because, as much as she was hoping no one else would
catch wind of her arrival, she knew the gossip mill around
town was probably already aflame.

"I'm glad this wasn't destroyed," Mel said lamely once
she slid into the passenger seat, picking up her suitcase in the
process. She placed it on her lap.

She remembered leaving her apartment with it, but not
what she'd packed inside. At least now she could change out
of her hospital gown.

Sterling slid into his truck like a knife through butter.

The man could make anything look good.

"I didn't see your car, but Deputy Rossi said it looked like someone hit your back end," he said once the door was shut. "Whoever hit you probably got spooked and took off. We're looking for them, though, so don't worry."

Mel's stomach moved a little at that last part.

"Don't worry" in Sterling's voice used to be the soundtrack to her life. A comforting repetition that felt like it could fix everything.

She played with the zipper on her suitcase.

"I guess I'll deal with the technical stuff tomorrow. Not sure what my insurance is going to say about the whole situation. I suppose it depends on how many cases of amnesia they get."

Sterling shrugged. He was such a big man that even the most subtle movements drew attention.

"I'm sure you'll do fine with them," he said.

She decided talking about her past was as bad as talking about theirs, so she looked out the window and tried to pretend for a moment that nothing had changed.

That she hadn't married Rider Partridge.

That she hadn't waited so long to divorce him.

That she hadn't fallen in love with Sterling.

That she hadn't—

Mel sat up straighter.

She glanced at Sterling and found him already looking at her.

She smiled.

It wasn't returned.

Don't miss
Accidental Amnesia *by Tyler Anne Snell,*
available May 2022 wherever
Harlequin Intrigue books and ebooks are sold.

Harlequin.com

HIEXP0322

Love Harlequin romance?

DISCOVER.

Be the first to find out about promotions, news and exclusive content!

f Facebook.com/HarlequinBooks

🐦 Twitter.com/HarlequinBooks

📷 Instagram.com/HarlequinBooks

📌 Pinterest.com/HarlequinBooks

▶ YouTube.com/HarlequinBooks

ReaderService.com

EXPLORE.

Sign up for the Harlequin e-newsletter and download a free book from any series at **TryHarlequin.com**

CONNECT.

Join our Harlequin community to share your thoughts and connect with other romance readers!
Facebook.com/groups/HarlequinConnection

◈ HARLEQUIN

HARLEQUIN

Heartfelt or thrilling, passionate or uplifting—Harlequin is more than just happily-ever-after.

With twelve different series to choose from and new books available every month, you are sure to find stories that will move you, uplift you, inspire and delight you.

HNEWS2021